ALSO AVAILABLE FROM 🐵 TOKYOPOP®

MANGA

.HACK//LEGEND OF THE TWILIGHT (September 2003)
@LARGE (COMING SOON)
ANGELIC LAYER*
BABY BIRTH* (September 2003)
BATTLE ROYALE*
BRAIN POWERED*
BRIGADOON* (August 2003)
CARDCAPTOR SAKURA
CARDCAPTOR SAKURA: MASTER OF THE CLOW*
CHOBITS*
CHRONICLES OF THE CURSED SWORD
CLAMP SCHOOL DETECTIVES*
CLOVER
CONFIDENTIAL CONFESSIONS*
CORRECTOR YUI
COWBOY BEBOP*
COWBOY BEBOP: SHOOTING STAR*
DEMON DIARY
DIGIMON*
DRAGON HUNTER
DRAGON KNIGHTS*
DUKLYON: CLAMP SCHOOL DEFENDERS*
ERICA SAKURAZAWA*
FAKE*
FLCL* (September 2003)
FORBIDDEN DANCE* (August 2003)
GATE KEEPERS*
G GUNDAM*
GRAVITATION*
GTO*
GUNDAM WING
GUNDAM WING: BATTLEFIELD OF PACIFISTS
GUNDAM WING: ENDLESS WALTZ*
GUNDAM WING: THE LAST OUTPOST*
HAPPY MANIA*
HARLEM BEAT
I.N.V.U.
INITIAL D*
ISLAND
JING: KING OF BANDITS*
JULINE
KARE KANO*
KINDAICHI CASE FILES, THE*
KING OF HELL
KODOCHA: SANA'S STAGE*
LOVE HINA*
LUPIN III*
MAGIC KNIGHT RAYEARTH* (August 2003)
MAGIC KNIGHT RAYEARTH II* (COMING SOON)

MAN OF MANY FACES*
MARMALADE BOY*
MARS*
MIRACLE GIRLS
MIYUKI-CHAN IN WONDERLAND* (October 2003)
MONSTERS, INC.
PARADISE KISS*
PARASYTE
PEACH GIRL
PEACH GIRL: CHANGE OF HEART*
PET SHOP OF HORRORS*
PLANET LADDER*
PLANETES* (October 2003)
PRIEST
RAGNAROK
RAVE MASTER*
REALITY CHECK
REBIRTH
REBOUND*
RISING STARS OF MANGA
SABER MARIONETTE J*
SAILOR MOON
SAINT TAIL
SAMURAI DEEPER KYO*
SAMURAI GIRL: REAL BOUT HIGH SCHOOL*
SCRYED*
SHAOLIN SISTERS*
SHIRAHIME-SYO: SNOW GODDESS TALES* (Dec. 2003)
SHUTTERBOX (November 2003)
SORCERER HUNTERS
THE SKULL MAN*
THE VISION OF ESCAFLOWNE
TOKYO MEW MEW*
UNDER THE GLASS MOON
VAMPIRE GAME*
WILD ACT*
WISH*
WORLD OF HARTZ (COMING SOON)
X-DAY* (August 2003)
ZODIAC P.I. *

For more information visit www.TOKYOPOP.com

*INDICATES 100% AUTHENTIC MANGA (RIGHT-TO-LEFT FORMAT)

CINE-MANGA™

CARDCAPTORS
JACKIE CHAN ADVENTURES (COMING SOON)
JIMMY NEUTRON (September 2003)
KIM POSSIBLE
LIZZIE MCGUIRE
POWER RANGERS: NINJA STORM (August 2003)
SPONGEBOB SQUAREPANTS (September 2003)
SPY KIDS 2

NOVELS

KARMA CLUB (April 2004)
SAILOR MOON

TOKYOPOP KIDS

STRAY SHEEP (September 2003)

ART BOOKS

CARDCAPTOR SAKURA*
MAGIC KNIGHT RAYEARTH*

ANIME GUIDES

COWBOY BEBOP ANIME GUIDES
GUNDAM TECHNICAL MANUALS
SAILOR MOON SCOUT GUIDES

6-5-03

VOLUME 4

STORY AND ART BY WOO

LOS ANGELES • TOKYO • LONDON

Translator - Youngju Ryu
English Adaptation - Taliesin Jaffe
Associate Editor - Bryce P. Coleman
Retouch and Lettering - Caren McCaleb
Cover Layout - Patrick Hook

Editor - Luis Reyes
Managing Editor - Jill Freshney
Production Coordinator - Antonio DePietro
Production Manager - Jennifer Miller
Art Director - Matt Alford
Editorial Director - Jeremy Ross
VP of Production - Ron Klamert
President & C.O.O. - John Parker
Publisher & C.E.O. - Stuart Levy

Email: editor@TOKYOPOP.com
Come visit us online at www.TOKYOPOP.com

A  Manga

TOKYOPOP Inc.
5900 Wilshire Blvd. Suite 2000
Los Angeles, CA 90036

ISBN: 1-59182-219-X

First TOKYOPOP® printing: September 2003

10 9 8 7 6 5 4 3 2 1

Printed in the USA

REBIRTH

Vol 4

STORY THUS FAR

After traveling to a remote Buddhist monastery to learn the secrets of The Power of Light, Deshwitat and his wary companions are faced with a startling revelation. According to Master Tae, high-priestess of the Nagamil sect, the vampire is none other than the "seed to the line of the Great Spirit," a creature alluded to in the ancient prophecies of Nostradamus and destined to alter the fate of the world. Unable to instruct the reluctant savior in the Power of Light, Master Tae sends the unlikely team to the one place that can — The Vatican. But even in the holy city, Deshwitat cannot deny his blood lust, nearly ending the mission before it begins. And when a church emissary approaches the vampire with a cryptic invitation, one can only wonder — is this the hand of fate or the harbinger of doom?

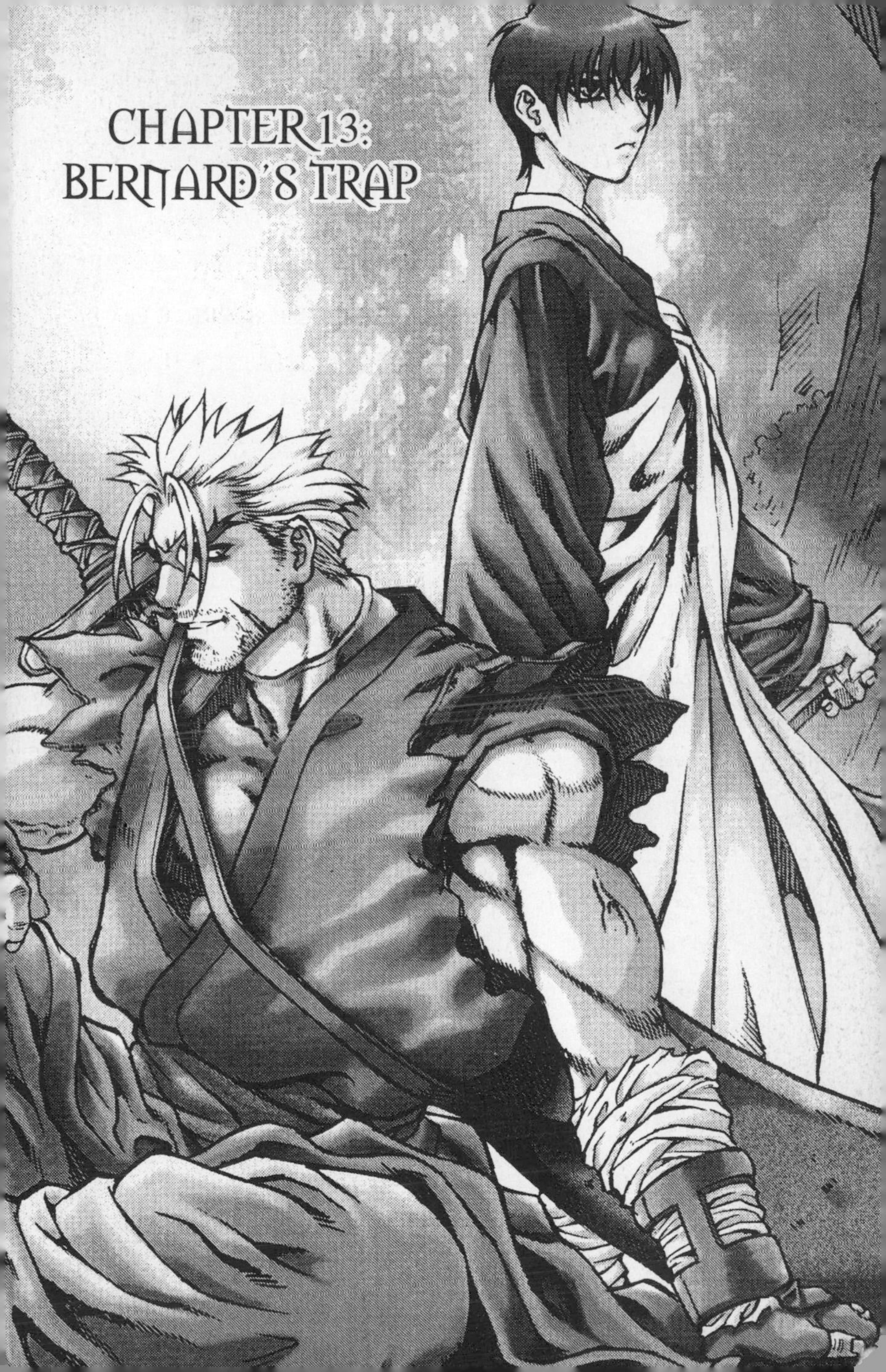
CHAPTER 13:
BERNARD'S TRAP

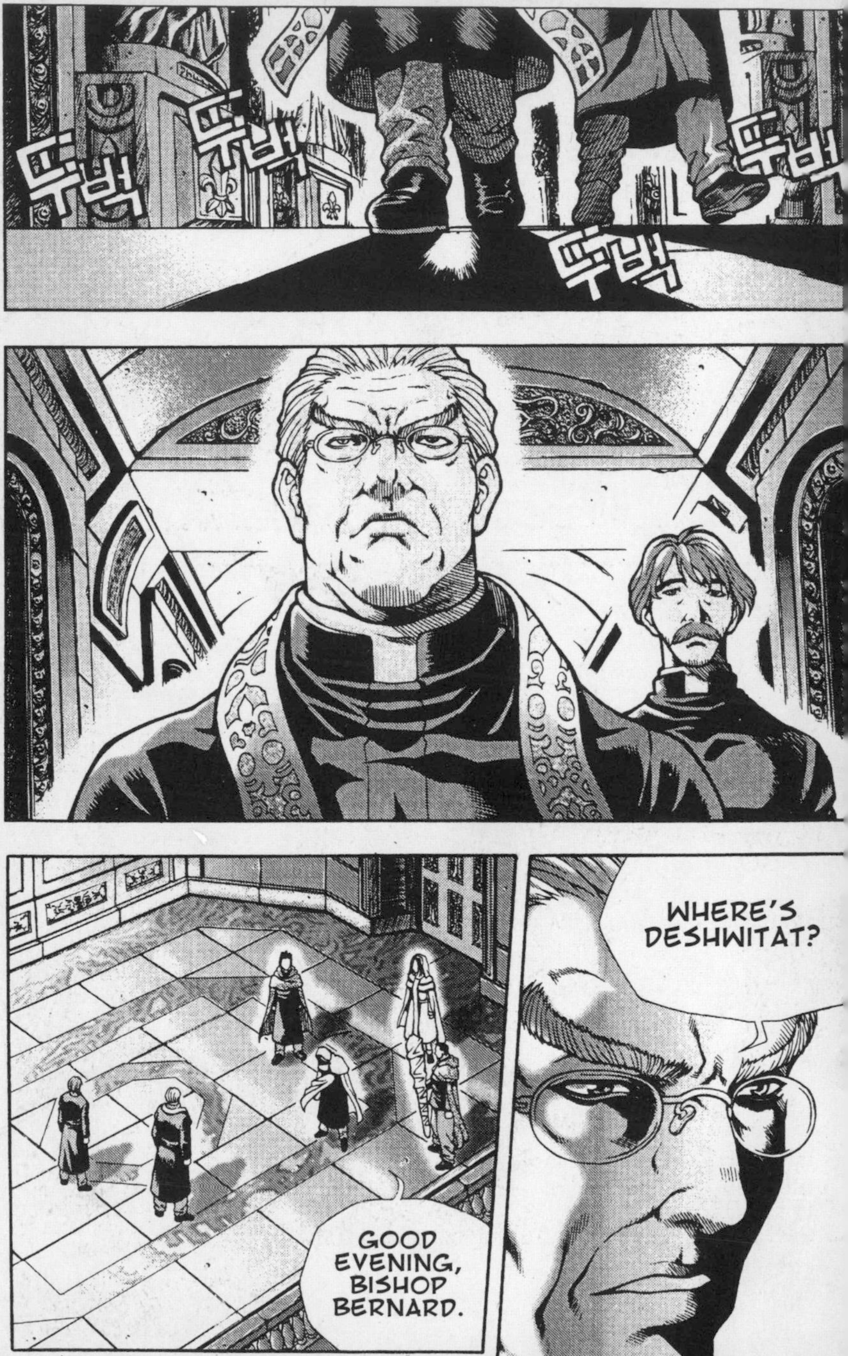
뚜벅
뚜벅
뚜벅
뚜벅
GOOD EVENING, BISHOP BERNARD.
WHERE'S DESHWITAT?

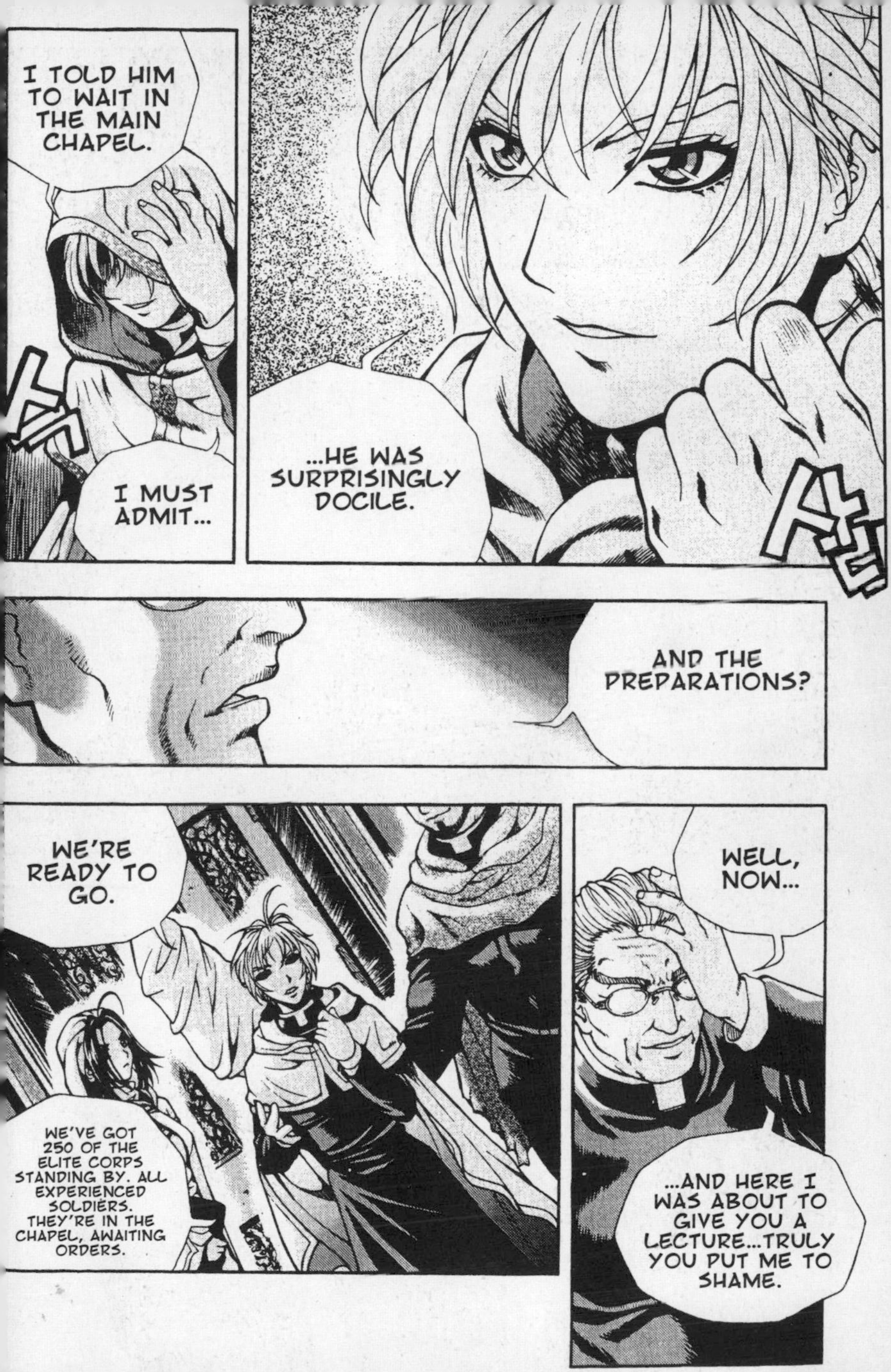
I TOLD HIM TO WAIT IN THE MAIN CHAPEL.
I MUST ADMIT...
...HE WAS SURPRISINGLY DOCILE.
AND THE PREPARATIONS?
WE'RE READY TO GO.
WE'VE GOT 250 OF THE ELITE CORPS STANDING BY. ALL EXPERIENCED SOLDIERS. THEY'RE IN THE CHAPEL, AWAITING ORDERS.
WELL, NOW...
...AND HERE I WAS ABOUT TO GIVE YOU A LECTURE...TRULY YOU PUT ME TO SHAME.

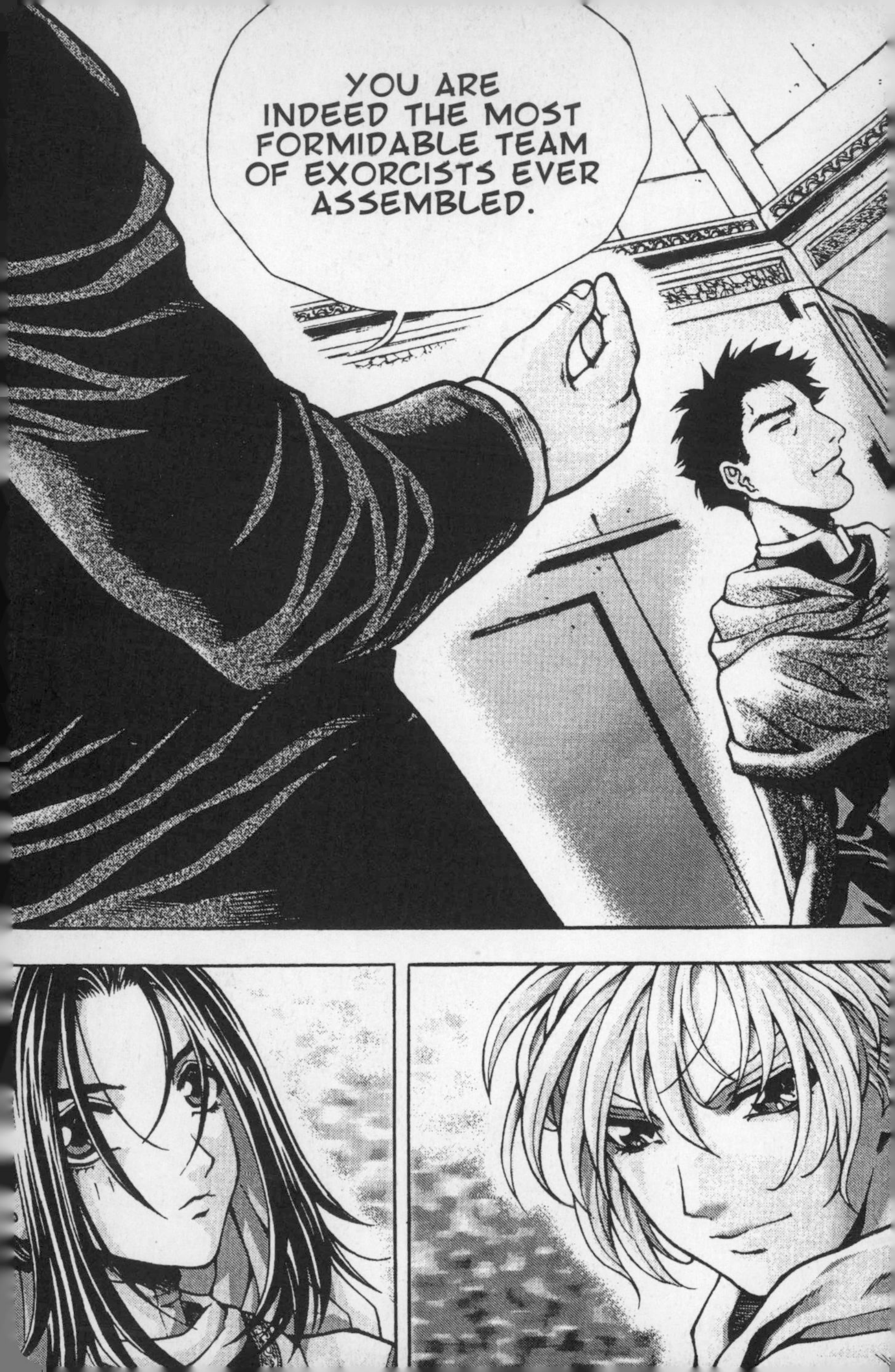
YOU ARE INDEED THE MOST FORMIDABLE TEAM OF EXORCISTS EVER ASSEMBLED.

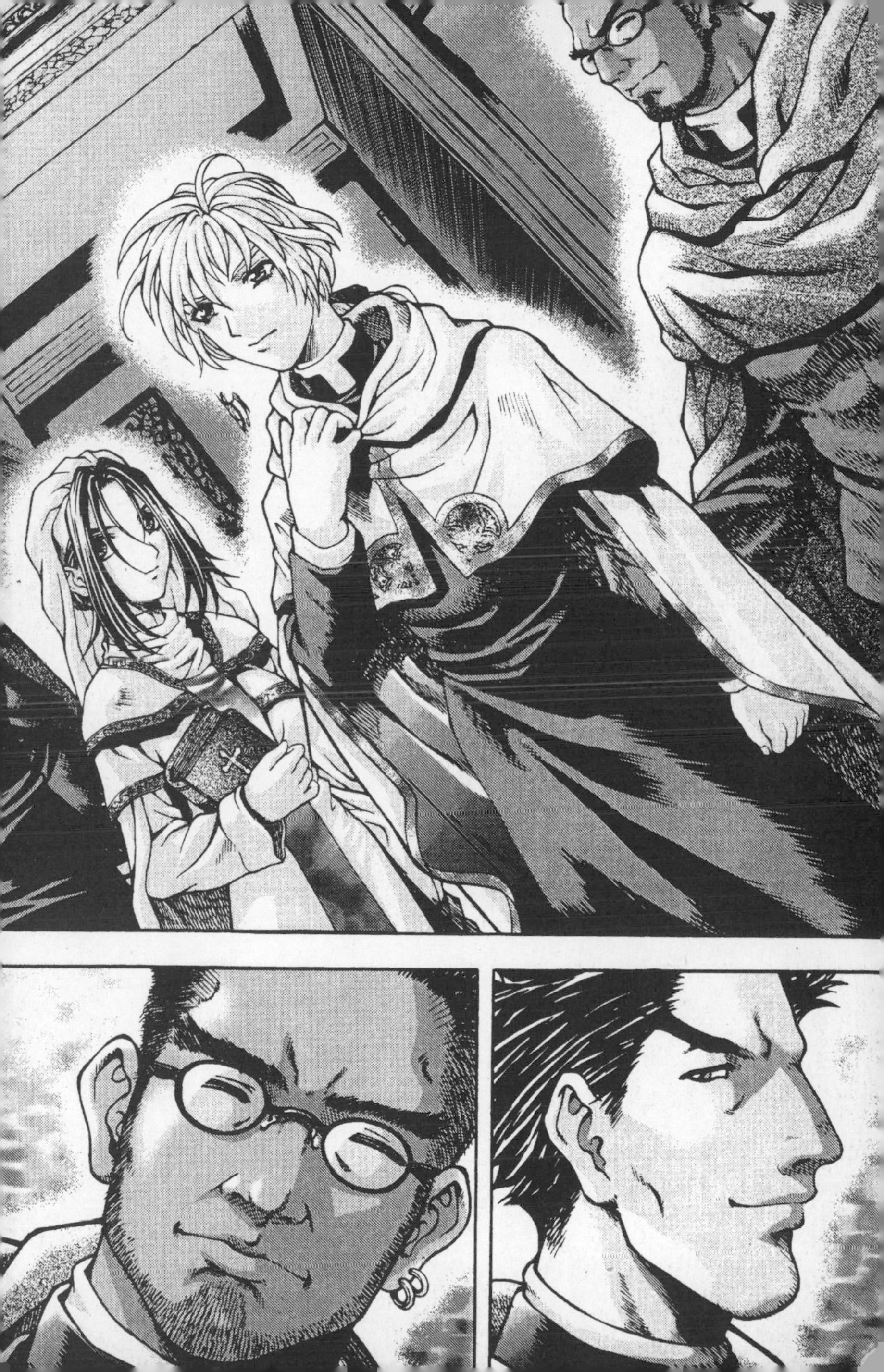

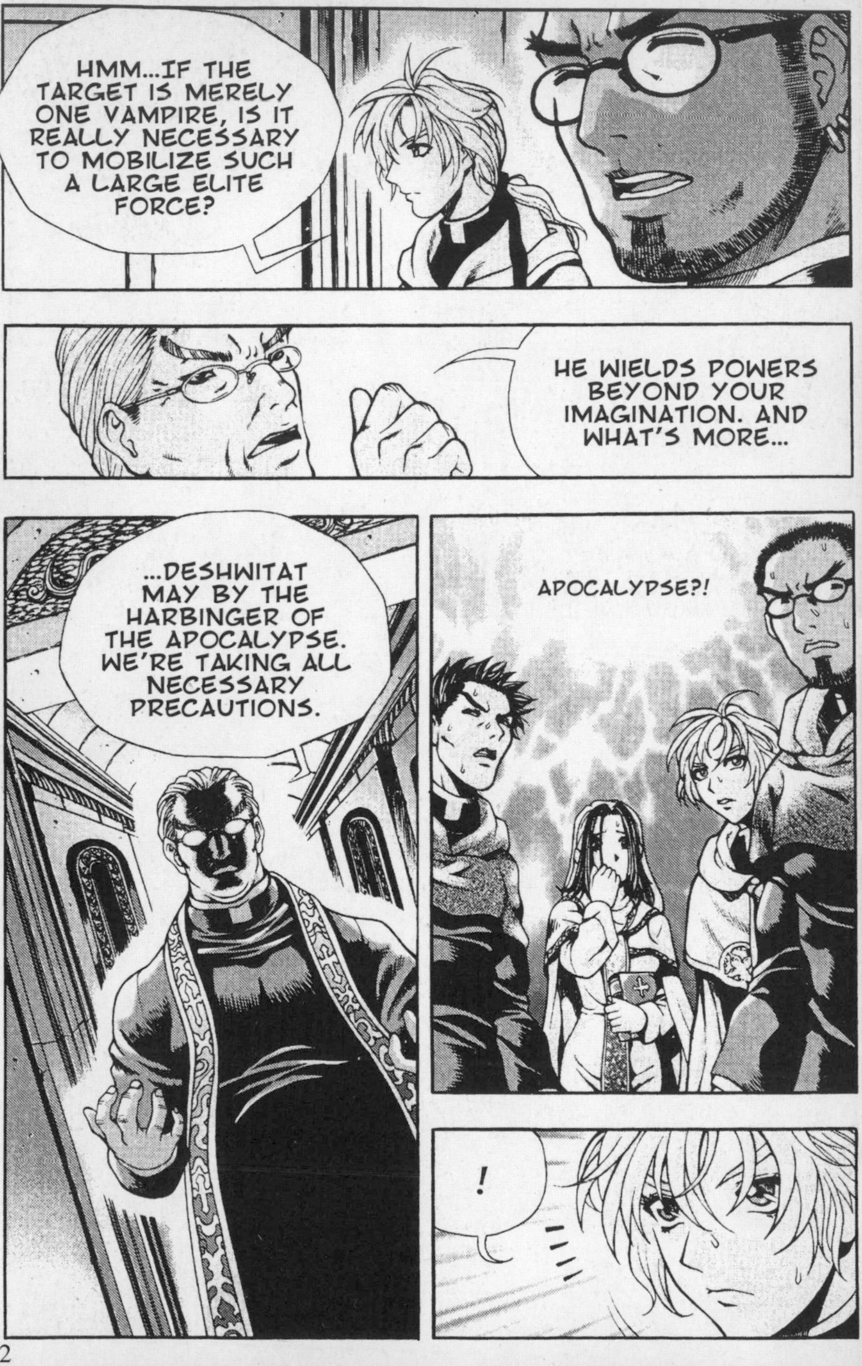
HMM...IF THE TARGET IS MERELY ONE VAMPIRE, IS IT REALLY NECESSARY TO MOBILIZE SUCH A LARGE ELITE FORCE?
HE WIELDS POWERS BEYOND YOUR IMAGINATION. AND WHAT'S MORE...
...DESHWITAT MAY BY THE HARBINGER OF THE APOCALYPSE. WE'RE TAKING ALL NECESSARY PRECAUTIONS.
APOCALYPSE?!
!

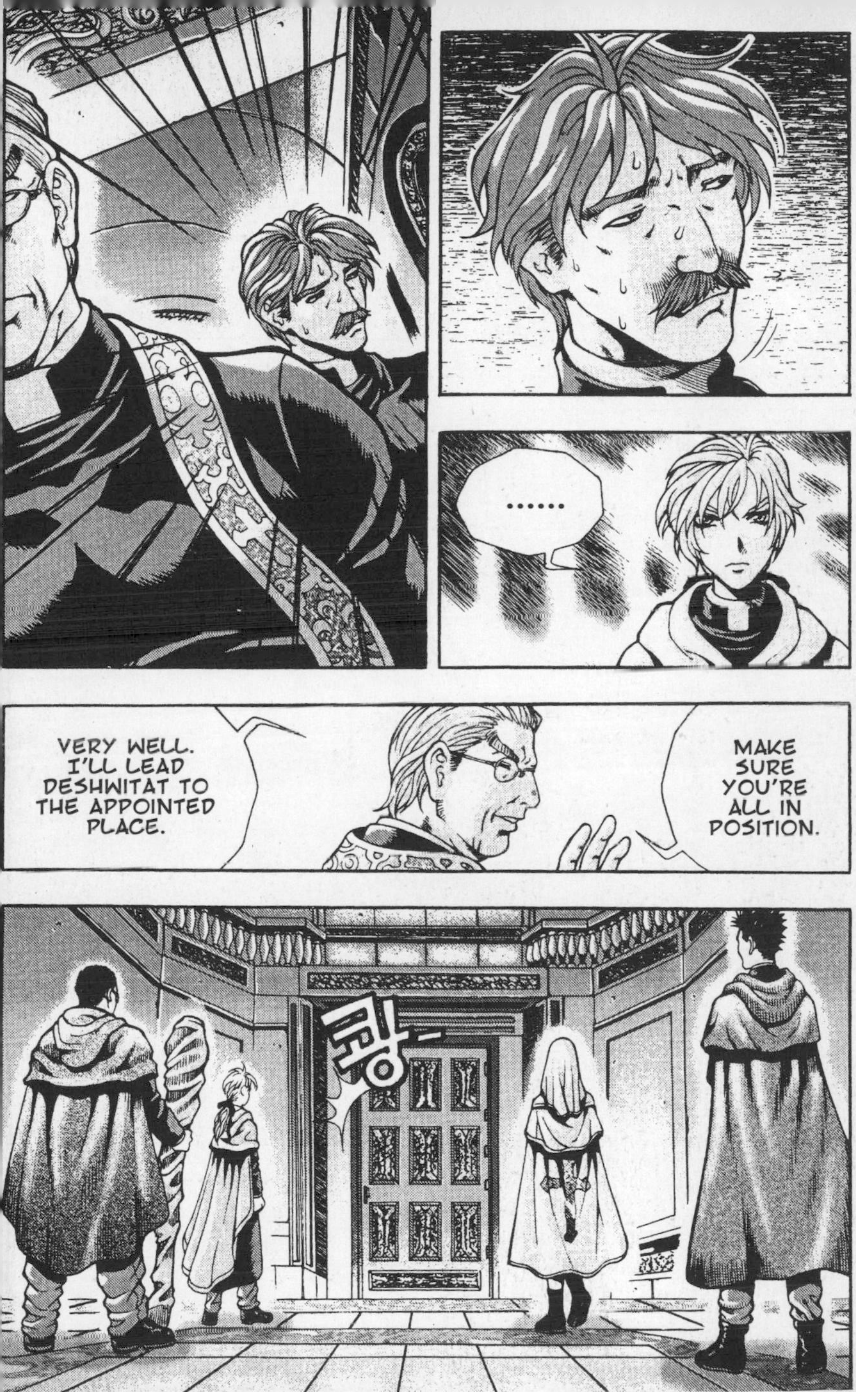

......
VERY WELL. I'LL LEAD DESHWITAT TO THE APPOINTED PLACE.
MAKE SURE YOU'RE ALL IN POSITION.
쾅-

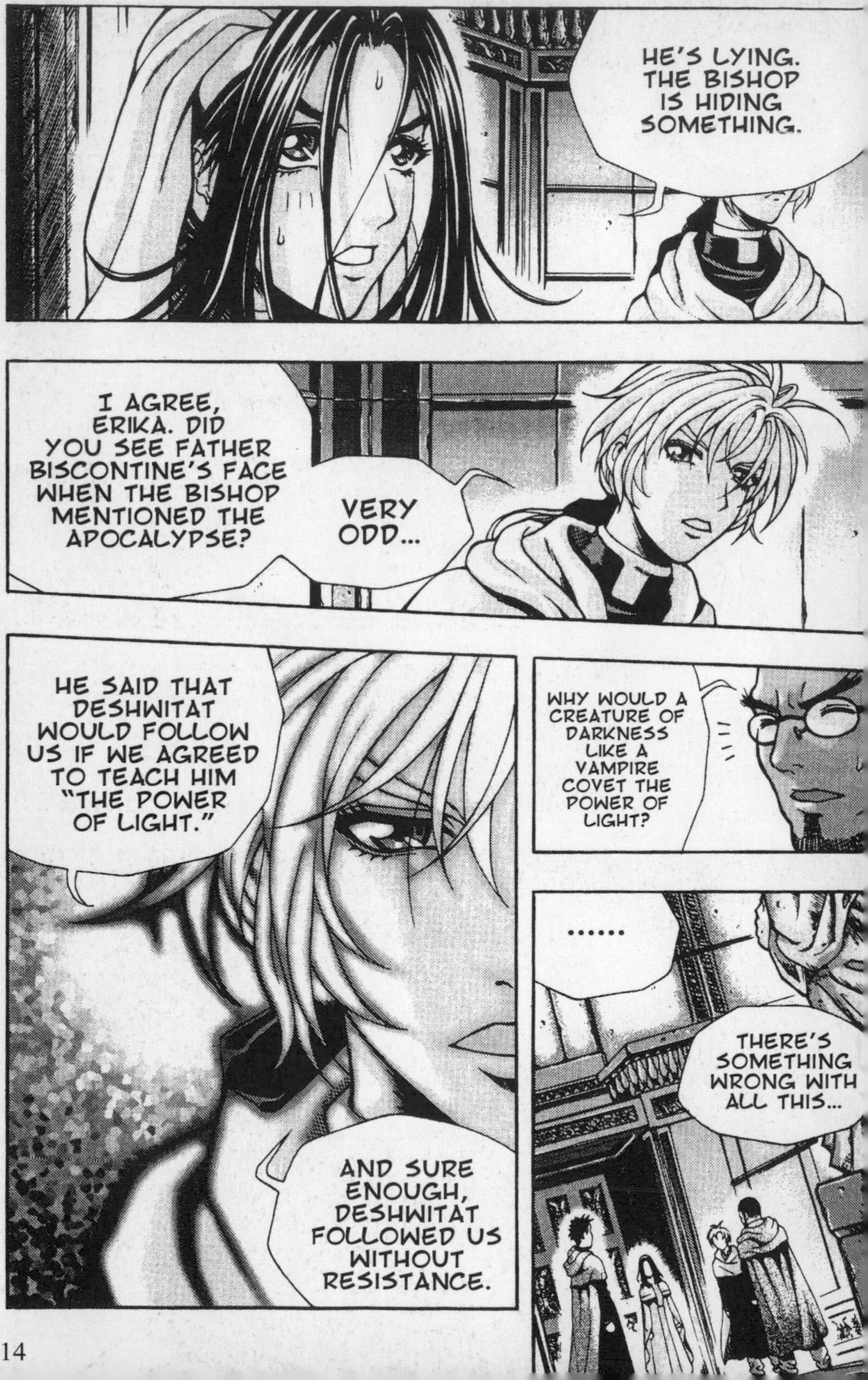
HE'S LYING. THE BISHOP IS HIDING SOMETHING.
I AGREE, ERIKA. DID YOU SEE FATHER BISCONTINE'S FACE WHEN THE BISHOP MENTIONED THE APOCALYPSE?
VERY ODD...
HE SAID THAT DESHWITAT WOULD FOLLOW US IF WE AGREED TO TEACH HIM "THE POWER OF LIGHT."
AND SURE ENOUGH, DESHWITAT FOLLOWED US WITHOUT RESISTANCE.
WHY WOULD A CREATURE OF DARKNESS LIKE A VAMPIRE COVET THE POWER OF LIGHT?
......
THERE'S SOMETHING WRONG WITH ALL THIS...

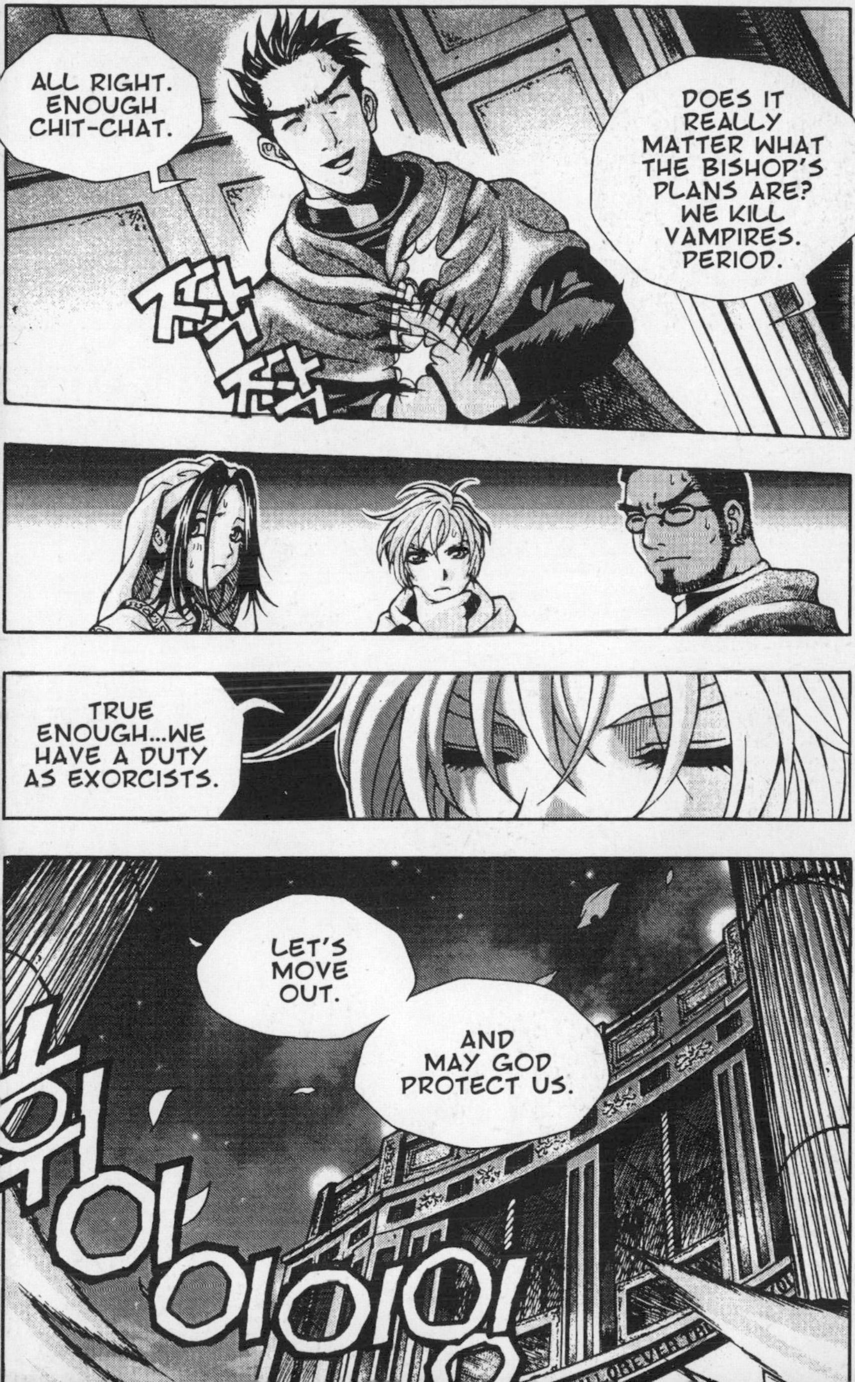
ALL RIGHT. ENOUGH CHIT-CHAT.
DOES IT REALLY MATTER WHAT THE BISHOP'S PLANS ARE? WE KILL VAMPIRES. PERIOD.
TRUE ENOUGH...WE HAVE A DUTY AS EXORCISTS.
LET'S MOVE OUT.
AND MAY GOD PROTECT US.

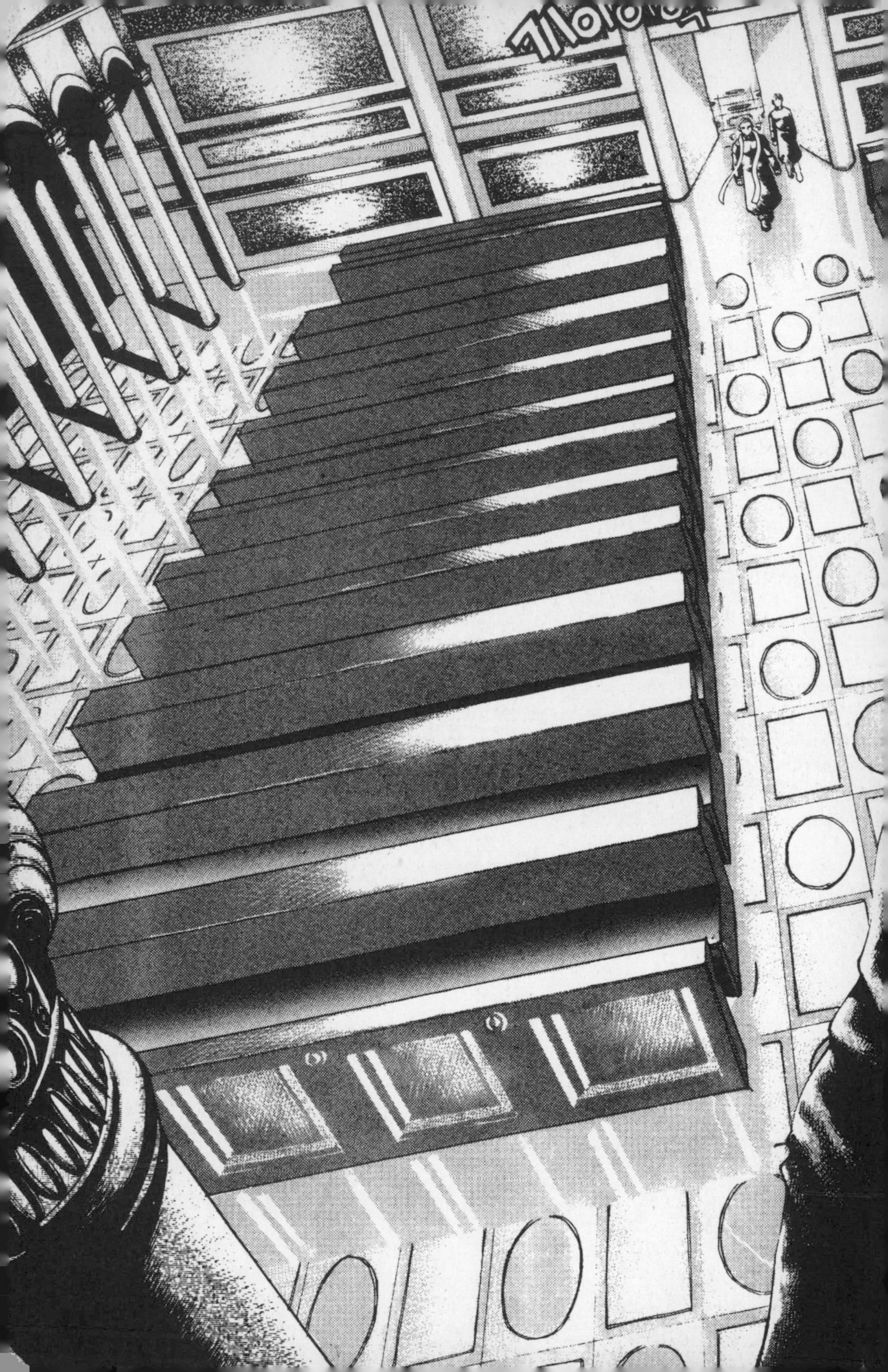
끼이이익

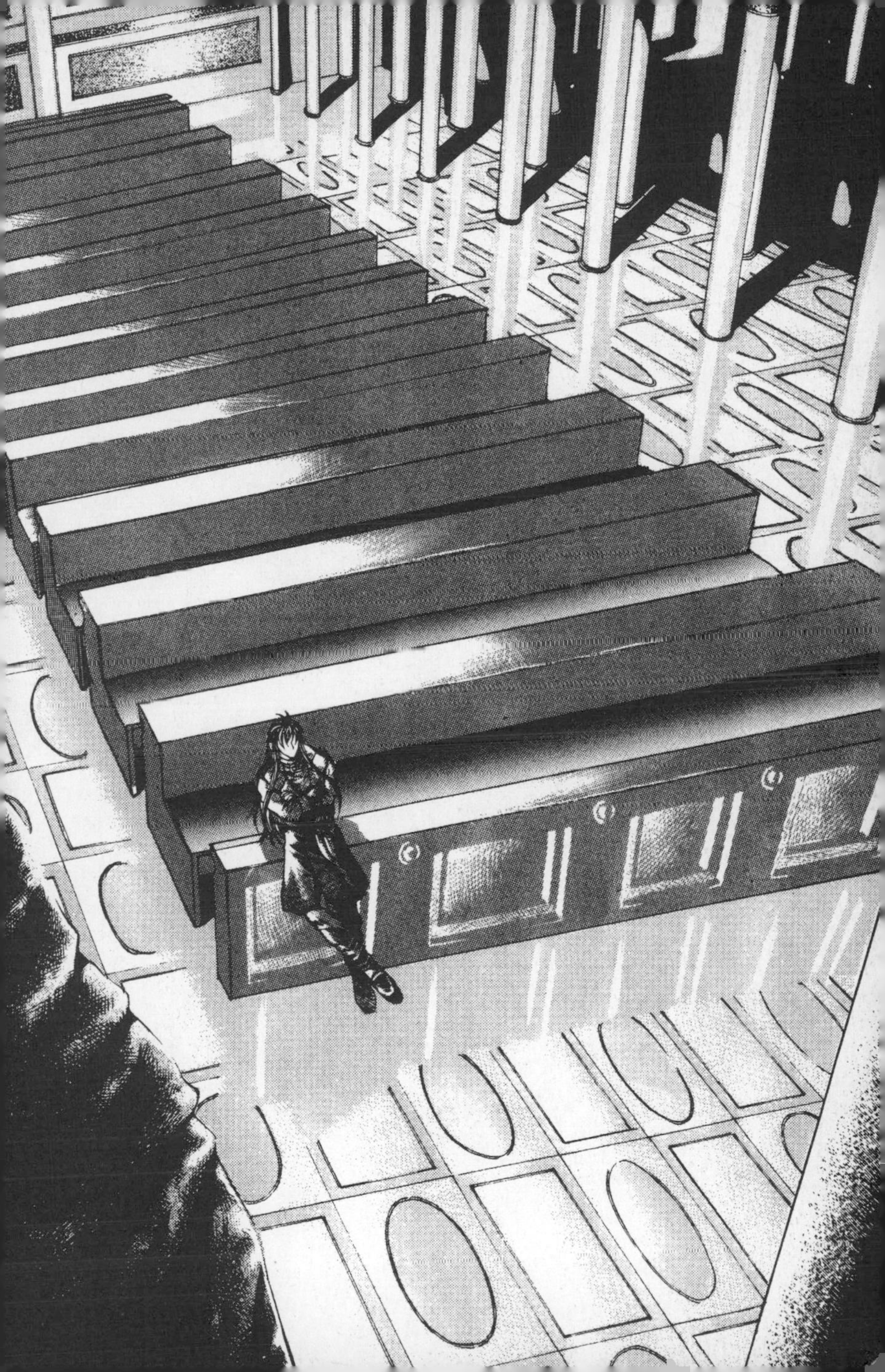

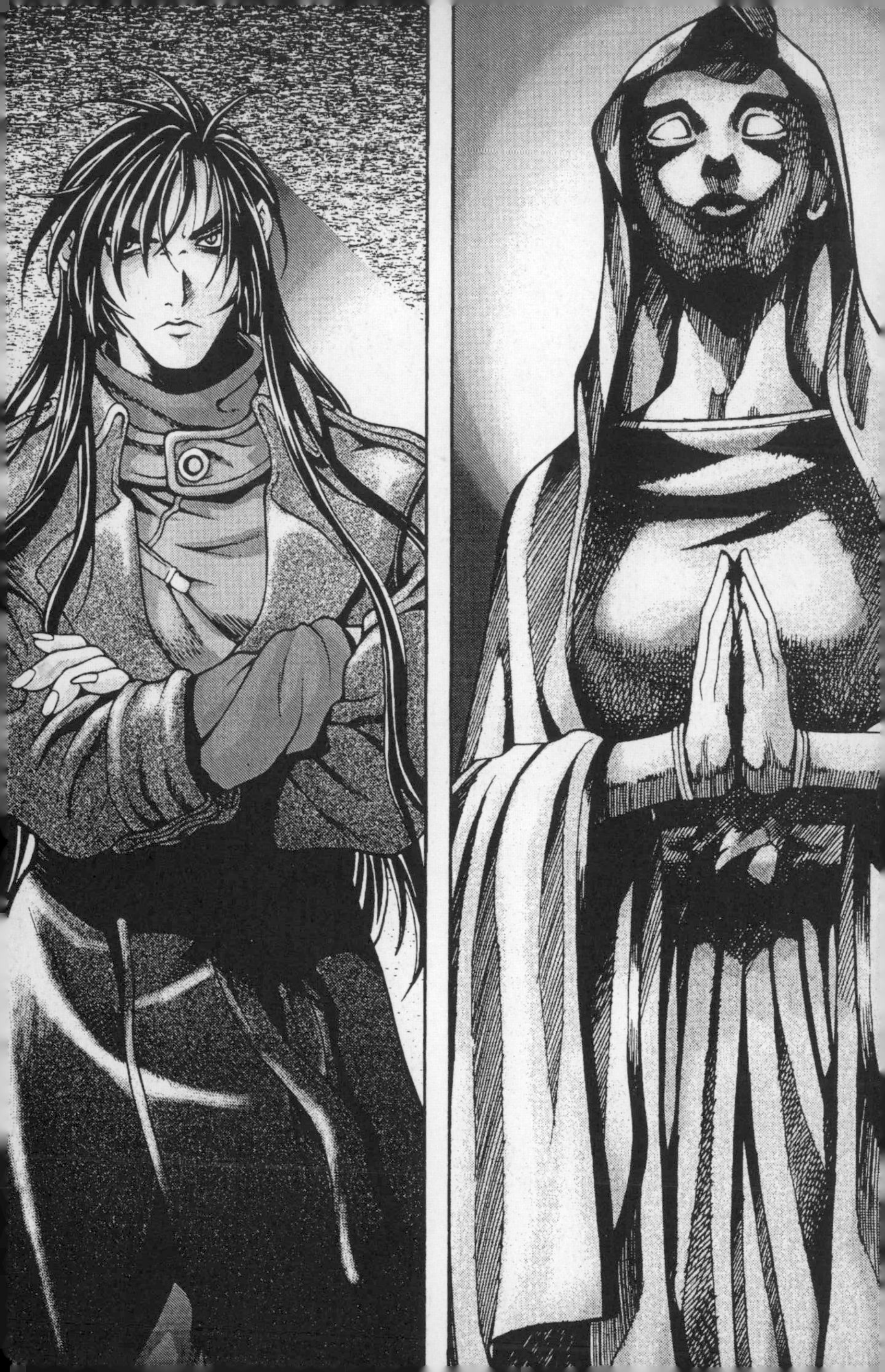

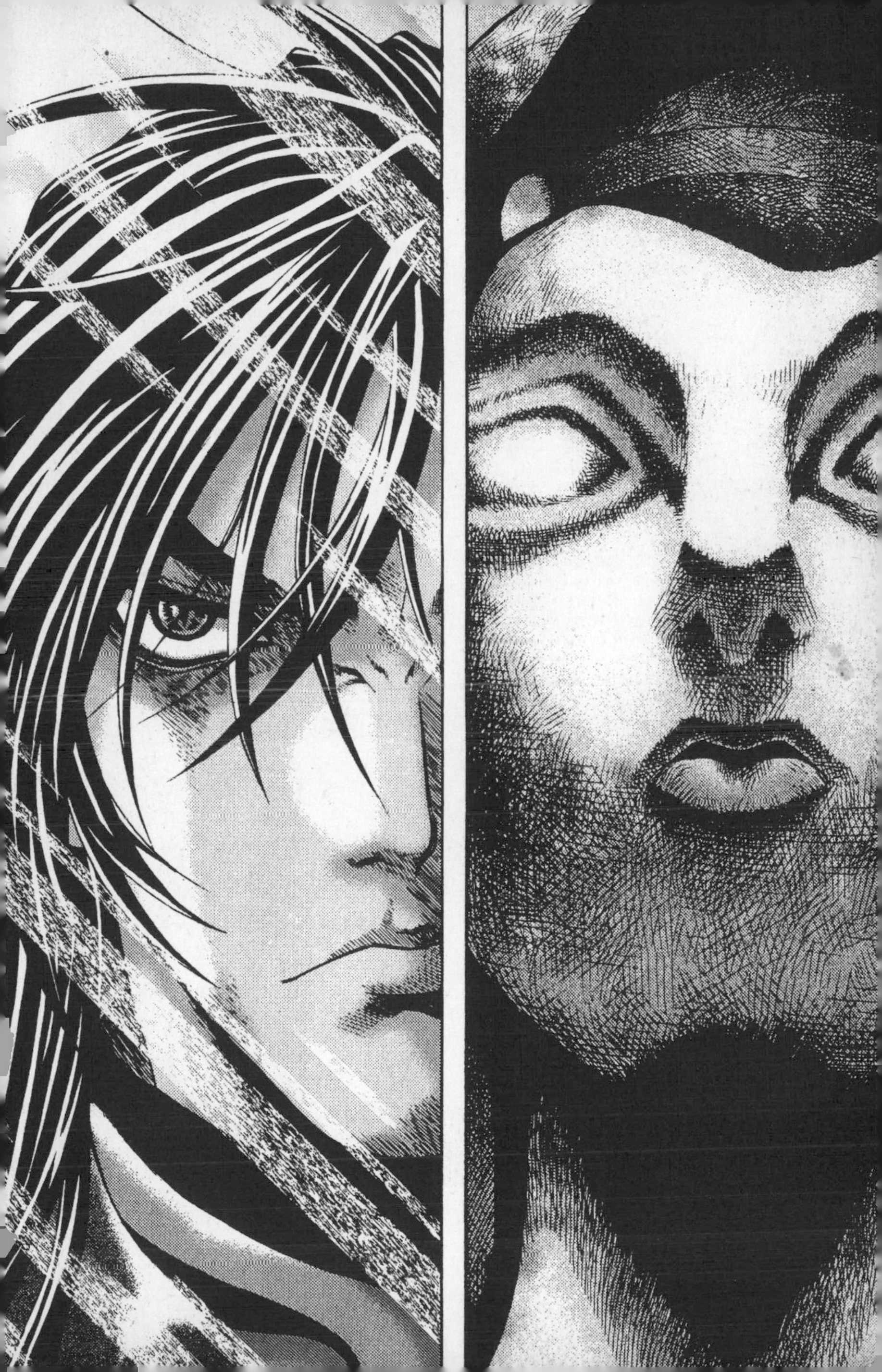

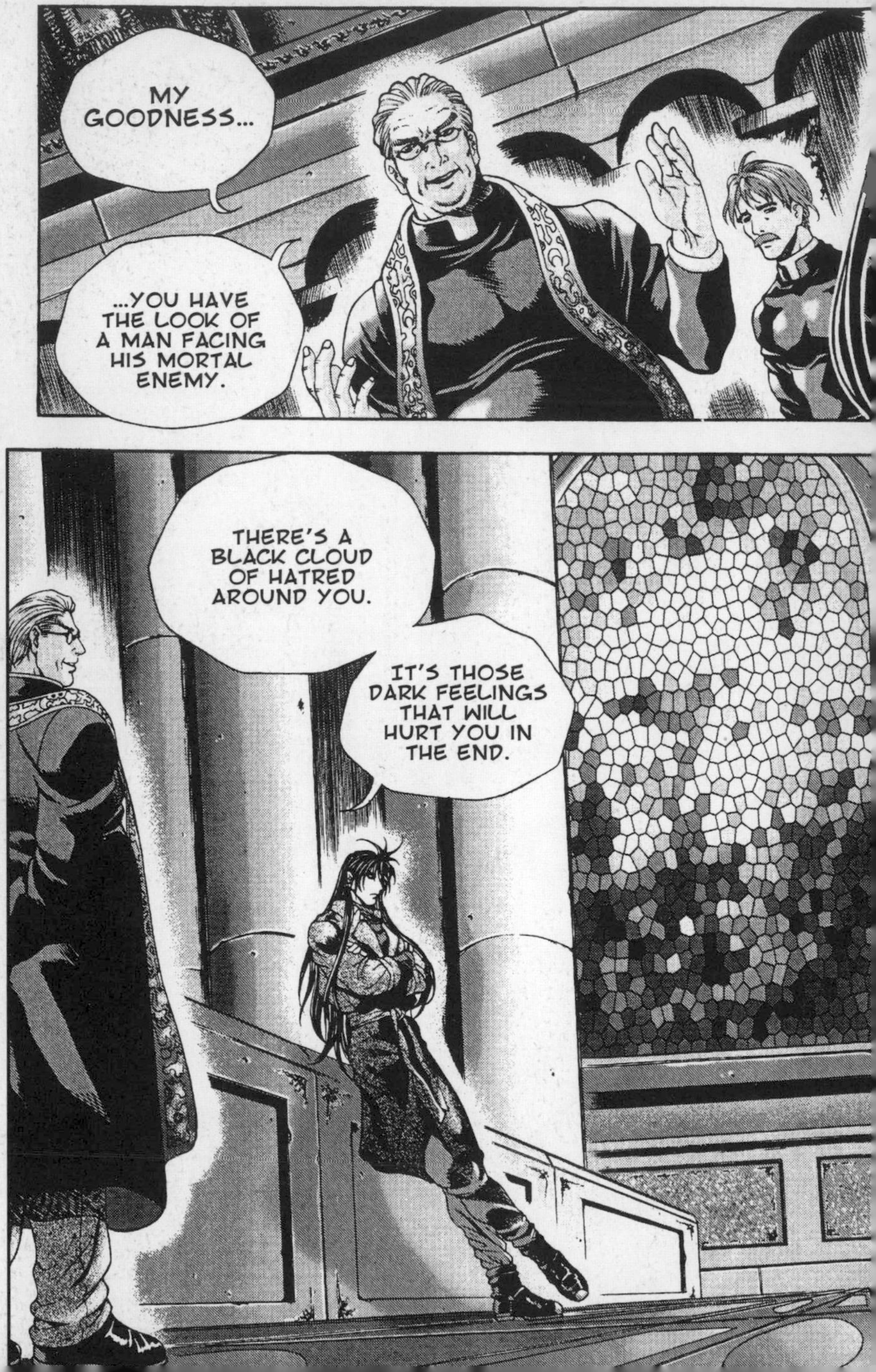
MY GOODNESS...
...YOU HAVE THE LOOK OF A MAN FACING HIS MORTAL ENEMY.
THERE'S A BLACK CLOUD OF HATRED AROUND YOU.
IT'S THOSE DARK FEELINGS THAT WILL HURT YOU IN THE END.

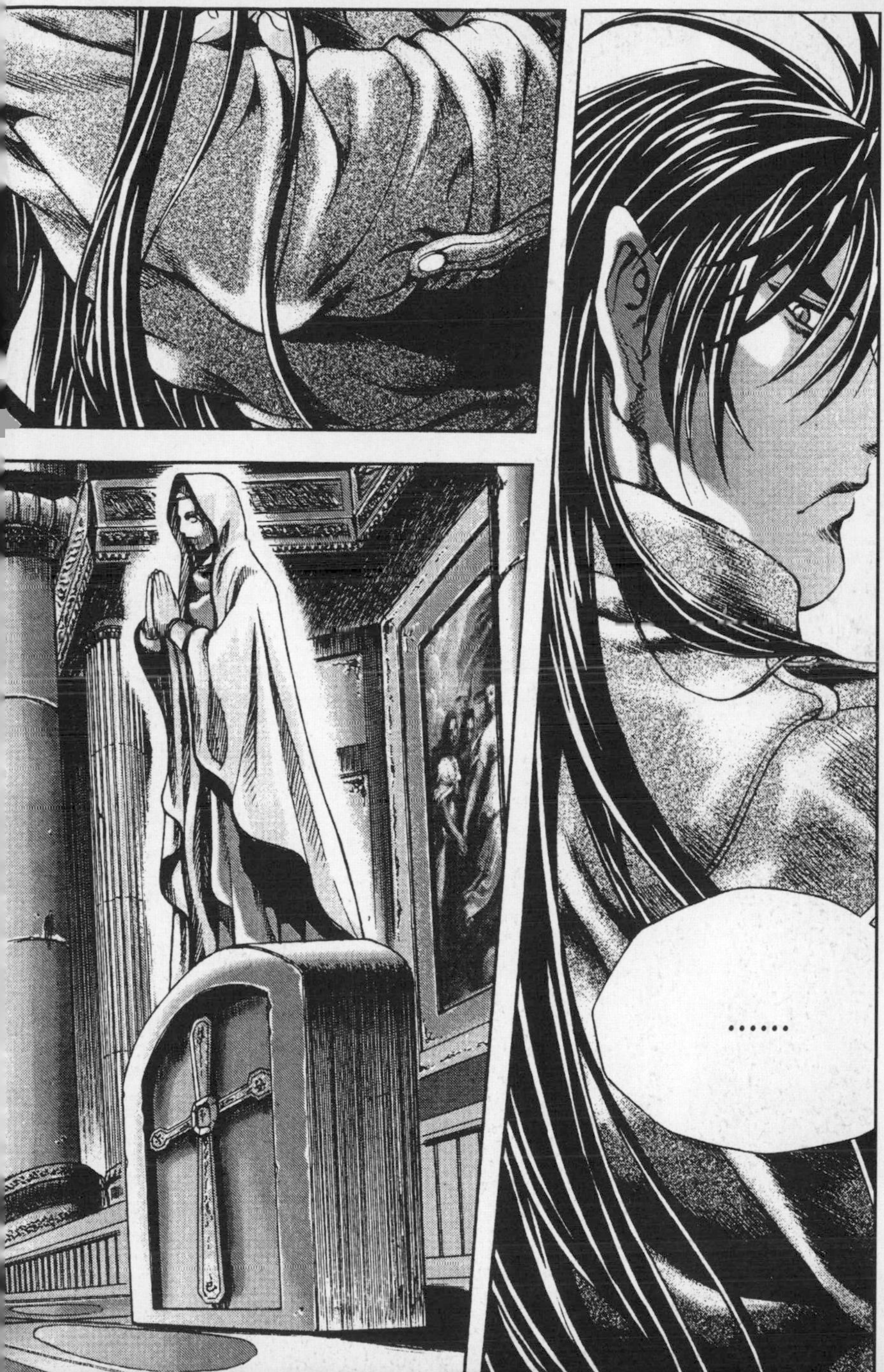
......

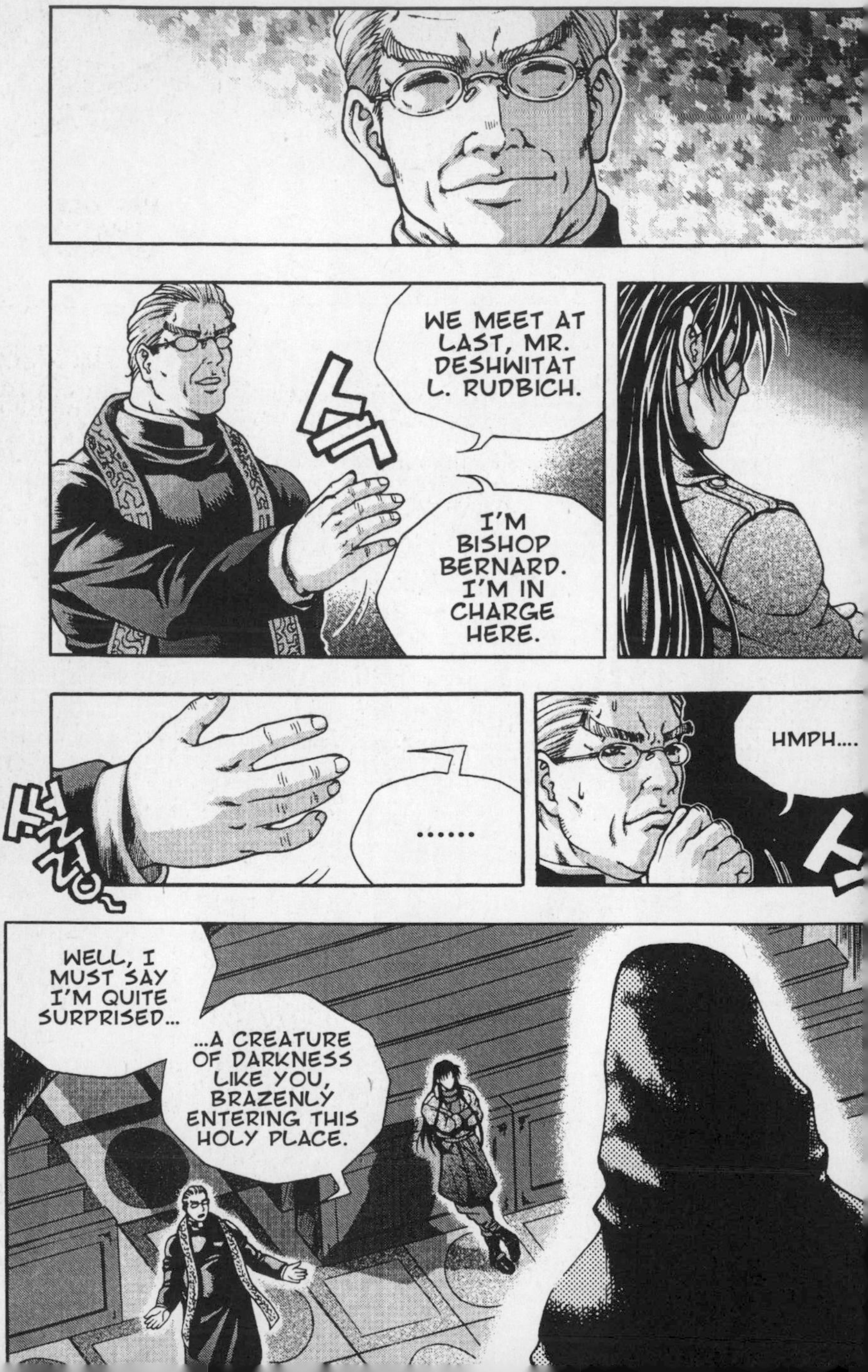
WE MEET AT LAST, MR. DESHWITAT L. RUDBICH.
I'M BISHOP BERNARD. I'M IN CHARGE HERE.
HMPH....
......
WELL, I MUST SAY I'M QUITE SURPRISED...
...A CREATURE OF DARKNESS LIKE YOU, BRAZENLY ENTERING THIS HOLY PLACE.

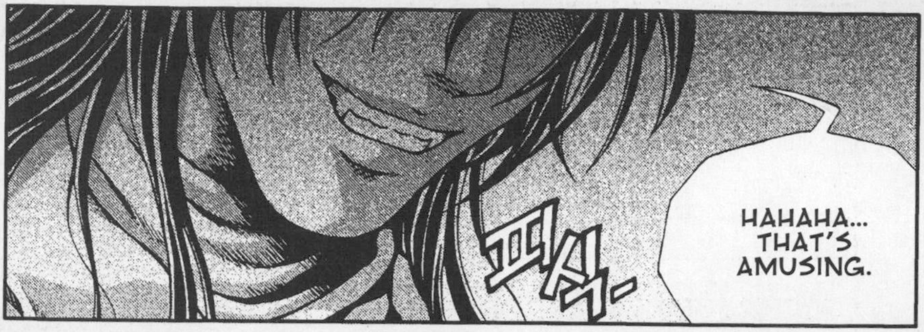
HAHAHA... THAT'S AMUSING.

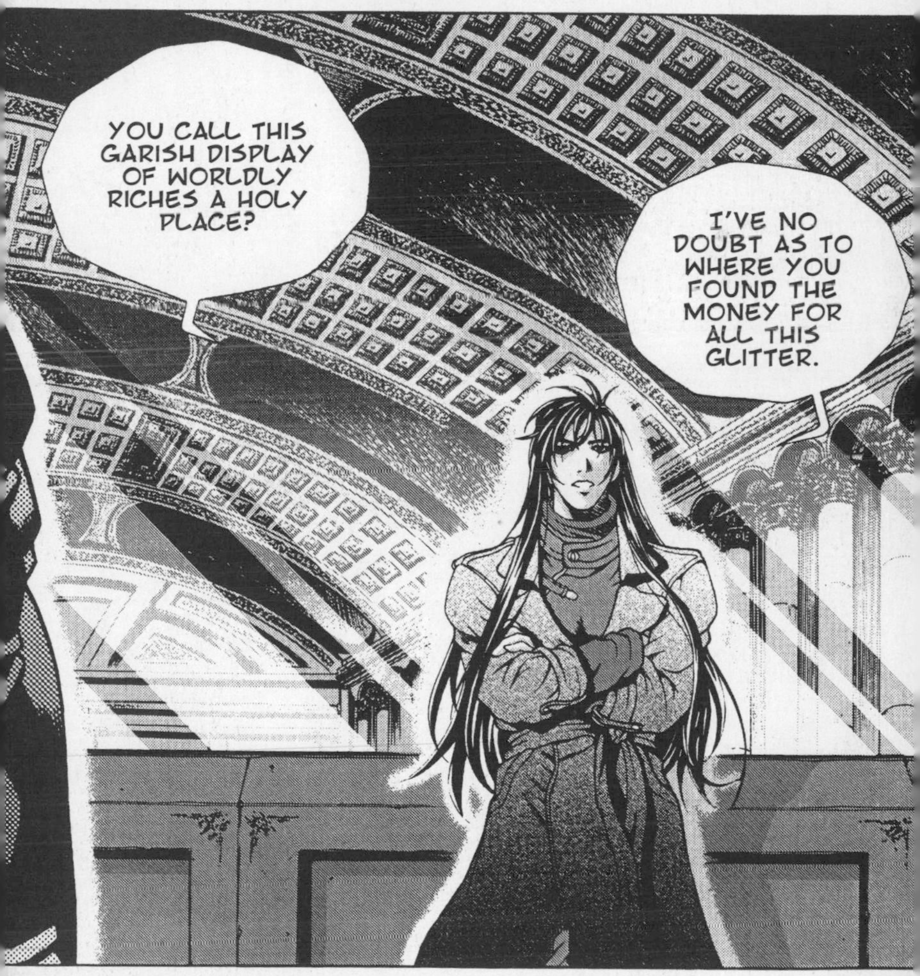
I'VE NO DOUBT AS TO WHERE YOU FOUND THE MONEY FOR ALL THIS GLITTER.
YOU CALL THIS GARISH DISPLAY OF WORLDLY RICHES A HOLY PLACE?

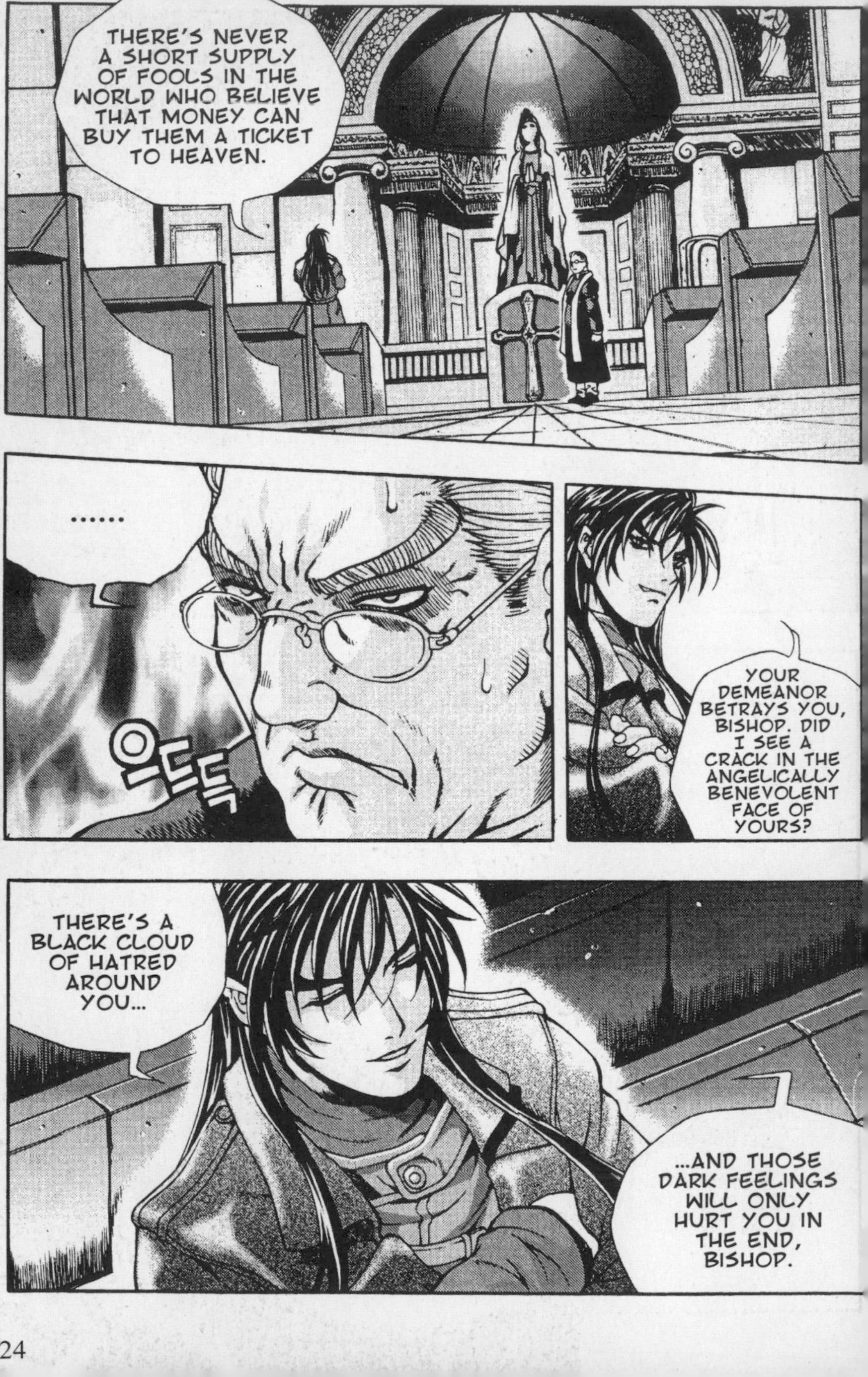
THERE'S NEVER A SHORT SUPPLY OF FOOLS IN THE WORLD WHO BELIEVE THAT MONEY CAN BUY THEM A TICKET TO HEAVEN.
......
YOUR DEMEANOR BETRAYS YOU, BISHOP. DID I SEE A CRACK IN THE ANGELICALLY BENEVOLENT FACE OF YOURS?
THERE'S A BLACK CLOUD OF HATRED AROUND YOU...
...AND THOSE DARK FEELINGS WILL ONLY HURT YOU IN THE END, BISHOP.

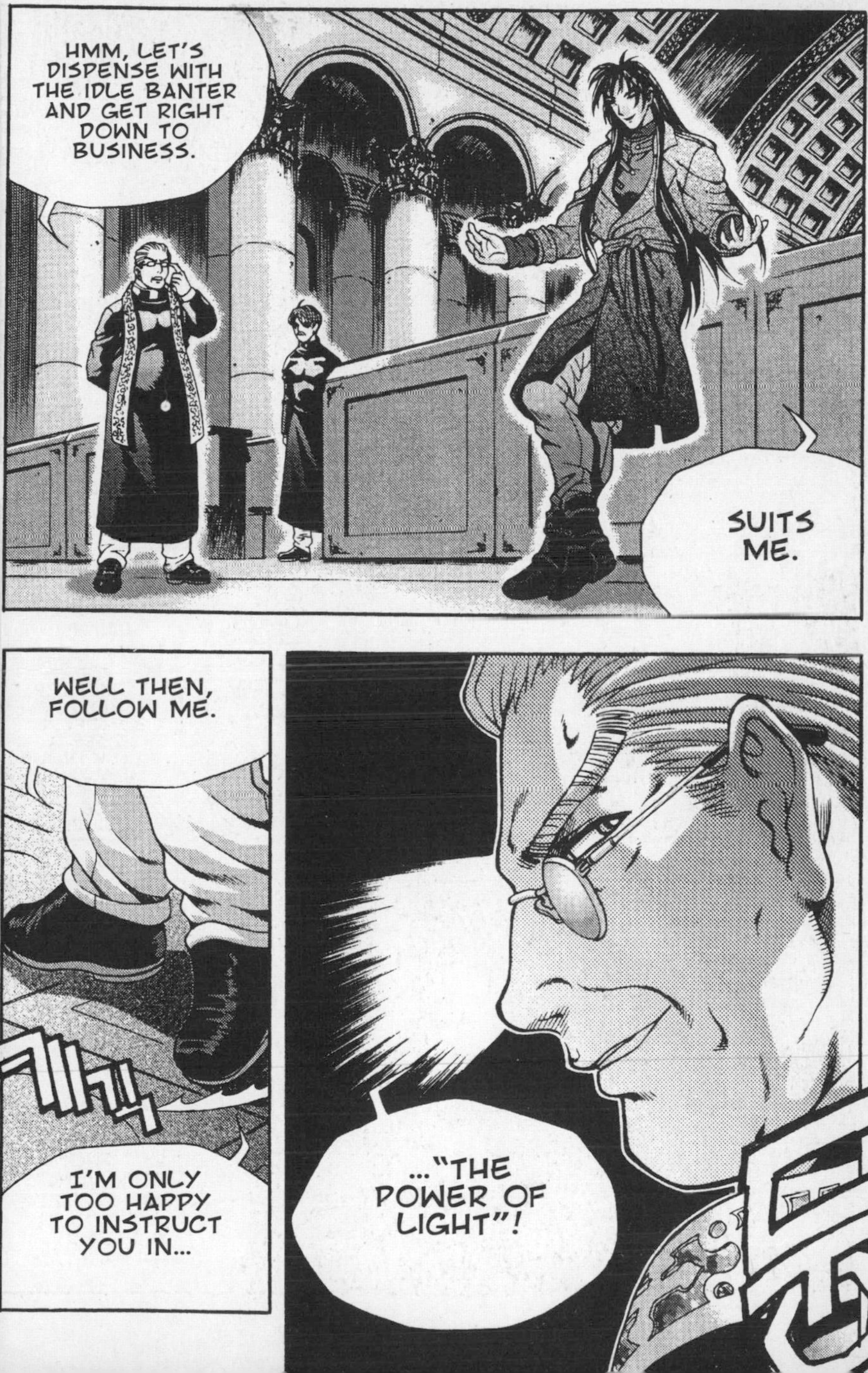
HMM, LET'S DISPENSE WITH THE IDLE BANTER AND GET RIGHT DOWN TO BUSINESS.
SUITS ME.
WELL THEN, FOLLOW ME.
I'M ONLY TOO HAPPY TO INSTRUCT YOU IN...
..."THE POWER OF LIGHT"!

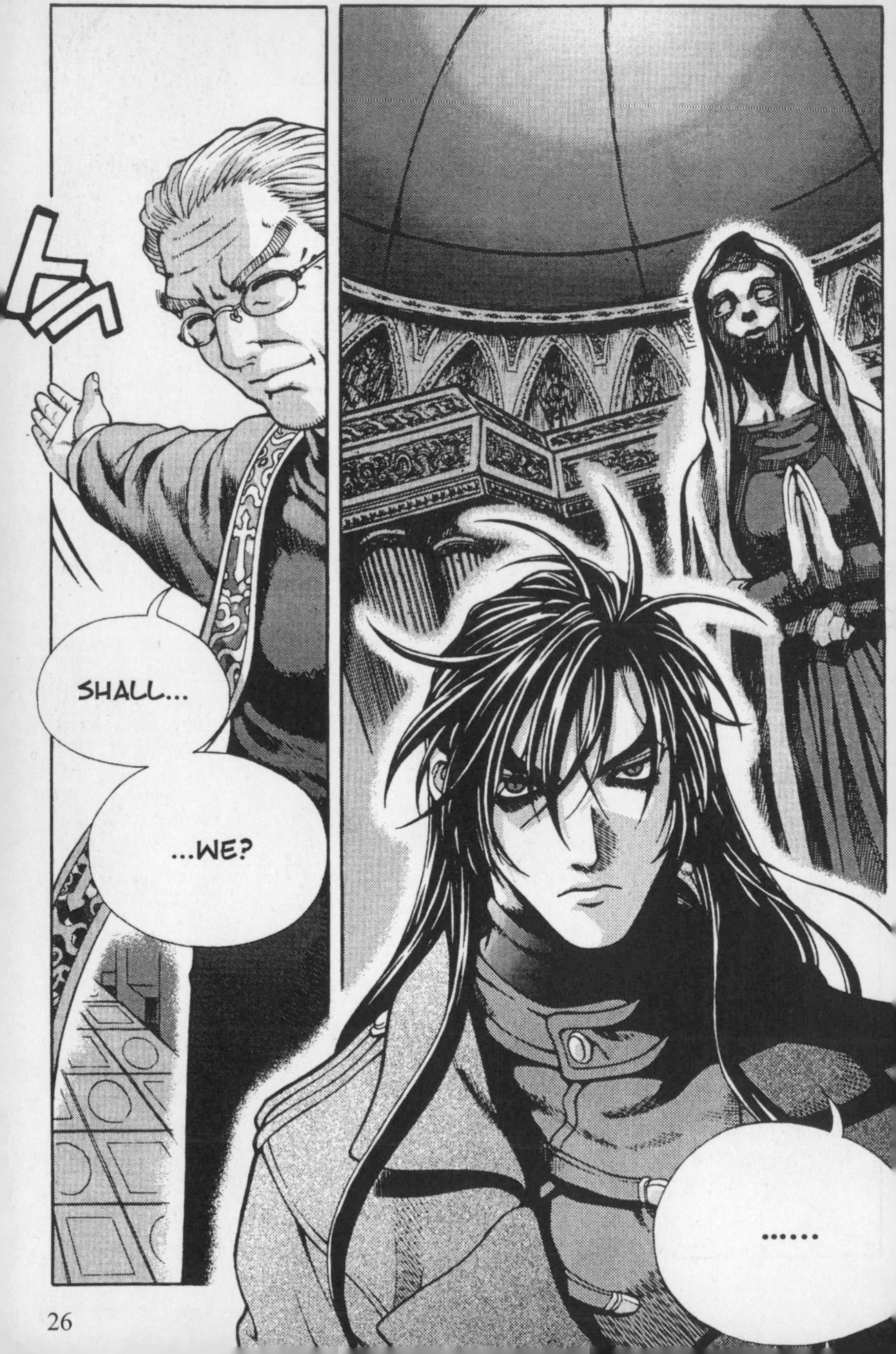
SHALL...
...WE?
......

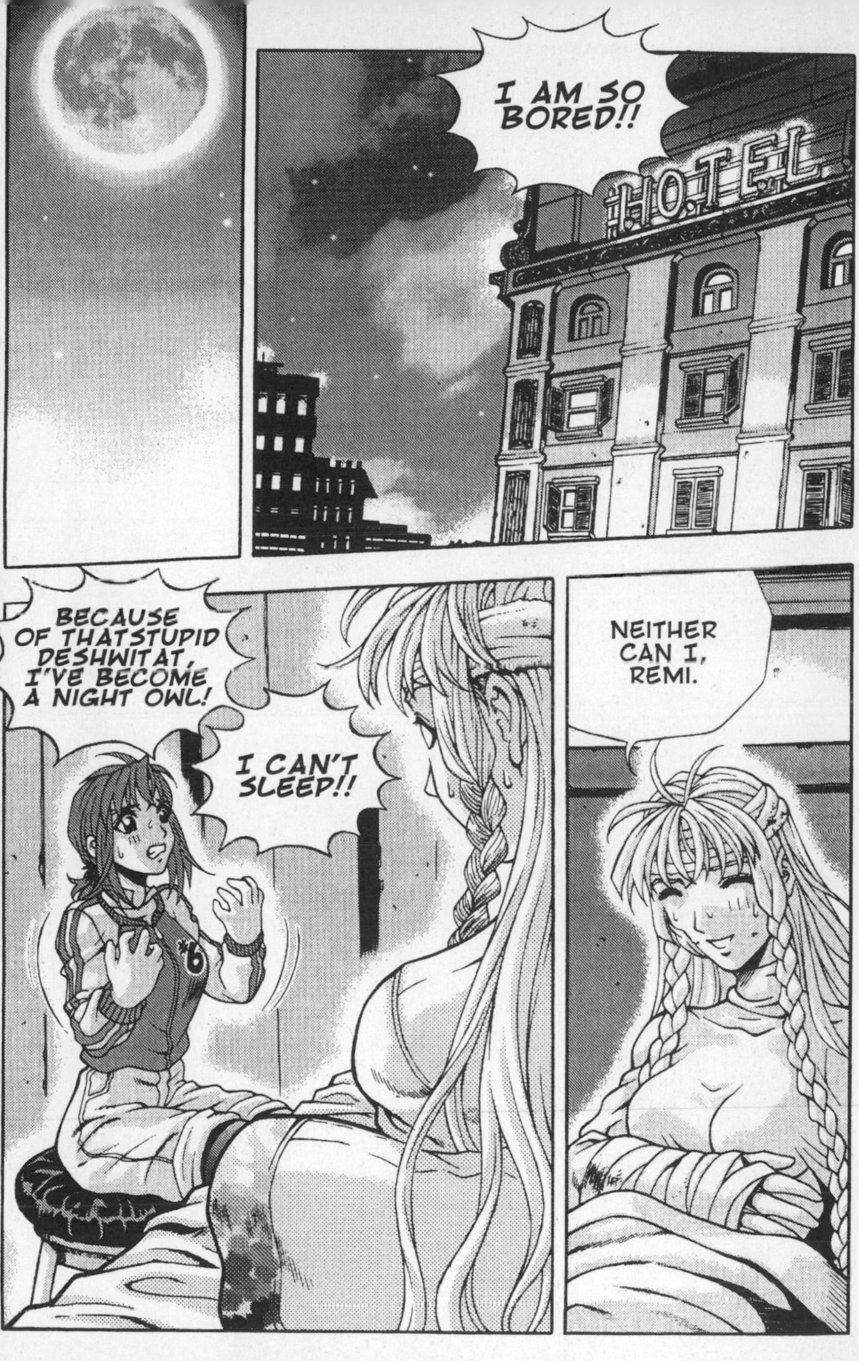
I AM SO BORED!!
HOTEL
BECAUSE OF THATSTUPID DESHWITAT, I'VE BECOME A NIGHT OWL!
I CAN'T SLEEP!!
NEITHER CAN I, REMI.

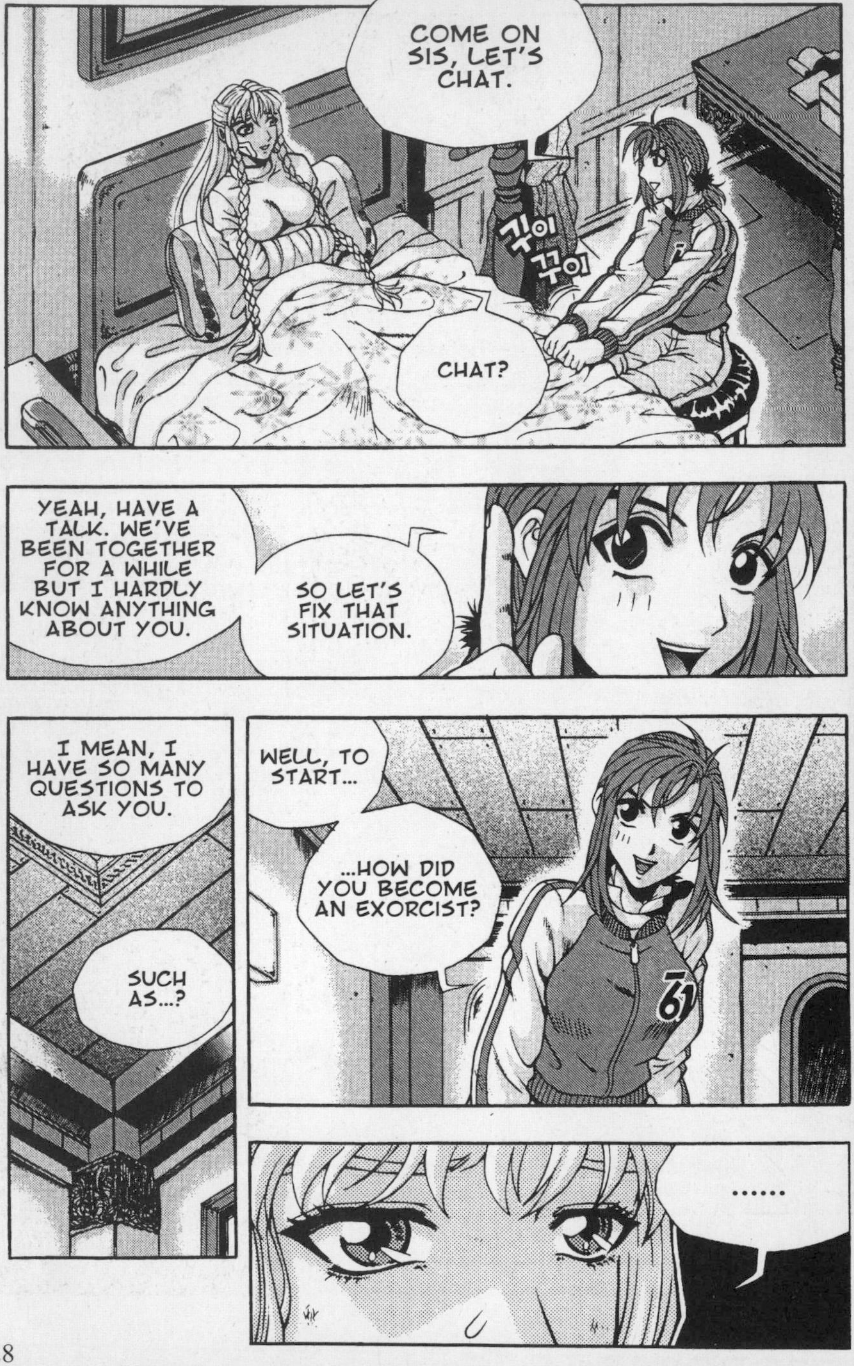
COME ON SIS, LET'S CHAT.
CHAT?
YEAH, HAVE A TALK. WE'VE BEEN TOGETHER FOR A WHILE BUT I HARDLY KNOW ANYTHING ABOUT YOU.
SO LET'S FIX THAT SITUATION.
I MEAN, I HAVE SO MANY QUESTIONS TO ASK YOU.
SUCH AS...?
WELL, TO START...
...HOW DID YOU BECOME AN EXORCIST?
......

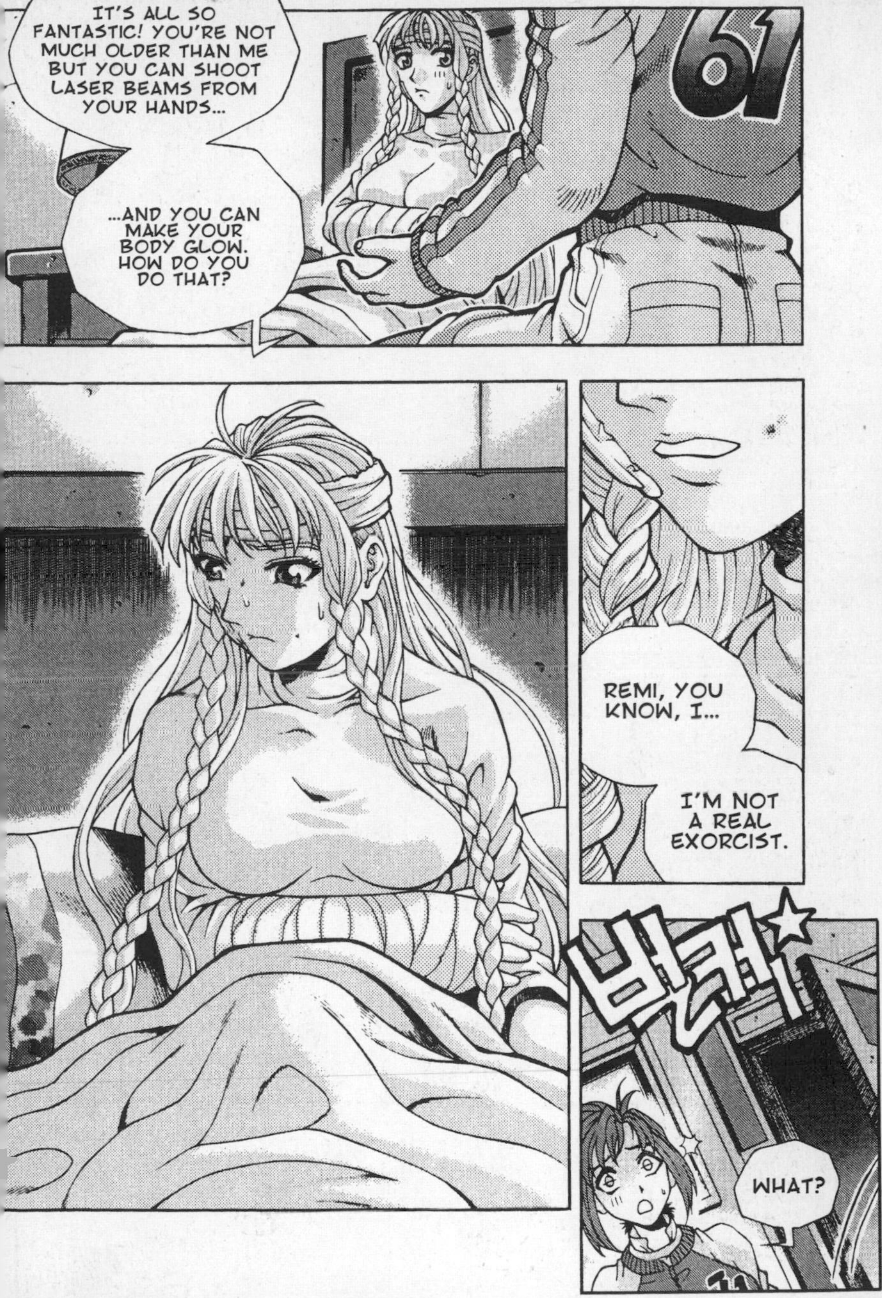
IT'S ALL SO FANTASTIC! YOU'RE NOT MUCH OLDER THAN ME BUT YOU CAN SHOOT LASER BEAMS FROM YOUR HANDS...
...AND YOU CAN MAKE YOUR BODY GLOW. HOW DO YOU DO THAT?
REMI, YOU KNOW, I...
I'M NOT A REAL EXORCIST.
WHAT?

RE... RETT?!

HOW RUDE! BARGING INTO A LADIES' BEDROOM!!

MIL

LEN

NE

AR

IT'S TIME FOR YOUR SHOT.

UM... YES!

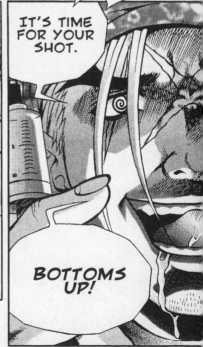

BOTTOMS UP!

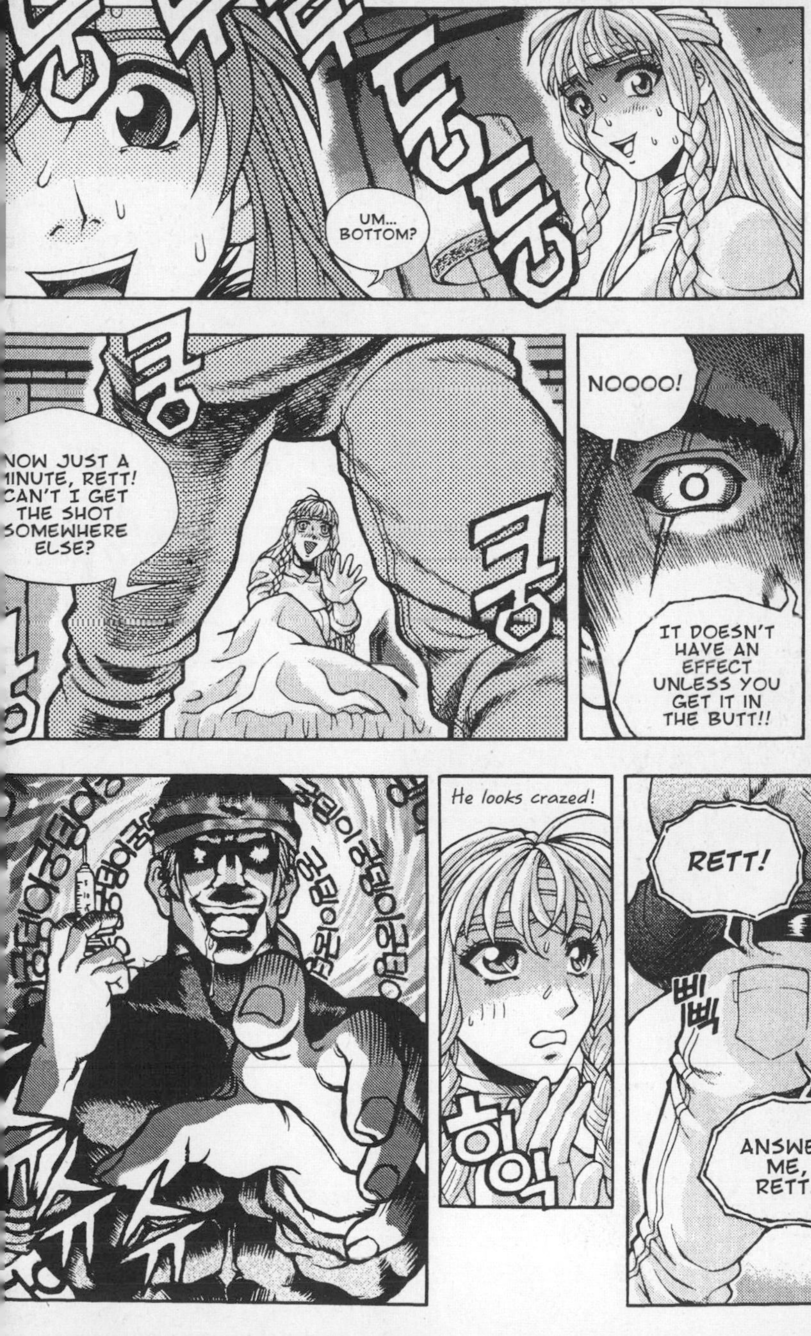
UM... BOTTOM?
쿵
NOW JUST A MINUTE, RETT! CAN'T I GET THE SHOT SOMEWHERE ELSE?
쿵
NOOOO!
IT DOESN'T HAVE AN EFFECT UNLESS YOU GET IT IN THE BUTT!!
He looks crazed!
히익
RETT!
빠빡
빡
ANSWER ME, RETT!

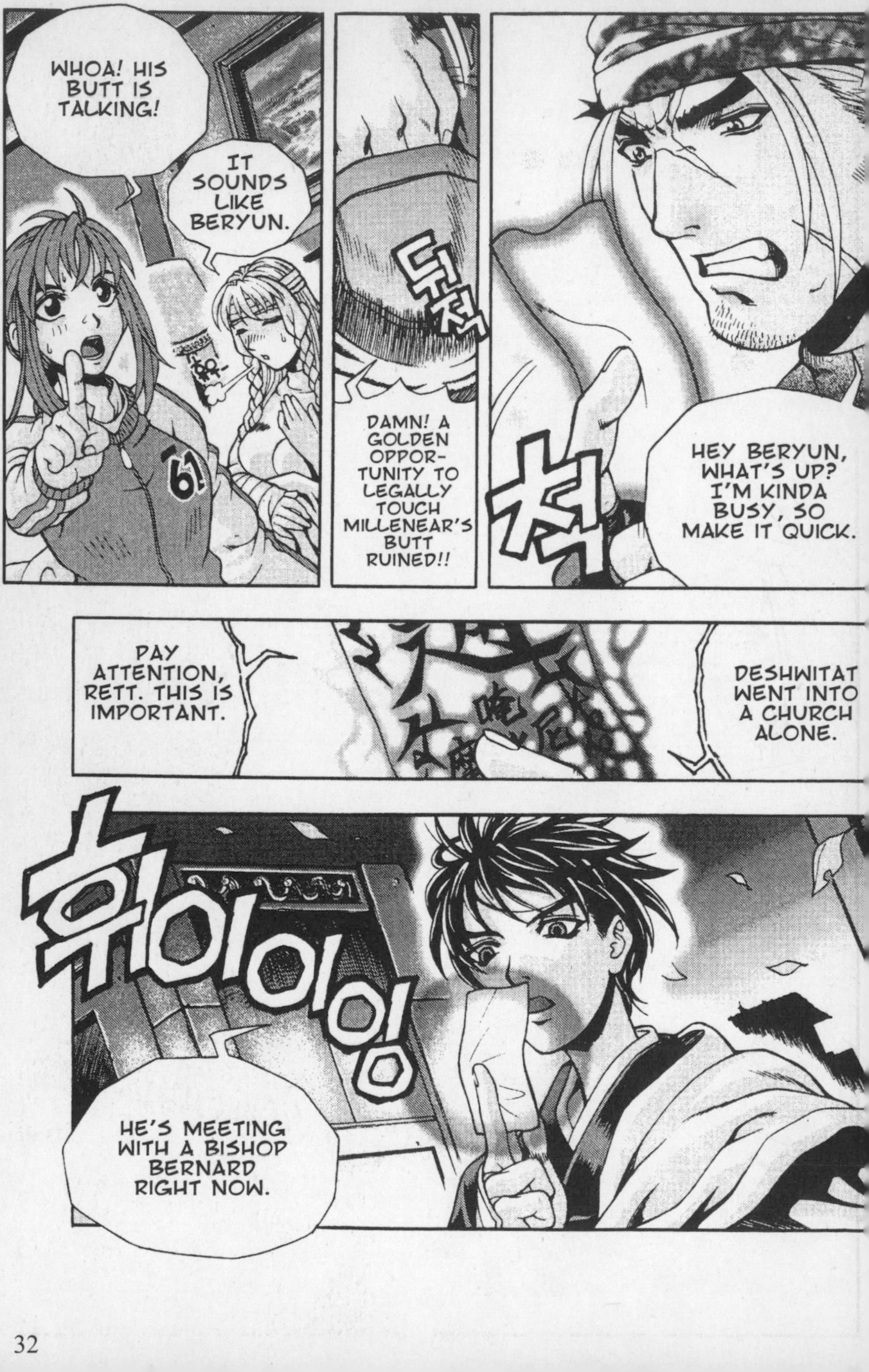
WHOA! HIS BUTT IS TALKING!
IT SOUNDS LIKE BERYUN.
DAMN! A GOLDEN OPPOR-TUNITY TO LEGALLY TOUCH MILLENEAR'S BUTT RUINED!!
척
HEY BERYUN, WHAT'S UP? I'M KINDA BUSY, SO MAKE IT QUICK.
PAY ATTENTION, RETT. THIS IS IMPORTANT.
DESHWITAT WENT INTO A CHURCH ALONE.
휘이이이잉
HE'S MEETING WITH A BISHOP BERNARD RIGHT NOW.

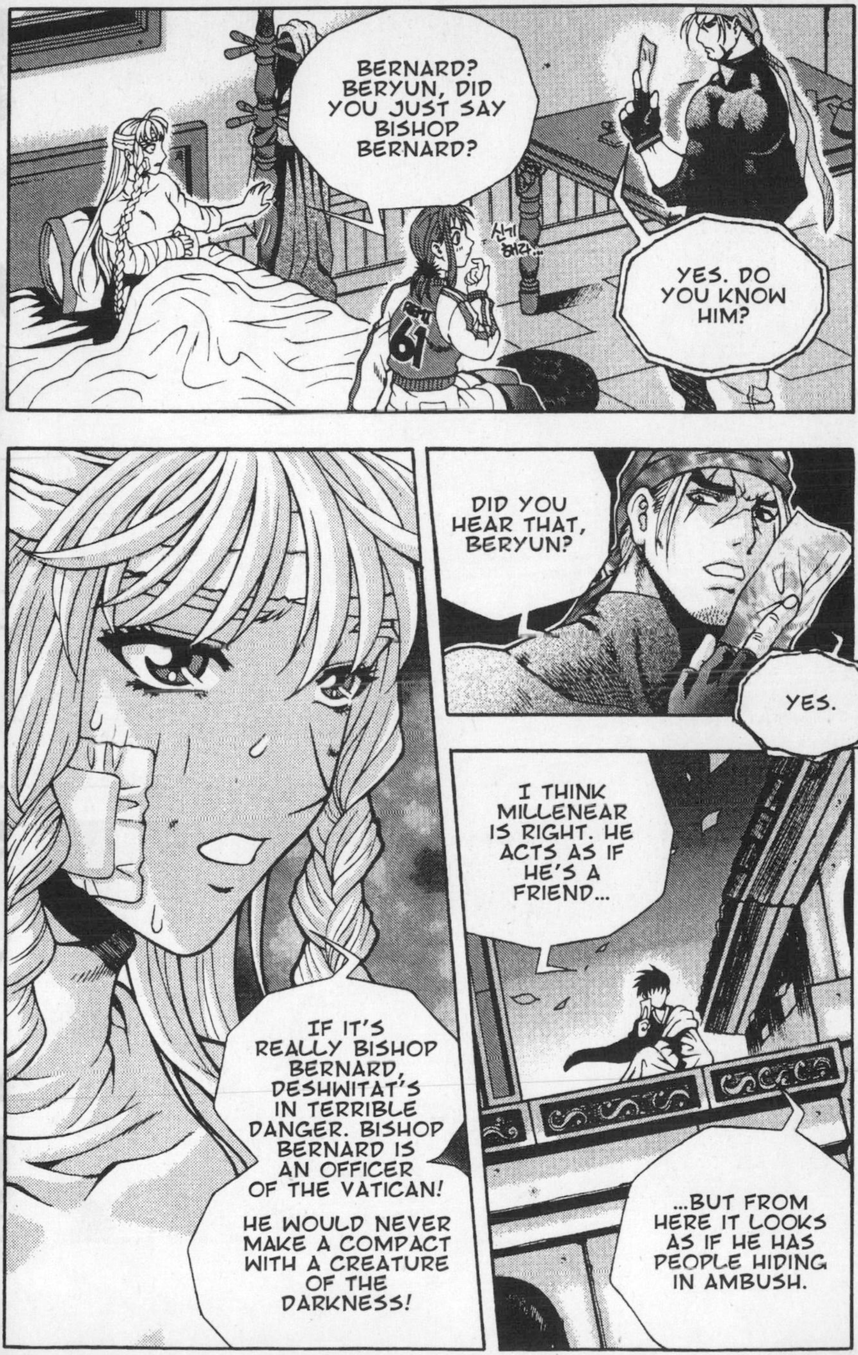
BERNARD? BERYUN, DID YOU JUST SAY BISHOP BERNARD?
신기해라...
YES. DO YOU KNOW HIM?
IF IT'S REALLY BISHOP BERNARD, DESHWITAT'S IN TERRIBLE DANGER. BISHOP BERNARD IS AN OFFICER OF THE VATICAN!
HE WOULD NEVER MAKE A COMPACT WITH A CREATURE OF THE DARKNESS!
DID YOU HEAR THAT, BERYUN?
YES.
I THINK MILLENEAR IS RIGHT. HE ACTS AS IF HE'S A FRIEND...
...BUT FROM HERE IT LOOKS AS IF HE HAS PEOPLE HIDING IN AMBUSH.

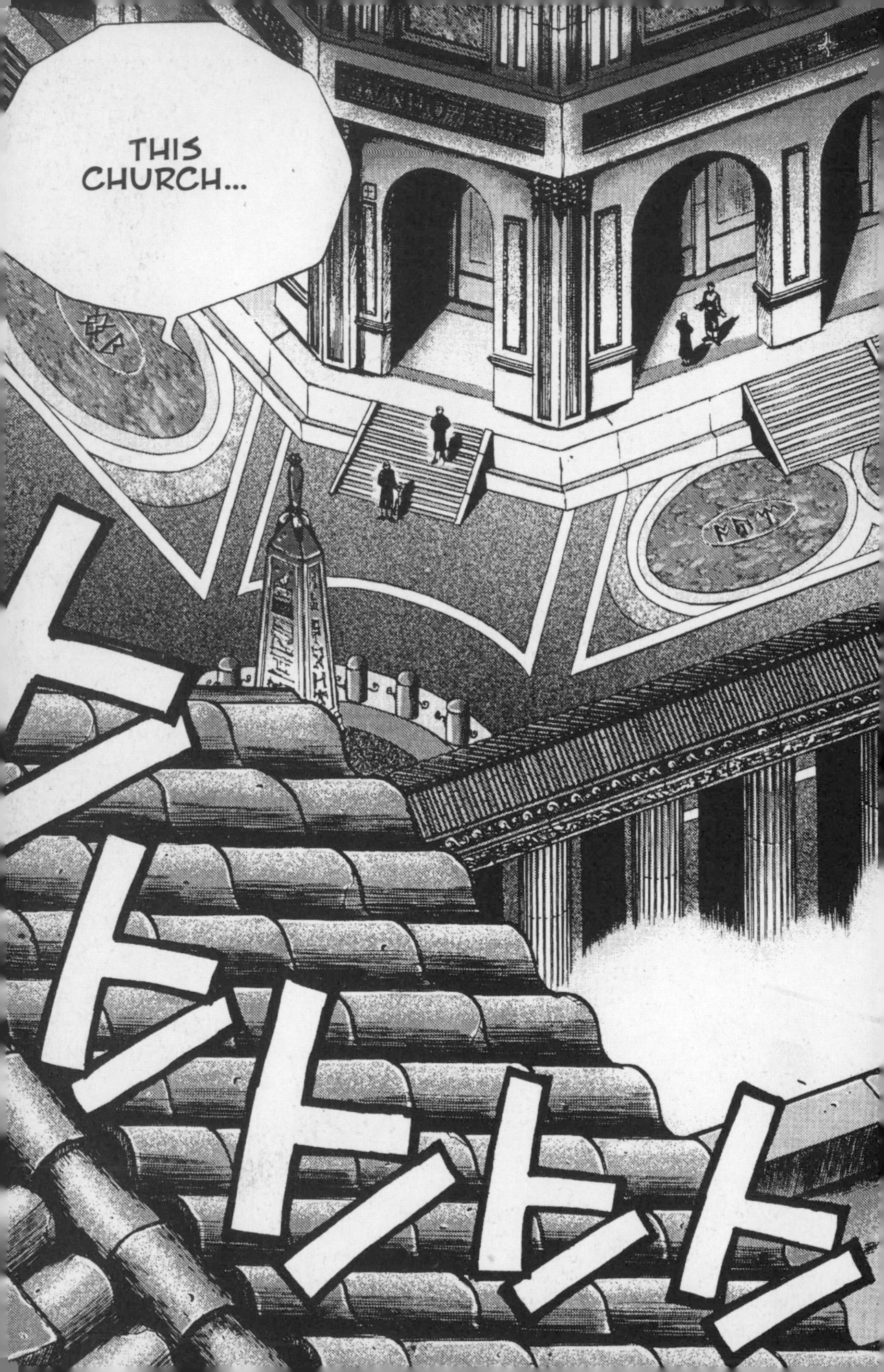
THIS CHURCH...
トトトト

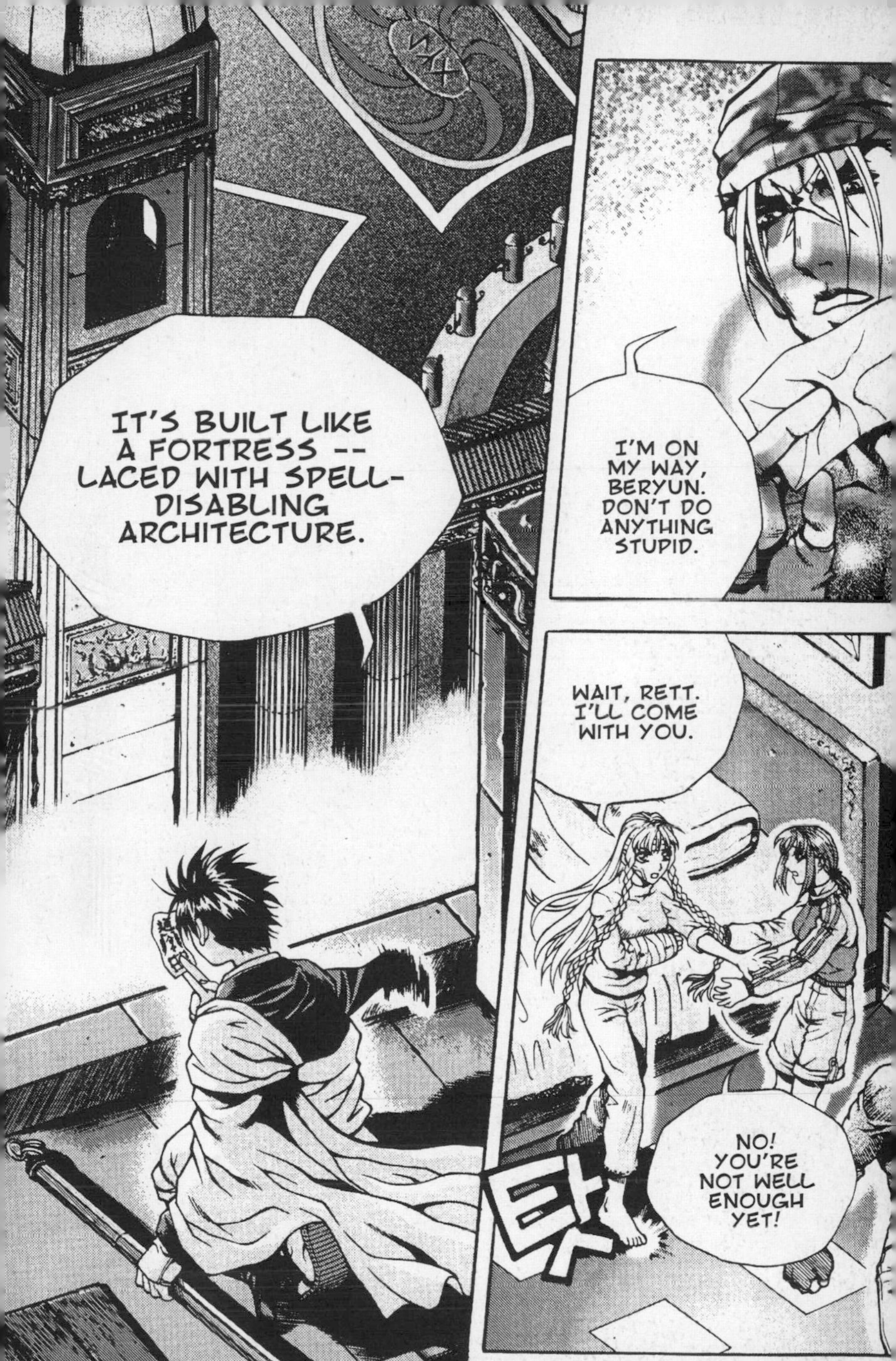
I'M ON MY WAY, BERYUN. DON'T DO ANYTHING STUPID.
WAIT, RETT. I'LL COME WITH YOU.
NO! YOU'RE NOT WELL ENOUGH YET!
IT'S BUILT LIKE A FORTRESS -- LACED WITH SPELL-DISABLING ARCHITECTURE.

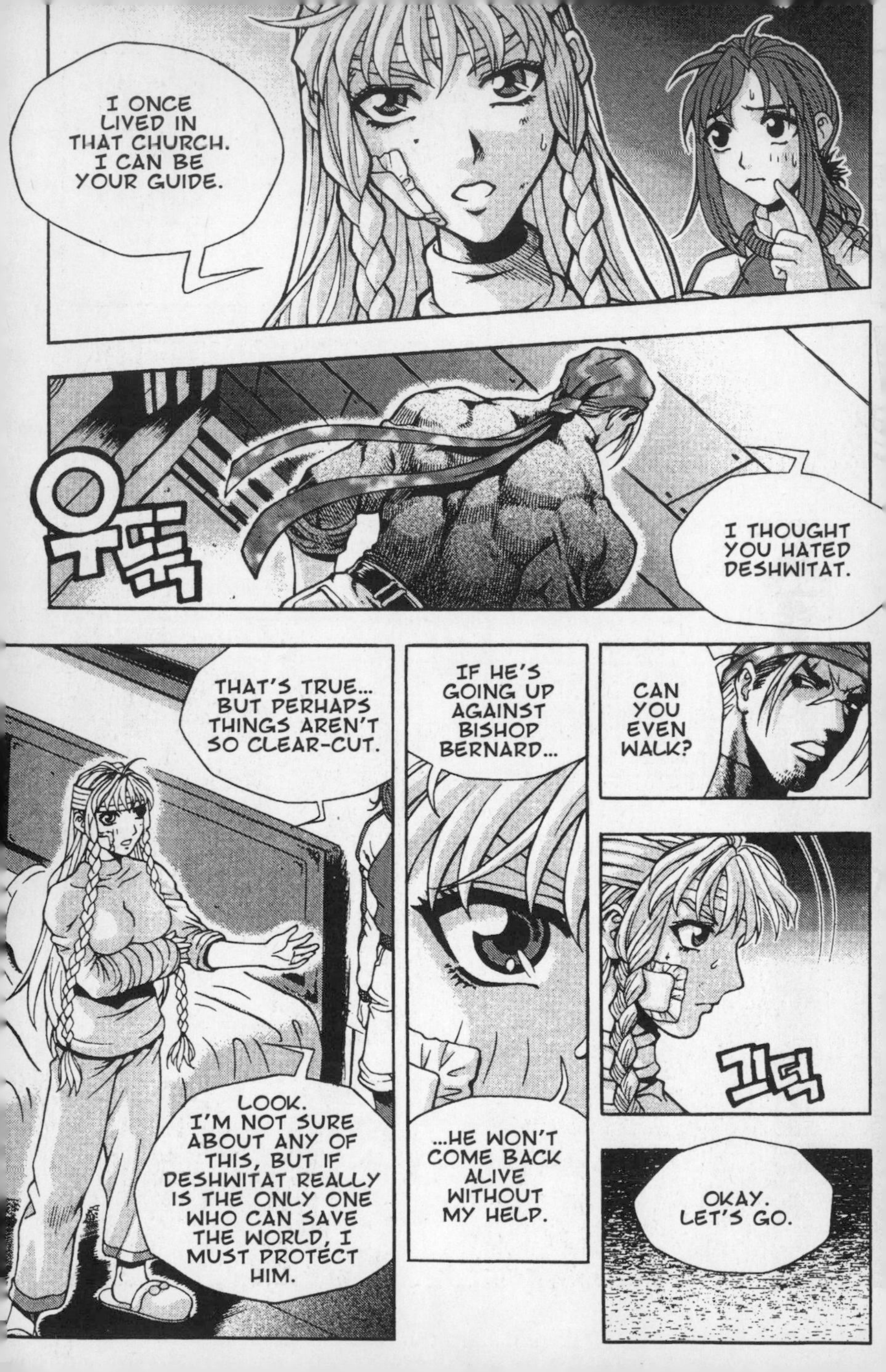
I ONCE LIVED IN THAT CHURCH. I CAN BE YOUR GUIDE.
I THOUGHT YOU HATED DESHWITAT.
THAT'S TRUE... BUT PERHAPS THINGS AREN'T SO CLEAR-CUT.
LOOK. I'M NOT SURE ABOUT ANY OF THIS, BUT IF DESHWITAT REALLY IS THE ONLY ONE WHO CAN SAVE THE WORLD, I MUST PROTECT HIM.
IF HE'S GOING UP AGAINST BISHOP BERNARD...
...HE WON'T COME BACK ALIVE WITHOUT MY HELP.
CAN YOU EVEN WALK?
끄덕
OKAY. LET'S GO.

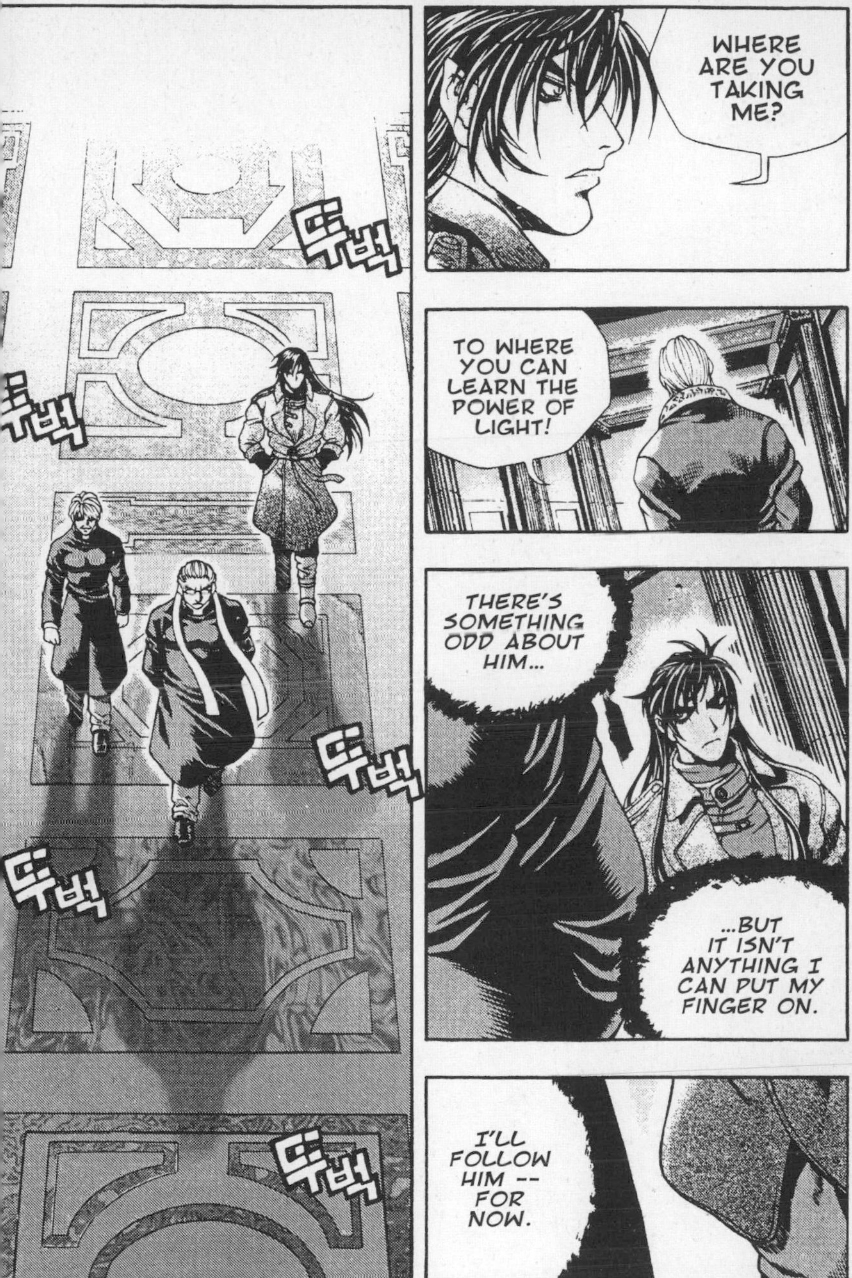

뚜벅
뚜벅
뚜벅
뚜벅
뚜벅
WHERE ARE YOU TAKING ME?
TO WHERE YOU CAN LEARN THE POWER OF LIGHT!
THERE'S SOMETHING ODD ABOUT HIM...
...BUT IT ISN'T ANYTHING I CAN PUT MY FINGER ON.
I'LL FOLLOW HIM -- FOR NOW.

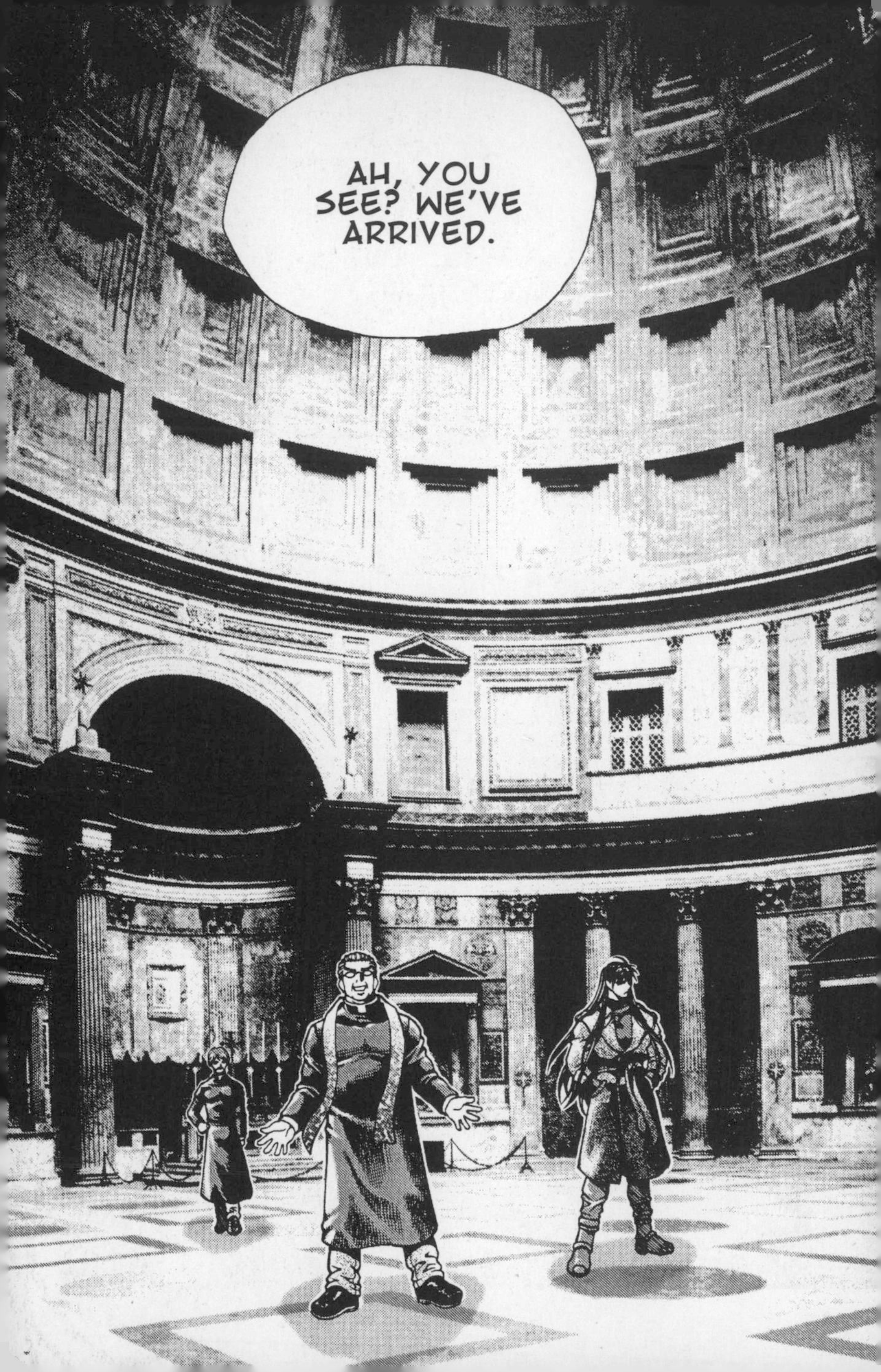
AH, YOU SEE? WE'VE ARRIVED.

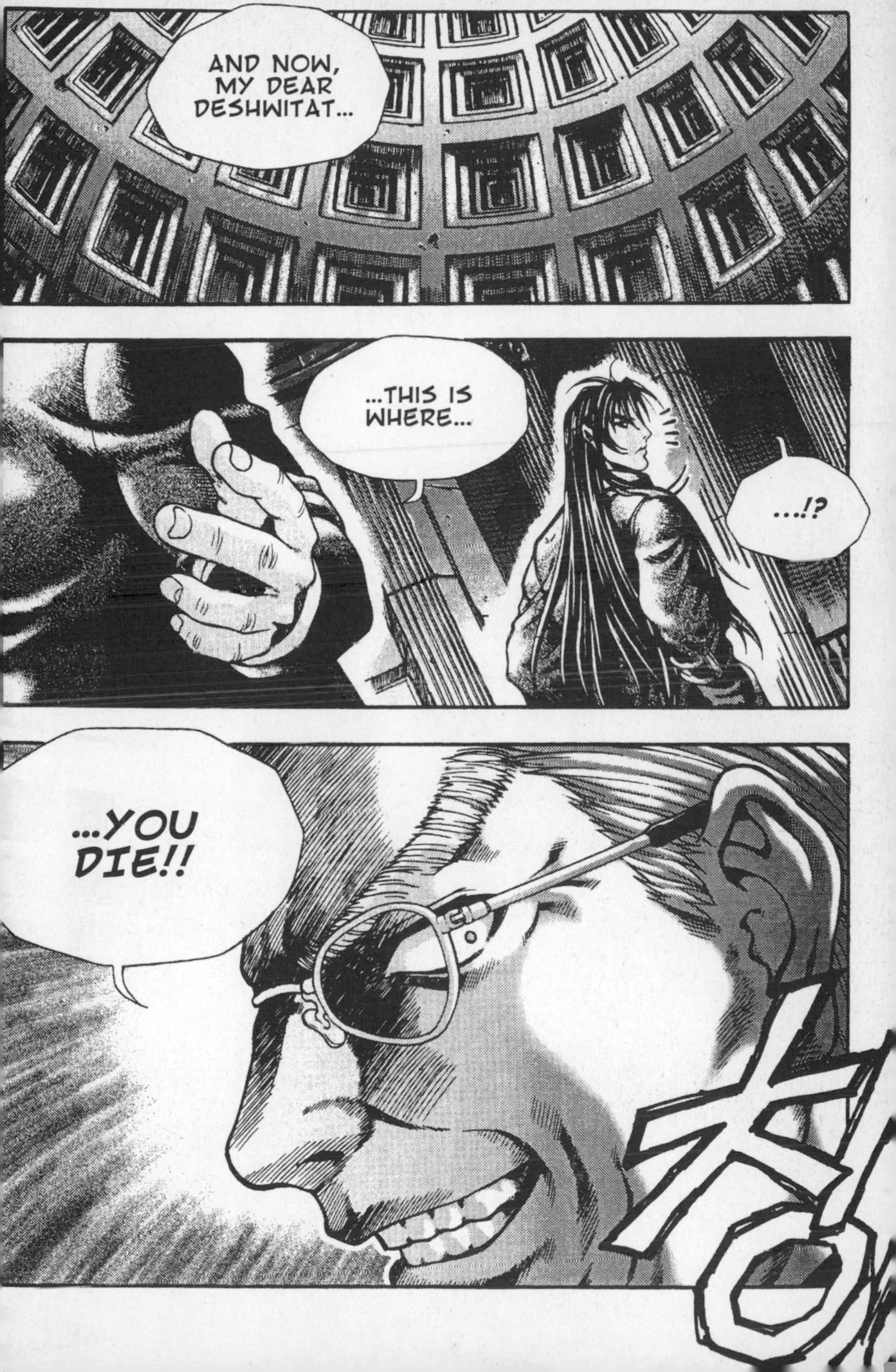
AND NOW, MY DEAR DESHWITAT...
...THIS IS WHERE...
...!?
...YOU DIE!!

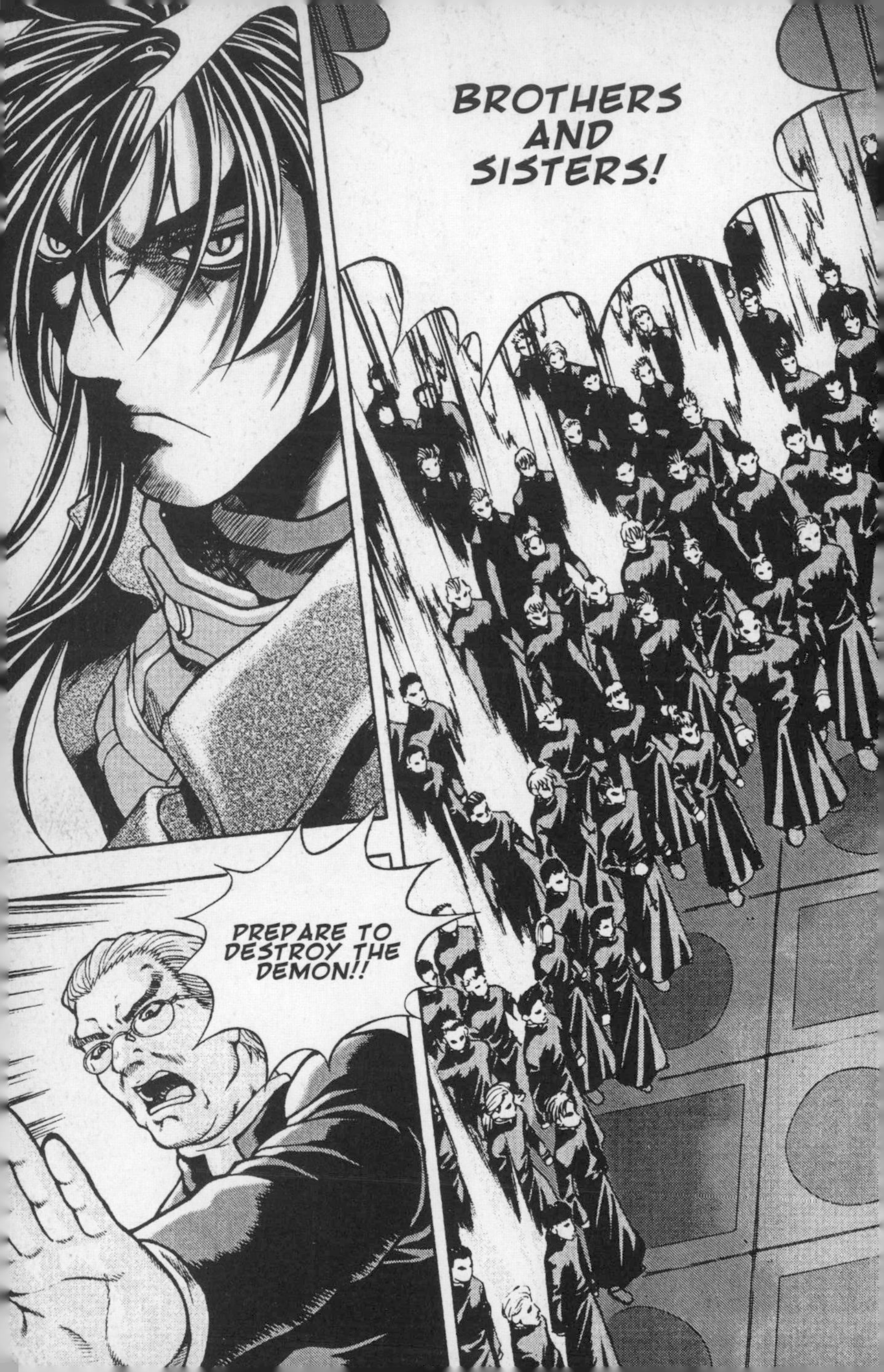
BROTHERS AND SISTERS!
PREPARE TO DESTROY THE DEMON!!

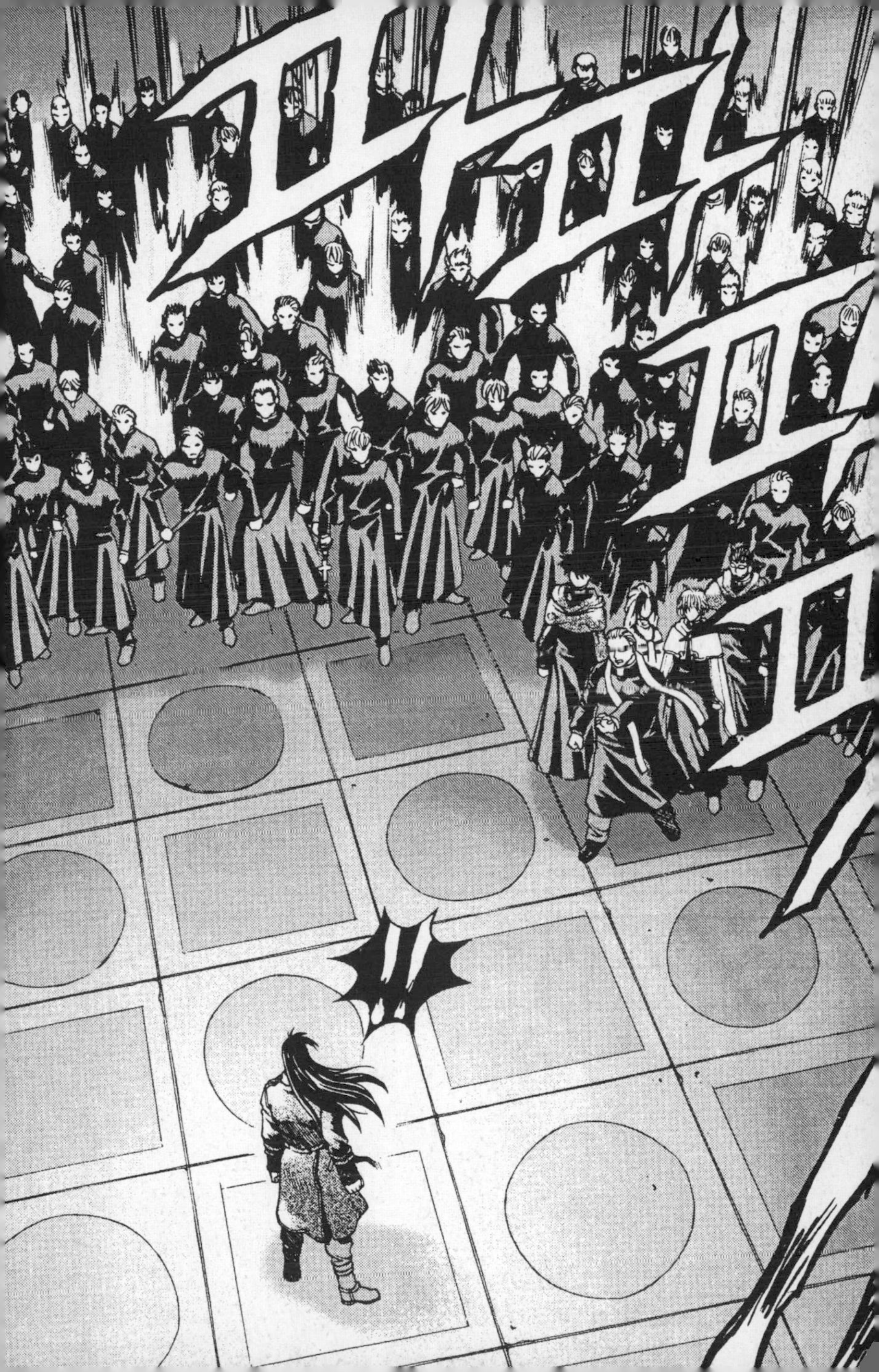
!!

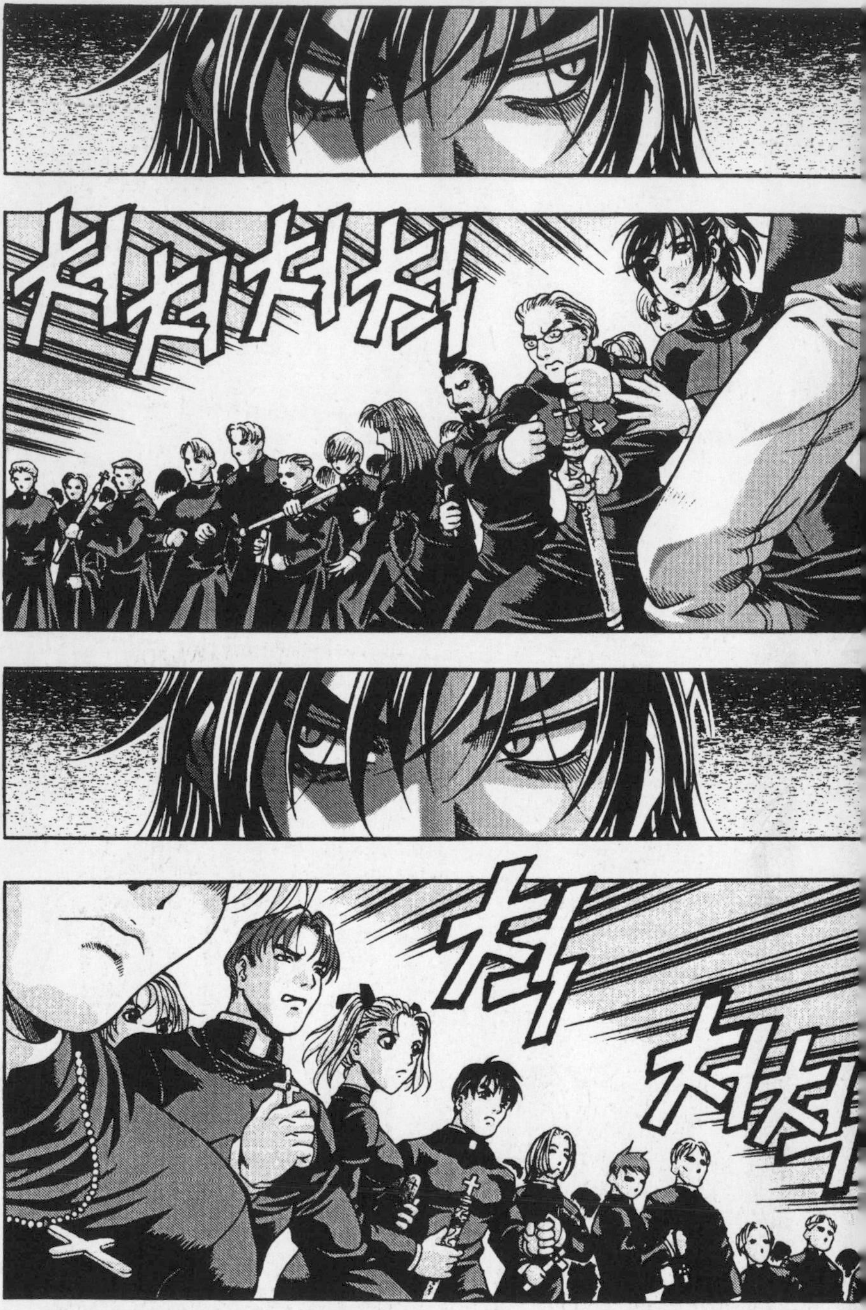

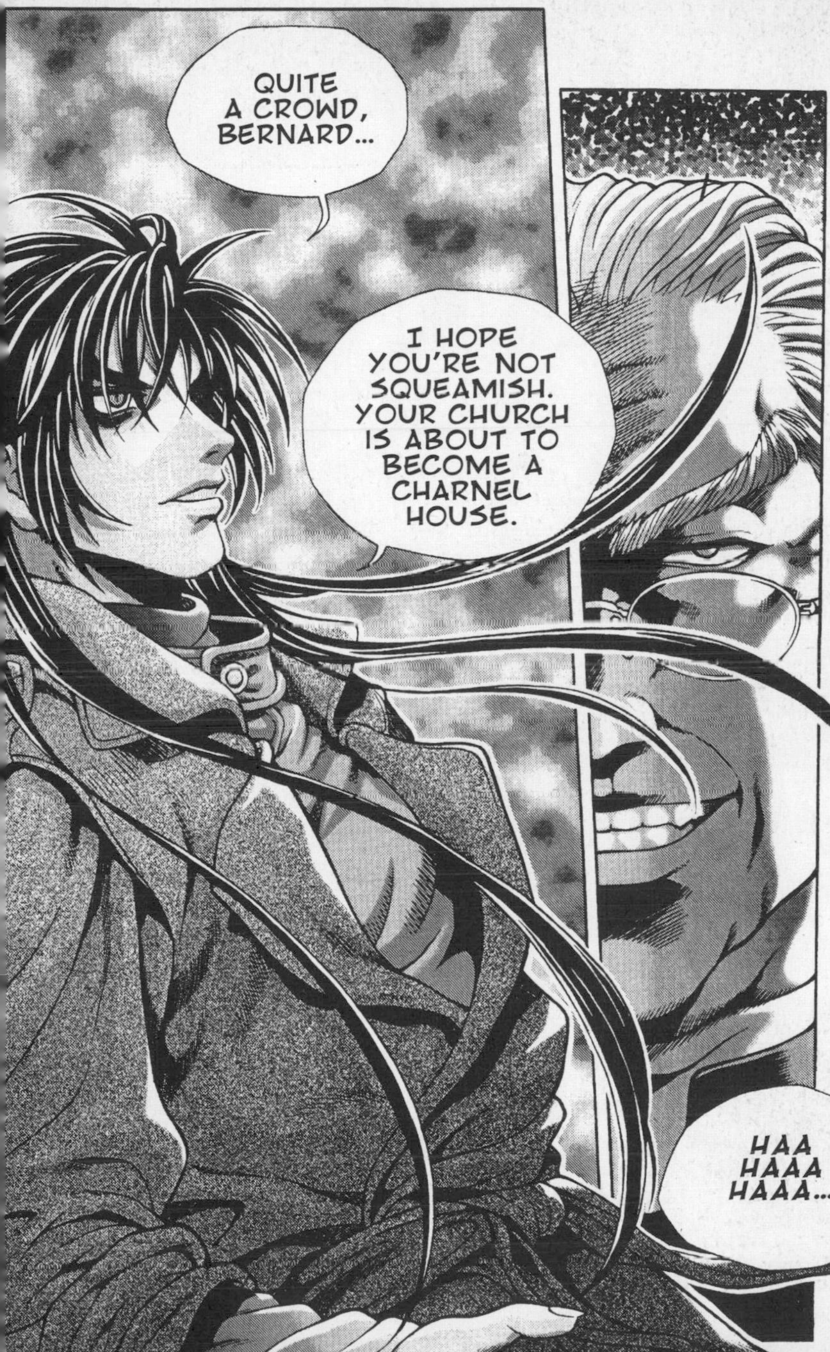
QUITE A CROWD, BERNARD...
I HOPE YOU'RE NOT SQUEAMISH. YOUR CHURCH IS ABOUT TO BECOME A CHARNEL HOUSE.
HAA HAAA HAAA...

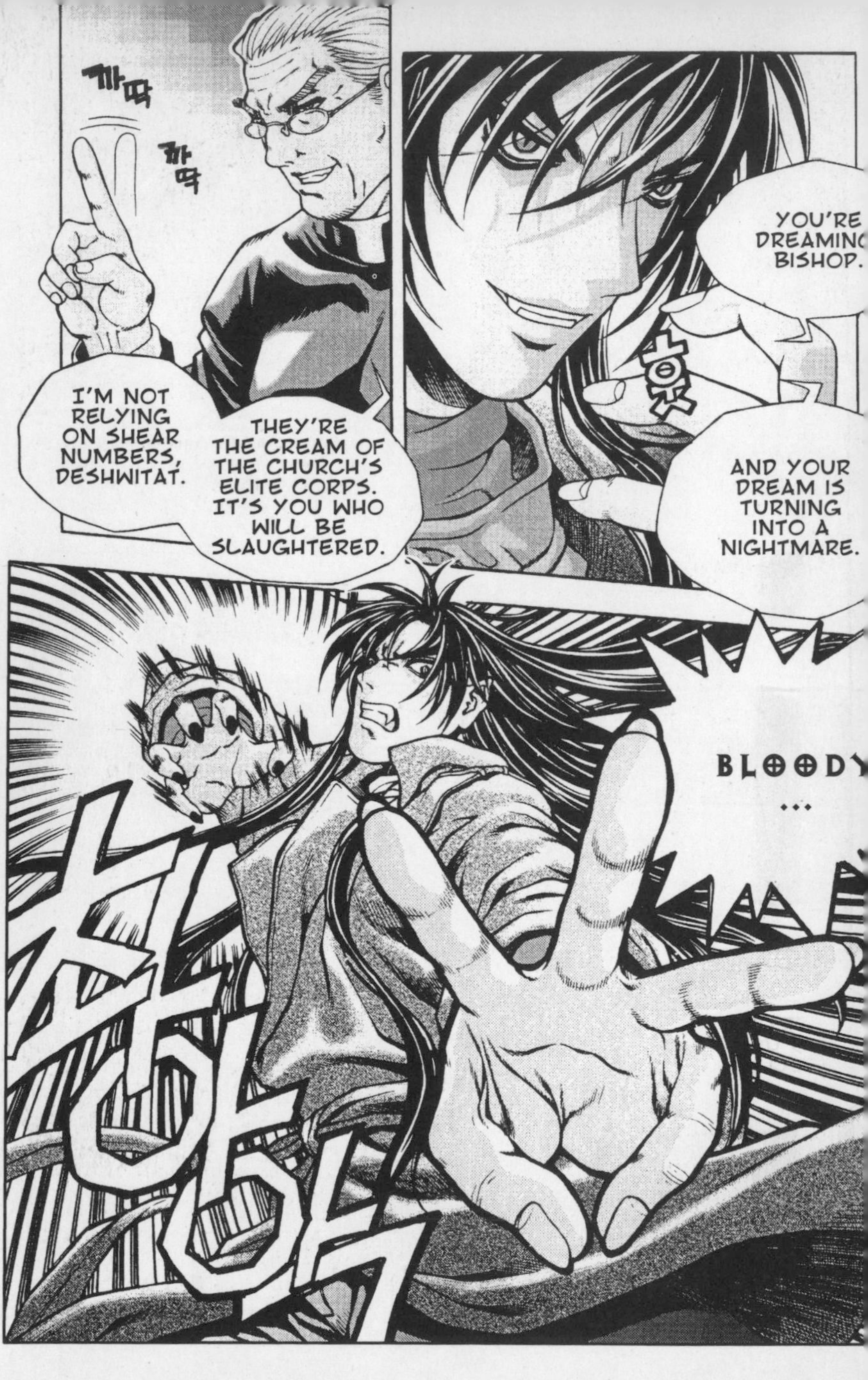
까딱
까딱
I'M NOT RELYING ON SHEAR NUMBERS, DESHWITAT.
THEY'RE THE CREAM OF THE CHURCH'S ELITE CORPS. IT'S YOU WHO WILL BE SLAUGHTERED.
YOU'RE DREAMING BISHOP.
AND YOUR DREAM IS TURNING INTO A NIGHTMARE.
BLOODY
...

WHAT? MY SPELL...

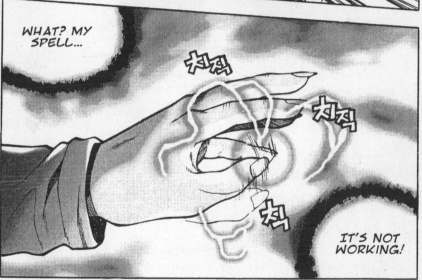

IT'S NOT WORKING!

TRYING TO USE A SPELL, EH?

LET ME BE THE FIRST TO INFORM YOU THAT IT'S USELESS.

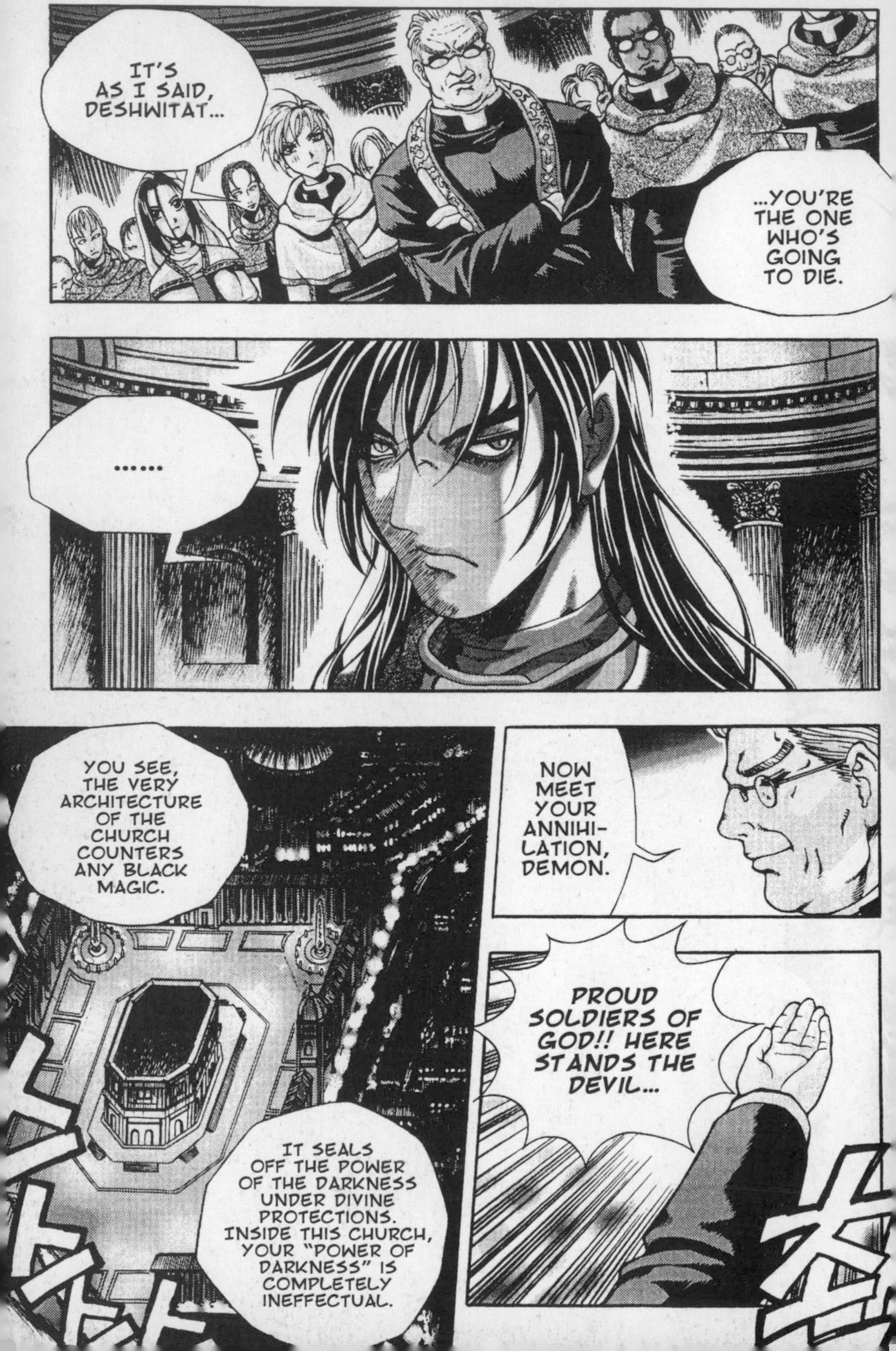
IT'S AS I SAID, DESHWITAT...
...YOU'RE THE ONE WHO'S GOING TO DIE.
......
YOU SEE, THE VERY ARCHITECTURE OF THE CHURCH COUNTERS ANY BLACK MAGIC.
IT SEALS OFF THE POWER OF THE DARKNESS UNDER DIVINE PROTECTIONS. INSIDE THIS CHURCH, YOUR "POWER OF DARKNESS" IS COMPLETELY INEFFECTUAL.
NOW MEET YOUR ANNIHILATION, DEMON.
PROUD SOLDIERS OF GOD!! HERE STANDS THE DEVIL...

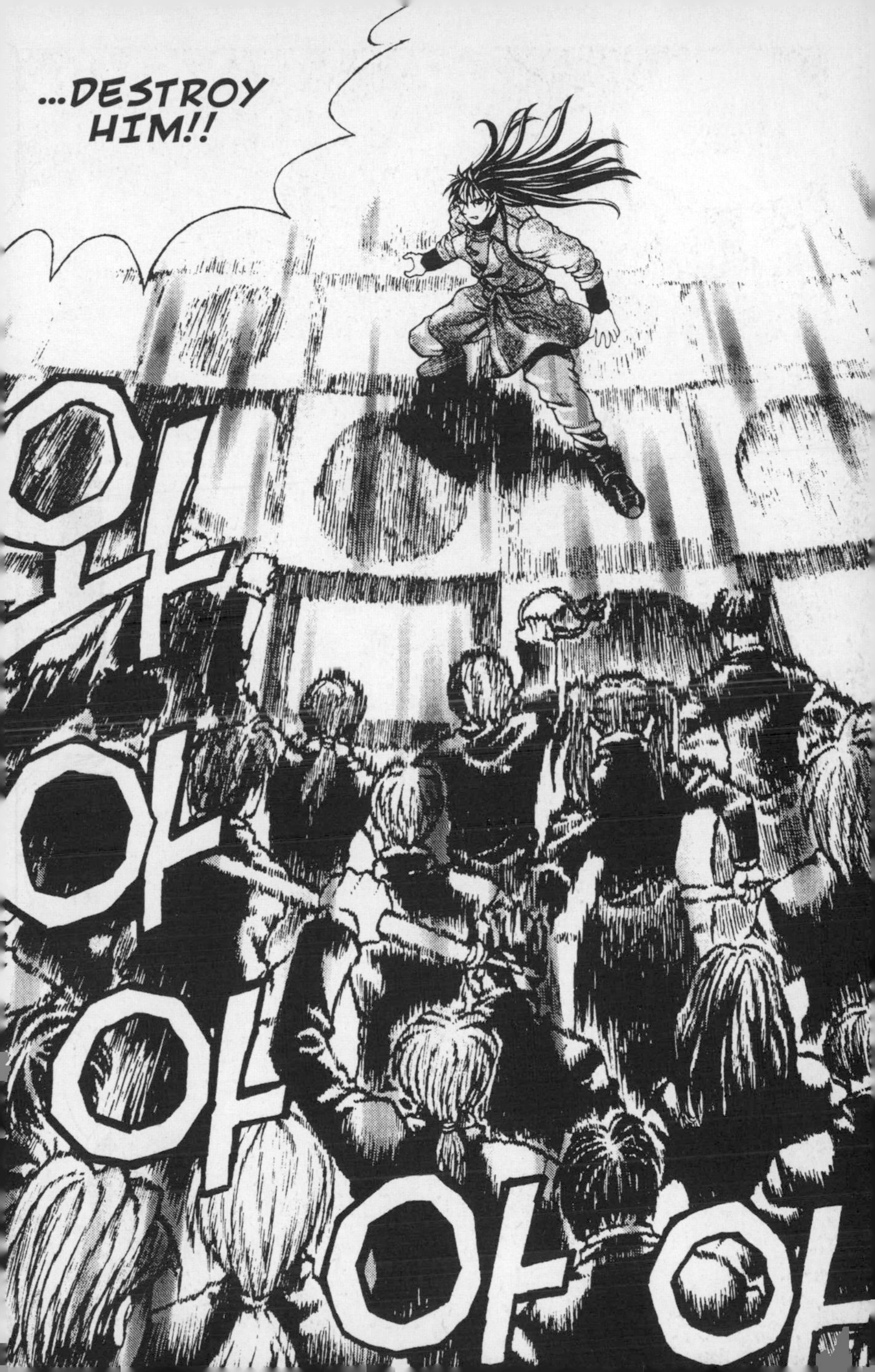
...DESTROY HIM!!
OH
OH
OH
OH
OH

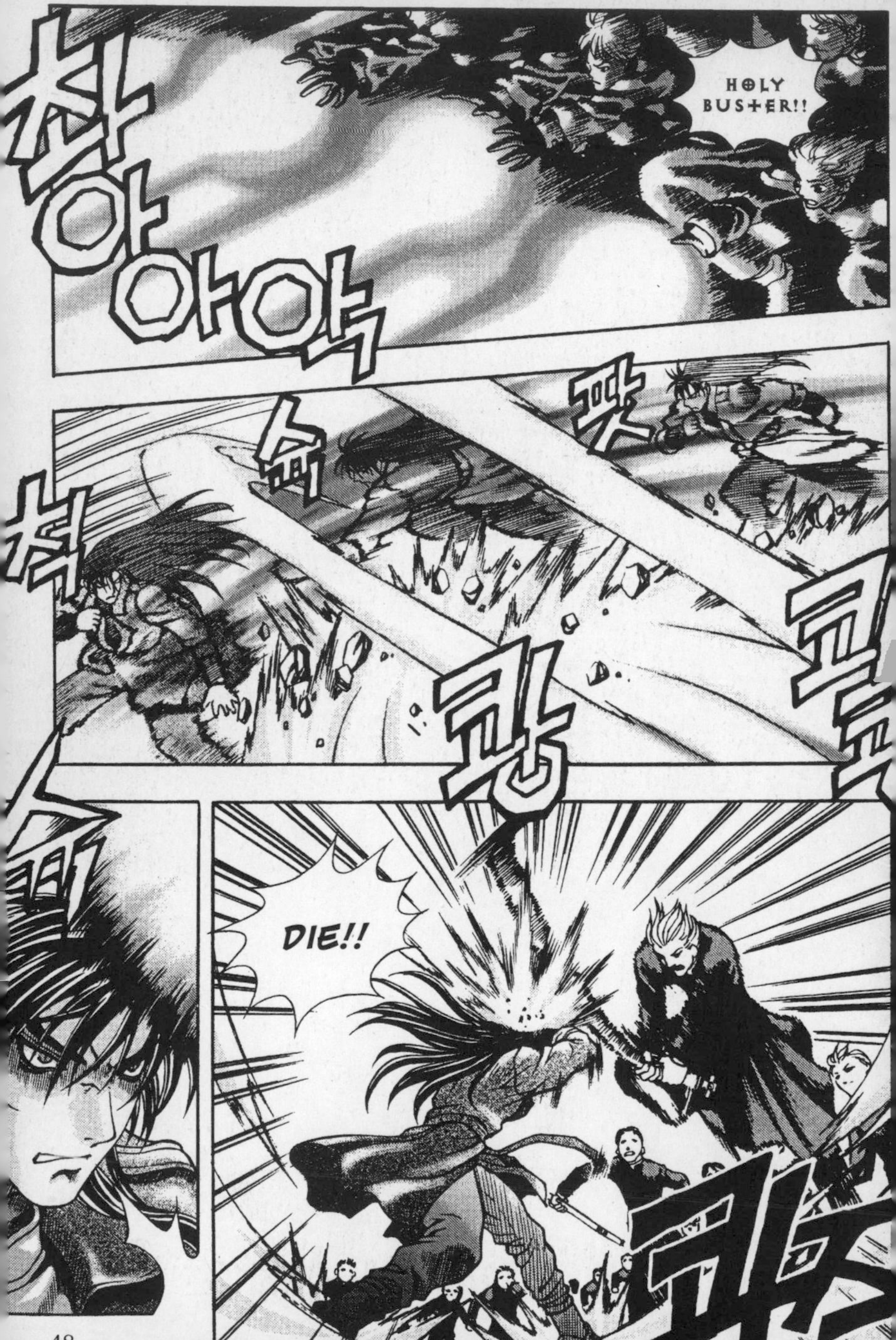
촤아아아악
HOLY BUSTER!!
팟
DIE!!

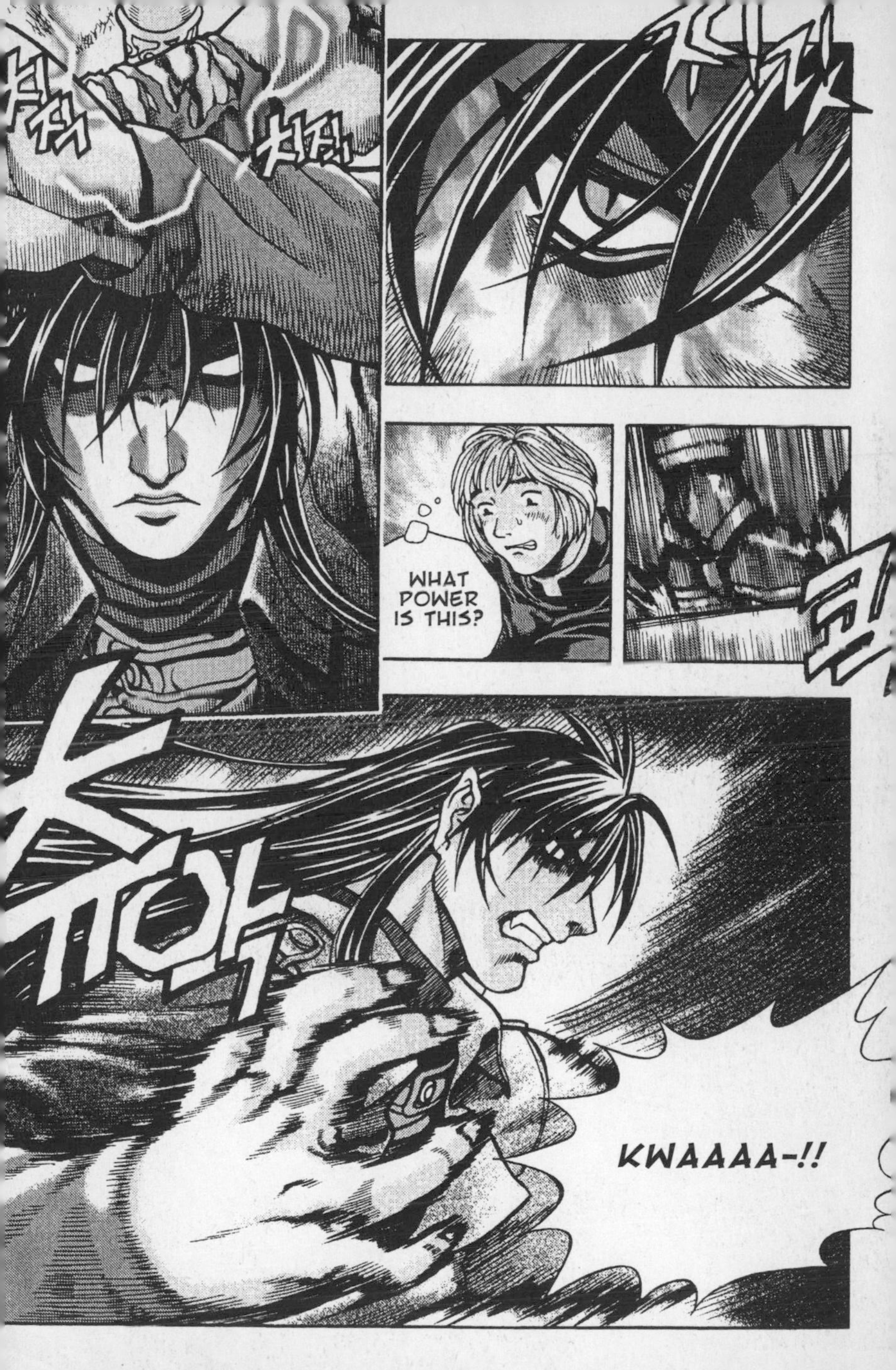
WHAT POWER IS THIS?
KWAAAA-!!

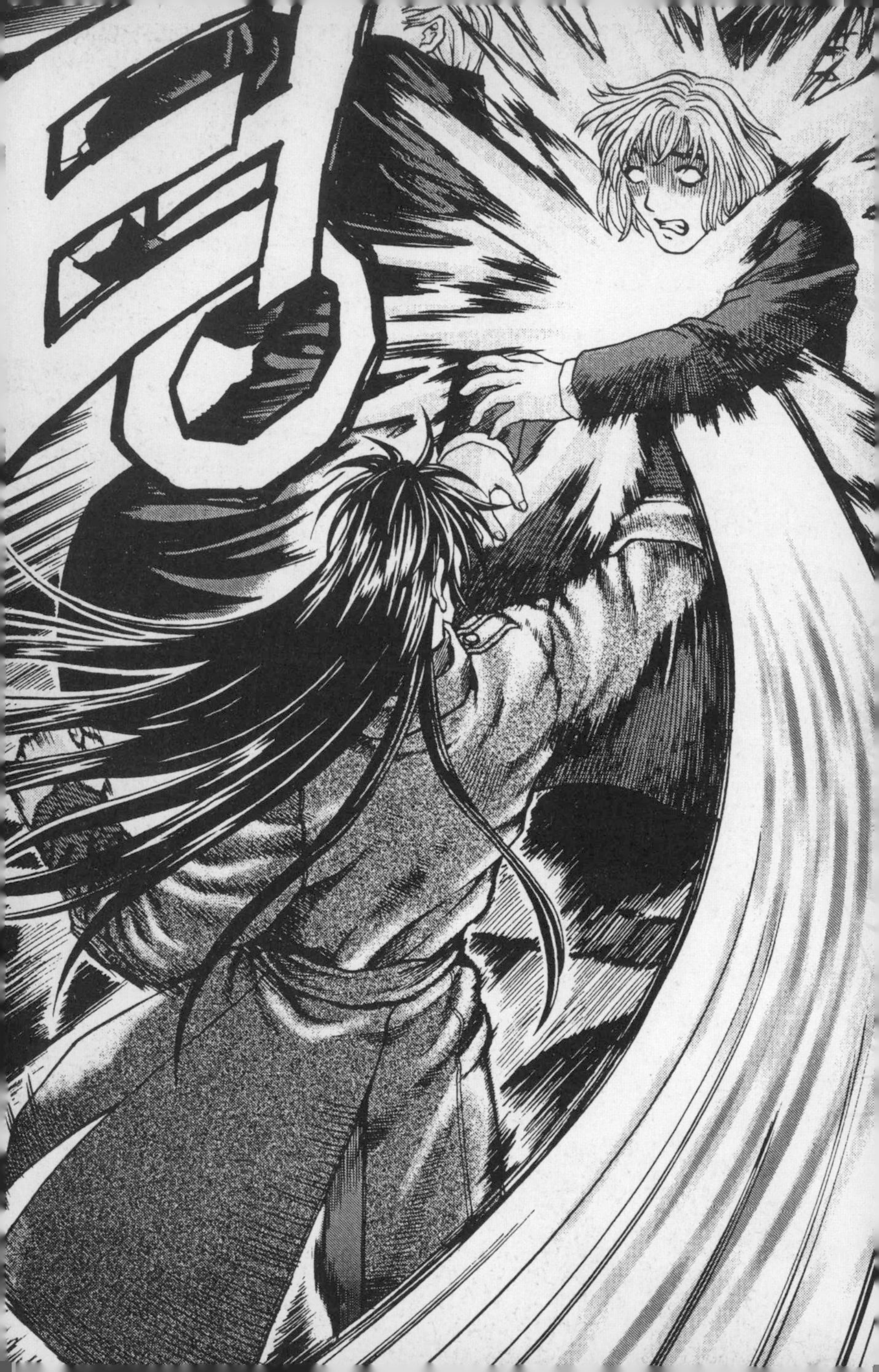

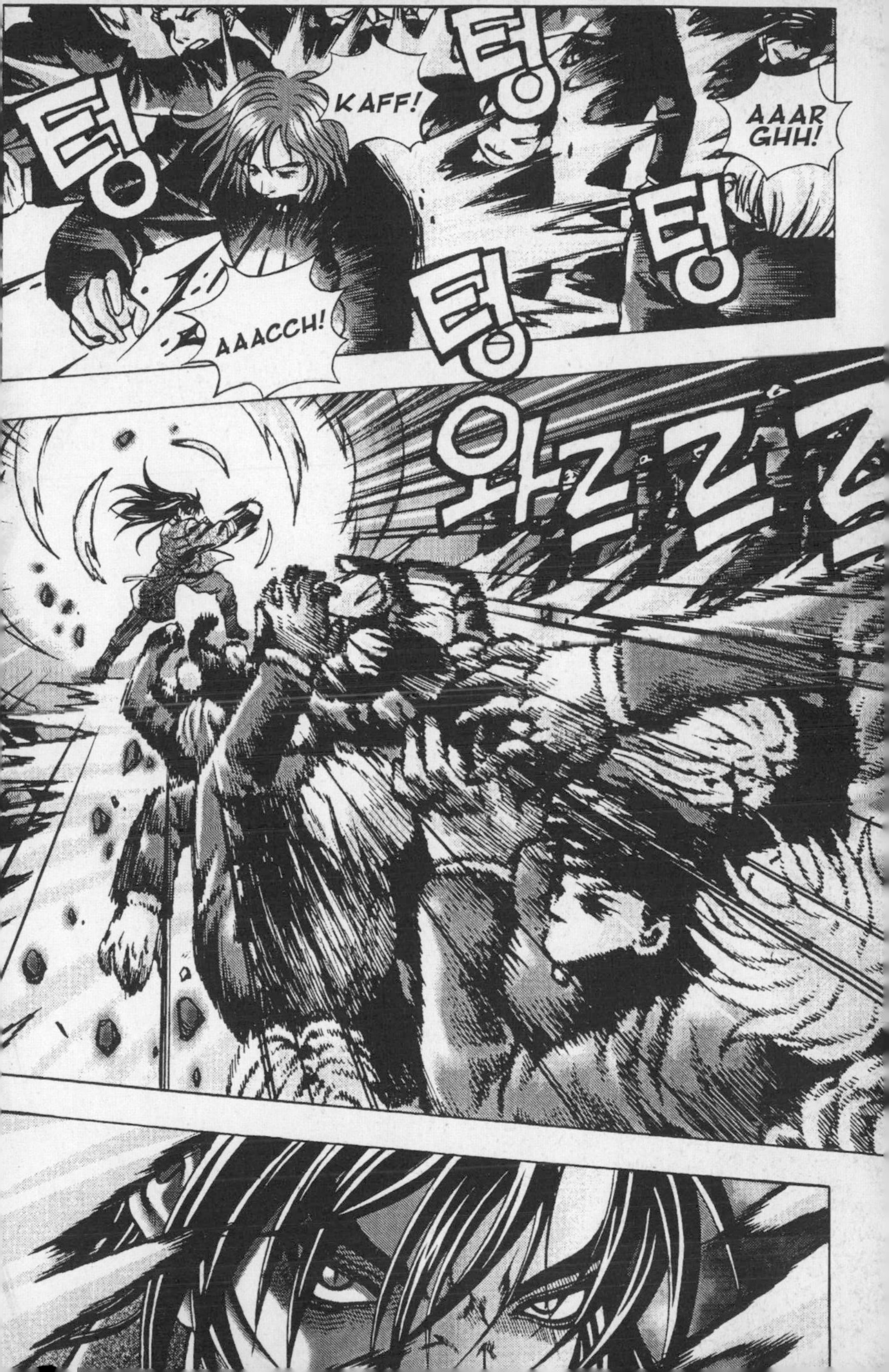
텅
KAFF!
텅
AAAR GHH!
AAACCH!
텅
텅

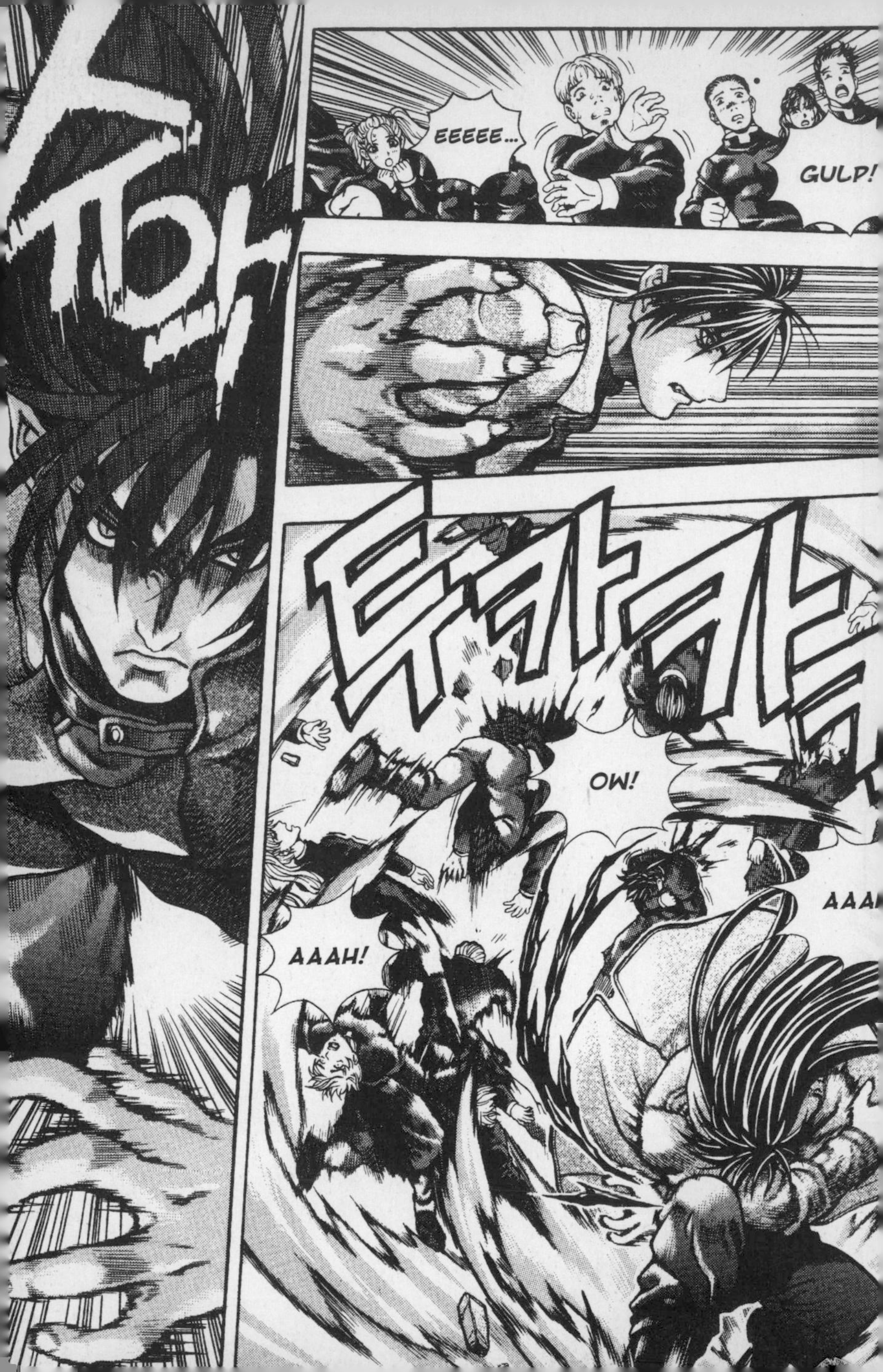

GULP!
EEEEE...
OW!
AAA
AAAH!

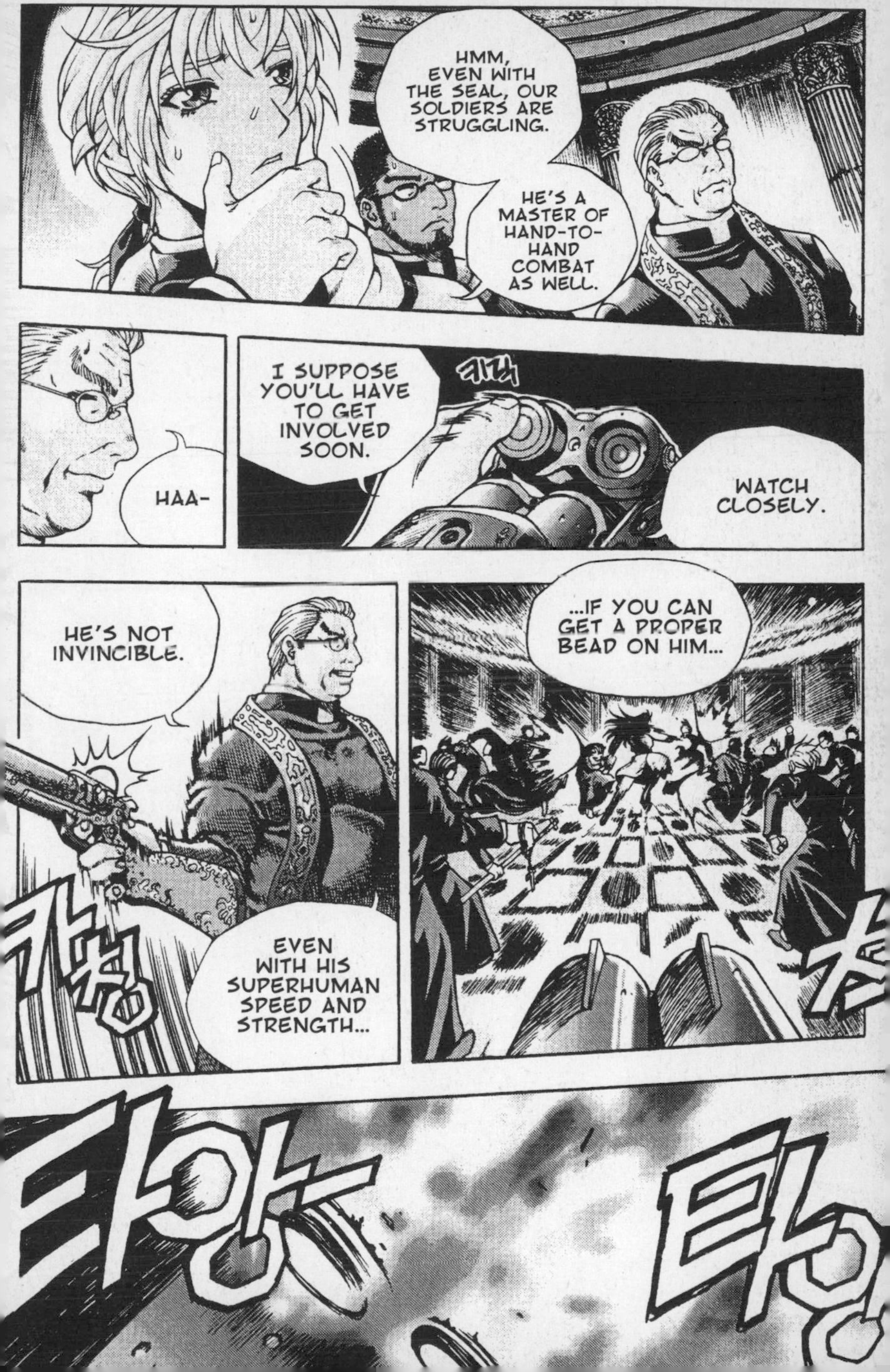
HMM, EVEN WITH THE SEAL, OUR SOLDIERS ARE STRUGGLING.
HE'S A MASTER OF HAND-TO-HAND COMBAT AS WELL.
HAA-
I SUPPOSE YOU'LL HAVE TO GET INVOLVED SOON.
WATCH CLOSELY.
HE'S NOT INVINCIBLE.
EVEN WITH HIS SUPERHUMAN SPEED AND STRENGTH...
...IF YOU CAN GET A PROPER BEAD ON HIM...

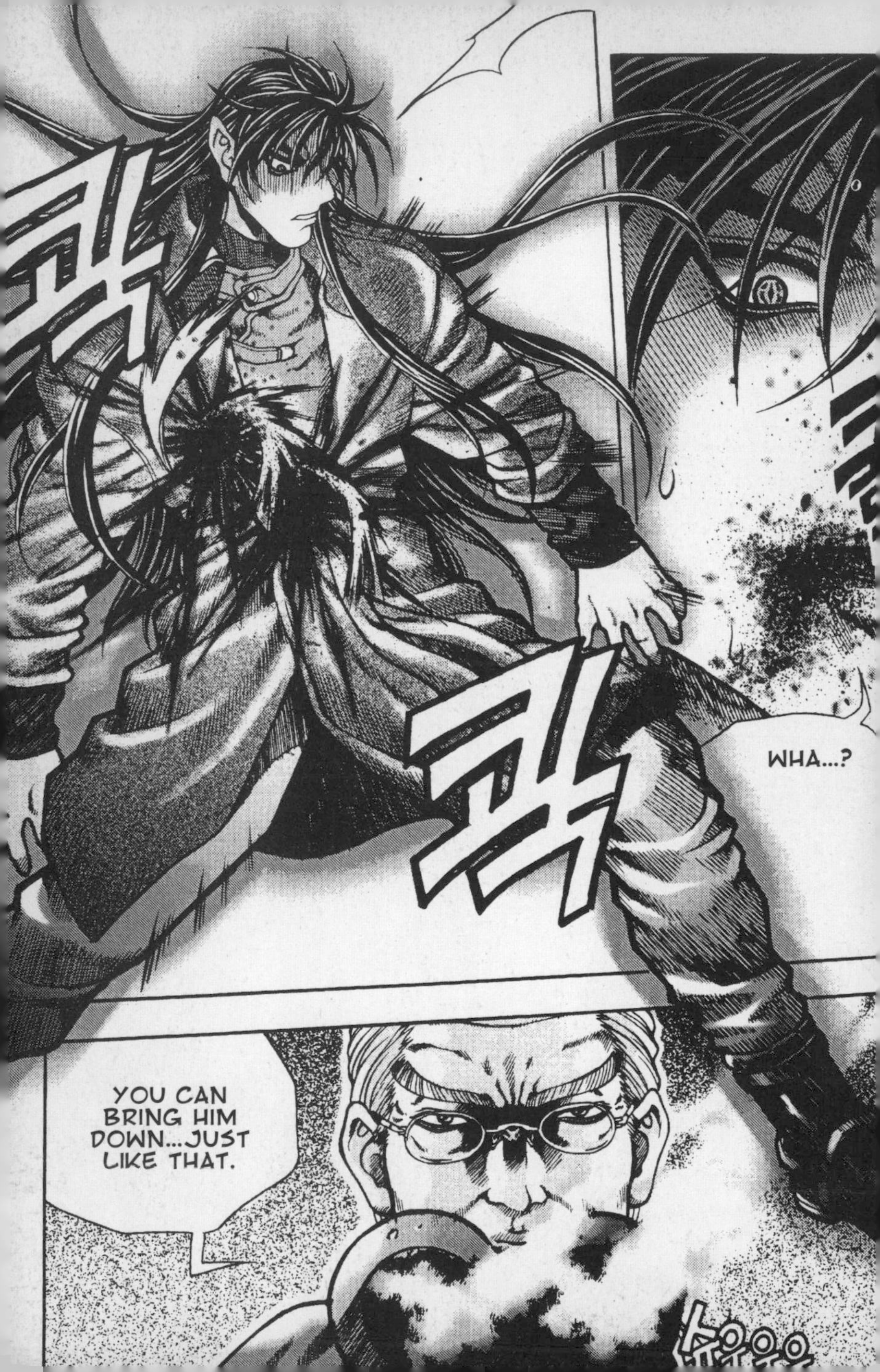
WHA...?
YOU CAN BRING HIM DOWN...JUST LIKE THAT.

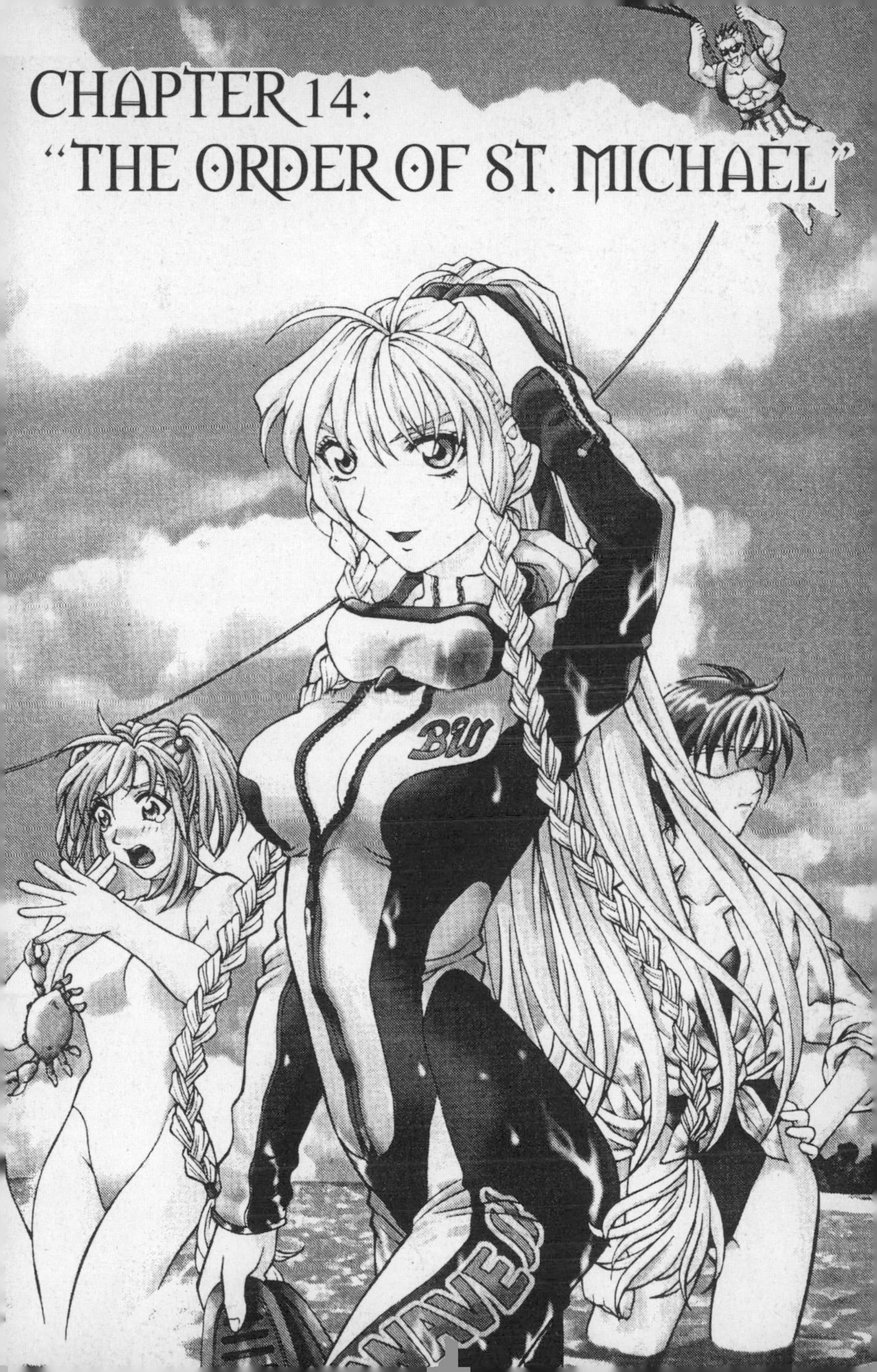
CHAPTER 14:
"THE ORDER OF ST. MICHAEL"
BW

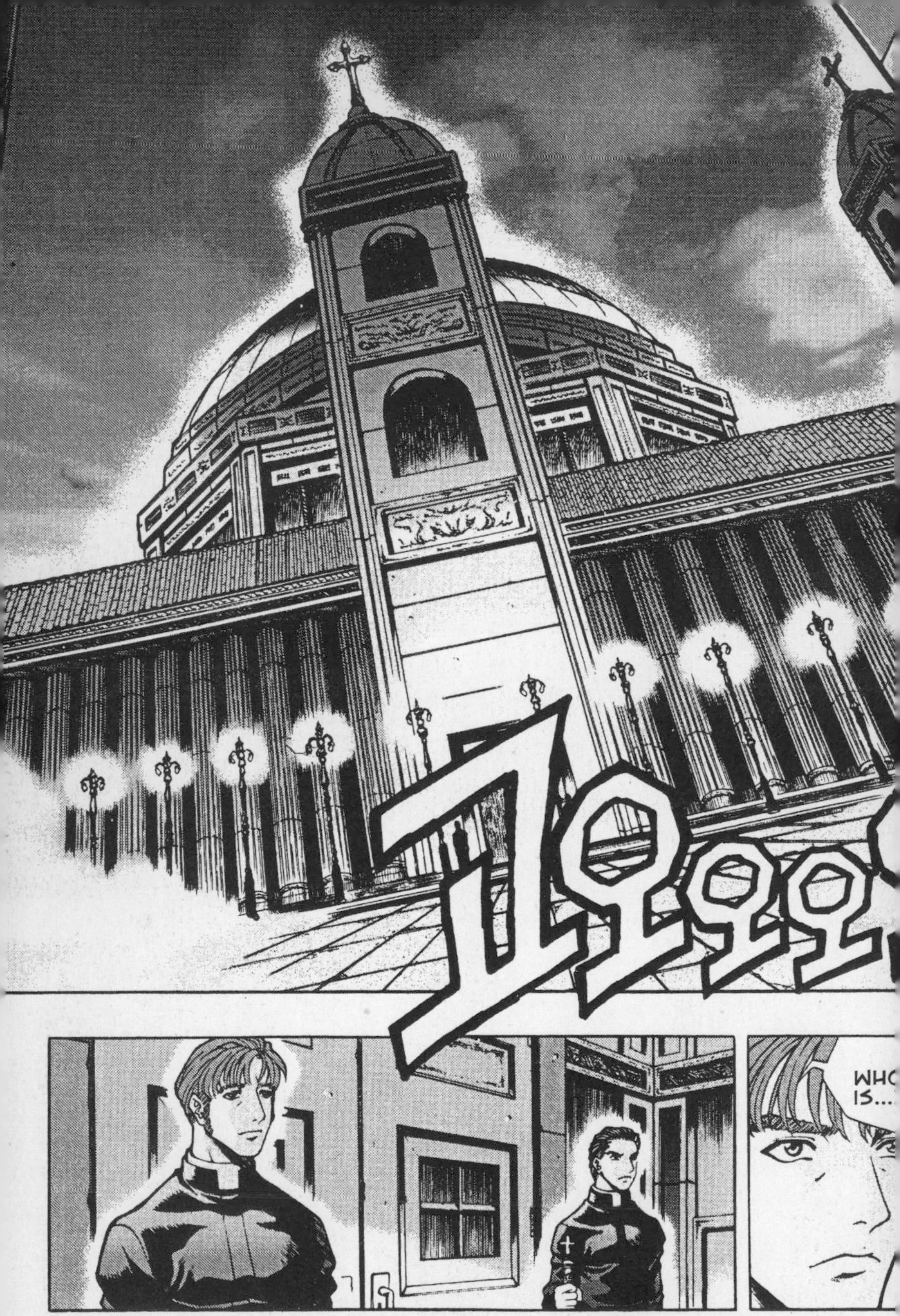
WHO IS...

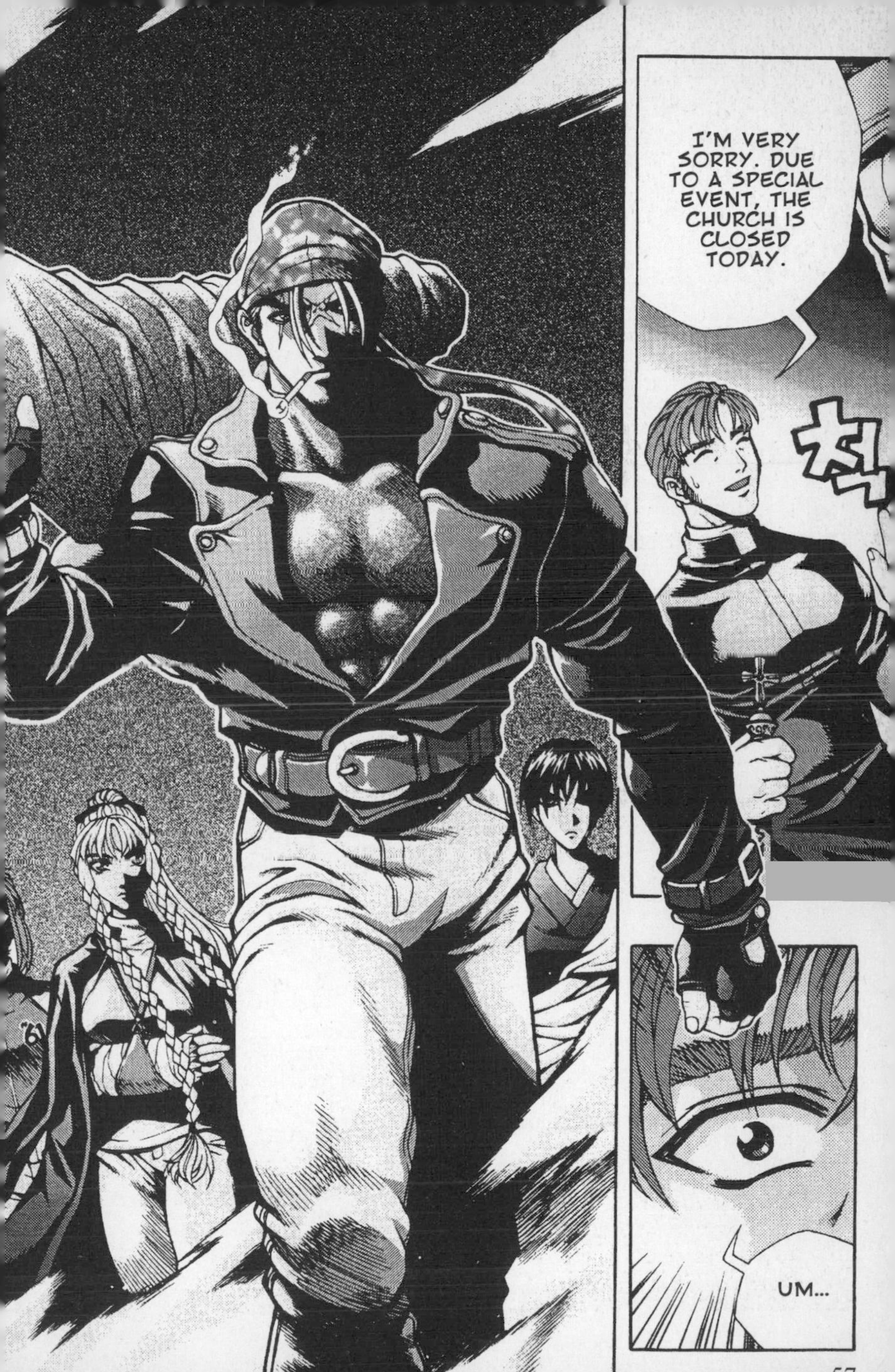
I'M VERY SORRY. DUE TO A SPECIAL EVENT, THE CHURCH IS CLOSED TODAY.
UM...

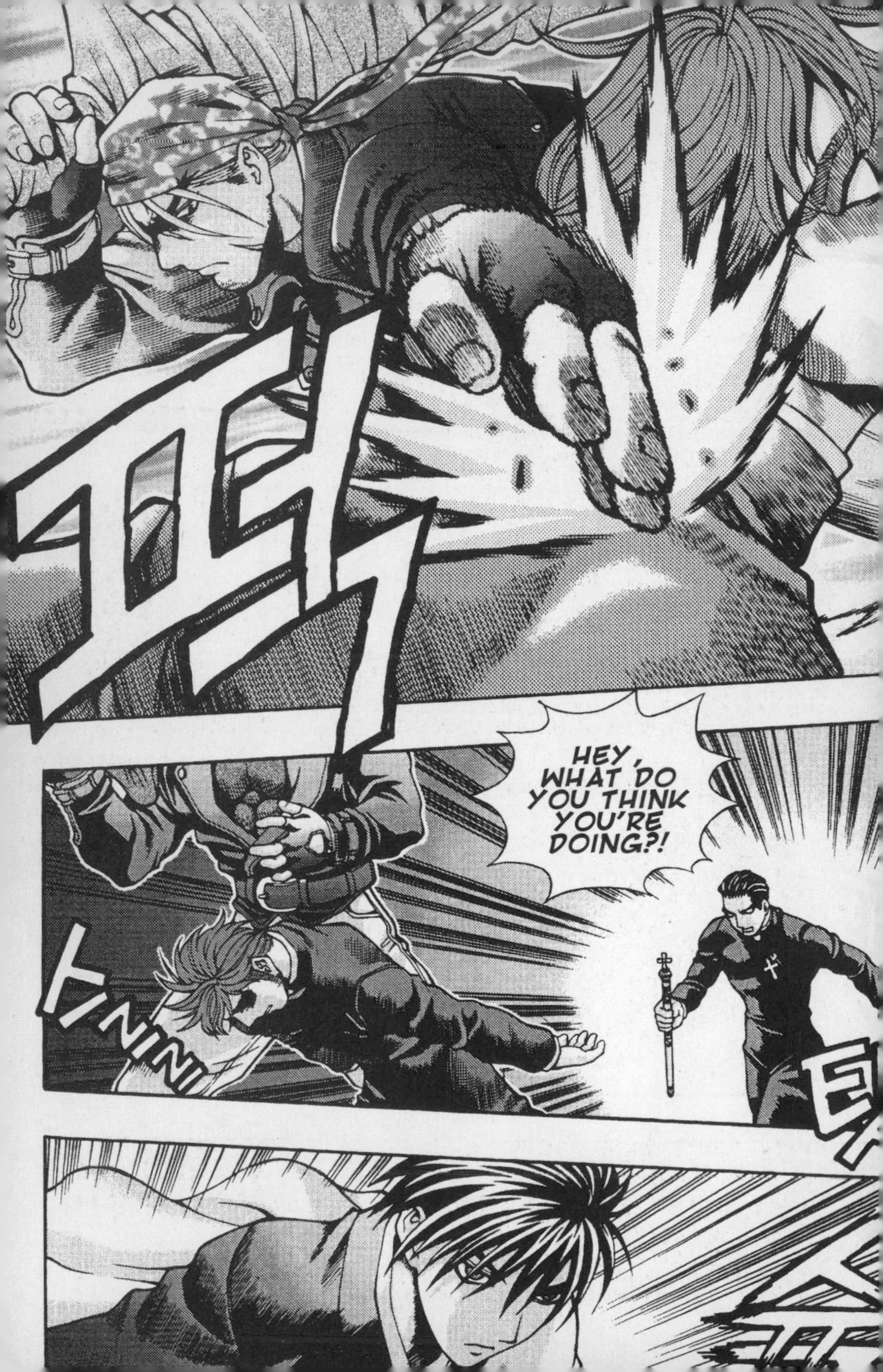
HEY, WHAT DO YOU THINK YOU'RE DOING?!

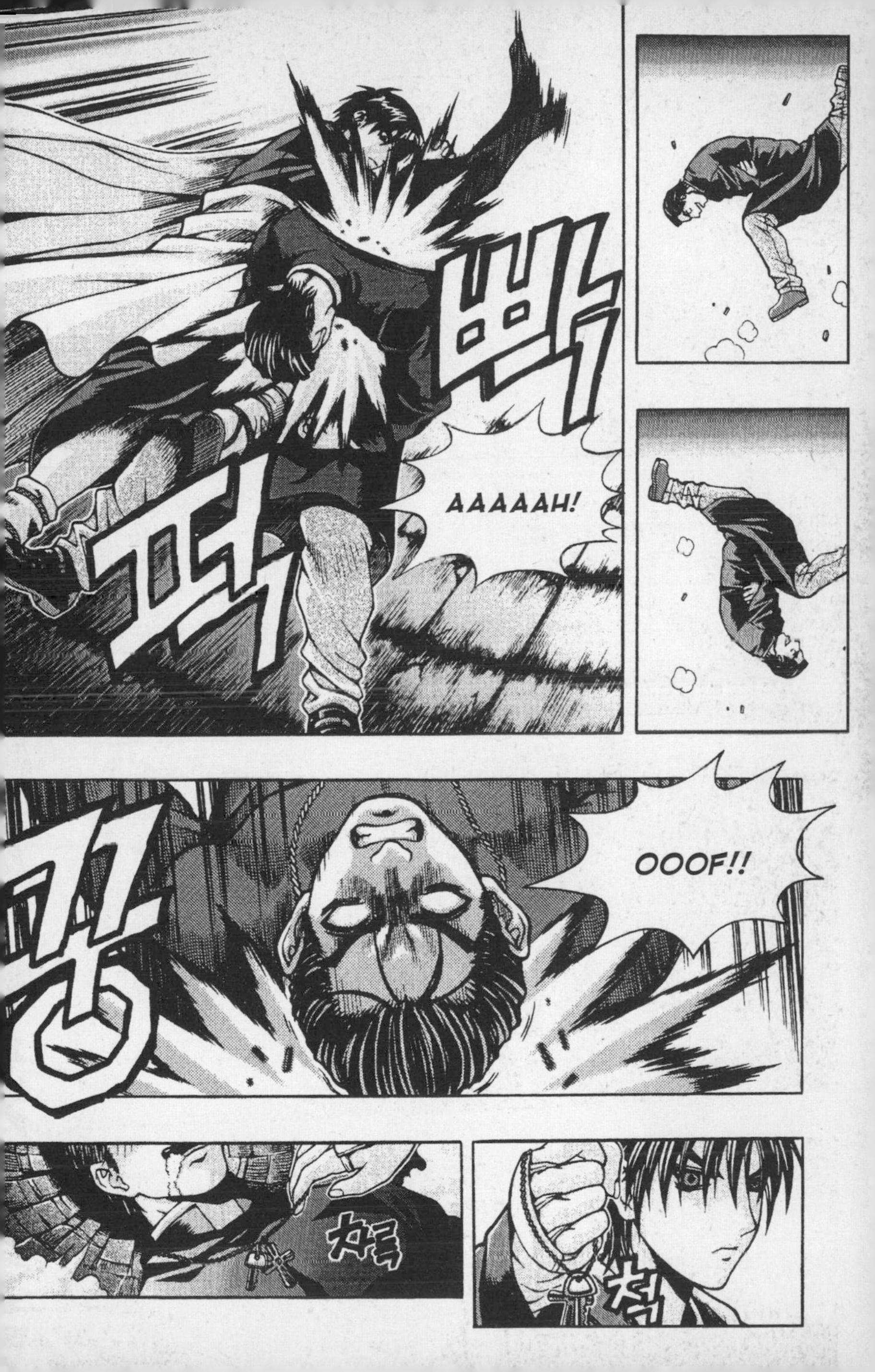
AAAAAH!
OOOF!!

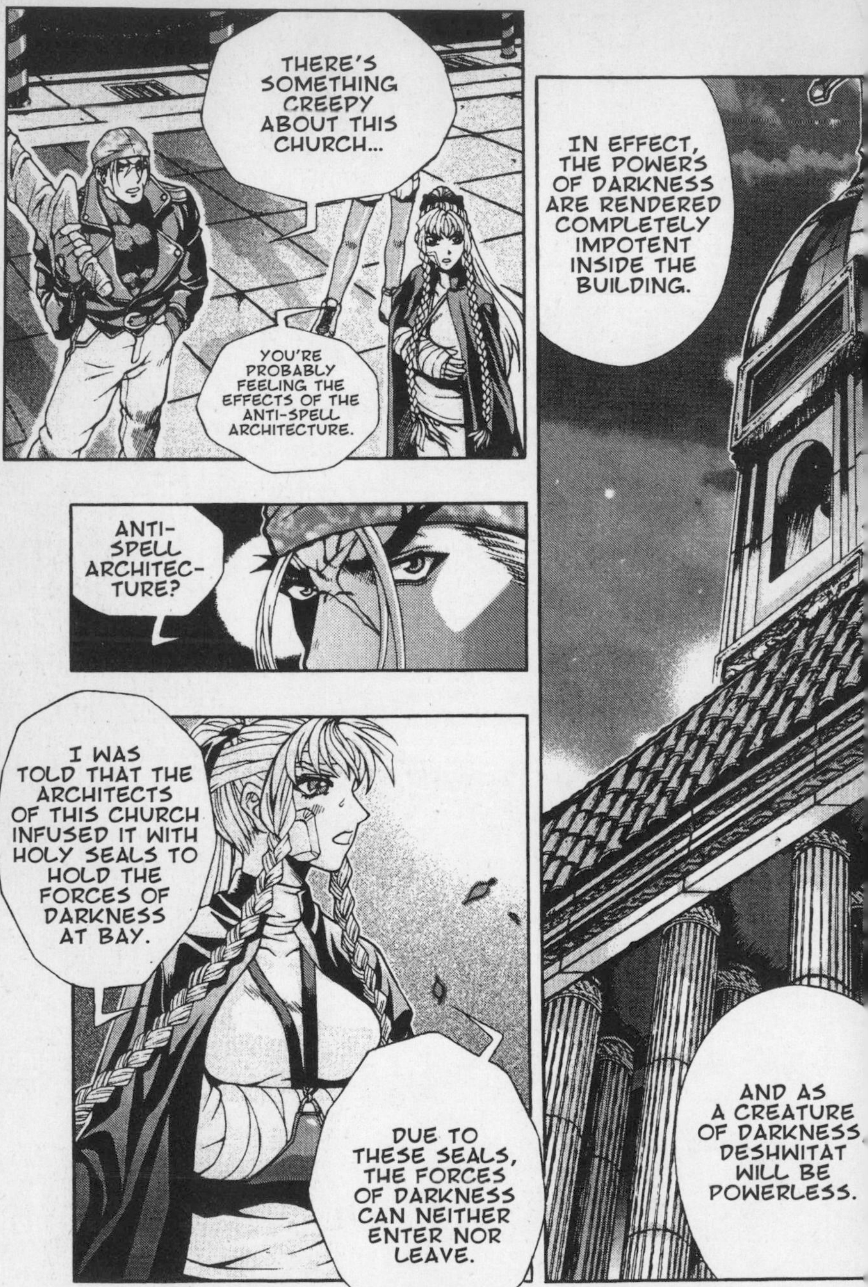
THERE'S SOMETHING CREEPY ABOUT THIS CHURCH...
YOU'RE PROBABLY FEELING THE EFFECTS OF THE ANTI-SPELL ARCHITECTURE.
ANTI-SPELL ARCHITEC-TURE?
I WAS TOLD THAT THE ARCHITECTS OF THIS CHURCH INFUSED IT WITH HOLY SEALS TO HOLD THE FORCES OF DARKNESS AT BAY.
DUE TO THESE SEALS, THE FORCES OF DARKNESS CAN NEITHER ENTER NOR LEAVE.
IN EFFECT, THE POWERS OF DARKNESS ARE RENDERED COMPLETELY IMPOTENT INSIDE THE BUILDING.
AND AS A CREATURE OF DARKNESS DESHWITAT WILL BE POWERLESS.

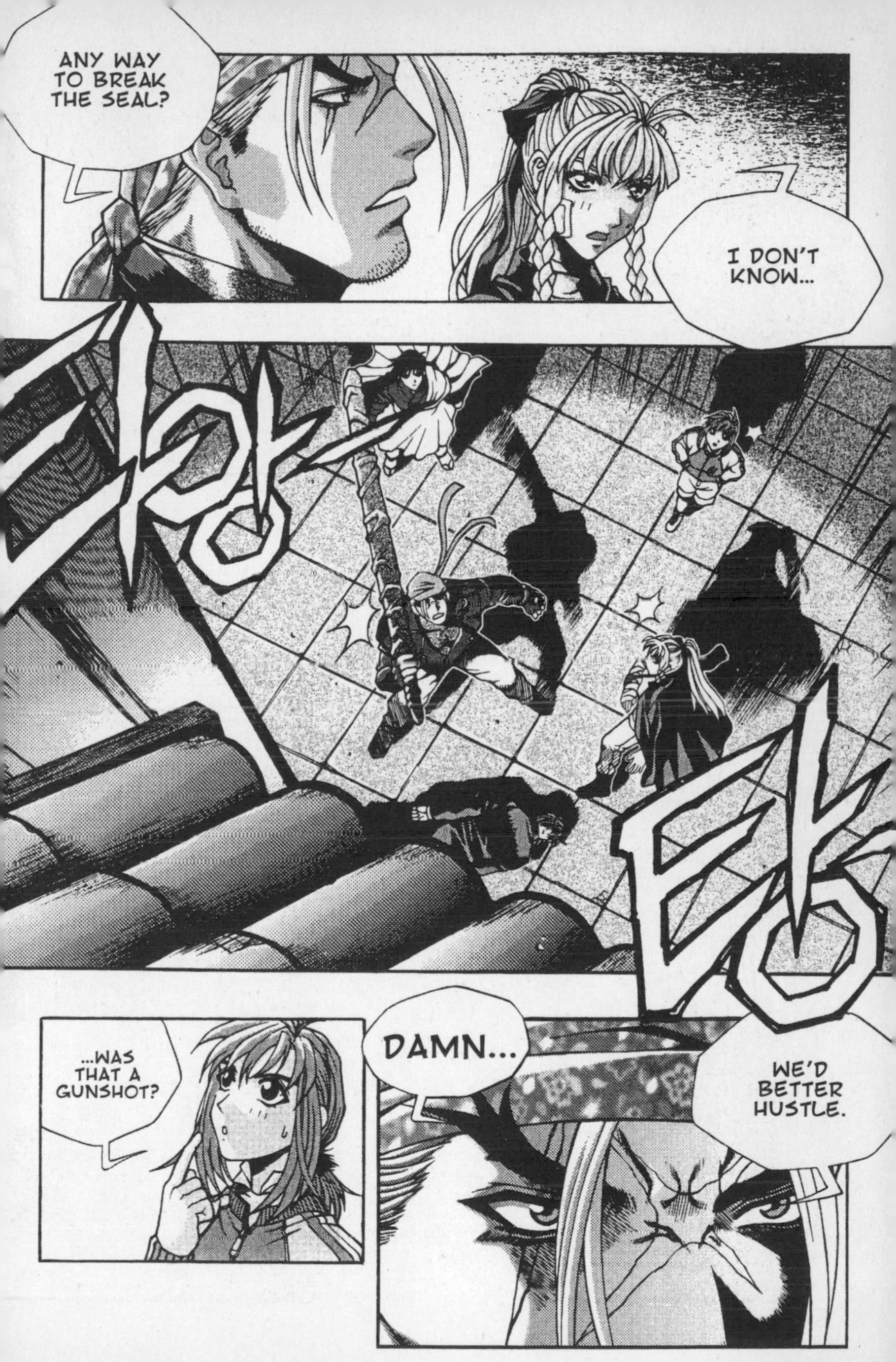

ANY WAY TO BREAK THE SEAL?
I DON'T KNOW...
...WAS THAT A GUNSHOT?
DAMN...
WE'D BETTER HUSTLE.

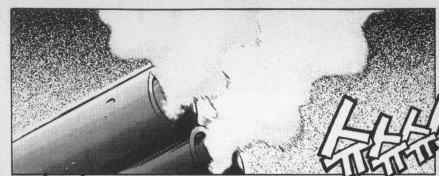

EXCELLENT...

WE'VE GOT HIM!

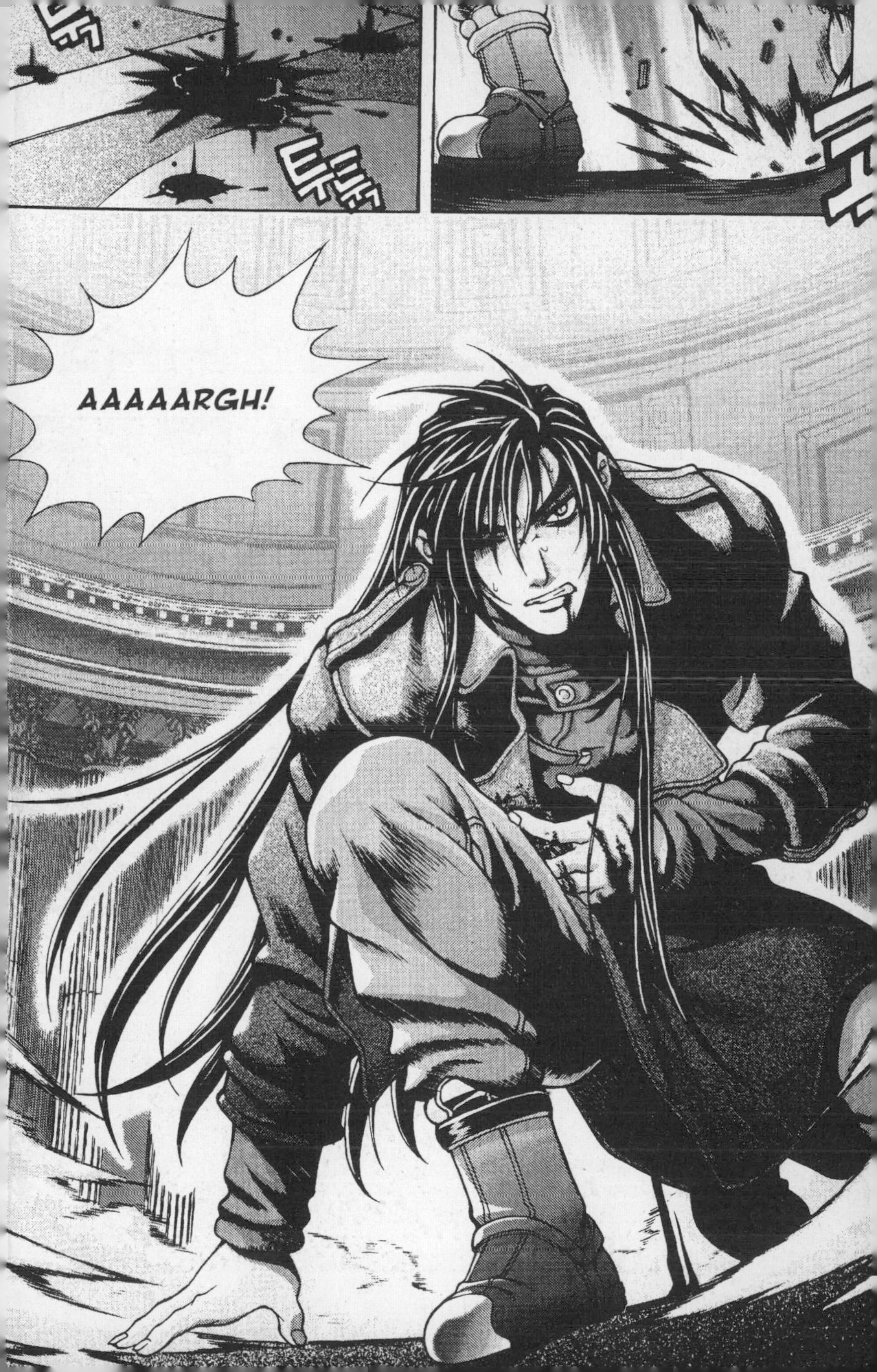
AAAAARGH!

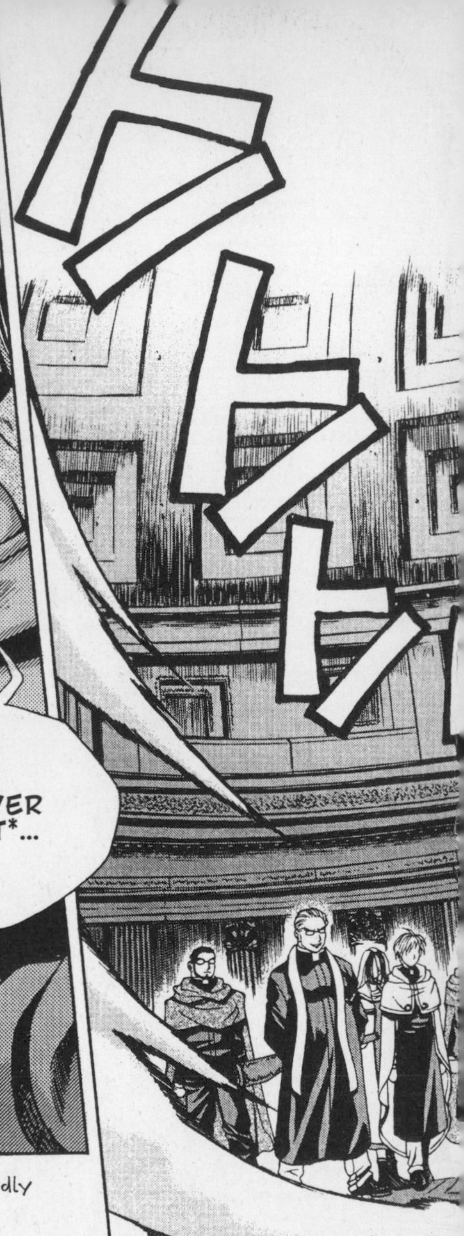
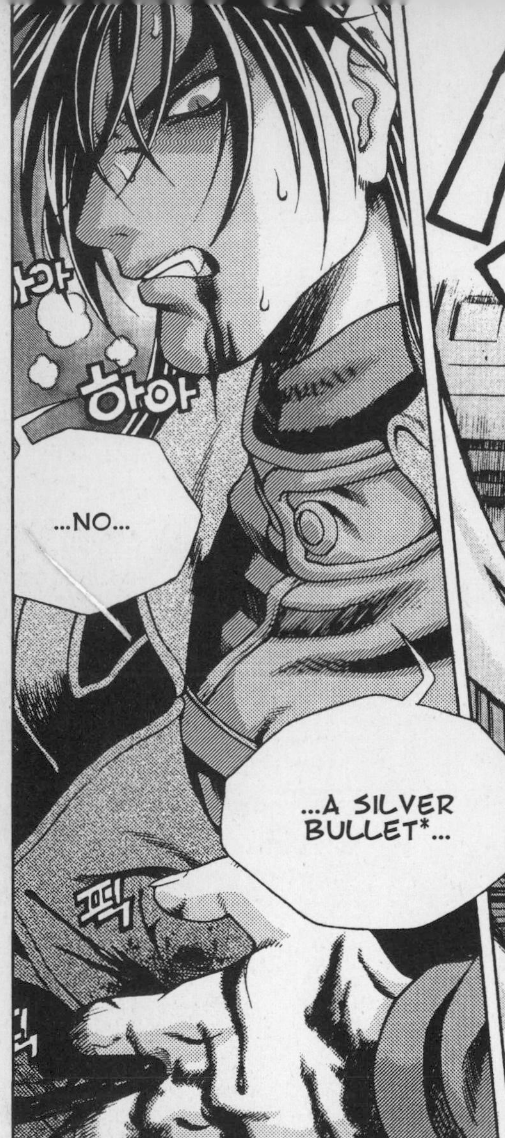
하아
하아
...NO...
...A SILVER BULLET*...
퍽

*Silver Bullets are known to be deadly to werewolves and vampires

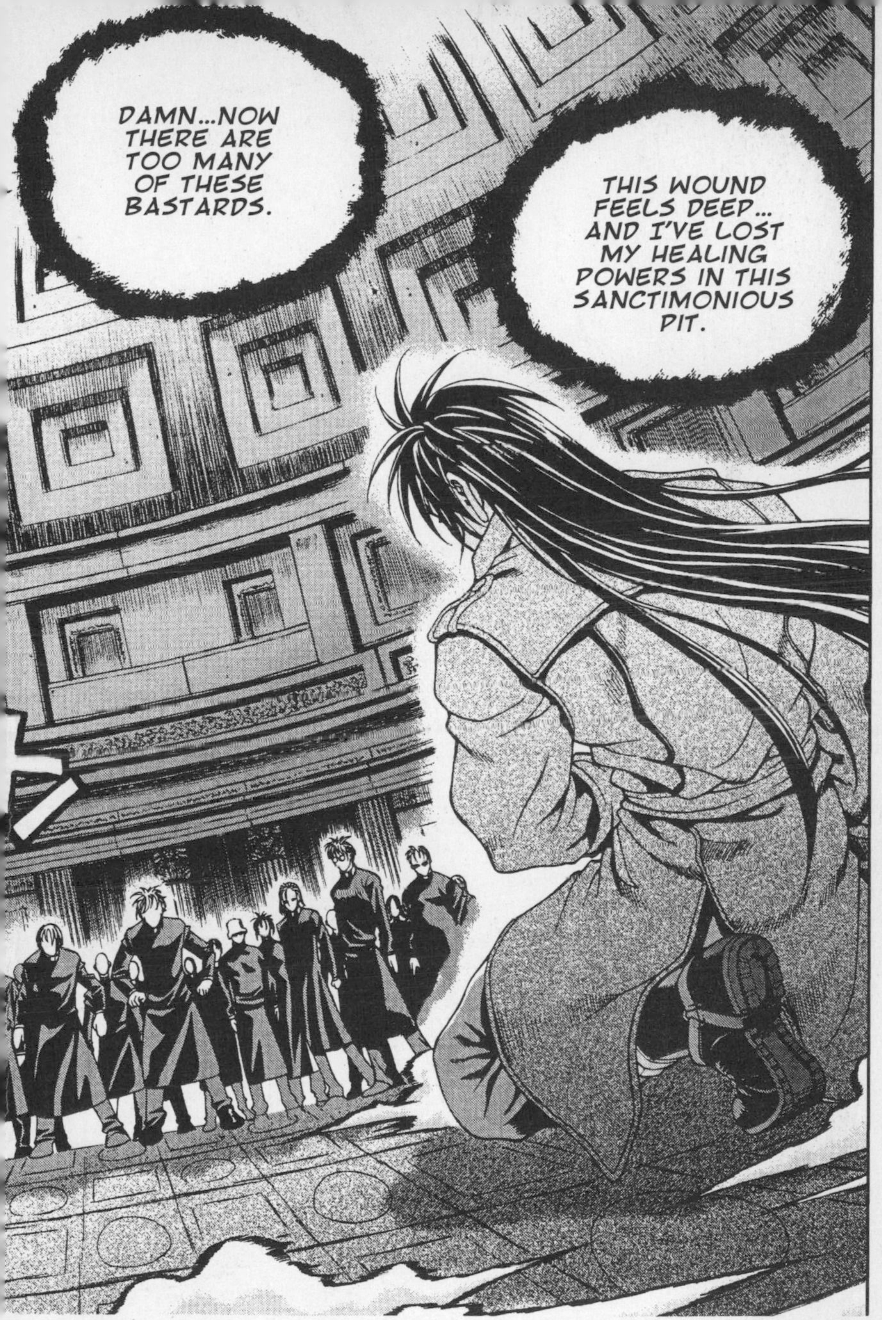
THIS WOUND FEELS DEEP... AND I'VE LOST MY HEALING POWERS IN THIS SANCTIMONIOUS PIT.
DAMN...NOW THERE ARE TOO MANY OF THESE BASTARDS.

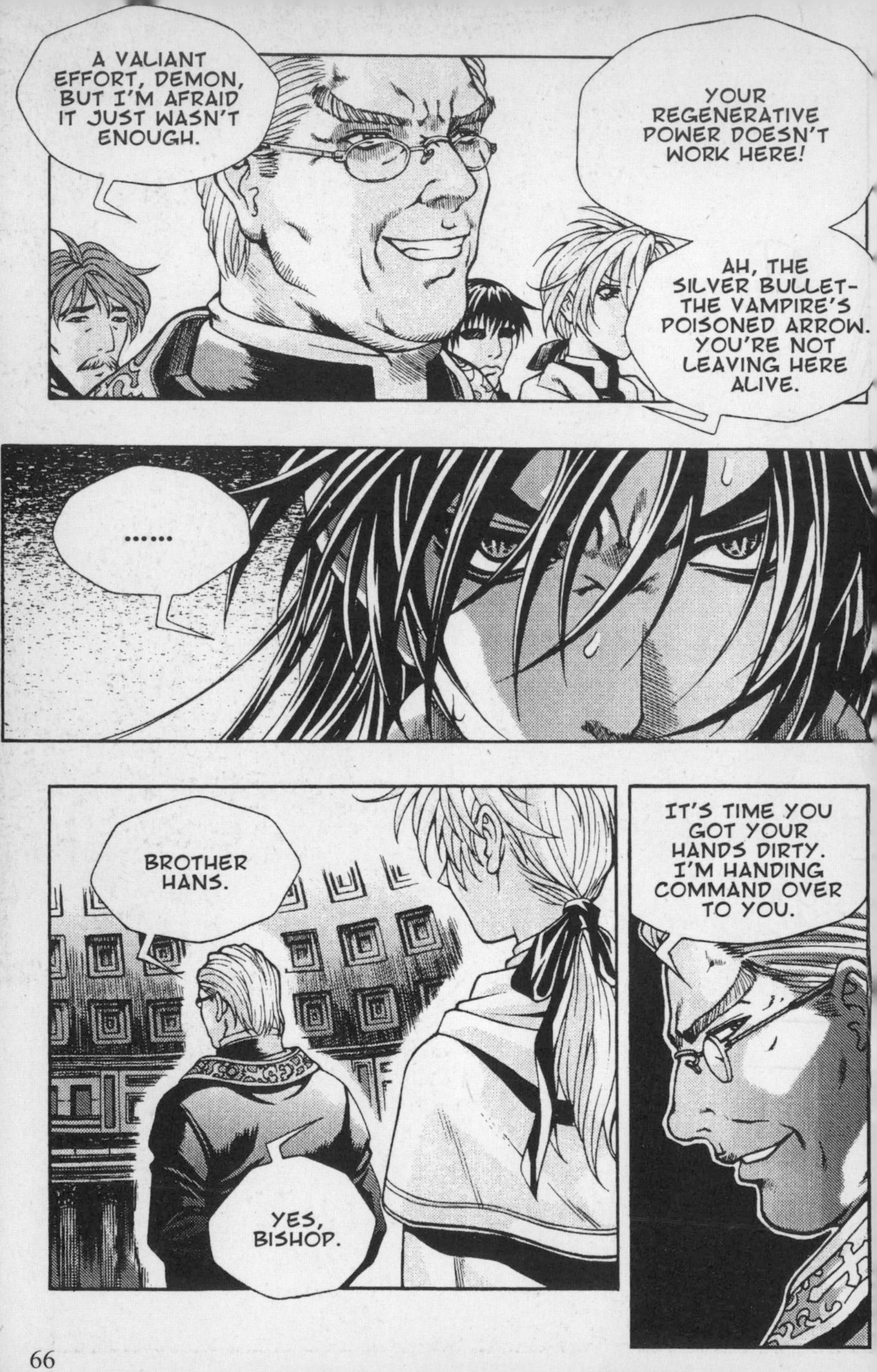
A VALIANT EFFORT, DEMON, BUT I'M AFRAID IT JUST WASN'T ENOUGH.
YOUR REGENERATIVE POWER DOESN'T WORK HERE!
AH, THE SILVER BULLET-THE VAMPIRE'S POISONED ARROW. YOU'RE NOT LEAVING HERE ALIVE.
......
BROTHER HANS.
IT'S TIME YOU GOT YOUR HANDS DIRTY. I'M HANDING COMMAND OVER TO YOU.
YES, BISHOP.

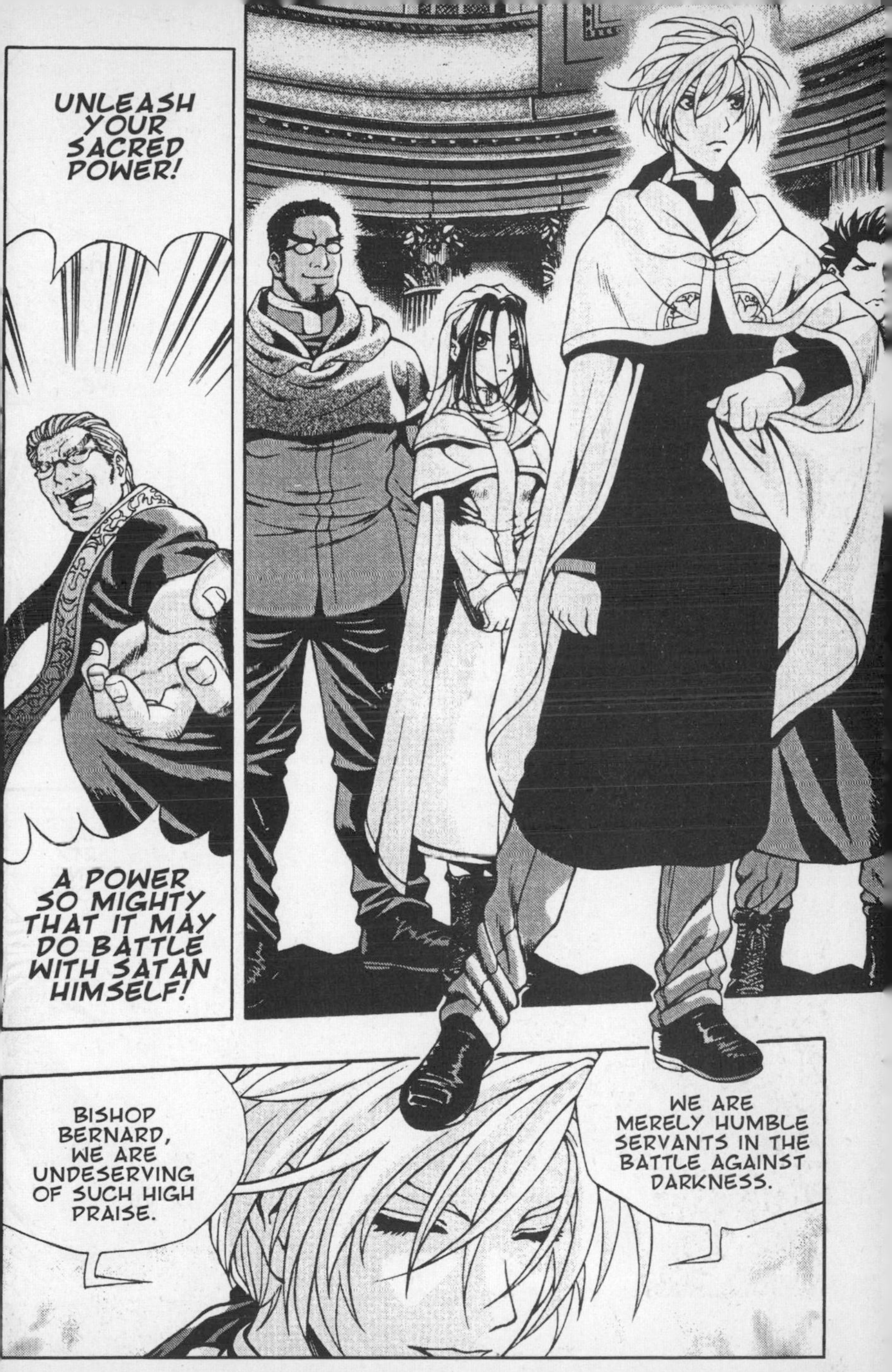
UNLEASH YOUR SACRED POWER!
A POWER SO MIGHTY THAT IT MAY DO BATTLE WITH SATAN HIMSELF!
BISHOP BERNARD, WE ARE UNDESERVING OF SUCH HIGH PRAISE.
WE ARE MERELY HUMBLE SERVANTS IN THE BATTLE AGAINST DARKNESS.

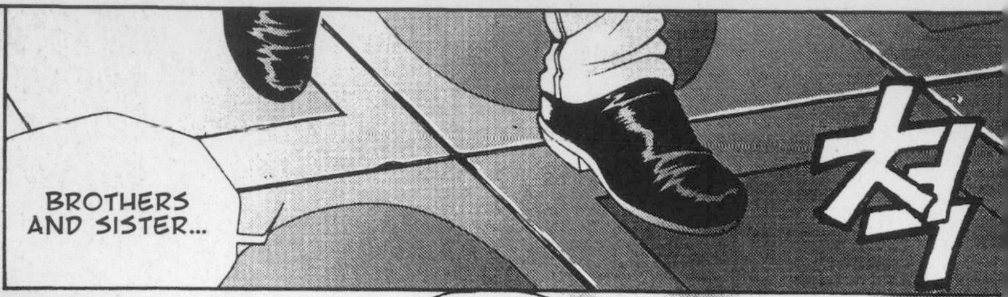
BROTHERS AND SISTER...
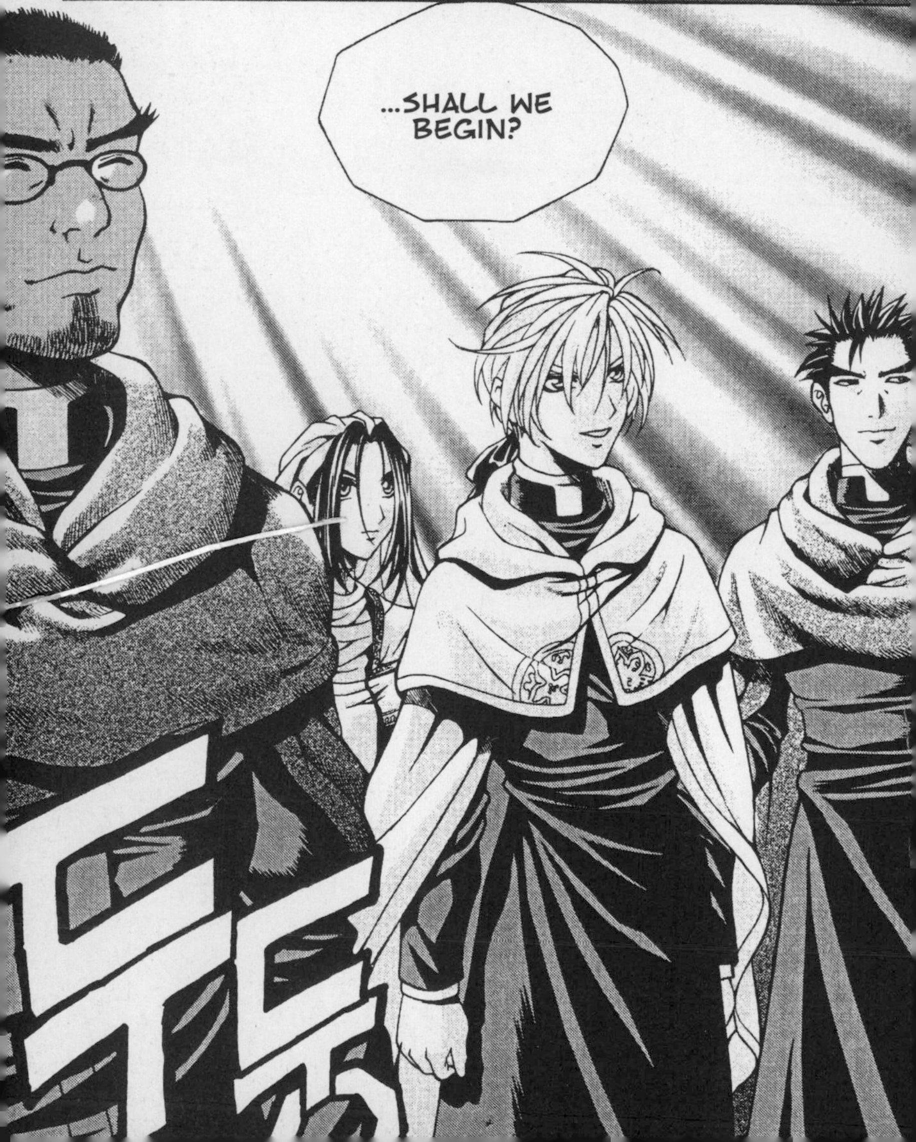
...SHALL WE BEGIN?

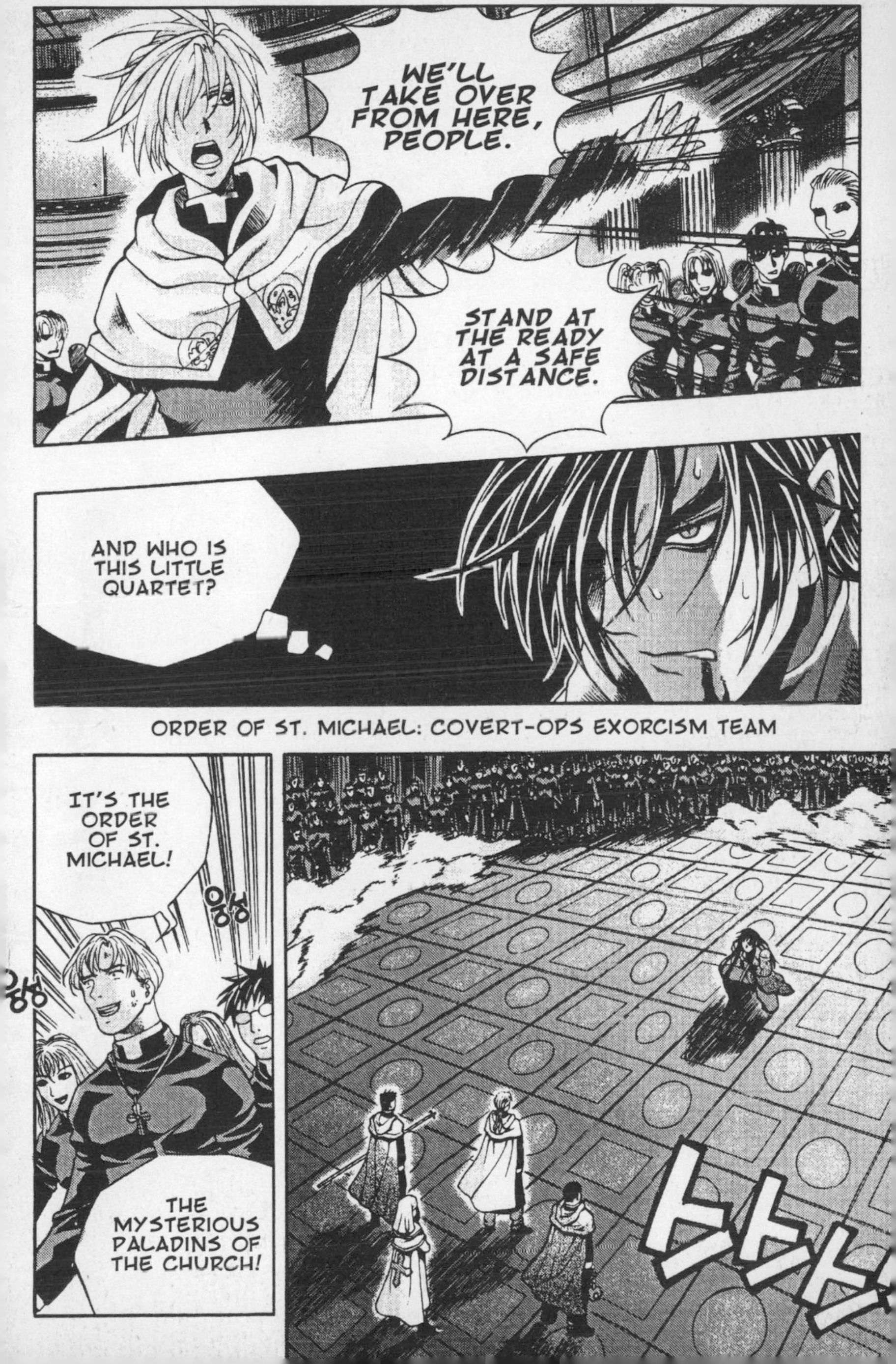
WE'LL TAKE OVER FROM HERE, PEOPLE.
STAND AT THE READY AT A SAFE DISTANCE.
AND WHO IS THIS LITTLE QUARTET?
ORDER OF ST. MICHAEL: COVERT-OPS EXORCISM TEAM
IT'S THE ORDER OF ST. MICHAEL!
THE MYSTERIOUS PALADINS OF THE CHURCH!

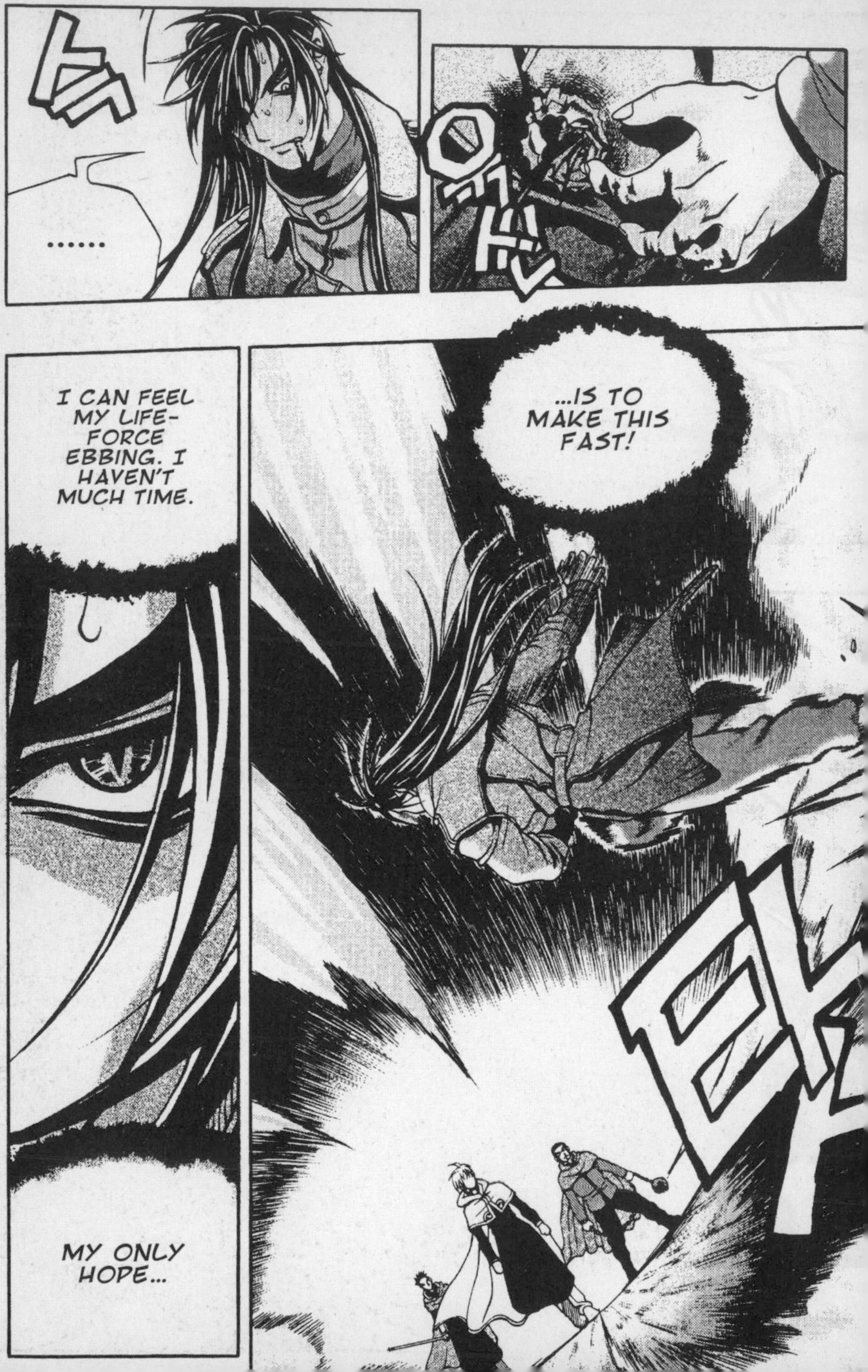
......
I CAN FEEL MY LIFE-FORCE EBBING. I HAVEN'T MUCH TIME.
MY ONLY HOPE...
...IS TO MAKE THIS FAST!

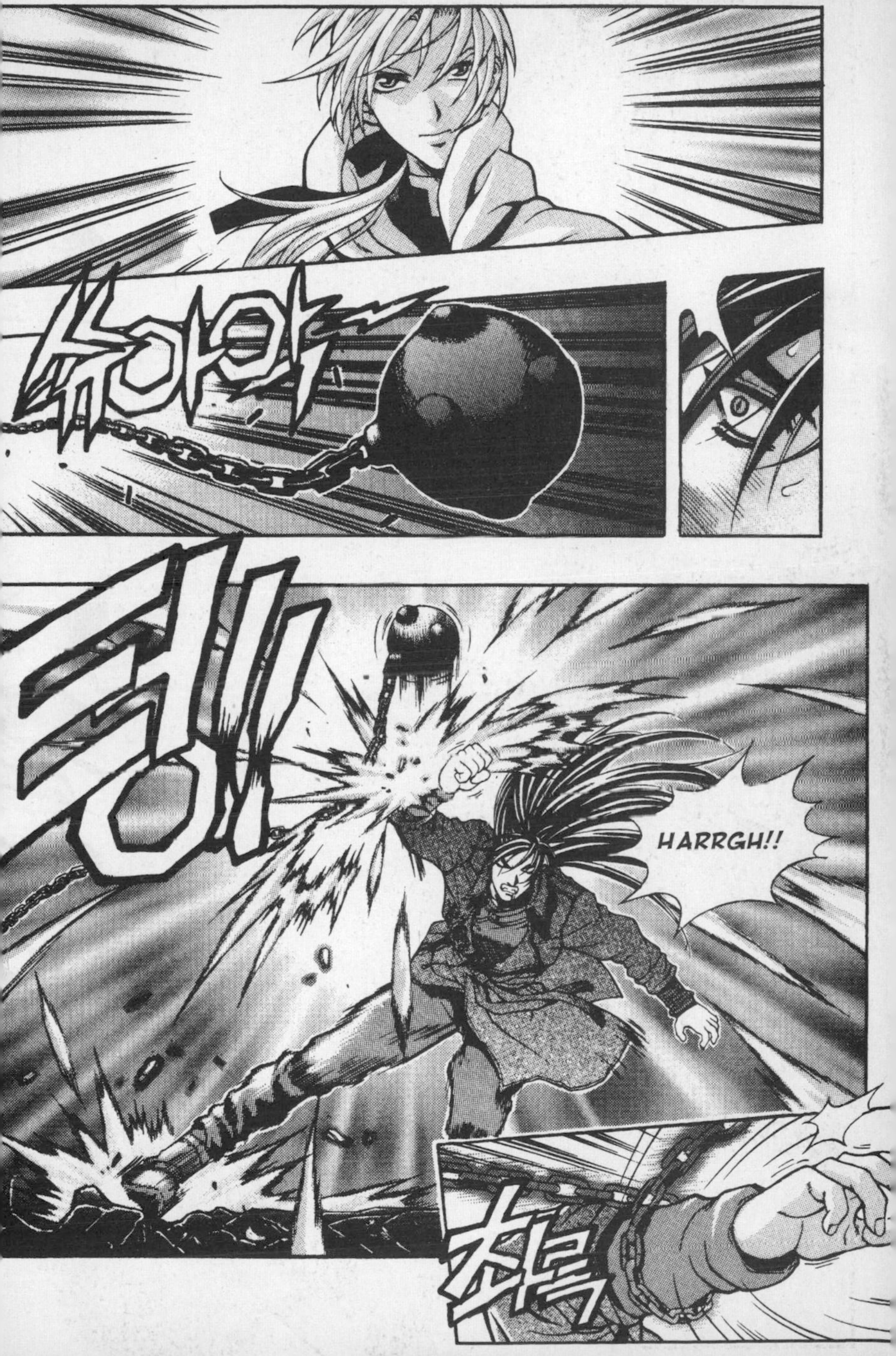
HARRGH!!

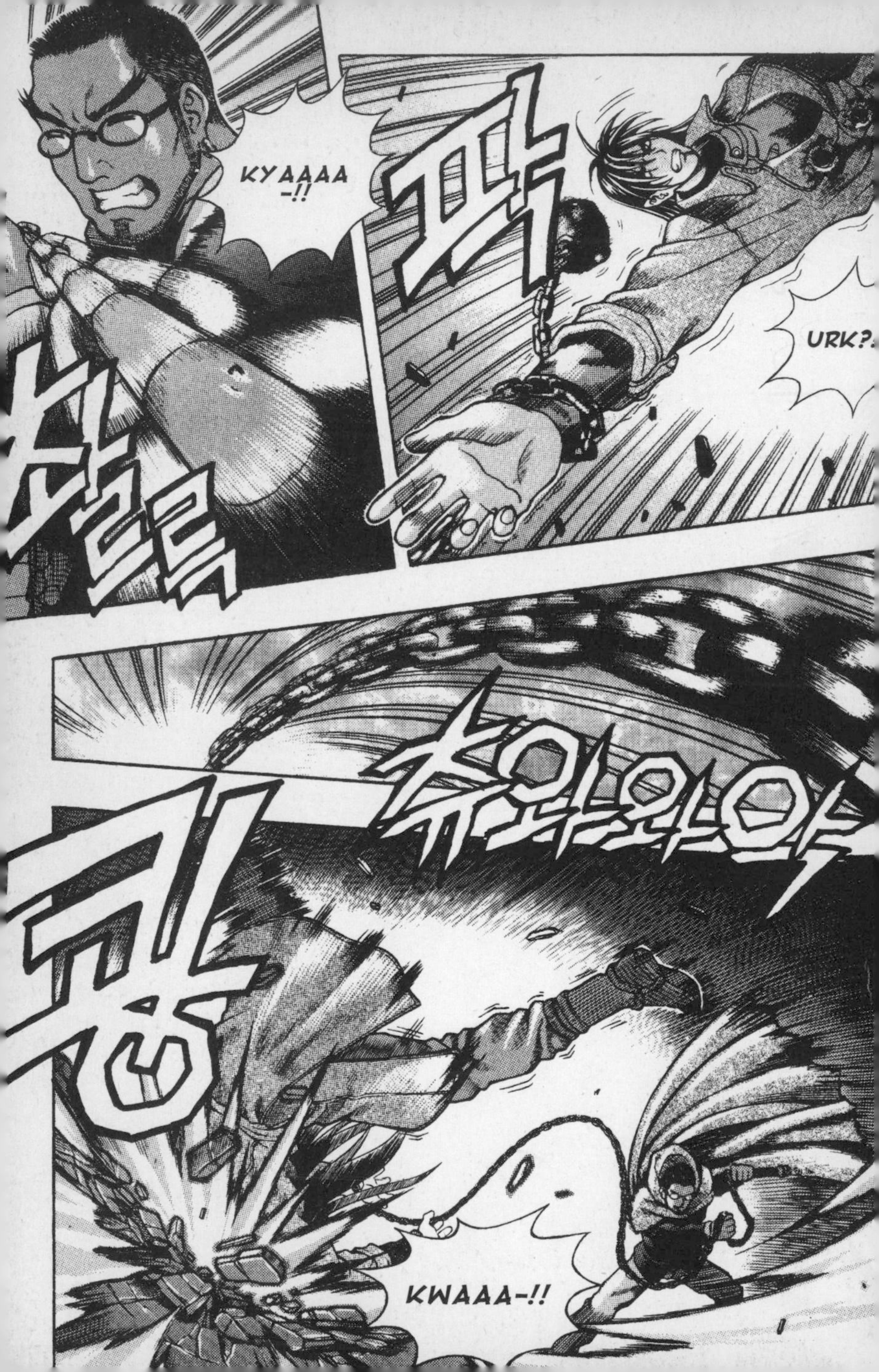
KYAAAA -!!
URK?..
KWAAA-!!

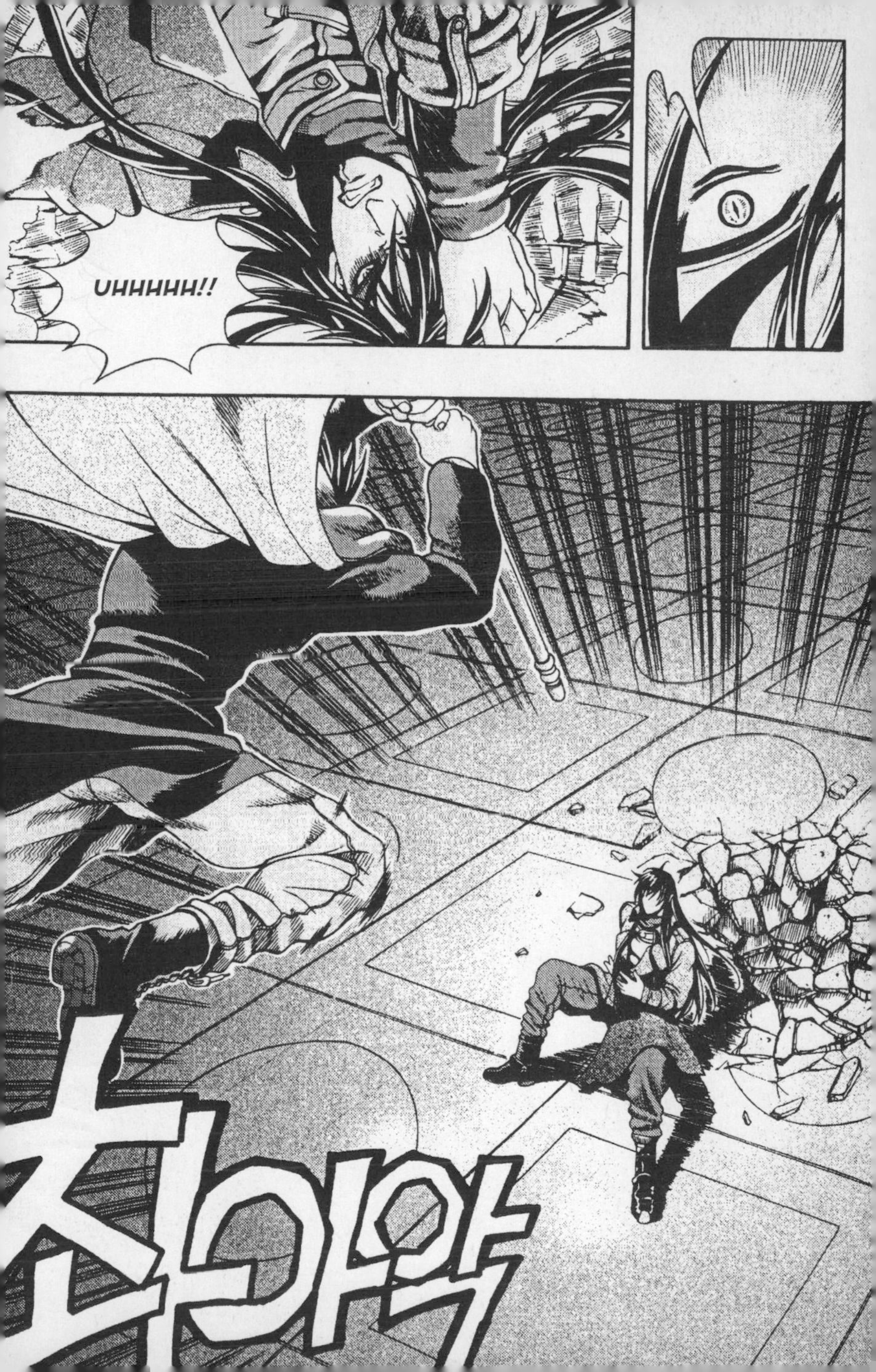
UHHHHH!!

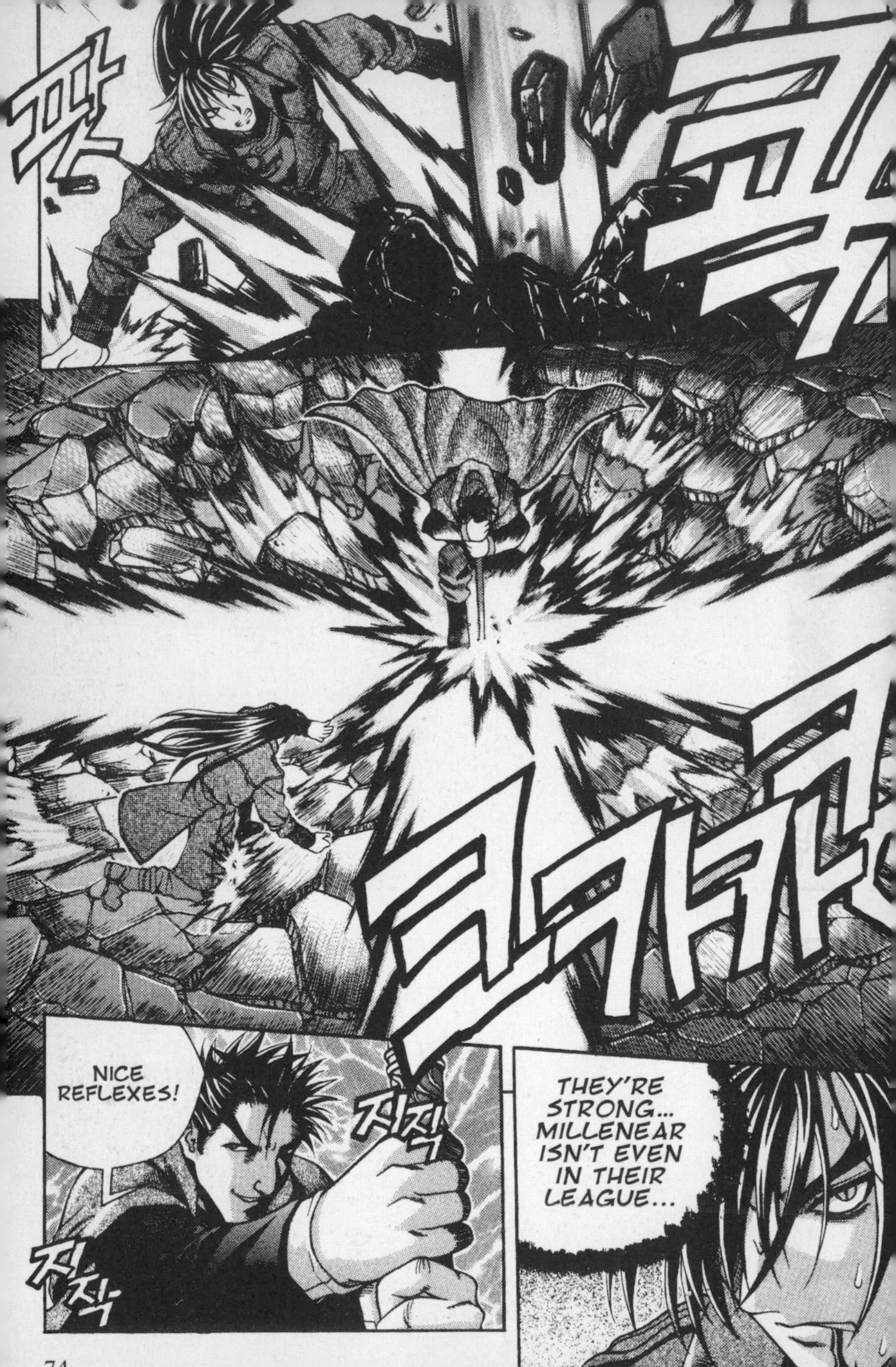
NICE REFLEXES!
지직
지직
THEY'RE STRONG... MILLENEAR ISN'T EVEN IN THEIR LEAGUE...

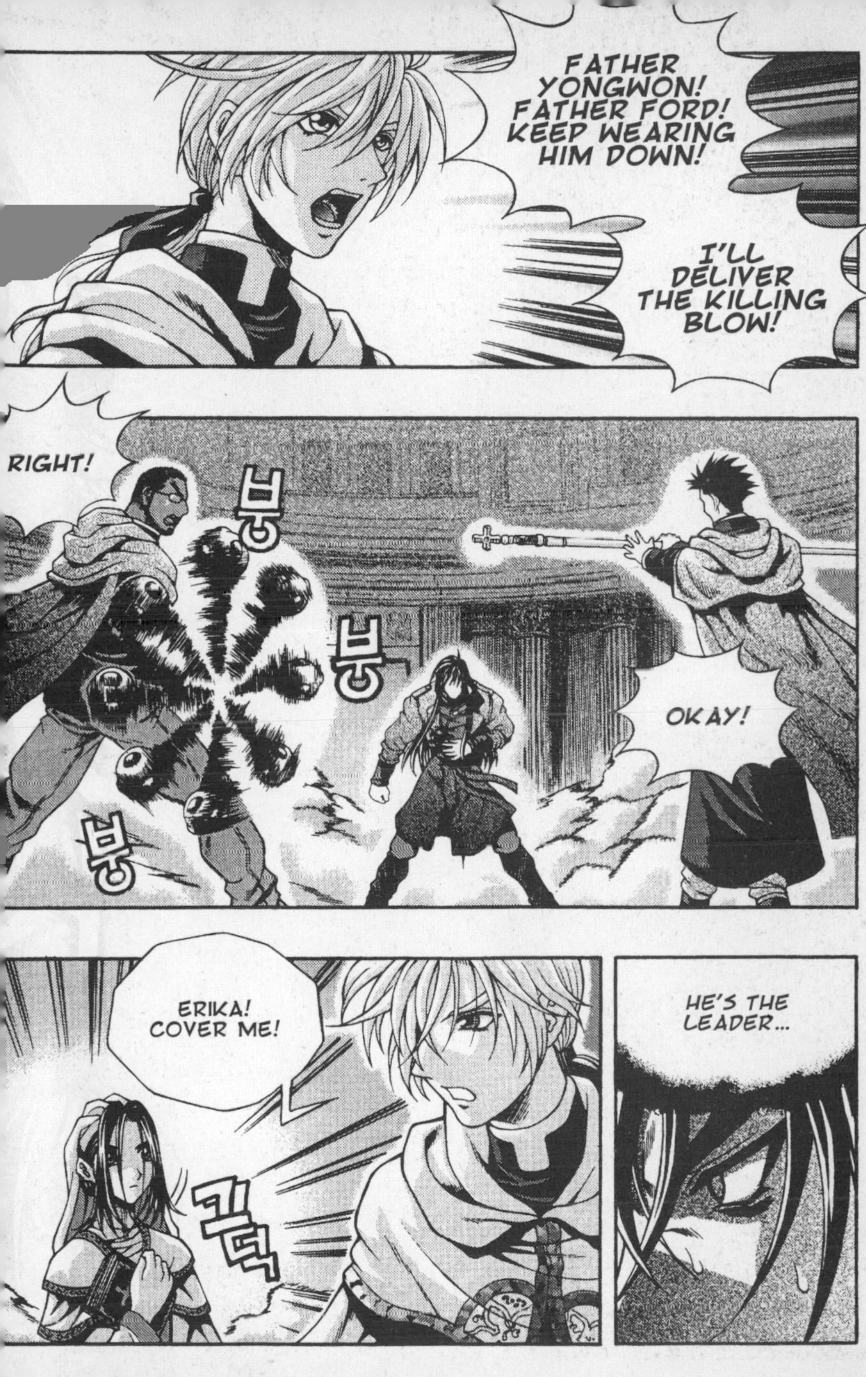
FATHER YONGWON! FATHER FORD! KEEP WEARING HIM DOWN!
I'LL DELIVER THE KILLING BLOW!
RIGHT!
붕
붕
붕
OKAY!
ERIKA! COVER ME!
끄덕
HE'S THE LEADER...

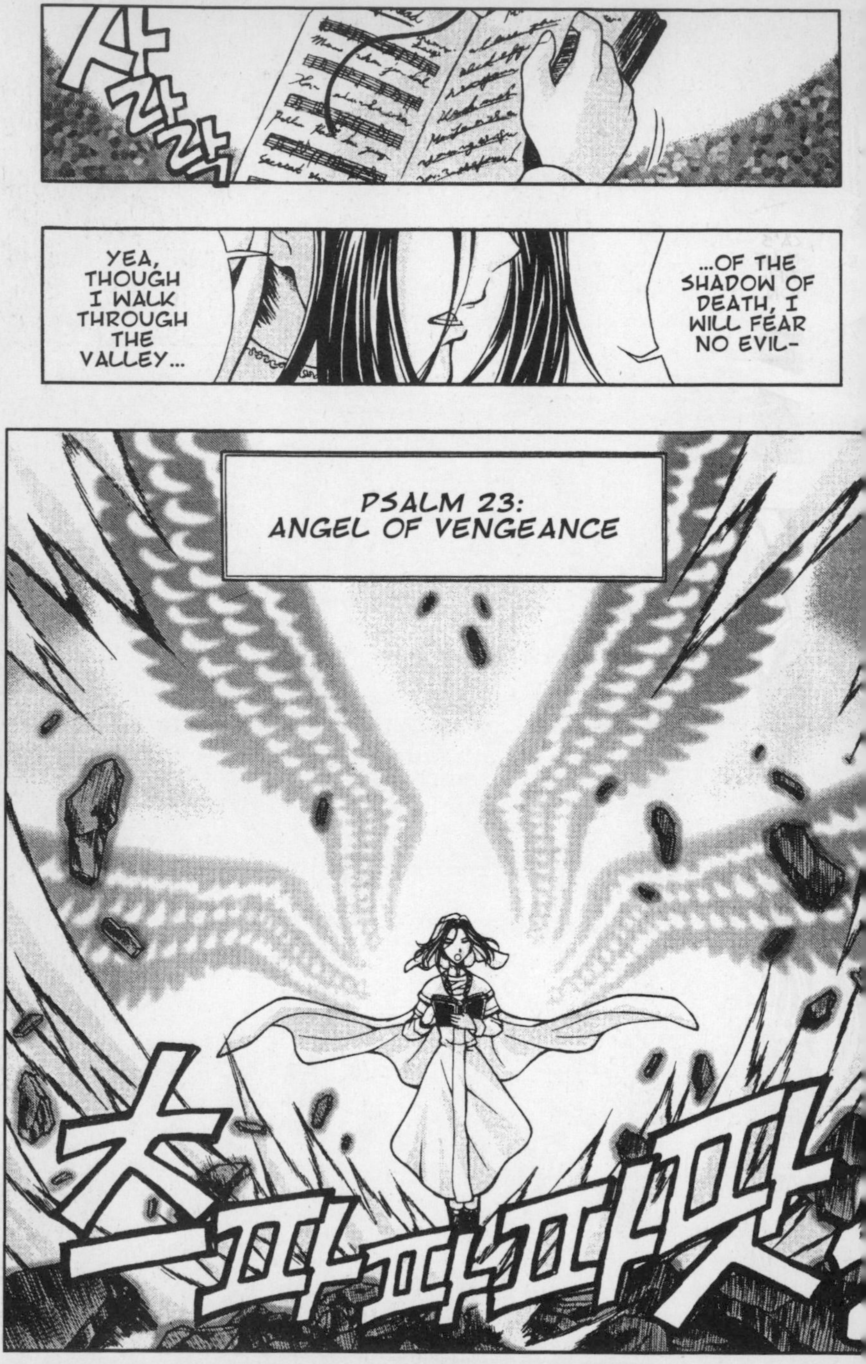
YEA, THOUGH I WALK THROUGH THE VALLEY...
...OF THE SHADOW OF DEATH, I WILL FEAR NO EVIL-
PSALM 23: ANGEL OF VENGEANCE

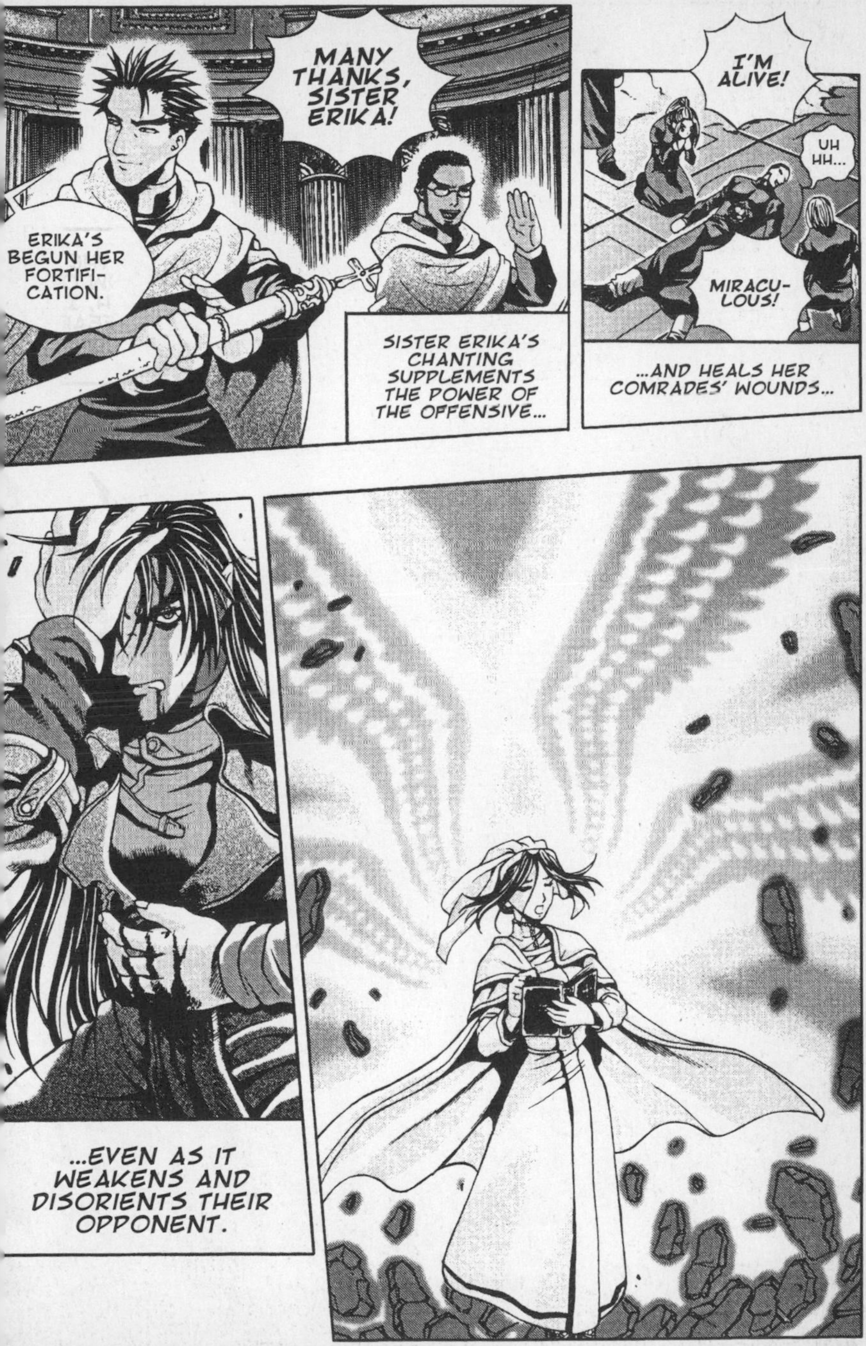
ERIKA'S BEGUN HER FORTIFI-CATION.
MANY THANKS, SISTER ERIKA!
SISTER ERIKA'S CHANTING SUPPLEMENTS THE POWER OF THE OFFENSIVE...
I'M ALIVE!
UH HH...
MIRACU-LOUS!
...AND HEALS HER COMRADES' WOUNDS...
...EVEN AS IT WEAKENS AND DISORIENTS THEIR OPPONENT.

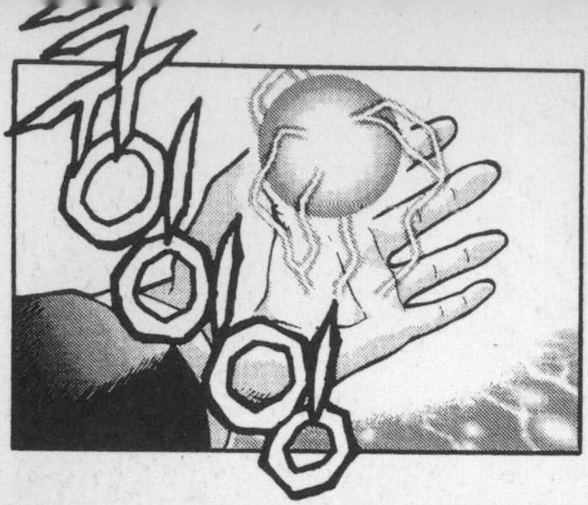
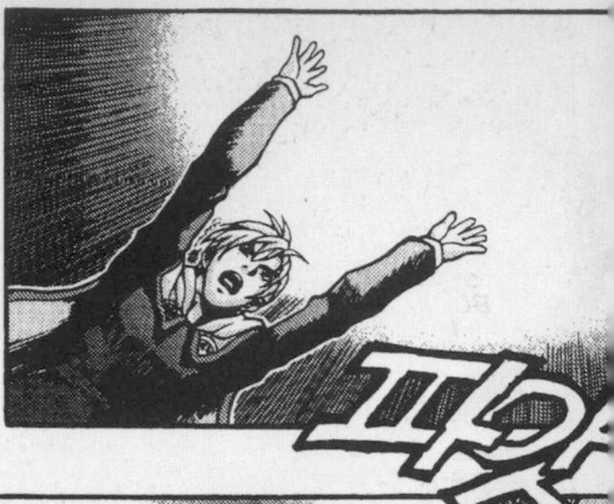
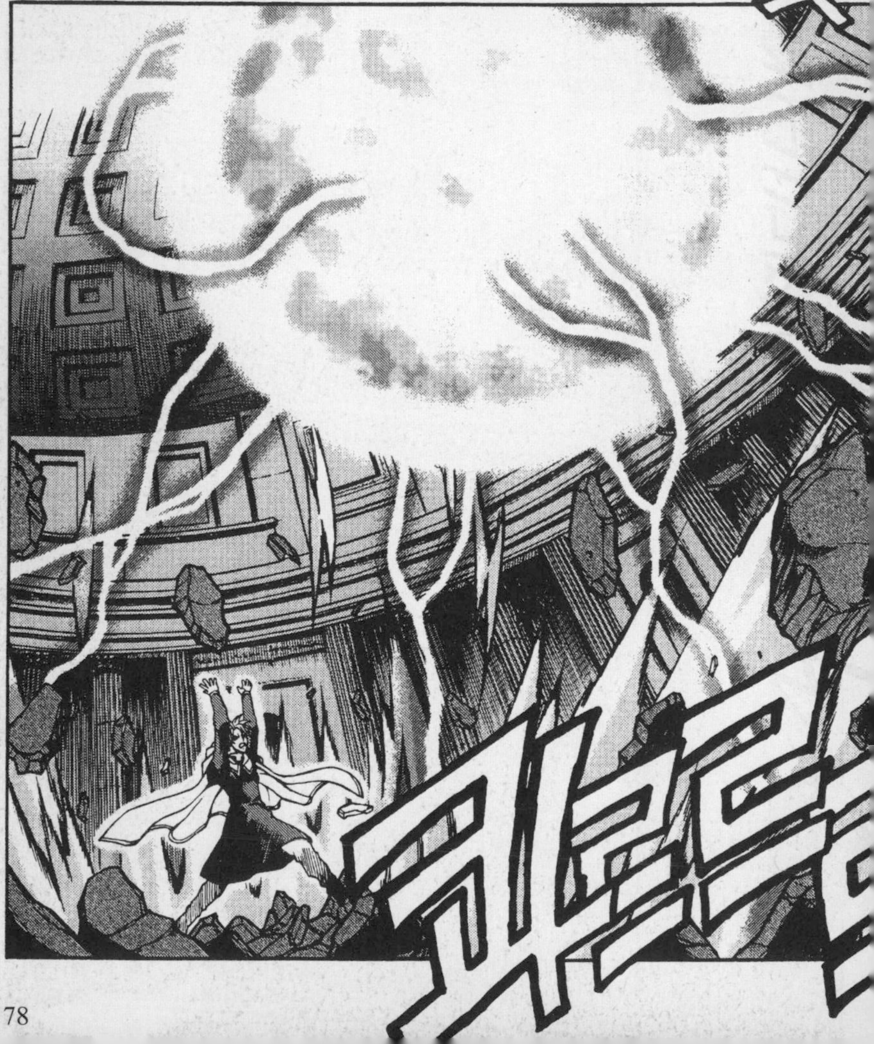

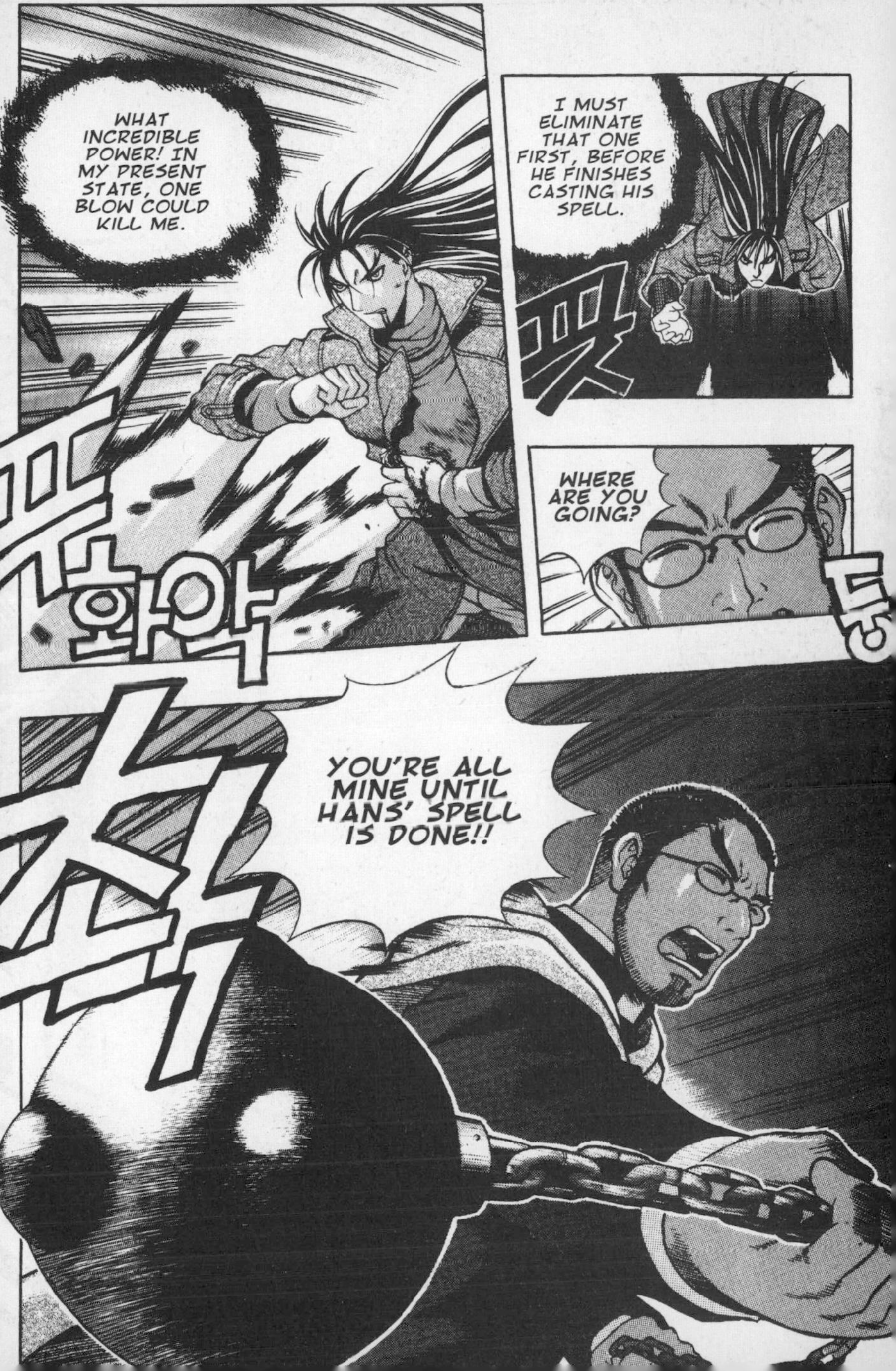
WHAT INCREDIBLE POWER! IN MY PRESENT STATE, ONE BLOW COULD KILL ME.
I MUST ELIMINATE THAT ONE FIRST, BEFORE HE FINISHES CASTING HIS SPELL.
WHERE ARE YOU GOING?
YOU'RE ALL MINE UNTIL HANS' SPELL IS DONE!!

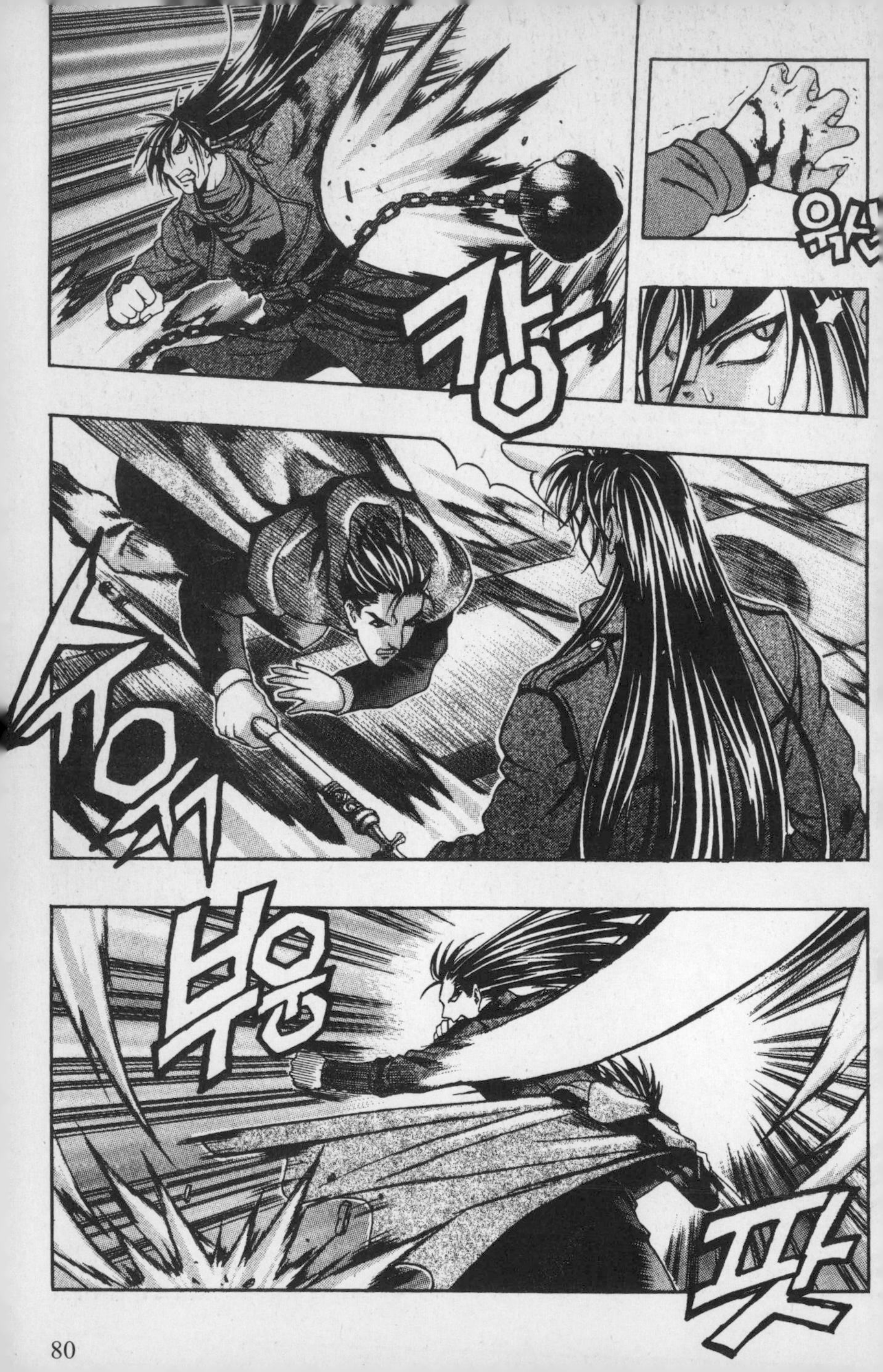
카앙
부웅
파앗

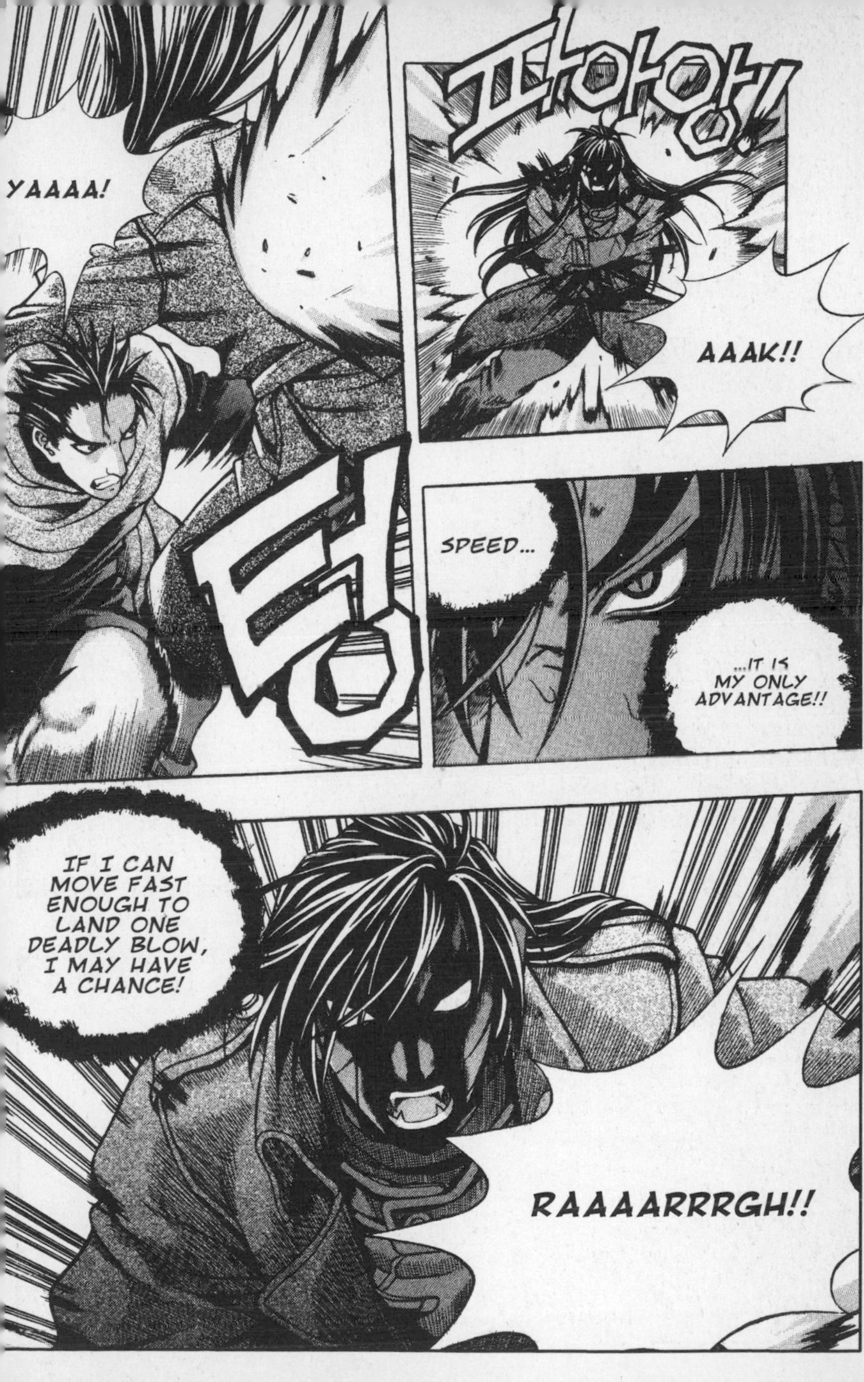
YAAAA!
AAAK!!
SPEED...
...IT IS MY ONLY ADVANTAGE!!
IF I CAN MOVE FAST ENOUGH TO LAND ONE DEADLY BLOW, I MAY HAVE A CHANCE!
RAAAARRRGH!!

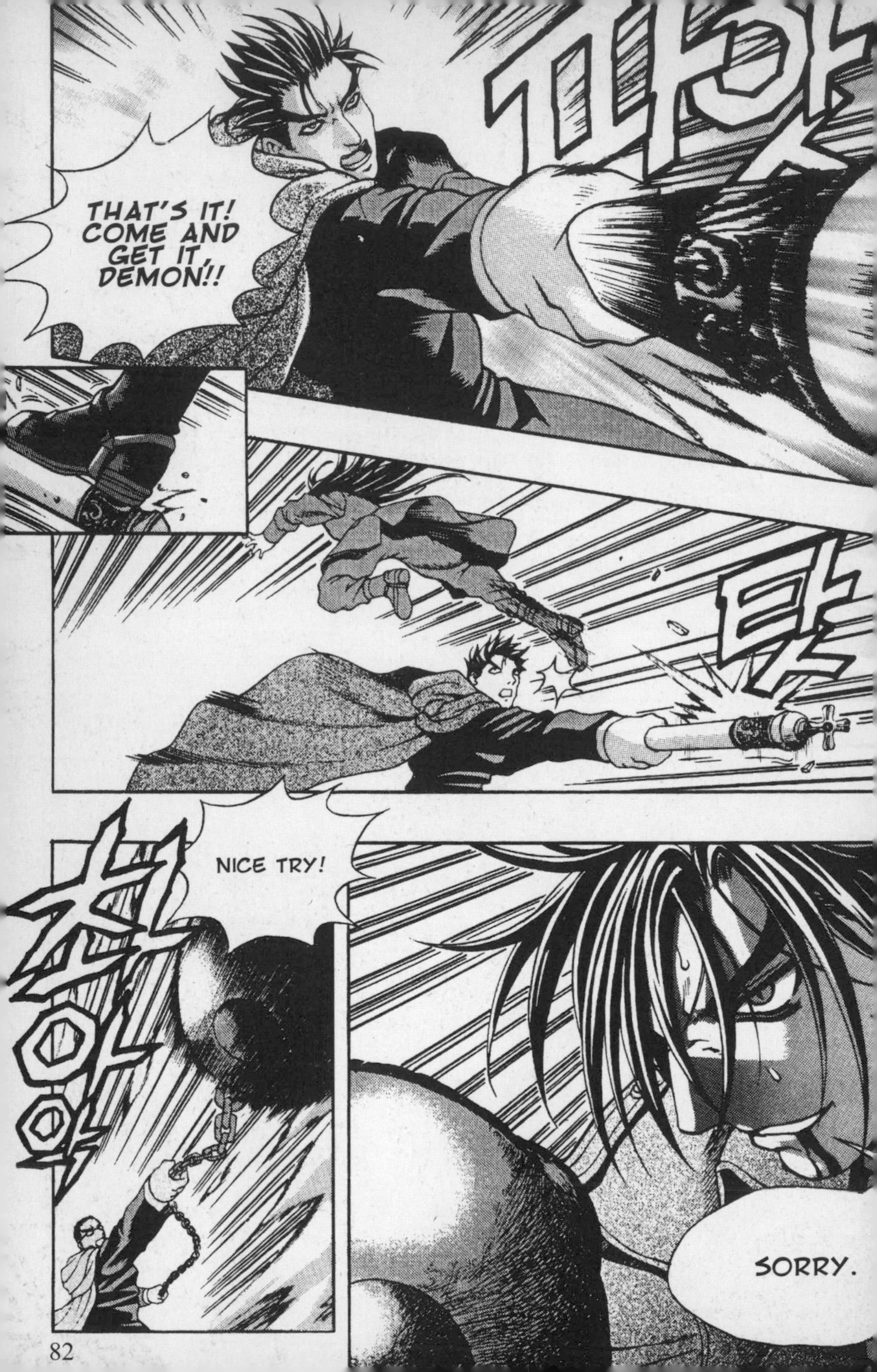
THAT'S IT! COME AND GET IT, DEMON!!
NICE TRY!
SORRY.

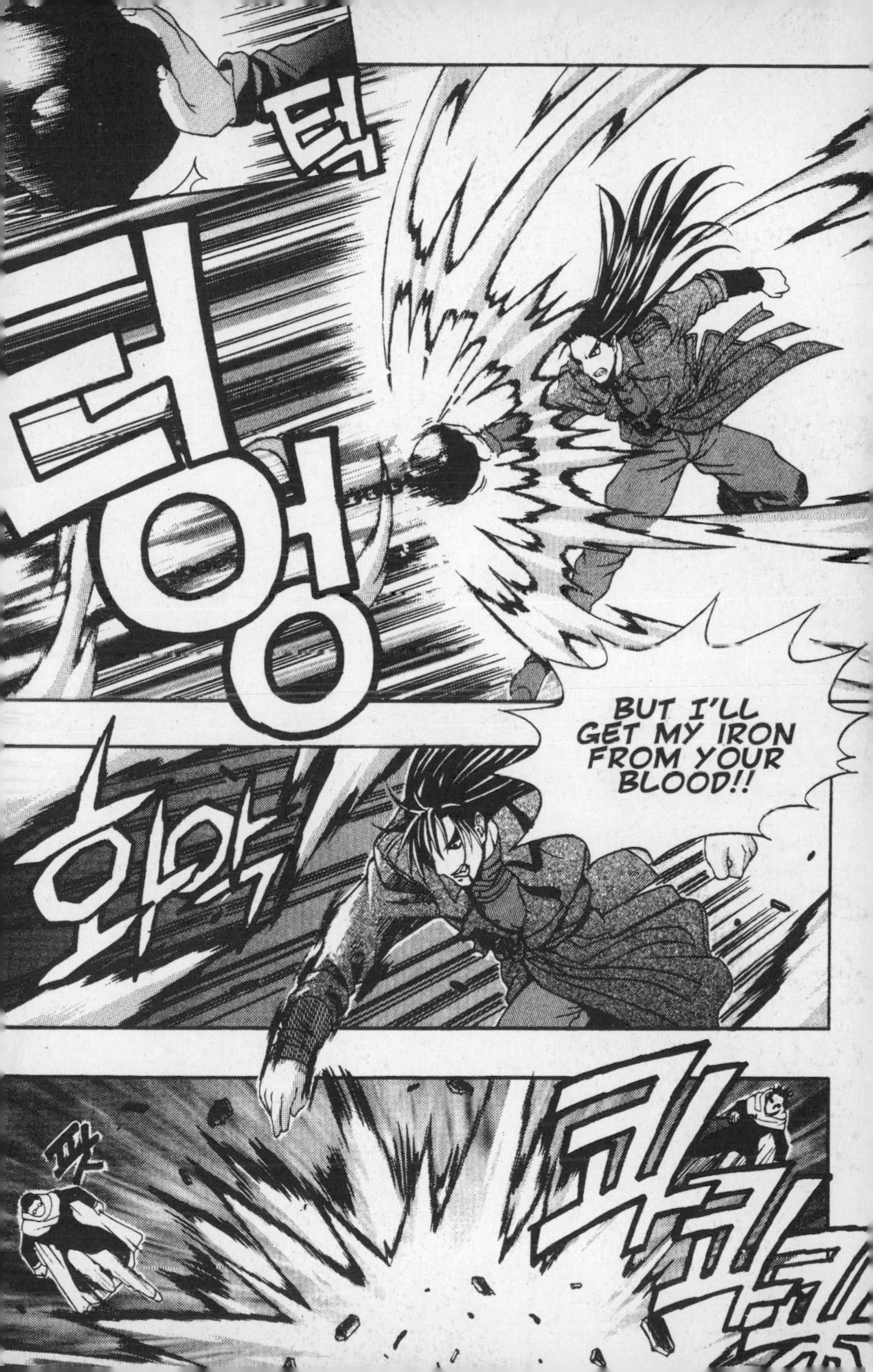
BUT I'LL GET MY IRON FROM YOUR BLOOD!!

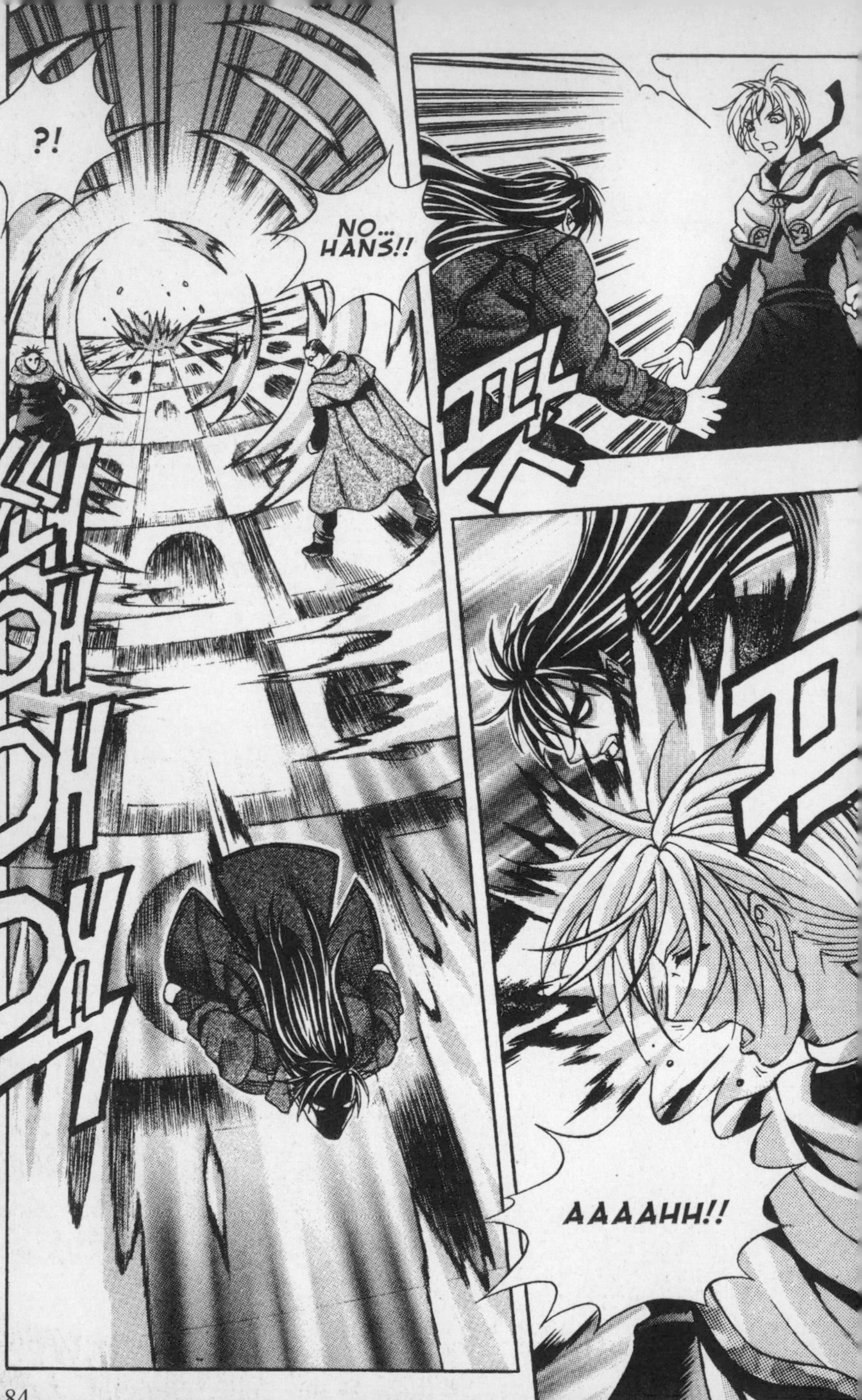
AAAAHH!!
?!
NO... HANS!!

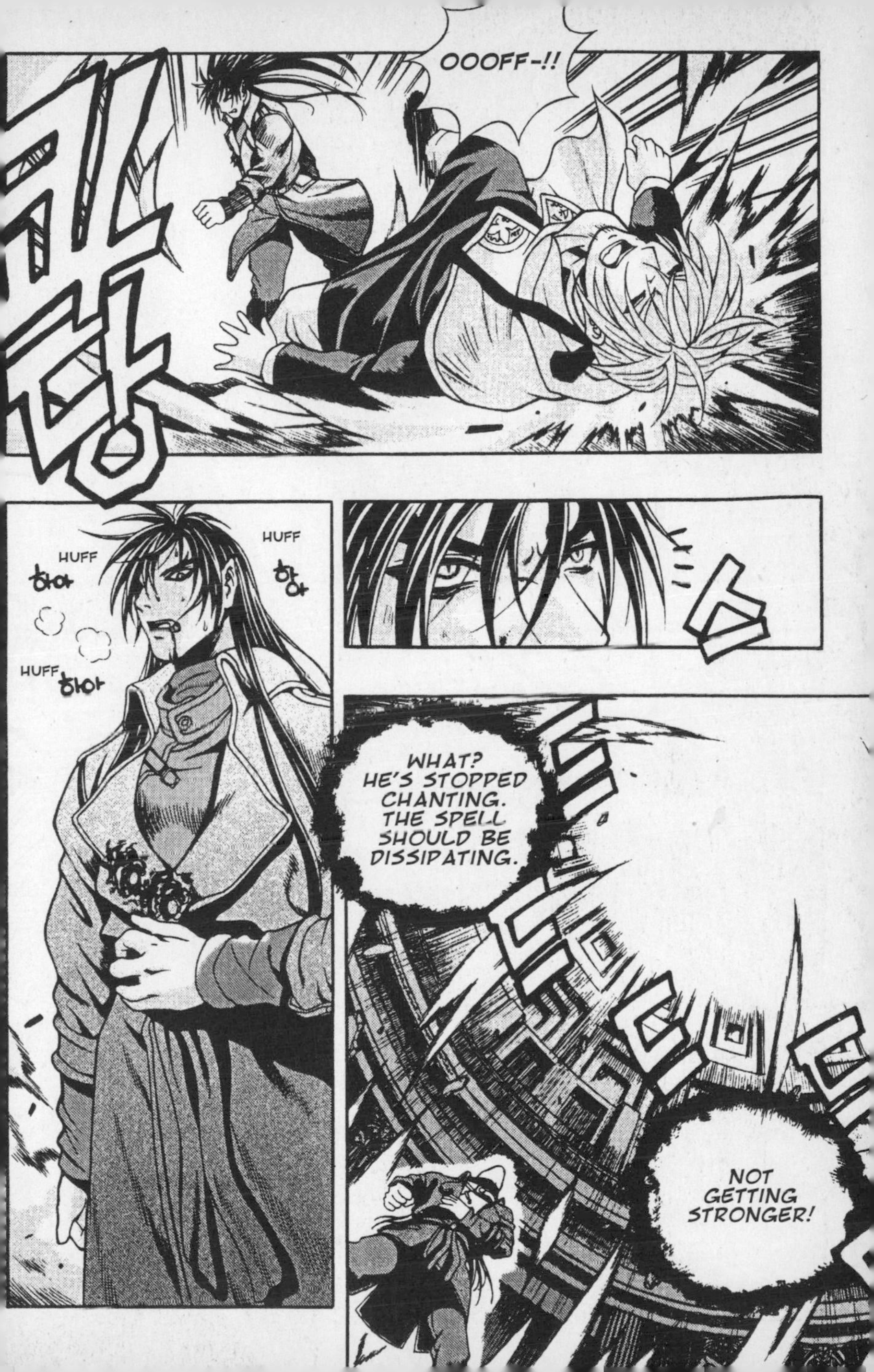
OOOFF-!!
HUFF 하아
HUFF 하아
HUFF 하아
WHAT? HE'S STOPPED CHANTING. THE SPELL SHOULD BE DISSIPATING.
NOT GETTING STRONGER!

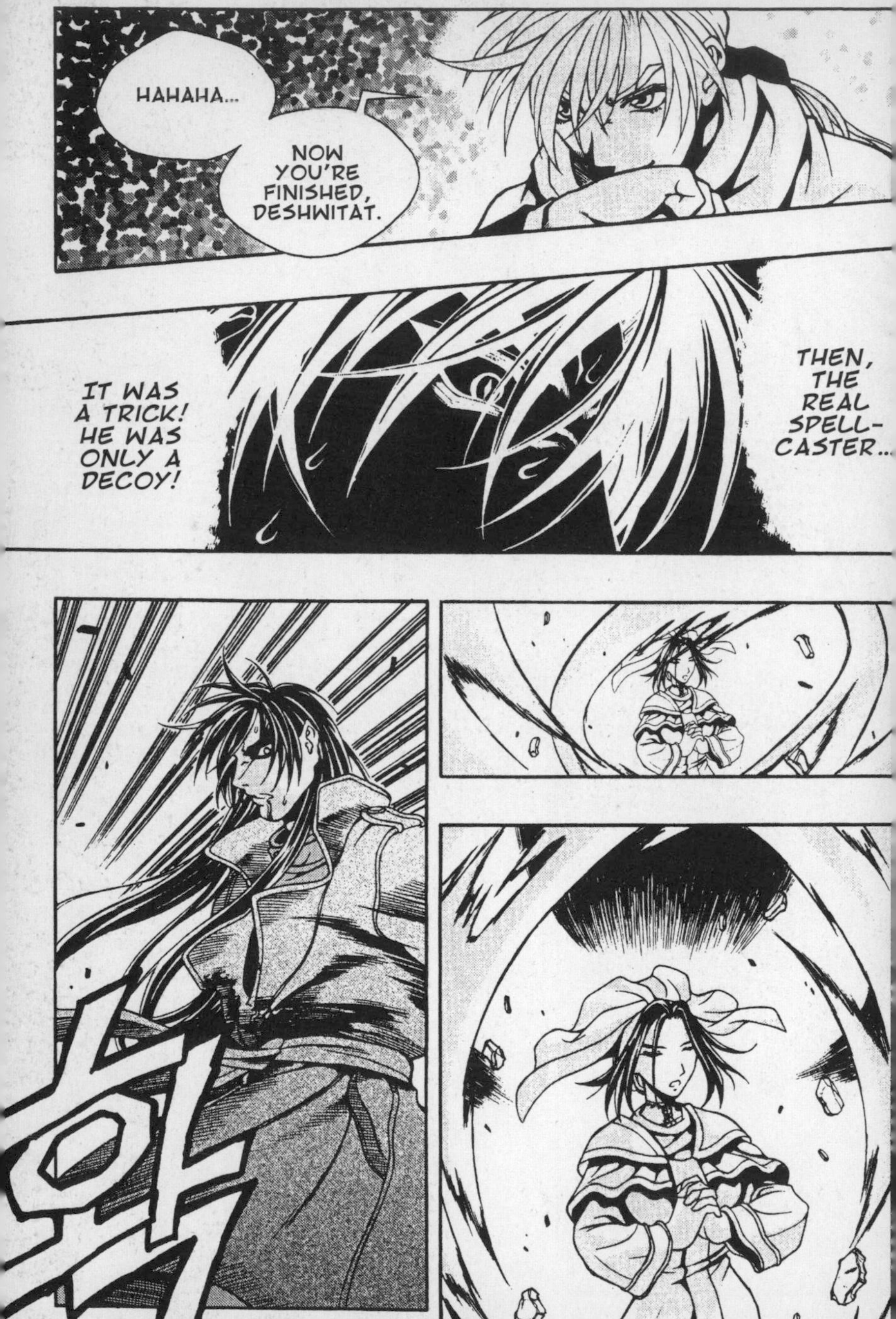
HAHAHA...
NOW YOU'RE FINISHED, DESHWITAT.
THEN, THE REAL SPELL-CASTER...
IT WAS A TRICK! HE WAS ONLY A DECOY!

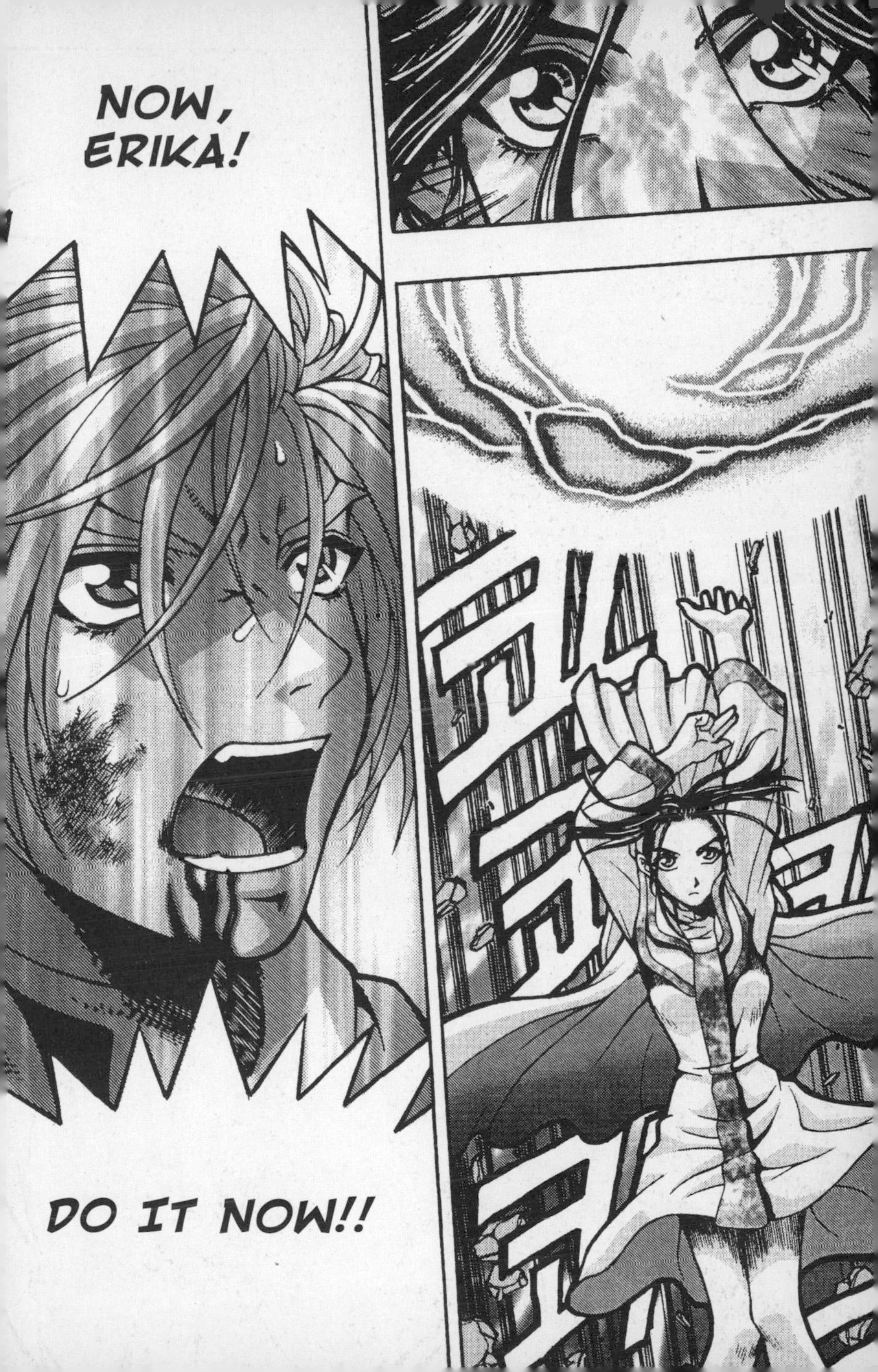
NOW, ERIKA!
DO IT NOW!!

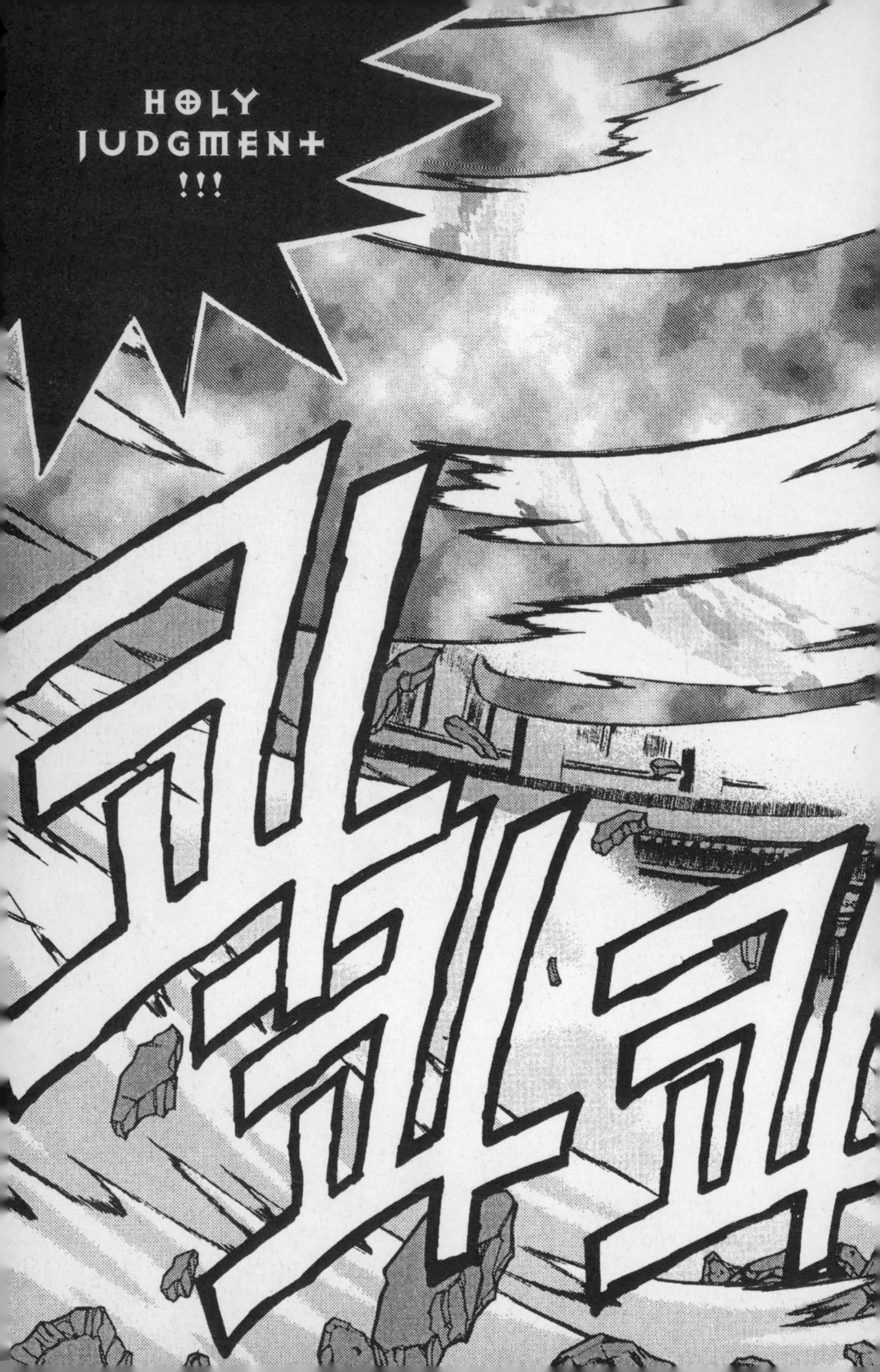
HOLY JUDGMENT !!!

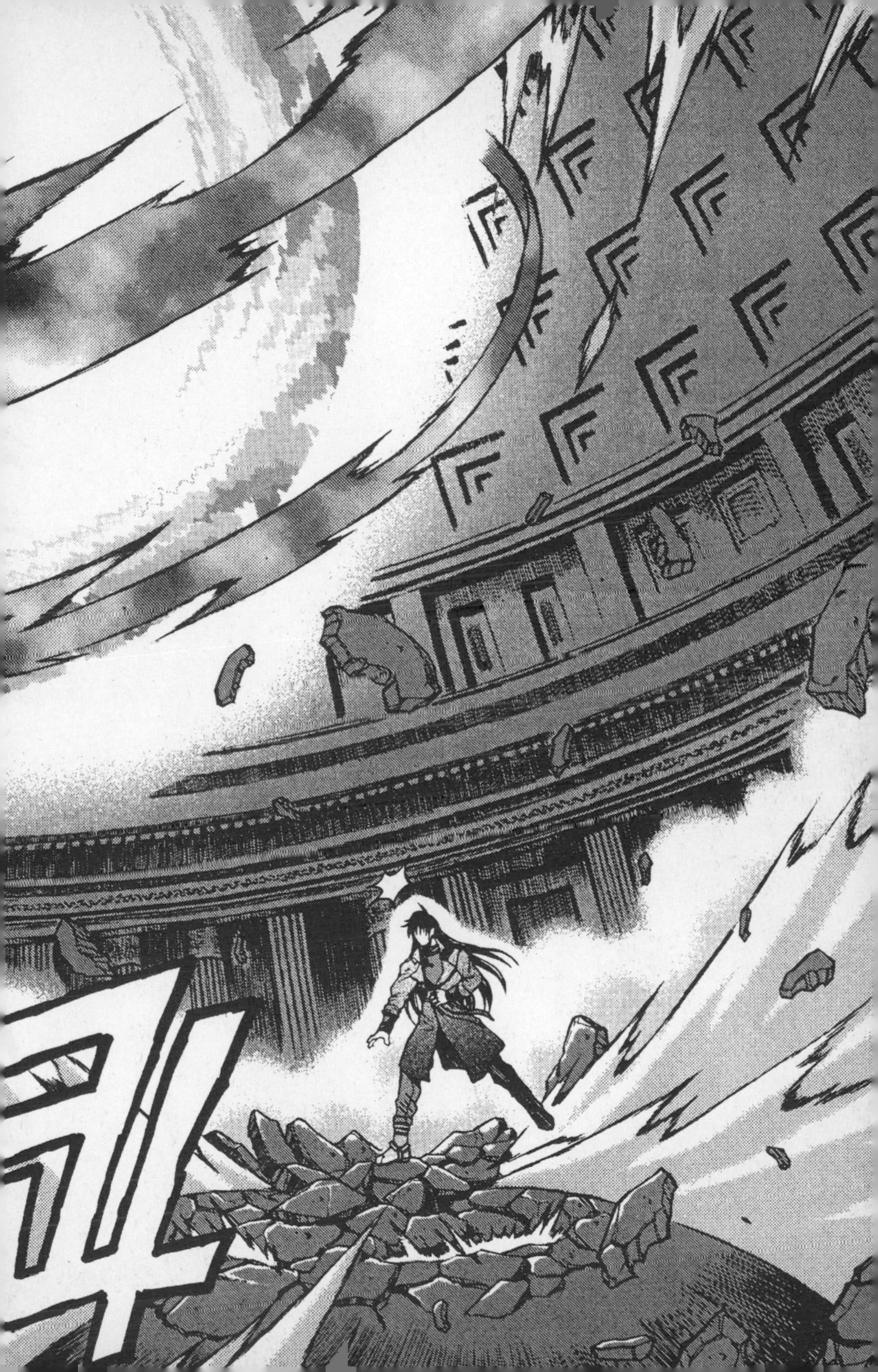

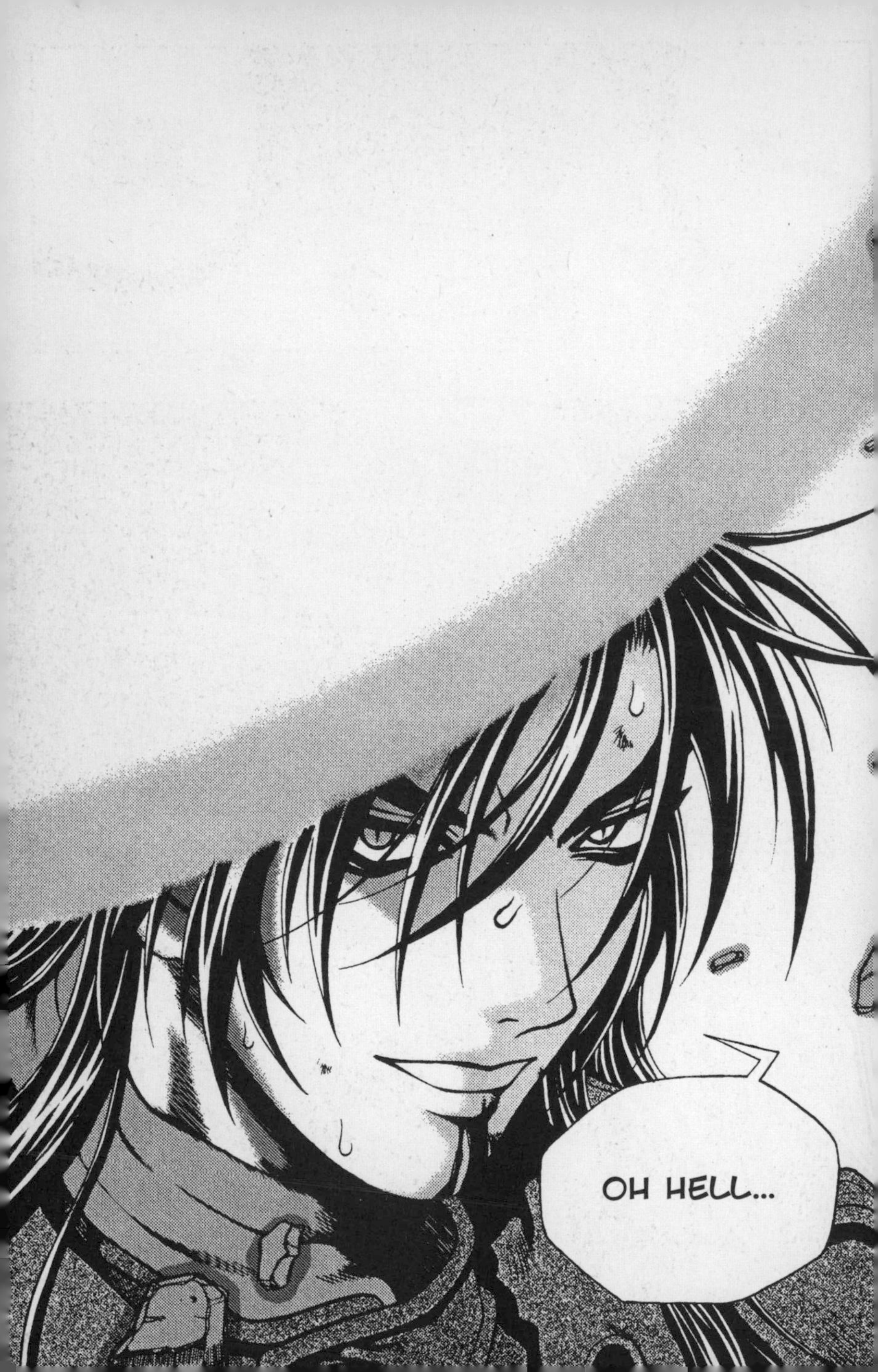
OH HELL...

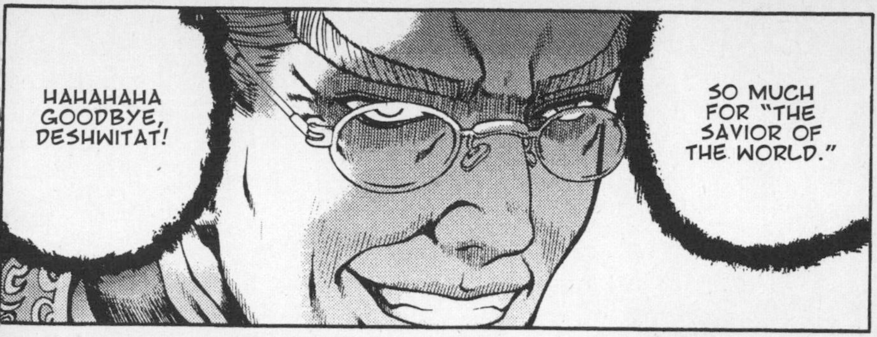
SO MUCH FOR "THE SAVIOR OF THE WORLD."
HAHAHAHA GOODBYE, DESHWITAT!

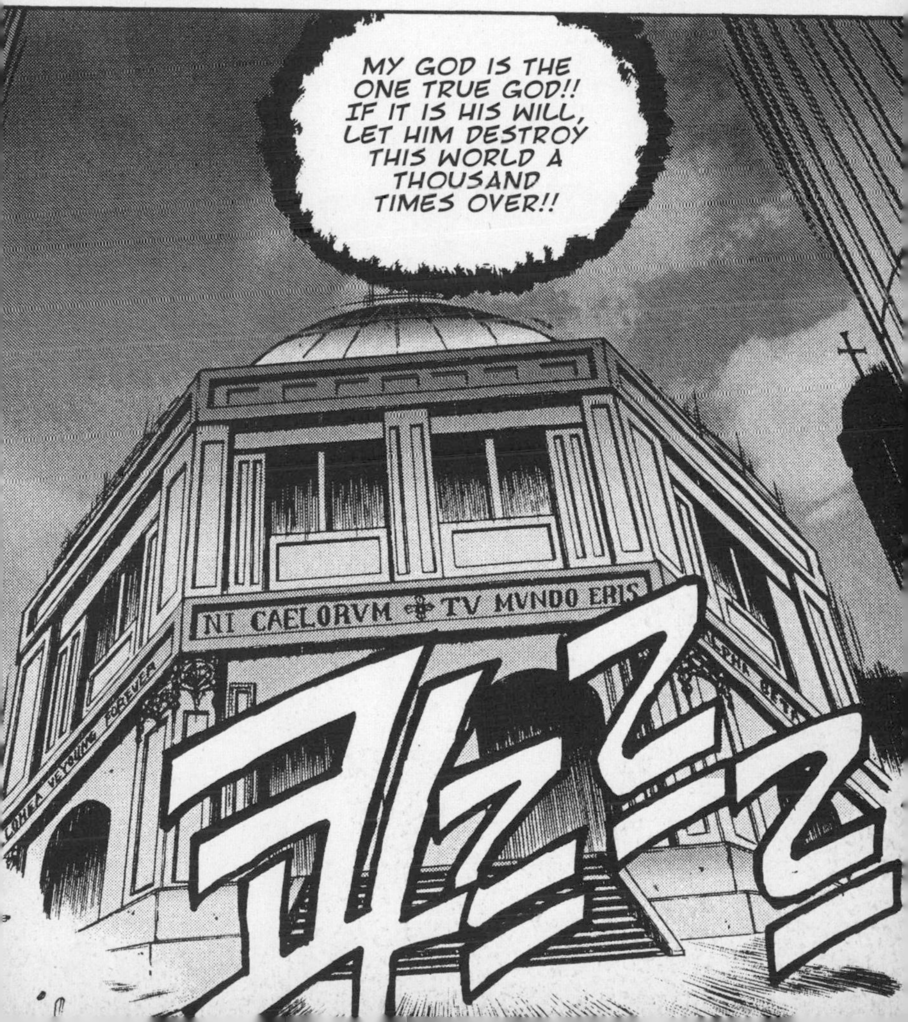
MY GOD IS THE ONE TRUE GOD!! IF IT IS HIS WILL, LET HIM DESTROY THIS WORLD A THOUSAND TIMES OVER!!
NI CAELORVM TV MVNDO ERIS

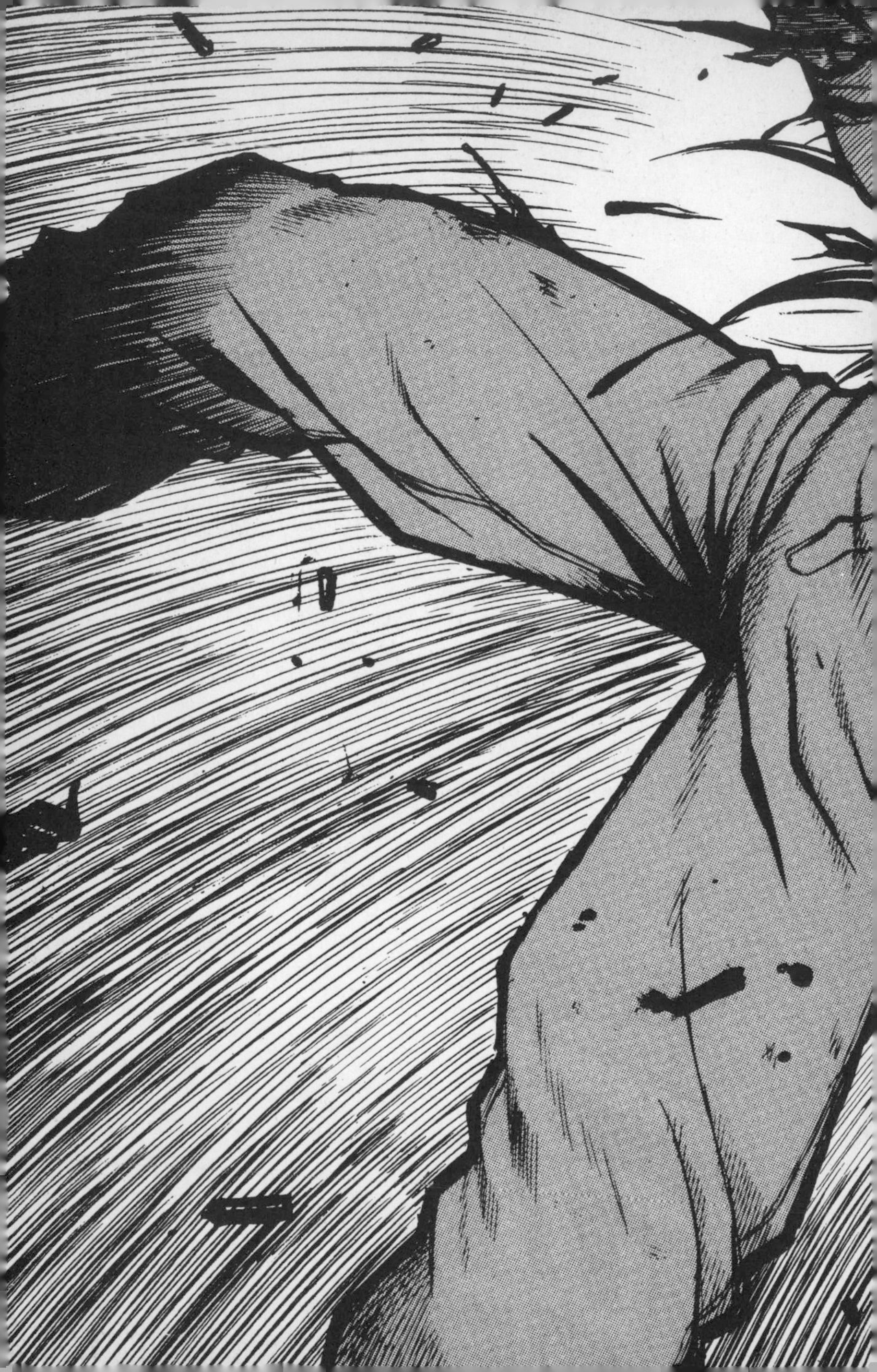

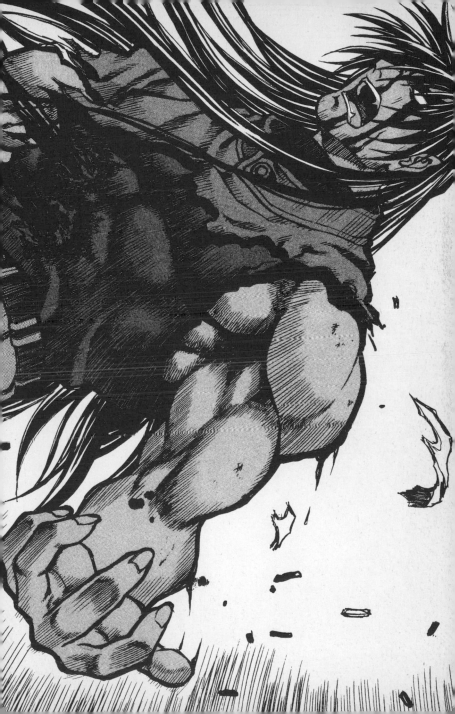

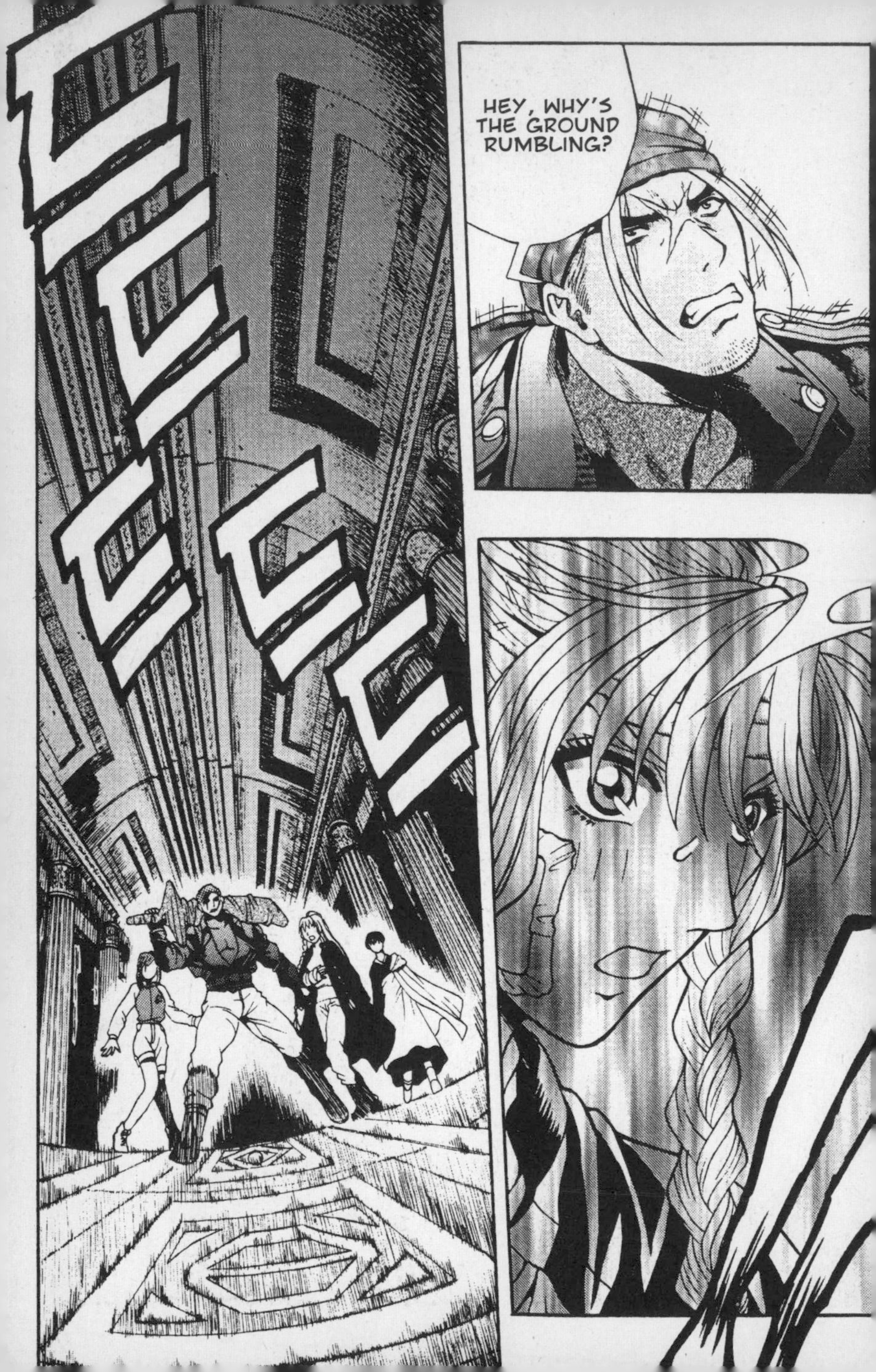
HEY, WHY'S THE GROUND RUMBLING?

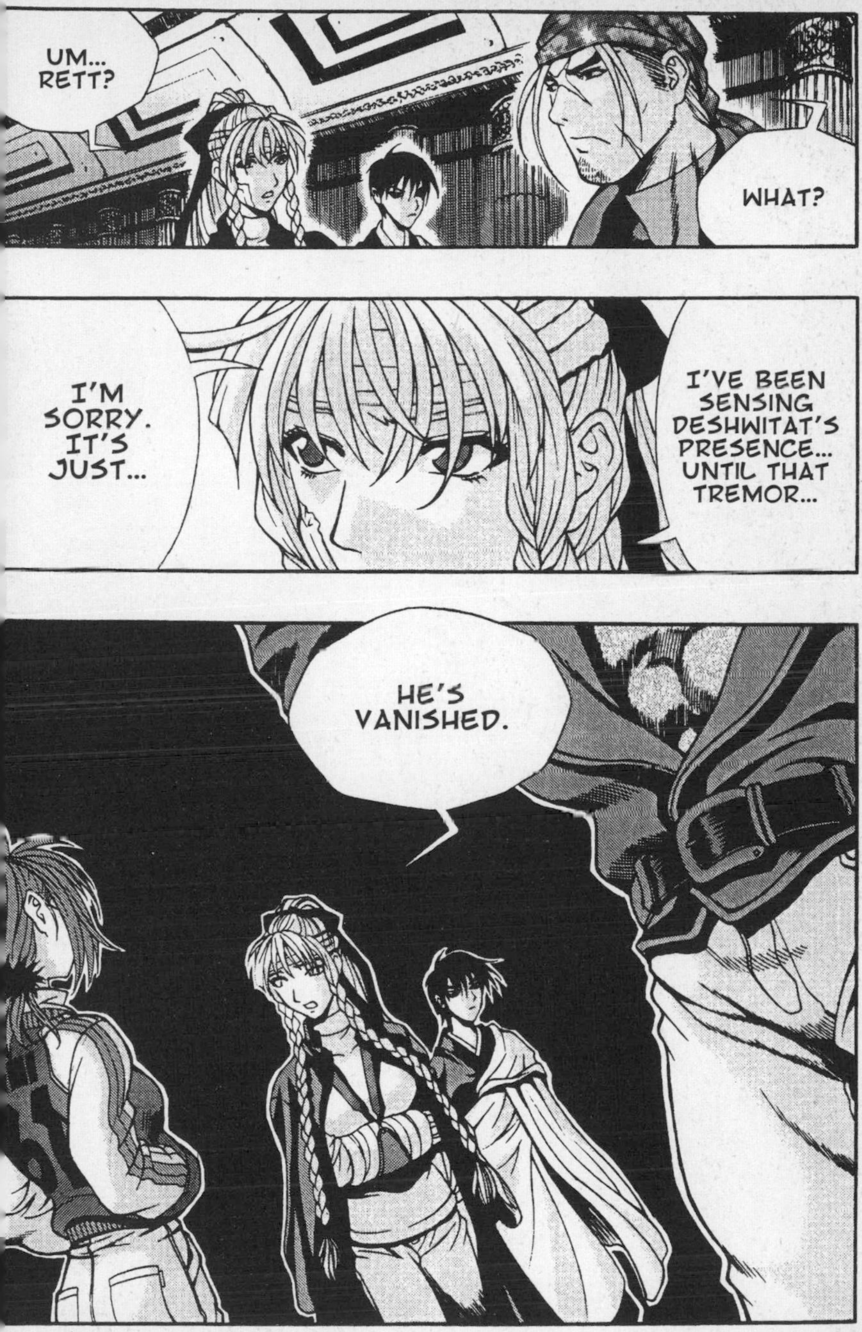
UM... RETT?
WHAT?
I'M SORRY. IT'S JUST...
I'VE BEEN SENSING DESHWITAT'S PRESENCE... UNTIL THAT TREMOR...
HE'S VANISHED.

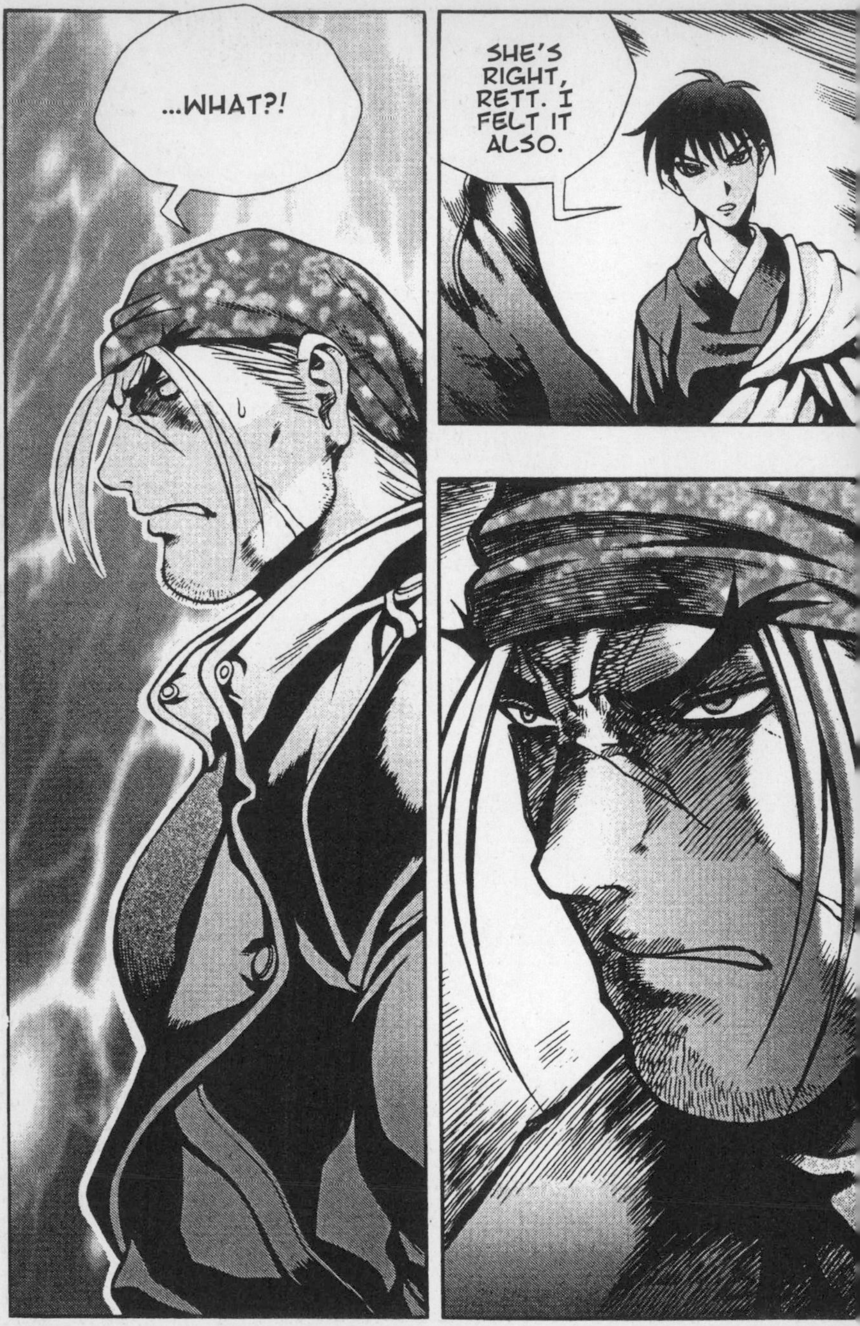
...WHAT?!
SHE'S RIGHT, RETT. I FELT IT ALSO.

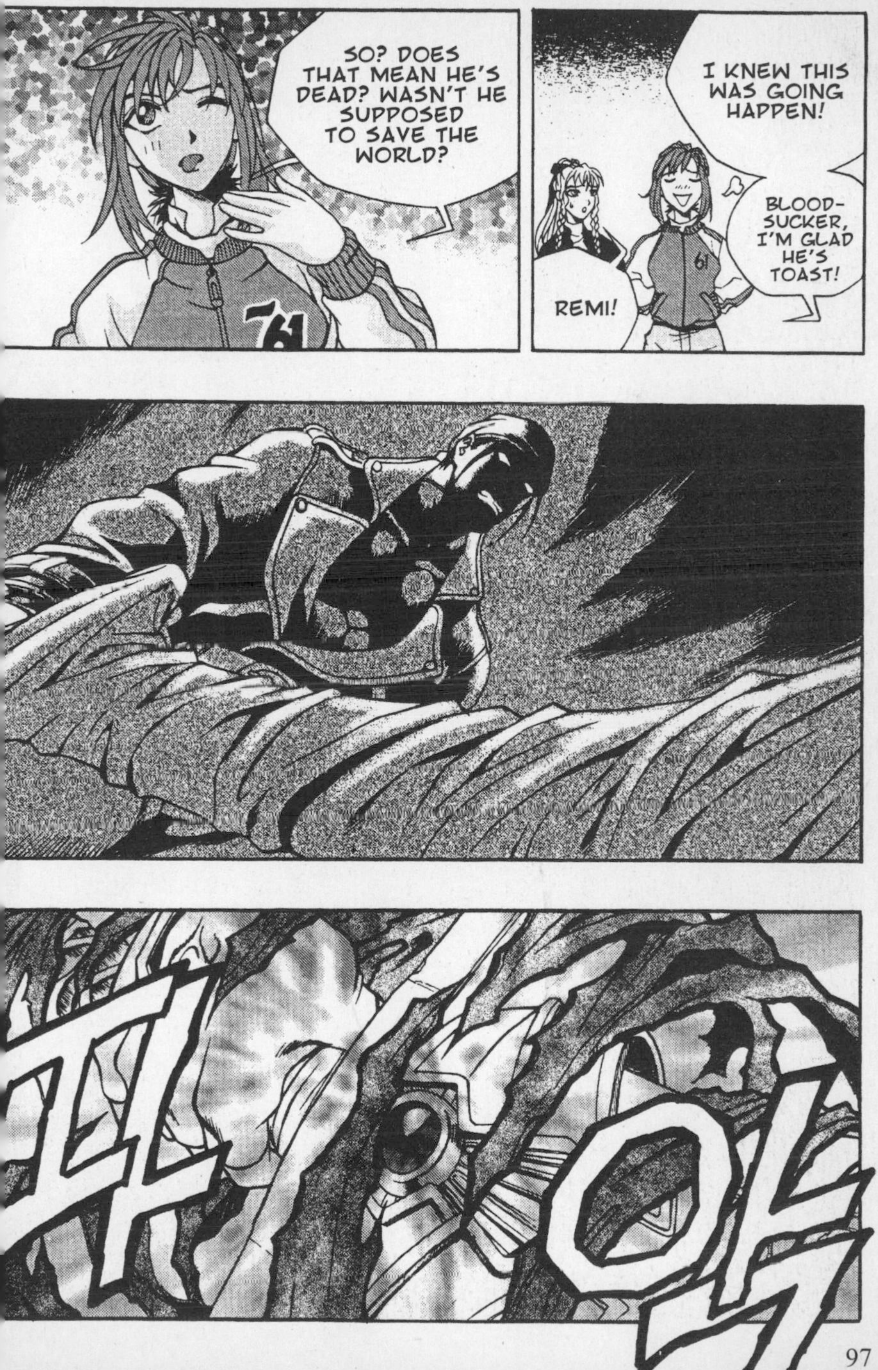
I KNEW THIS WAS GOING HAPPEN!
BLOOD-SUCKER, I'M GLAD HE'S TOAST!
REMI!
SO? DOES THAT MEAN HE'S DEAD? WASN'T HE SUPPOSED TO SAVE THE WORLD?

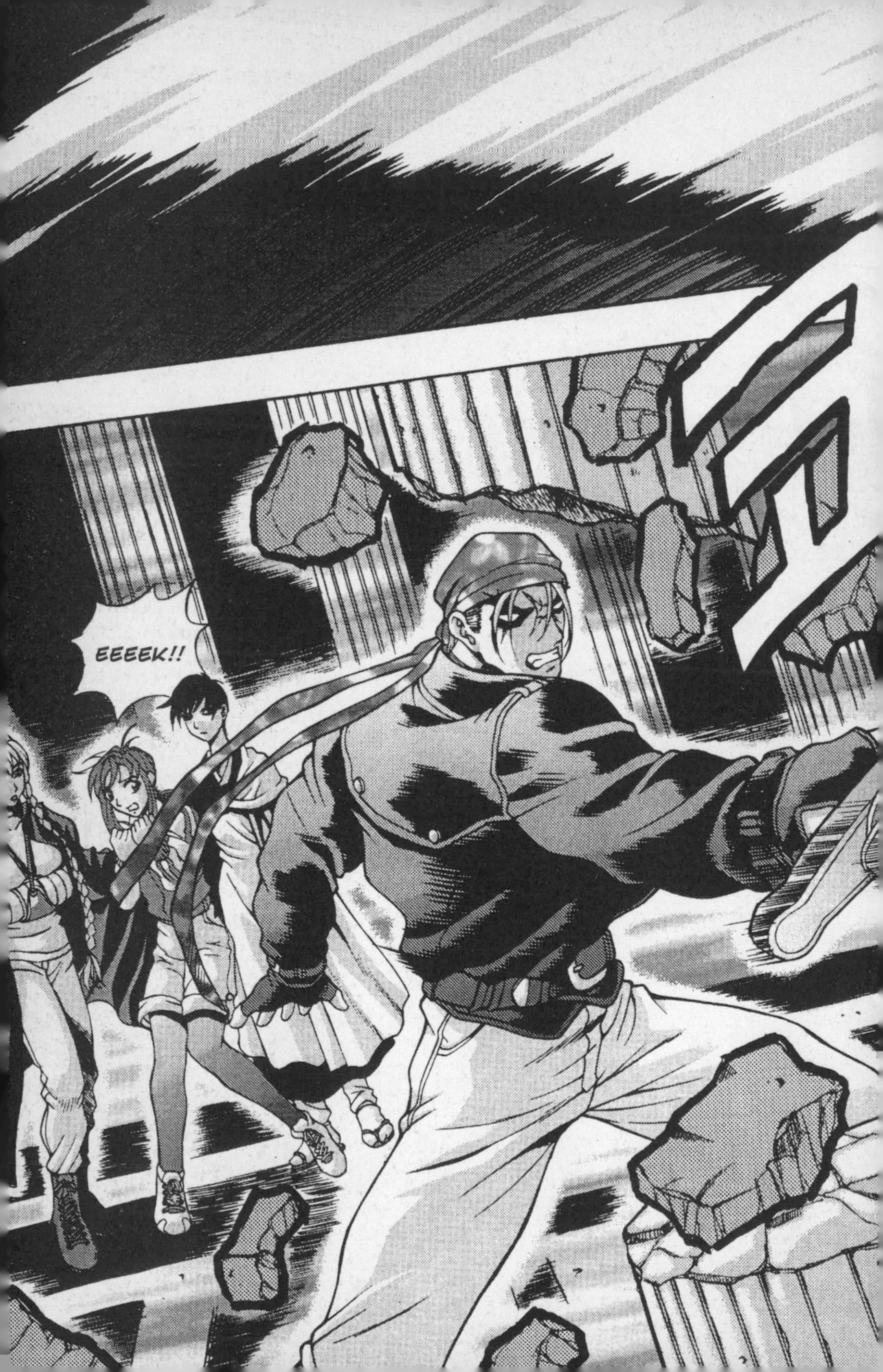
EEEEK!!

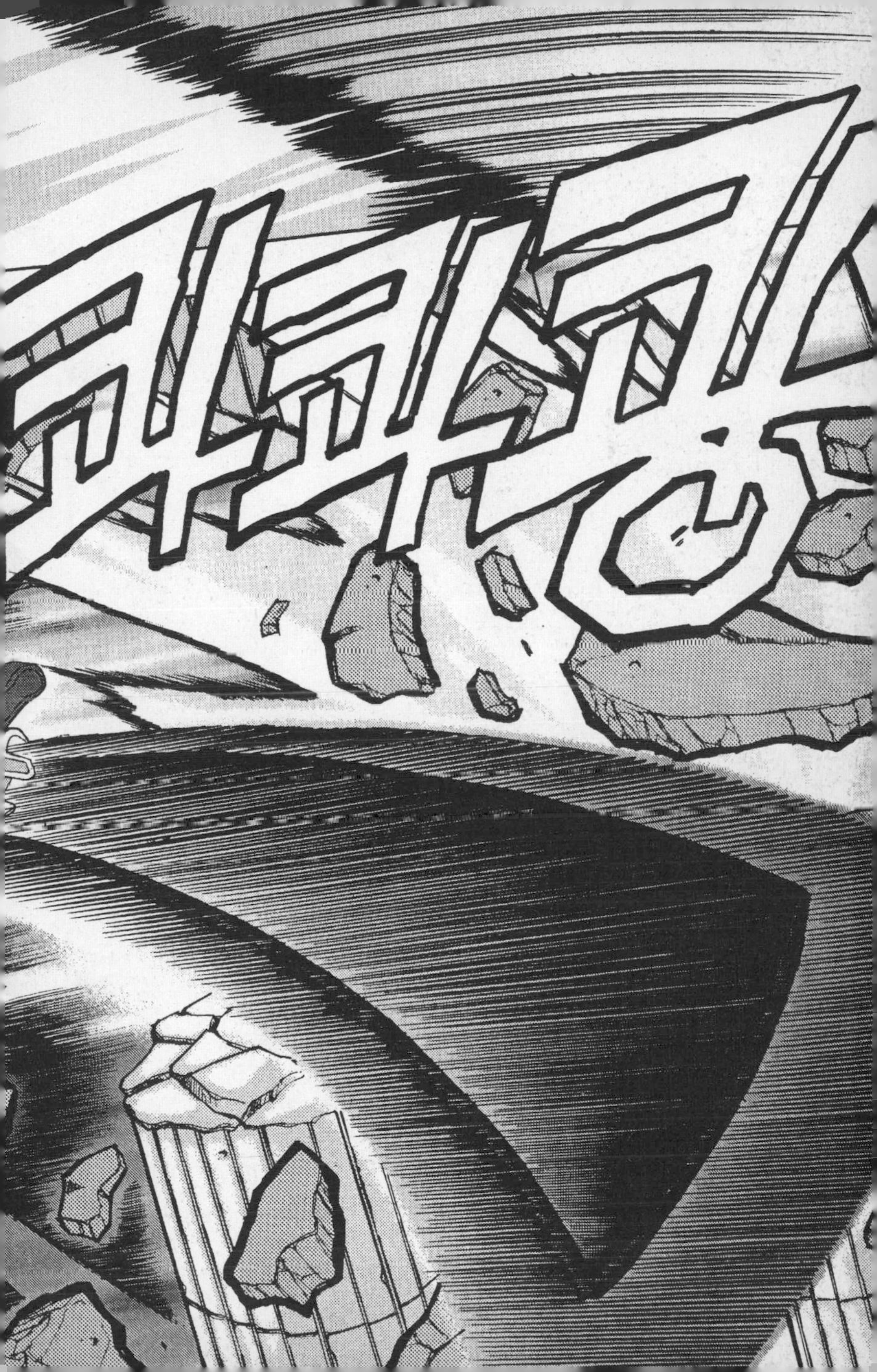

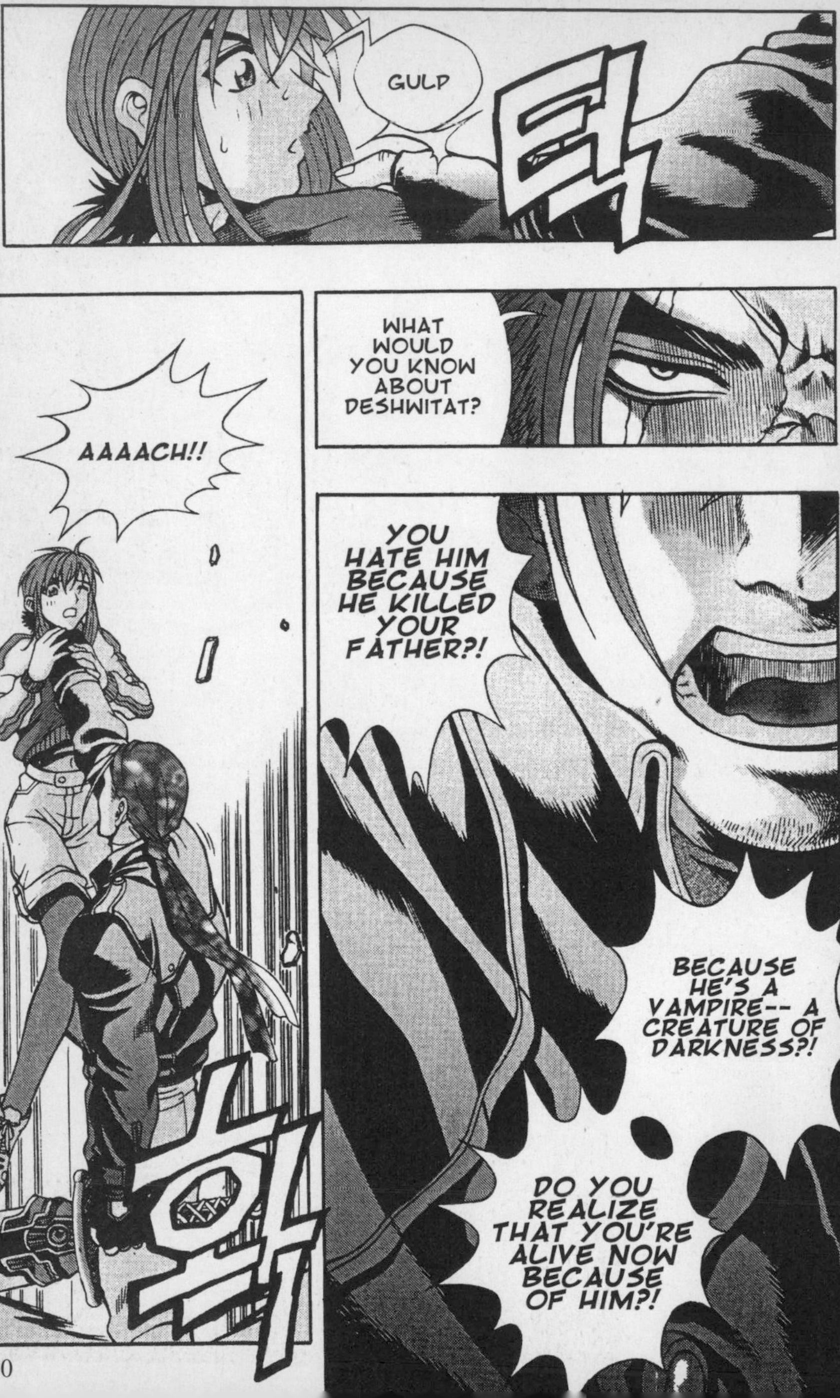
GULP
WHAT WOULD YOU KNOW ABOUT DESHWITAT?
YOU HATE HIM BECAUSE HE KILLED YOUR FATHER?!
BECAUSE HE'S A VAMPIRE-- A CREATURE OF DARKNESS?!
DO YOU REALIZE THAT YOU'RE ALIVE NOW BECAUSE OF HIM?!
AAAACH!!

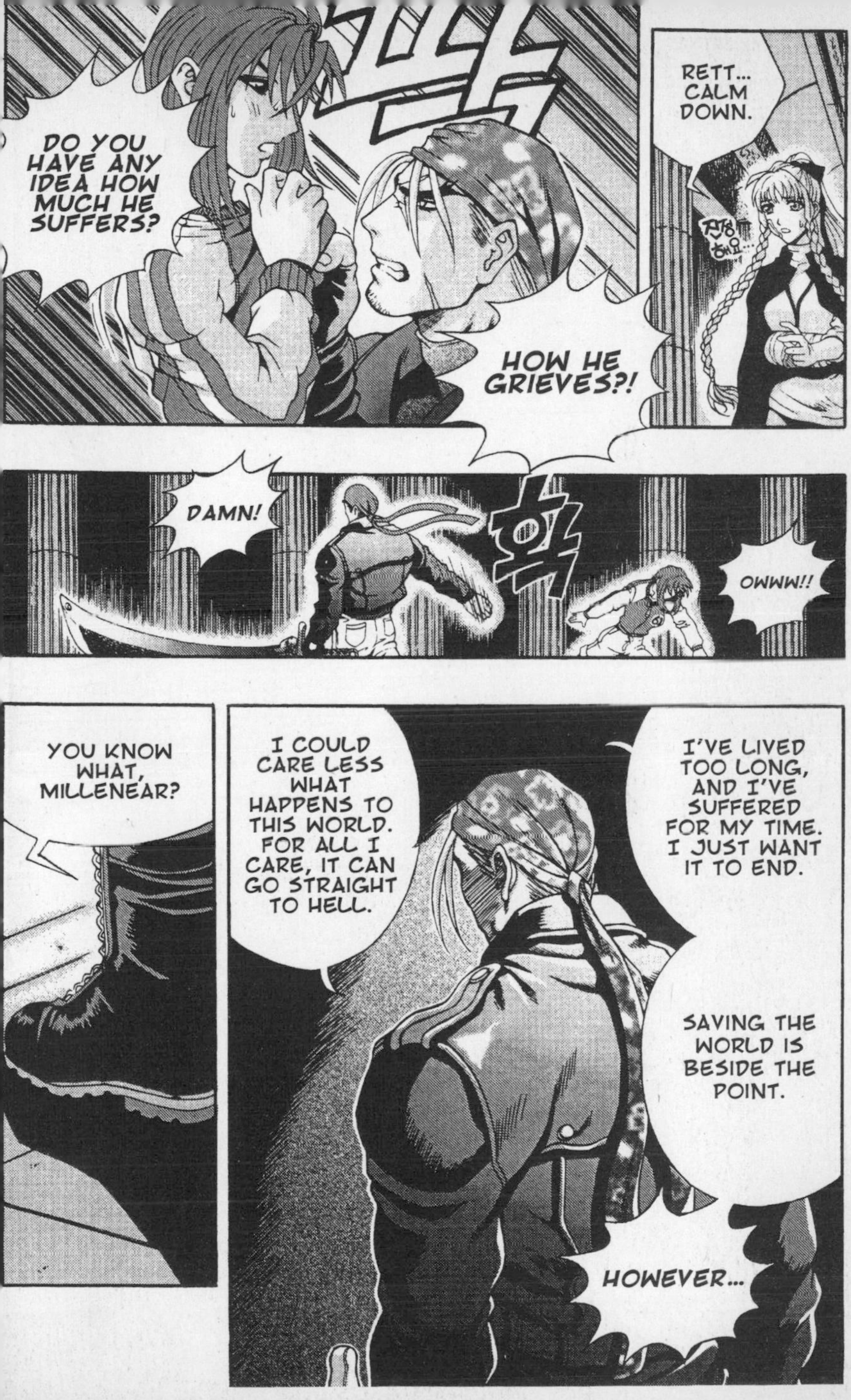
DO YOU HAVE ANY IDEA HOW MUCH HE SUFFERS?
HOW HE GRIEVES?!
RETT... CALM DOWN.
진정해요...
DAMN!
OWWW!!
YOU KNOW WHAT, MILLENEAR?
I COULD CARE LESS WHAT HAPPENS TO THIS WORLD. FOR ALL I CARE, IT CAN GO STRAIGHT TO HELL.
I'VE LIVED TOO LONG, AND I'VE SUFFERED FOR MY TIME. I JUST WANT IT TO END.
SAVING THE WORLD IS BESIDE THE POINT.
HOWEVER...

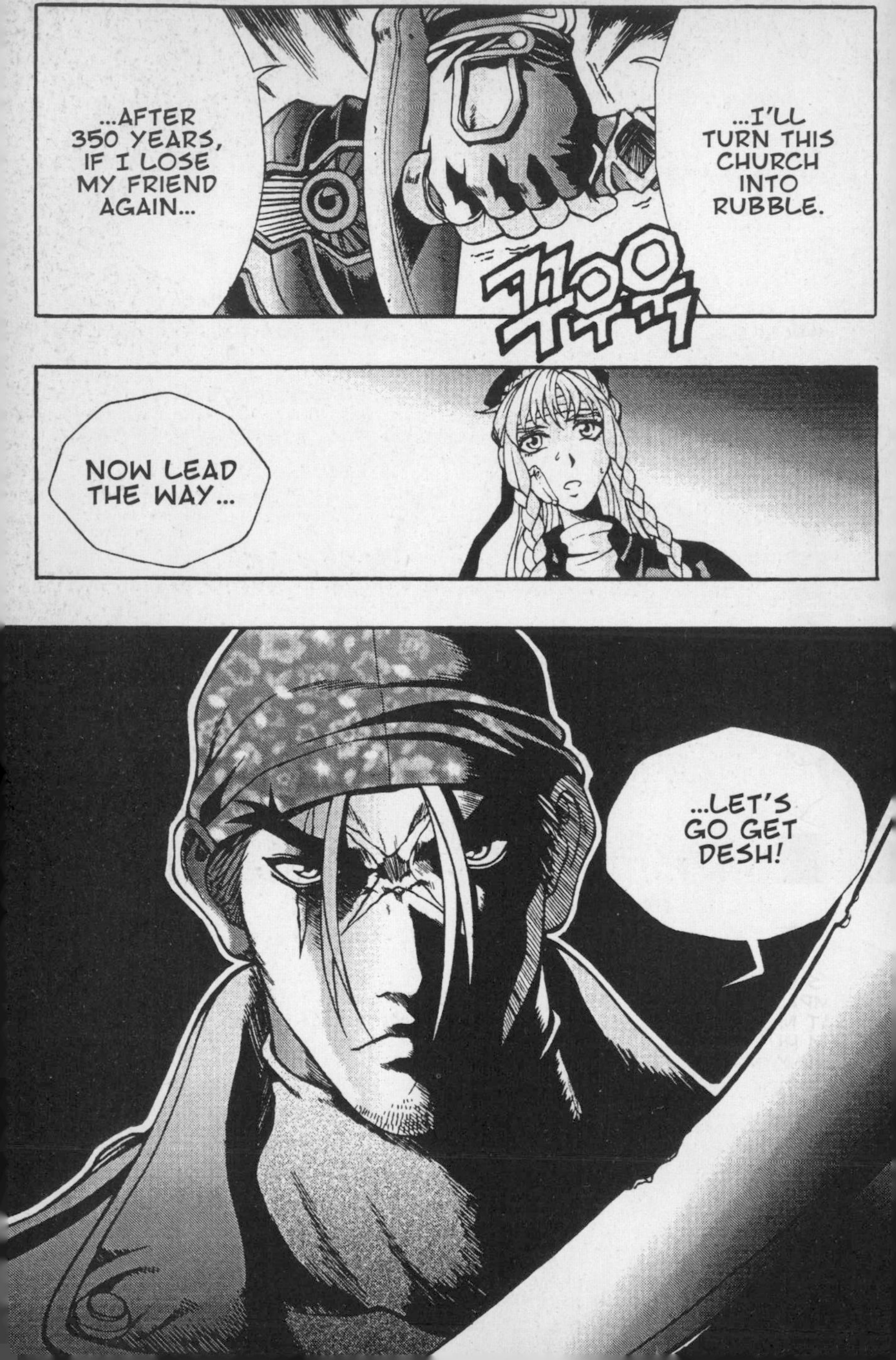
...AFTER 350 YEARS, IF I LOSE MY FRIEND AGAIN...
...I'LL TURN THIS CHURCH INTO RUBBLE.
NOW LEAD THE WAY...
...LET'S GO GET DESH!

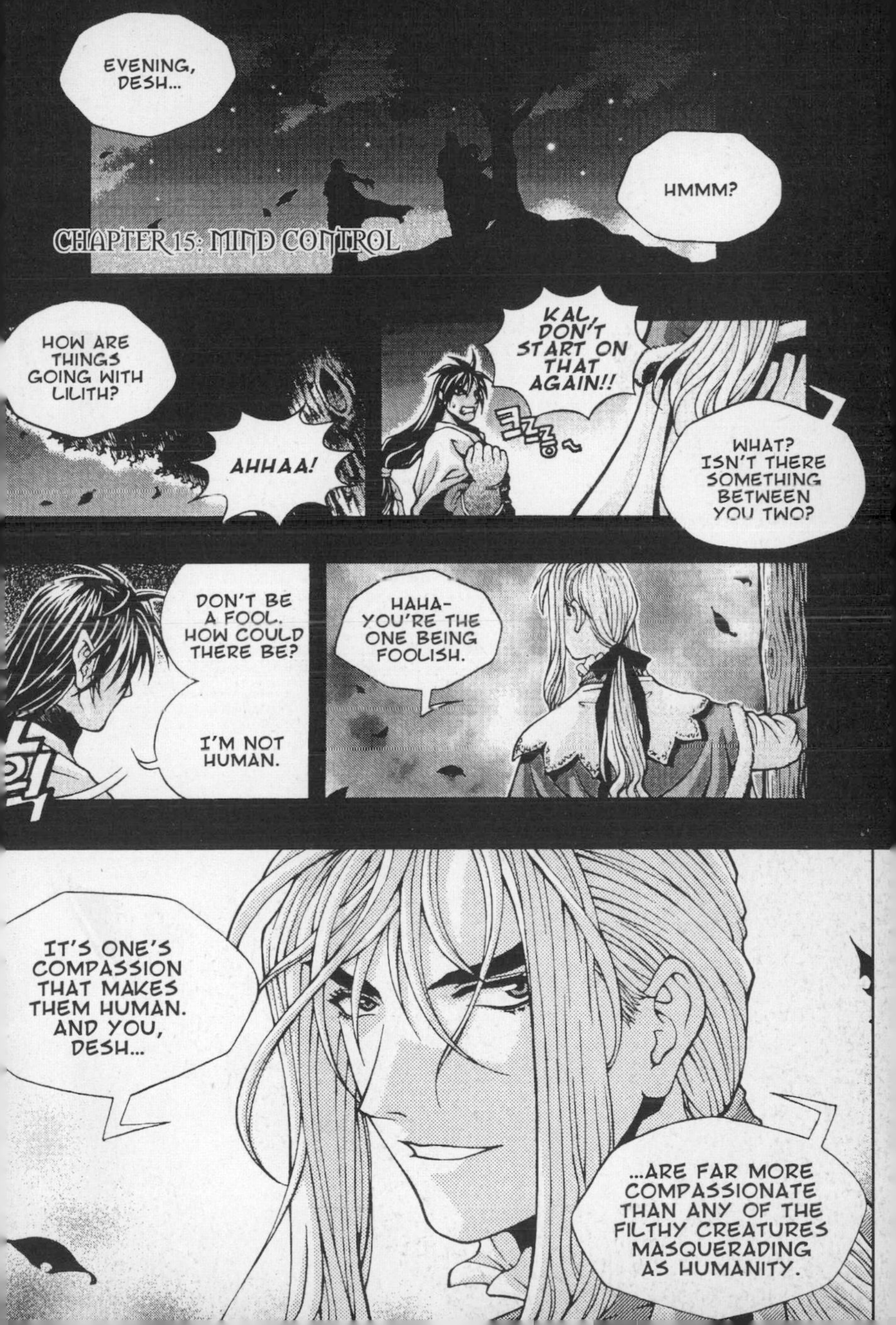
EVENING, DESH...
HMMM?
CHAPTER 15: MIND CONTROL
HOW ARE THINGS GOING WITH LILITH?
AHHAA!
KAL, DON'T START ON THAT AGAIN!!
WHAT? ISN'T THERE SOMETHING BETWEEN YOU TWO?
DON'T BE A FOOL. HOW COULD THERE BE?
I'M NOT HUMAN.
HAHA- YOU'RE THE ONE BEING FOOLISH.
IT'S ONE'S COMPASSION THAT MAKES THEM HUMAN. AND YOU, DESH...
...ARE FAR MORE COMPASSIONATE THAN ANY OF THE FILTHY CREATURES MASQUERADING AS HUMANITY.

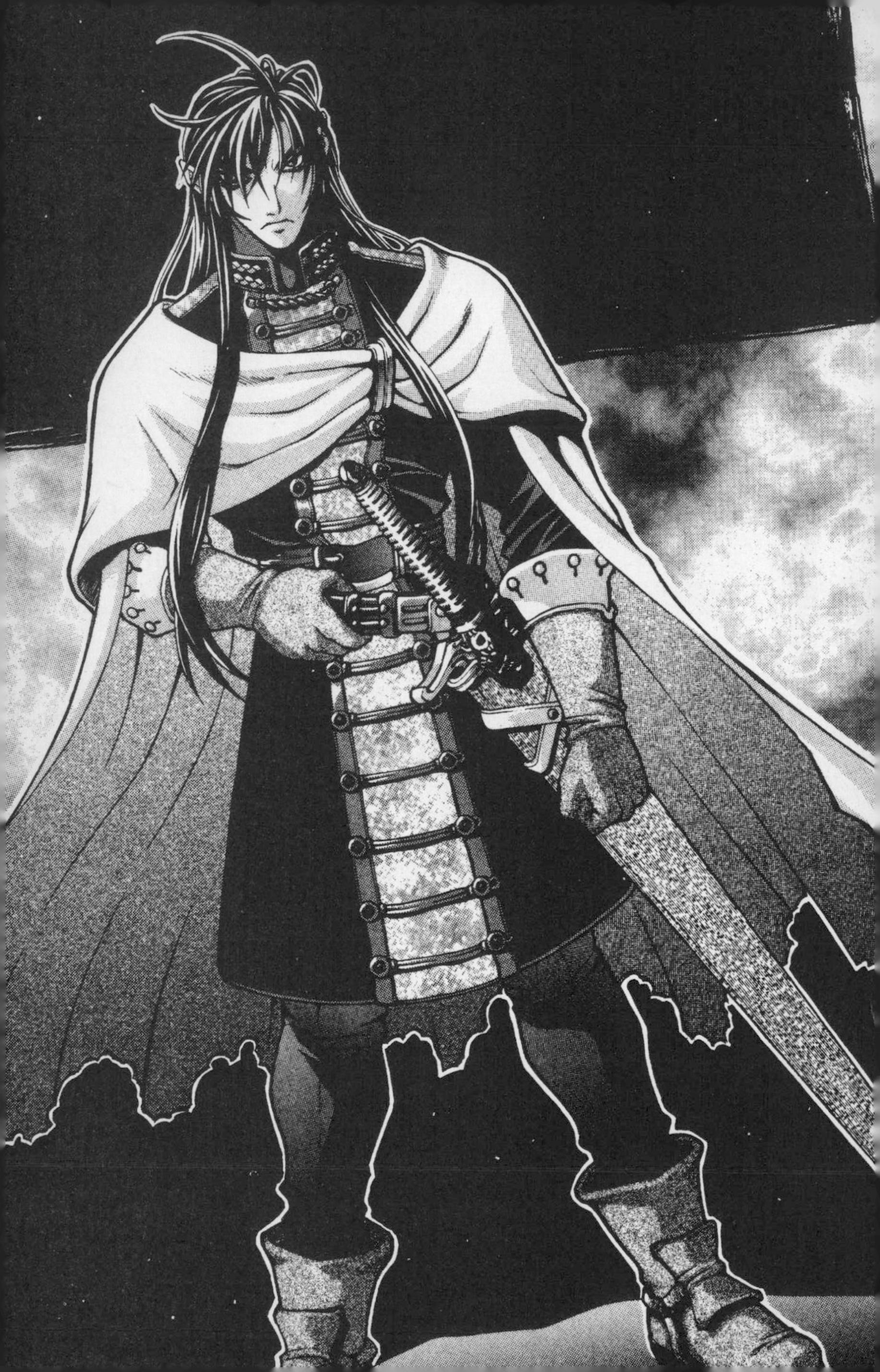

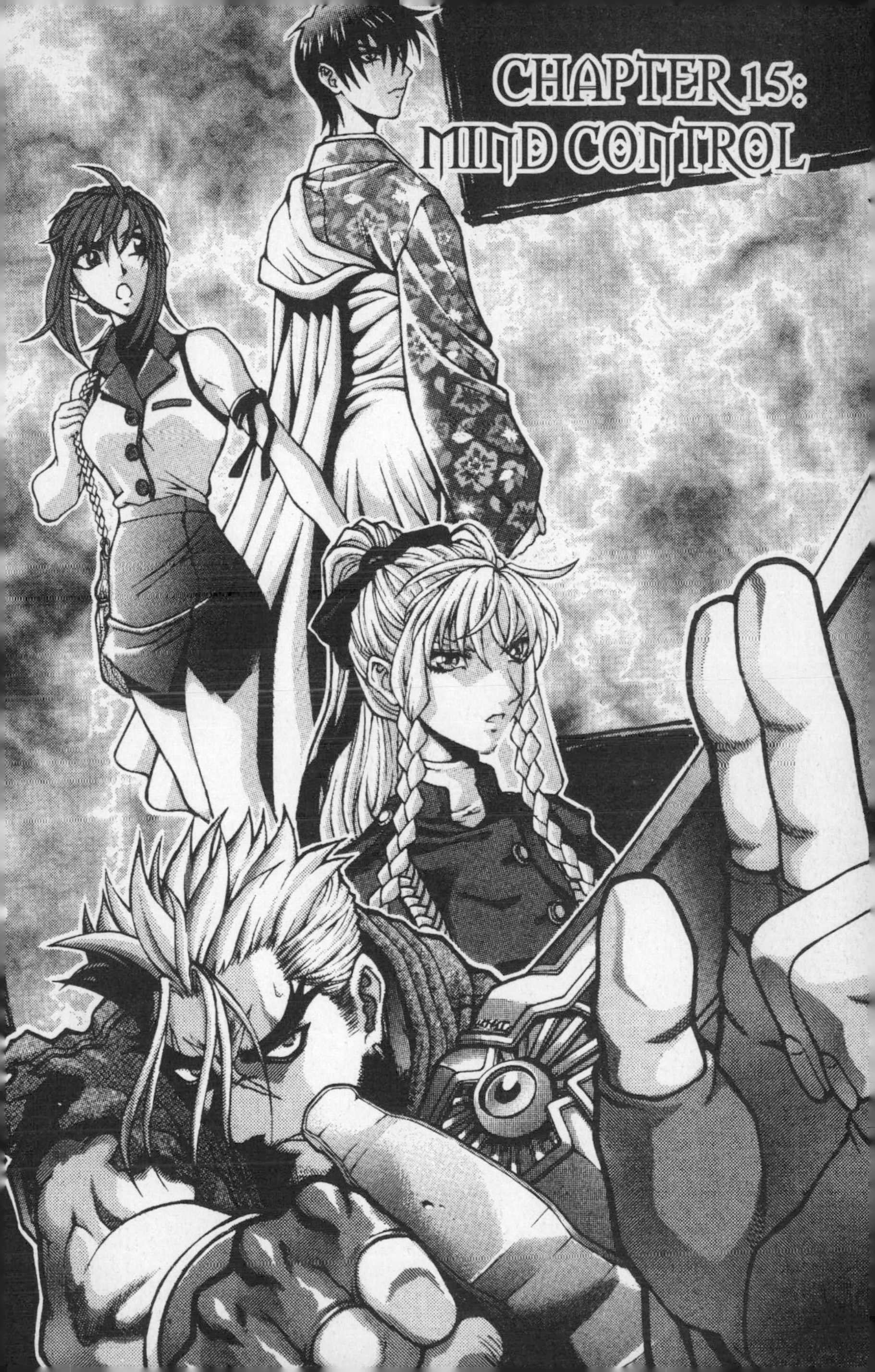
CHAPTER 15:
MIND CONTROL

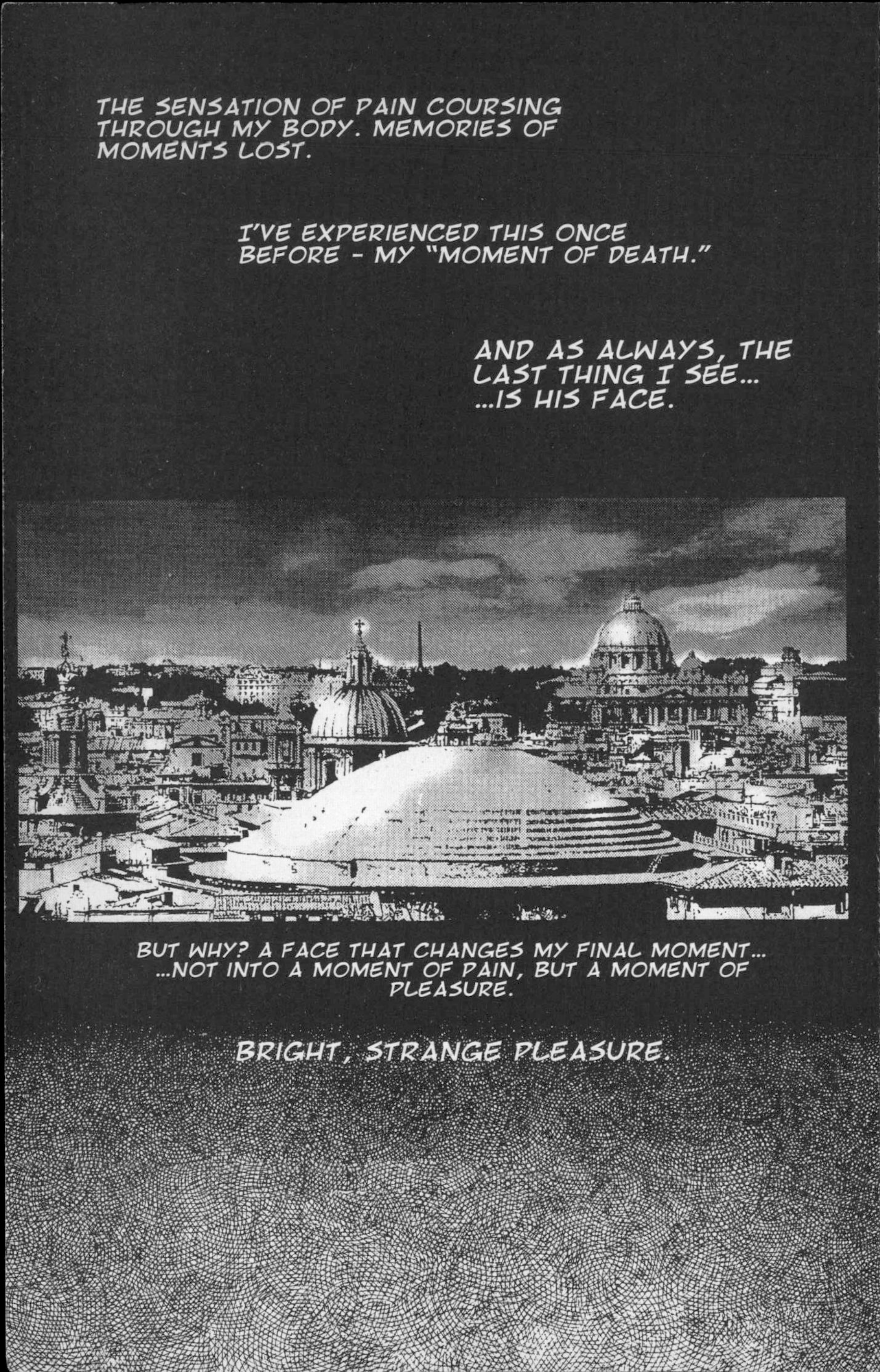
THE SENSATION OF PAIN COURSING THROUGH MY BODY. MEMORIES OF MOMENTS LOST.
I'VE EXPERIENCED THIS ONCE BEFORE - MY "MOMENT OF DEATH."
AND AS ALWAYS, THE LAST THING I SEE... ...IS HIS FACE.
BUT WHY? A FACE THAT CHANGES MY FINAL MOMENT... ...NOT INTO A MOMENT OF PAIN, BUT A MOMENT OF PLEASURE.
BRIGHT, STRANGE PLEASURE.

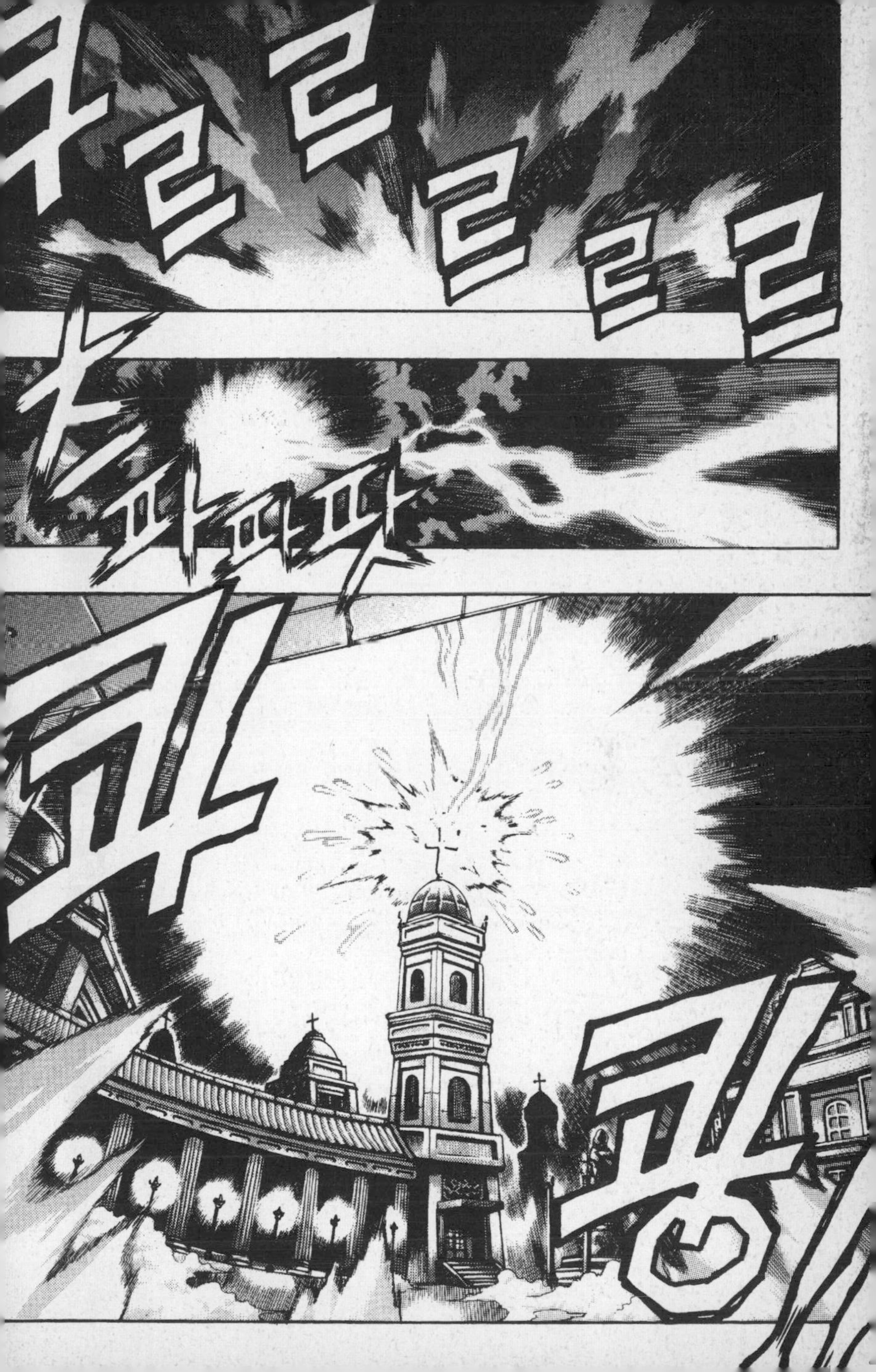
쿠르르르르르
꽈꽝

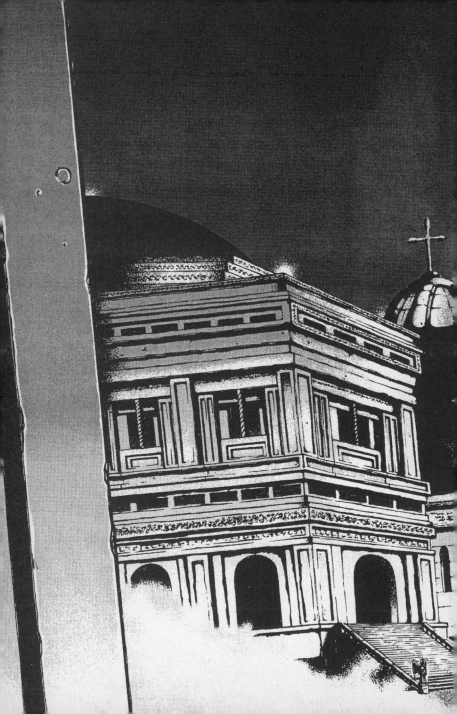

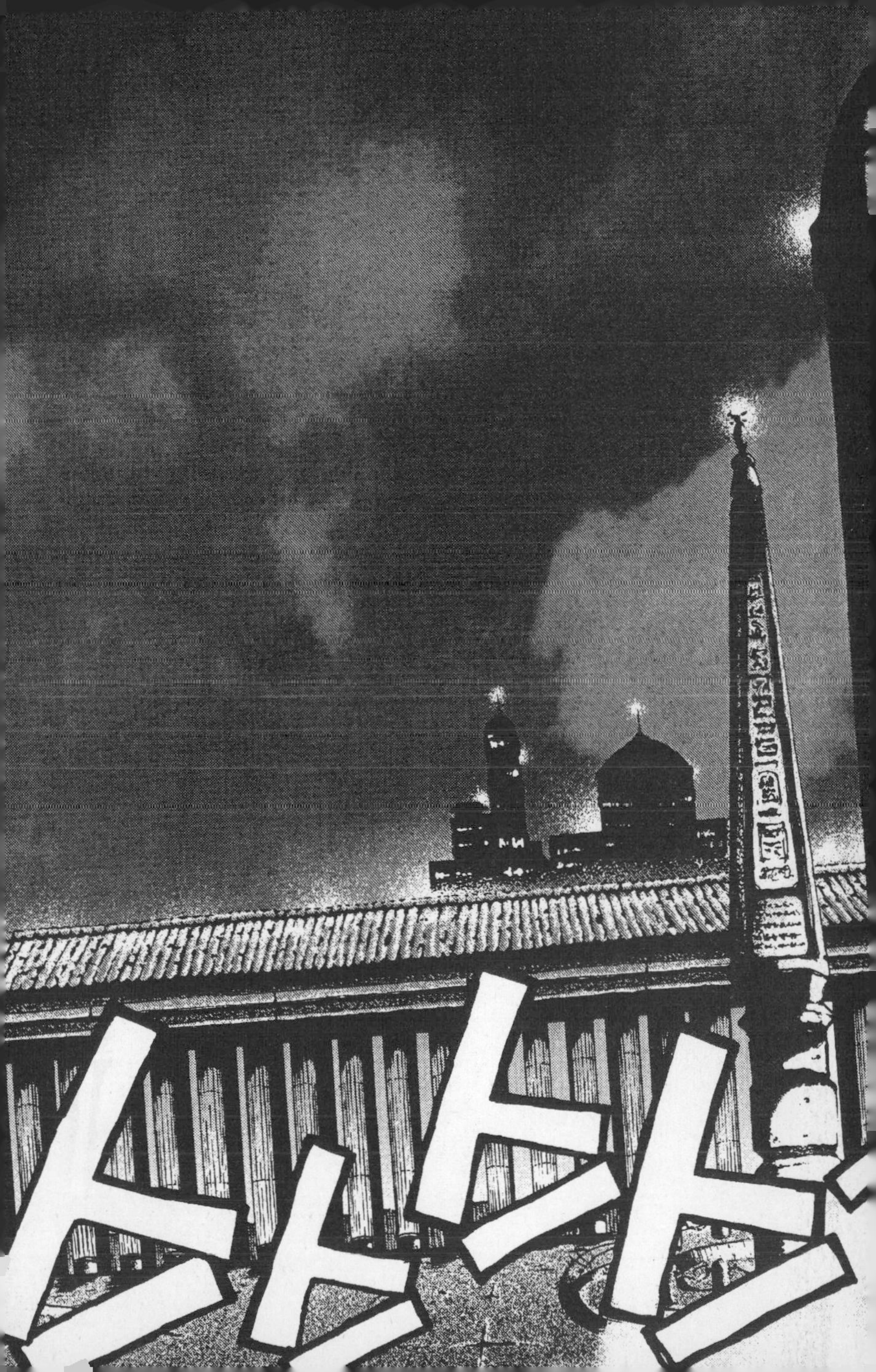
トトトド

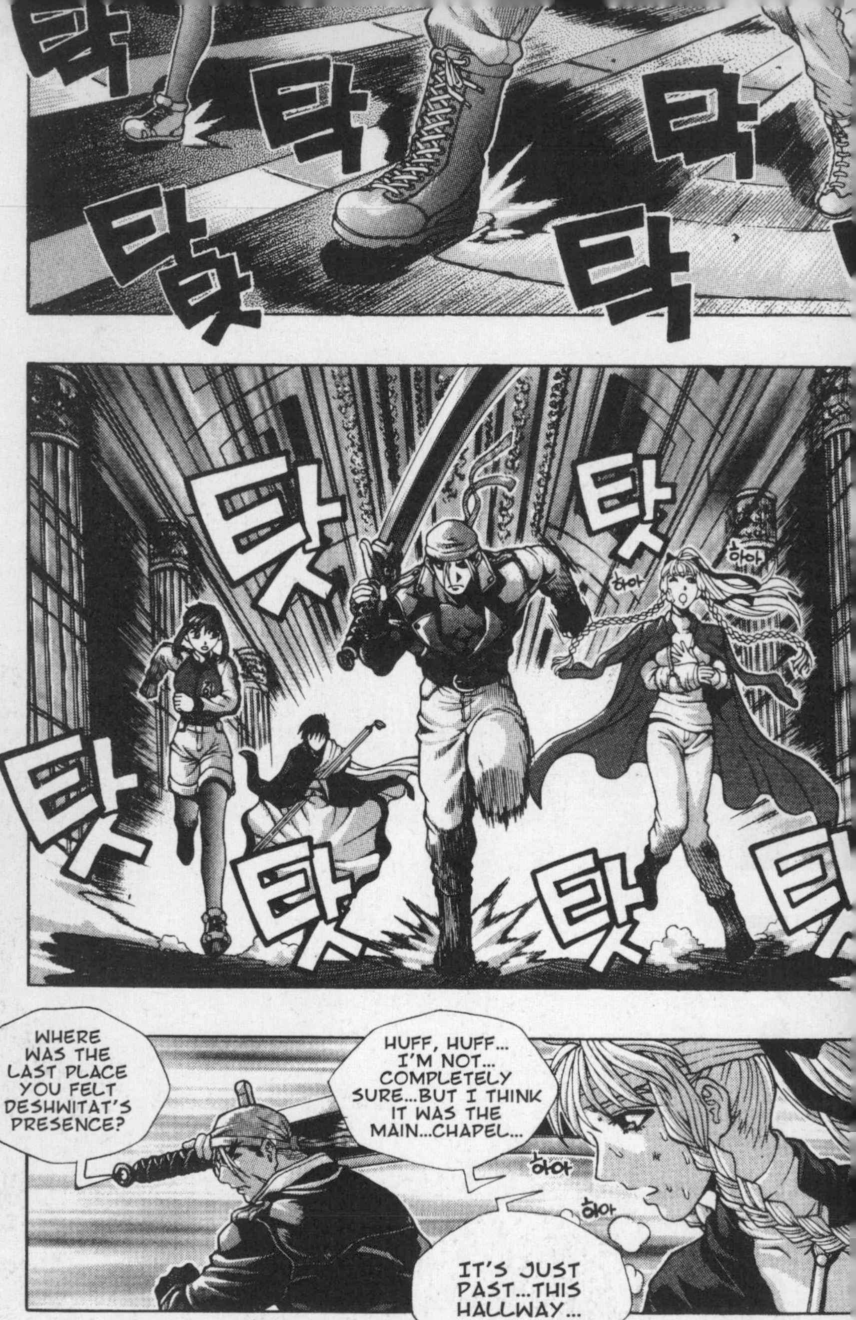

탁
탁
탁
탁
탁
탓
탓
하아
하아
탓
탓
탓
WHERE WAS THE LAST PLACE YOU FELT DESHWITAT'S PRESENCE?
HUFF, HUFF... I'M NOT... COMPLETELY SURE...BUT I THINK IT WAS THE MAIN...CHAPEL...
하아
하아
IT'S JUST PAST...THIS HALLWAY...

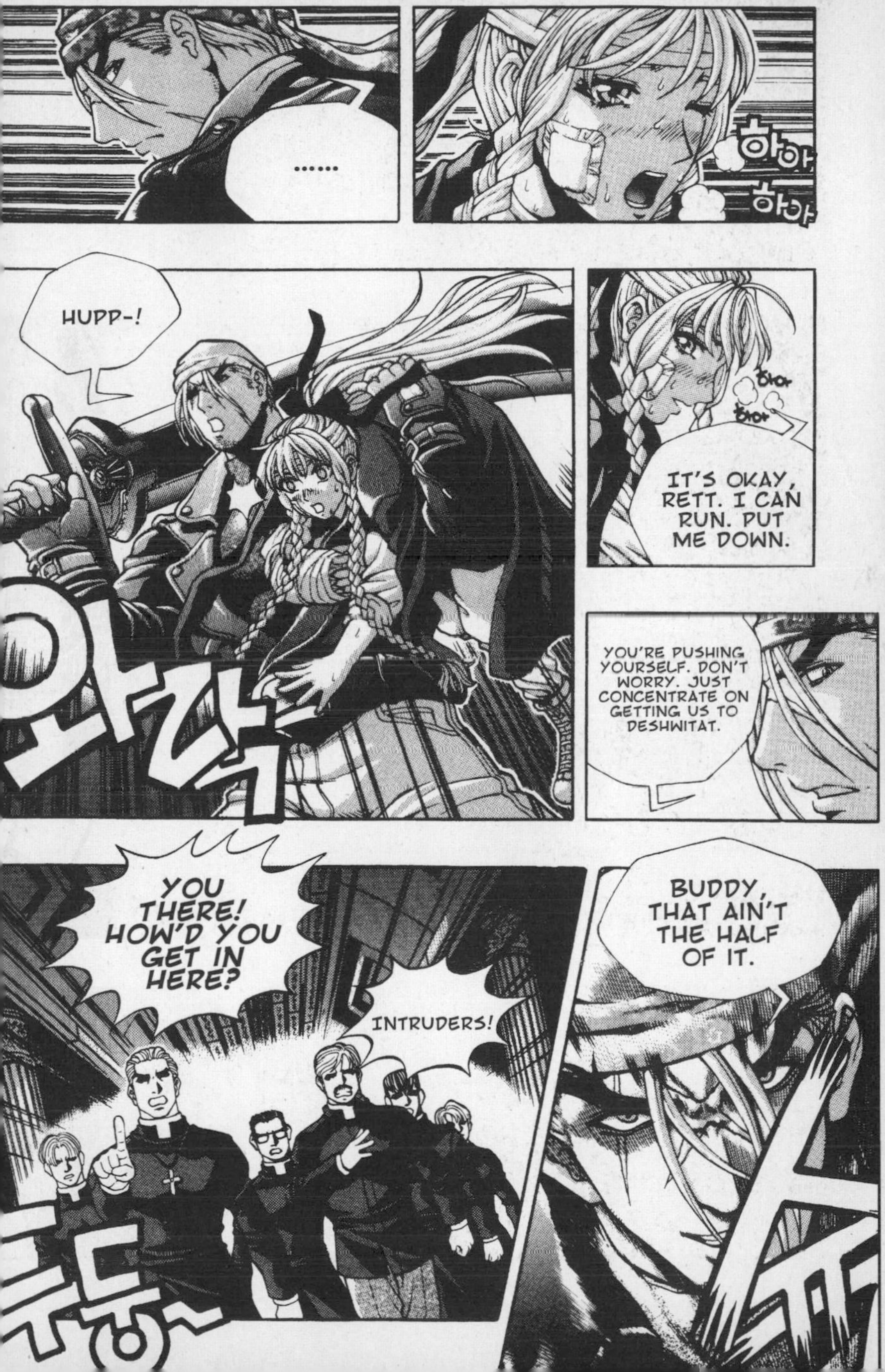
......
하아
하아
HUPP-!
하아
하아
IT'S OKAY, RETT. I CAN RUN. PUT ME DOWN.
YOU'RE PUSHING YOURSELF. DON'T WORRY. JUST CONCENTRATE ON GETTING US TO DESHWITAT.
YOU THERE! HOW'D YOU GET IN HERE?
INTRUDERS!
BUDDY, THAT AIN'T THE HALF OF IT.

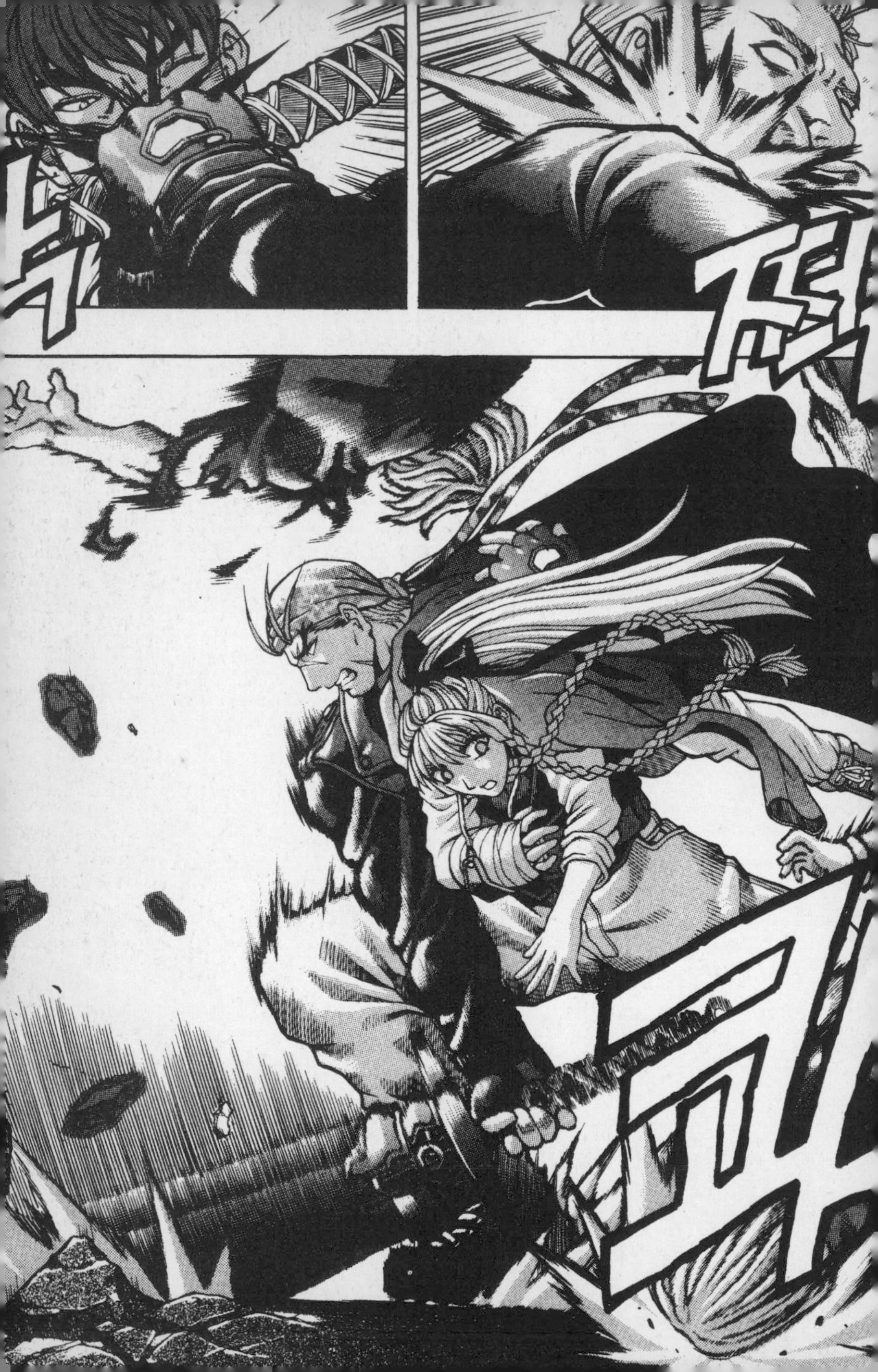

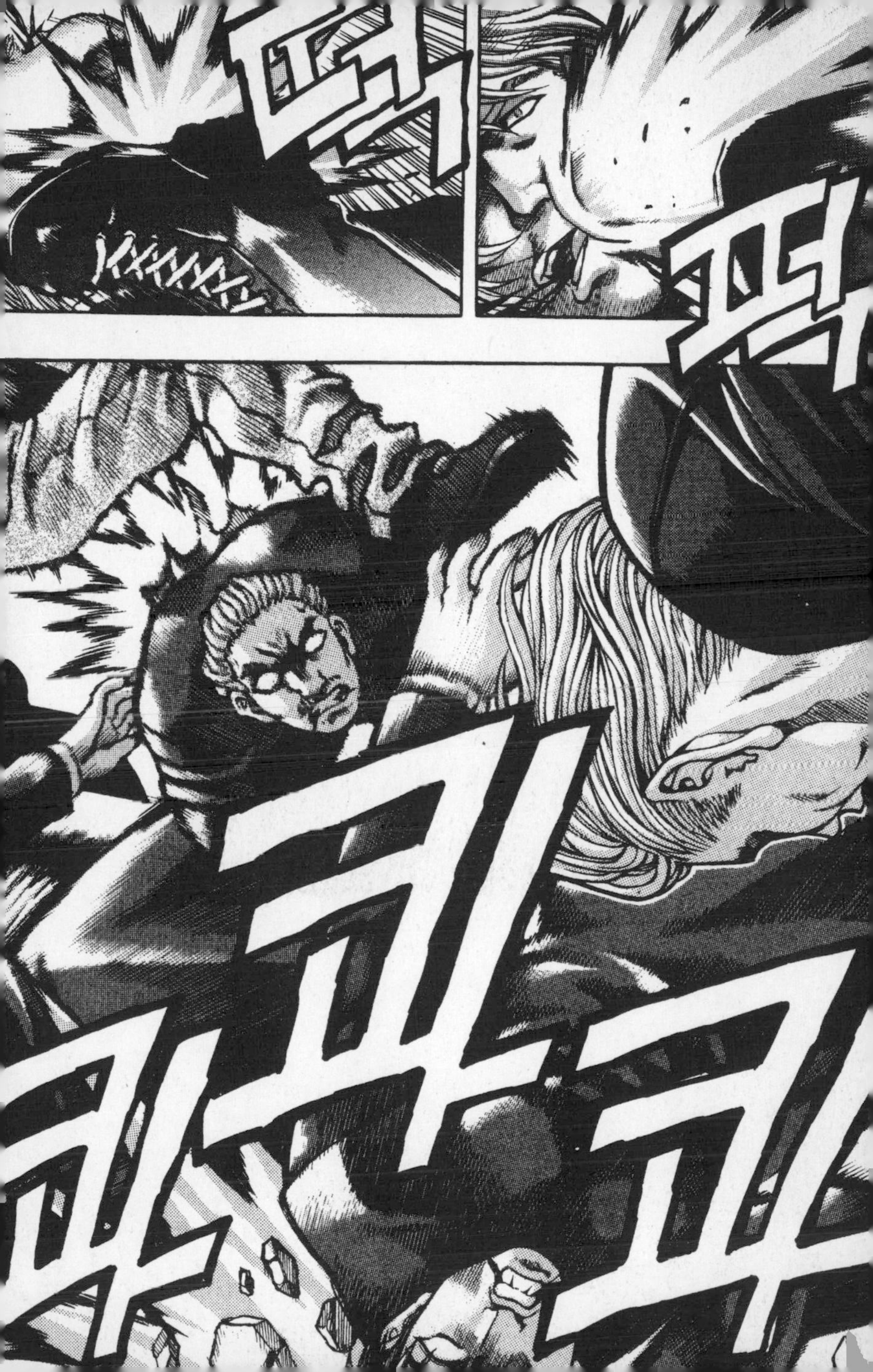

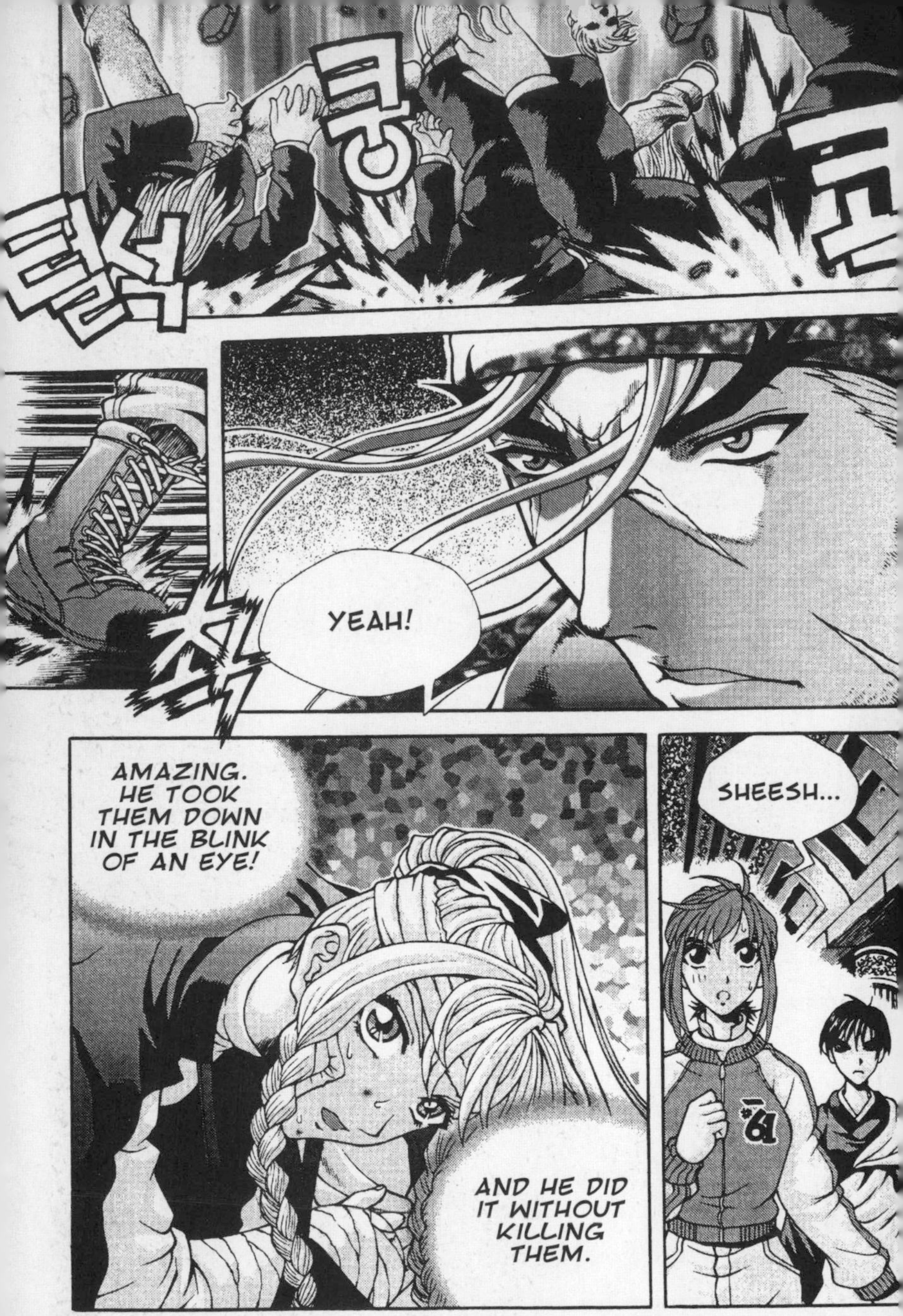

YEAH!
AMAZING. HE TOOK THEM DOWN IN THE BLINK OF AN EYE!
AND HE DID IT WITHOUT KILLING THEM.
SHEESH...

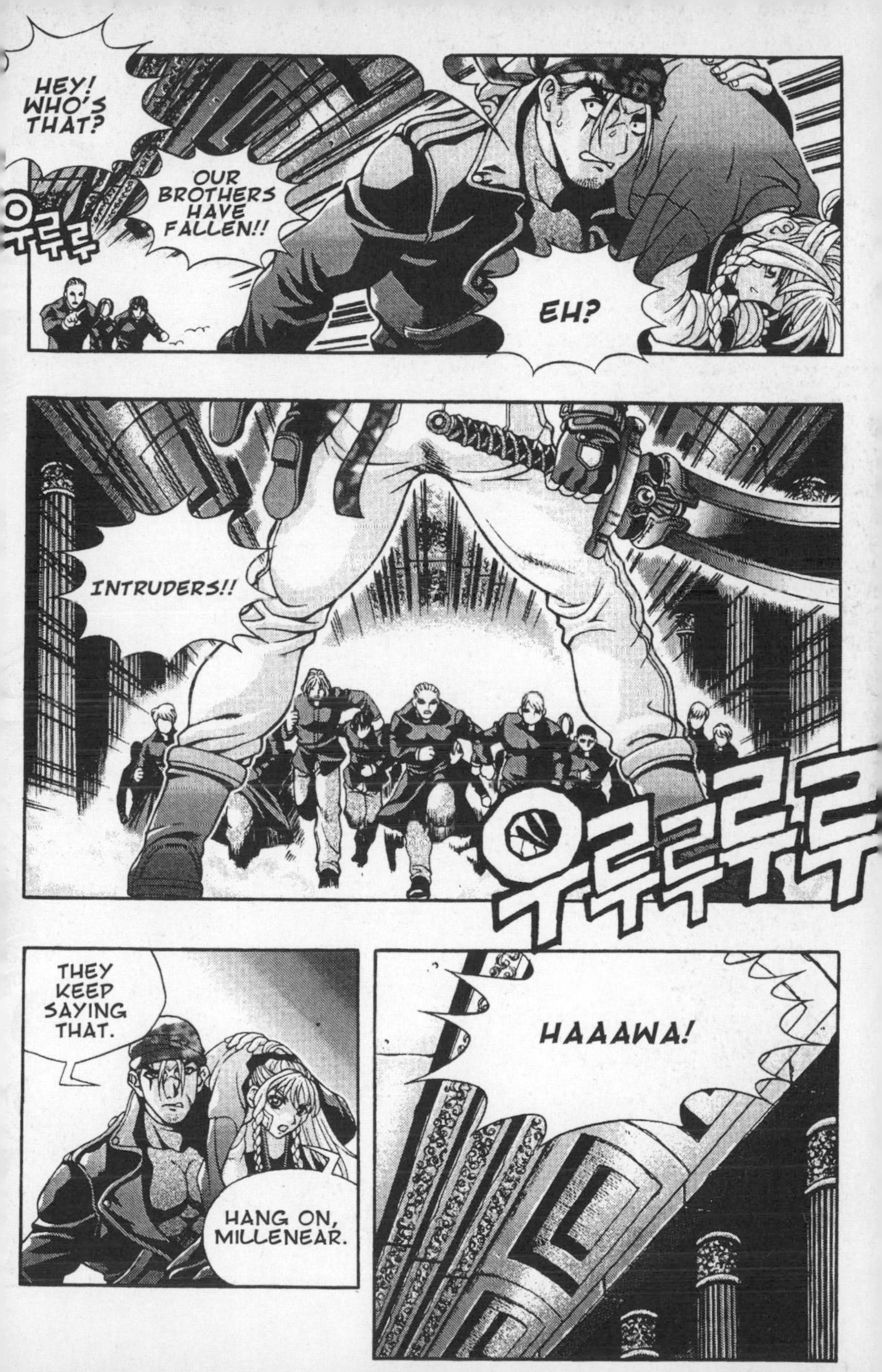
HEY! WHO'S THAT?
OUR BROTHERS HAVE FALLEN!!
EH?
INTRUDERS!!
THEY KEEP SAYING THAT.
HANG ON, MILLENEAR.
HAAAWA!

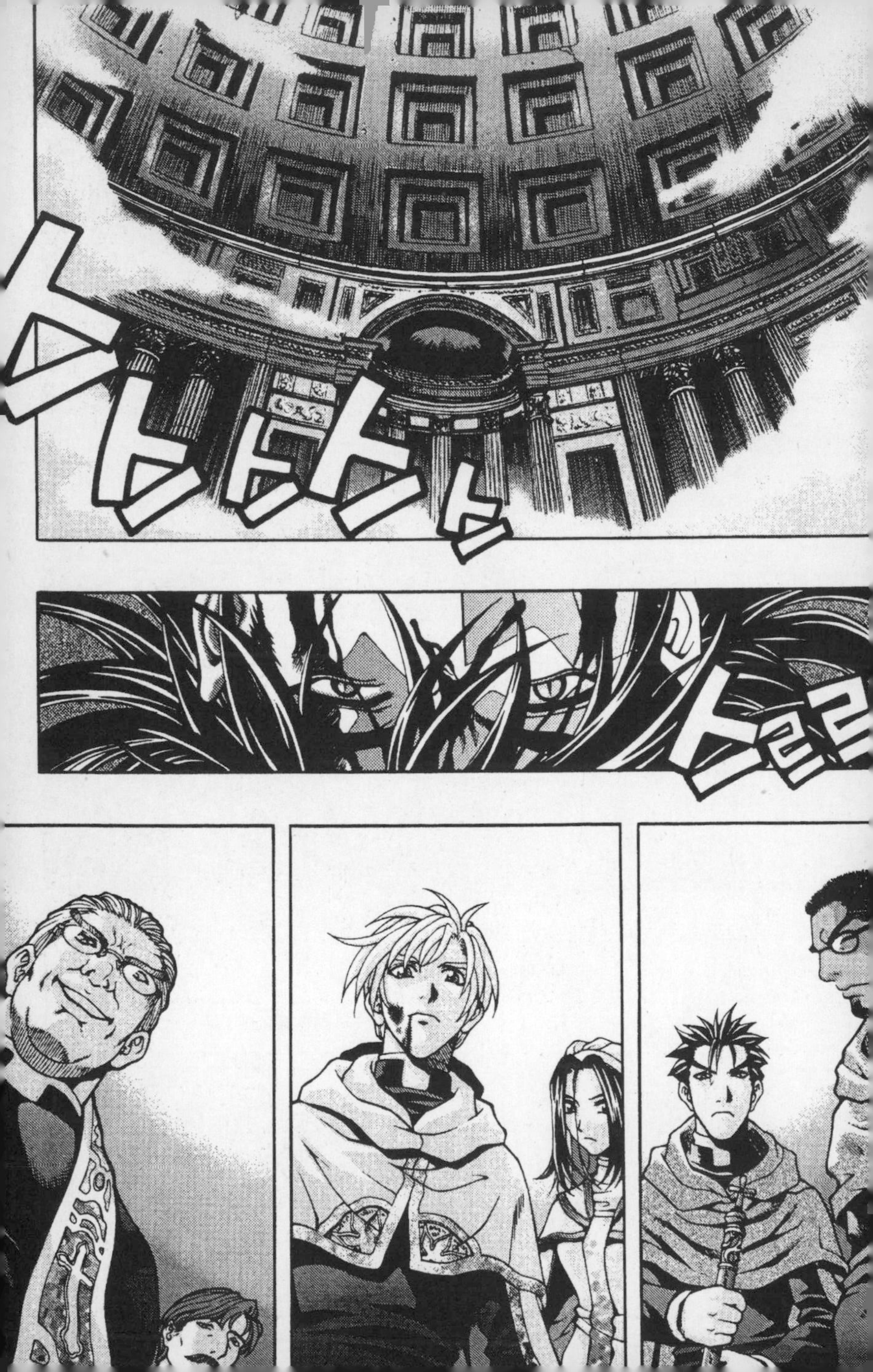

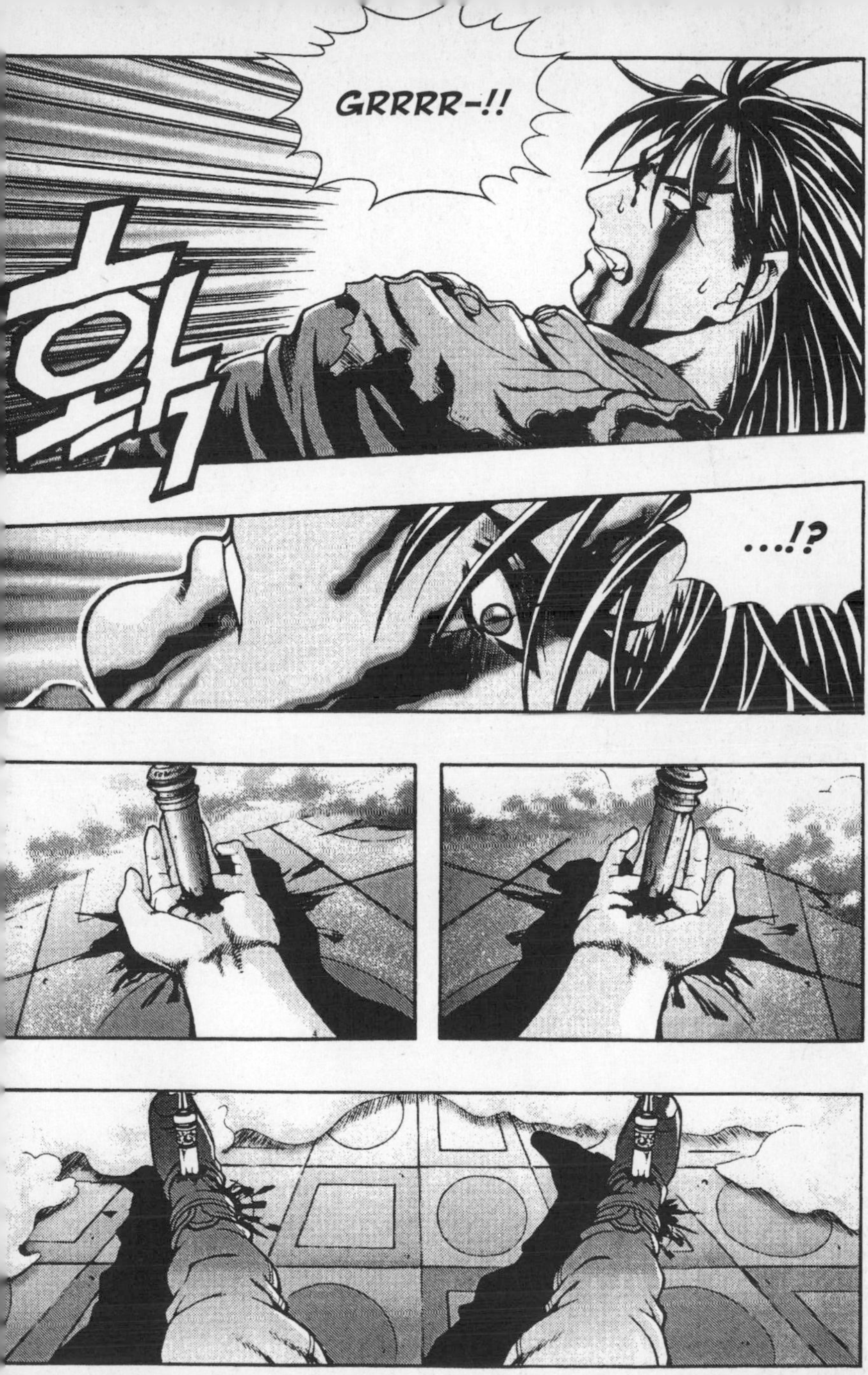
GRRRR-!!
학
...!?

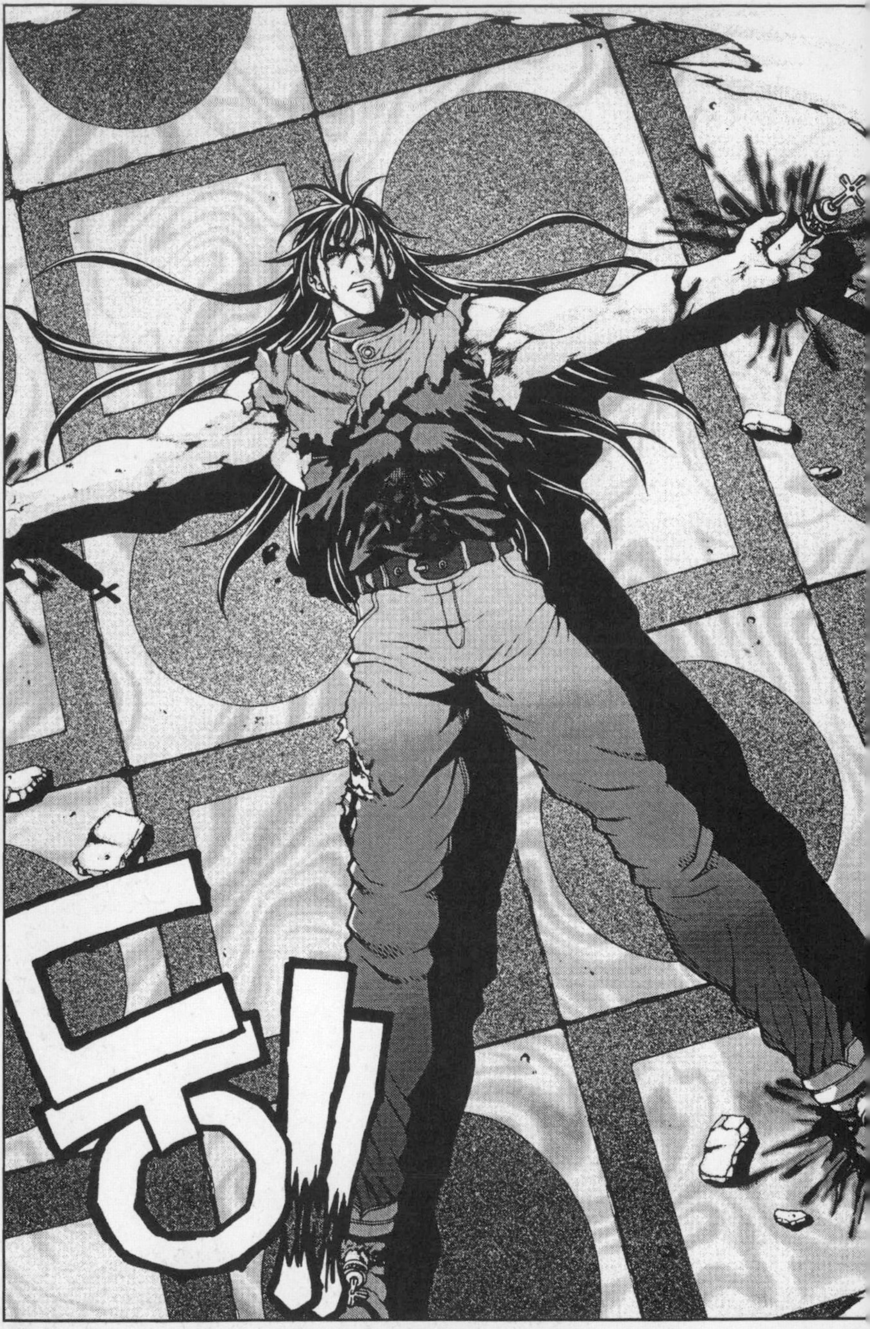

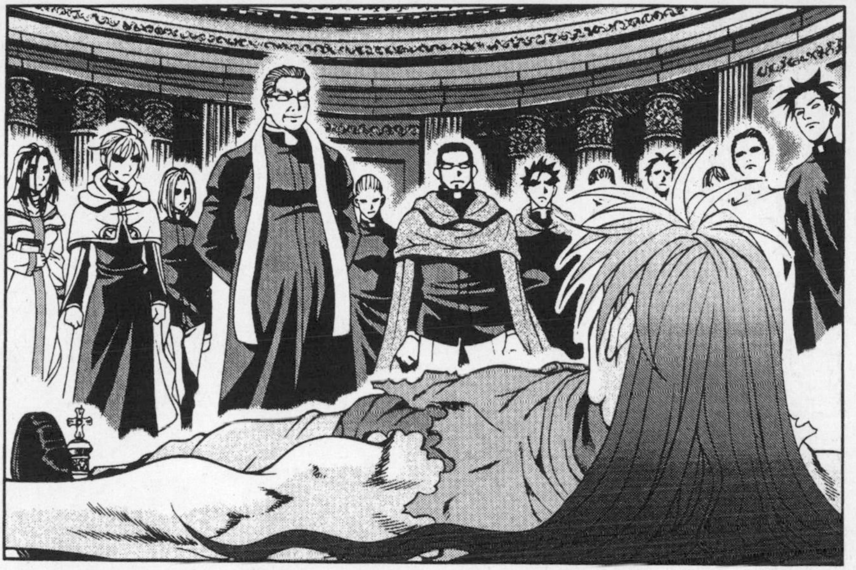

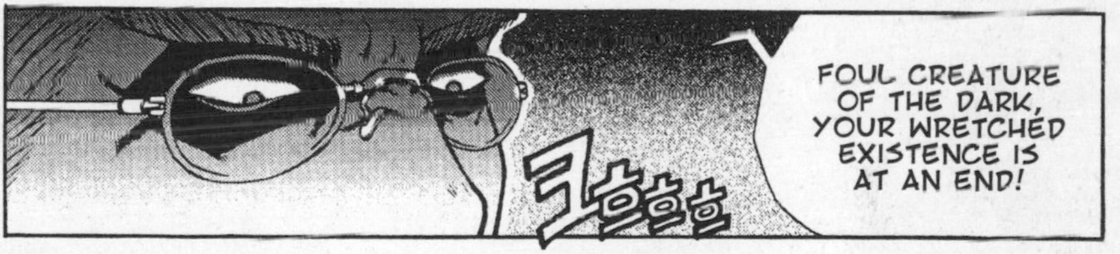
FOUL CREATURE OF THE DARK, YOUR WRETCHED EXISTENCE IS AT AN END!

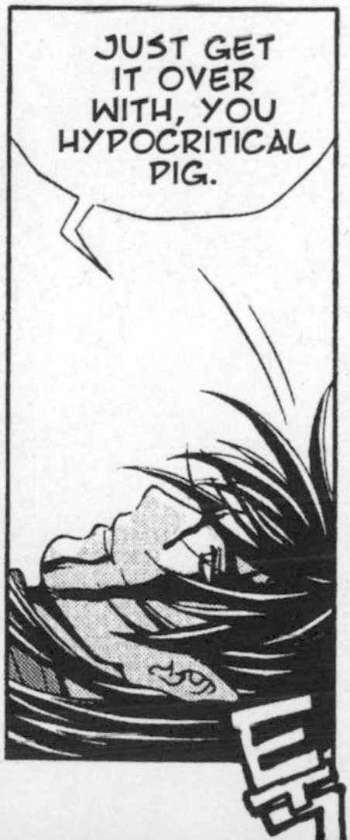
JUST GET IT OVER WITH, YOU HYPOCRITICAL PIG.

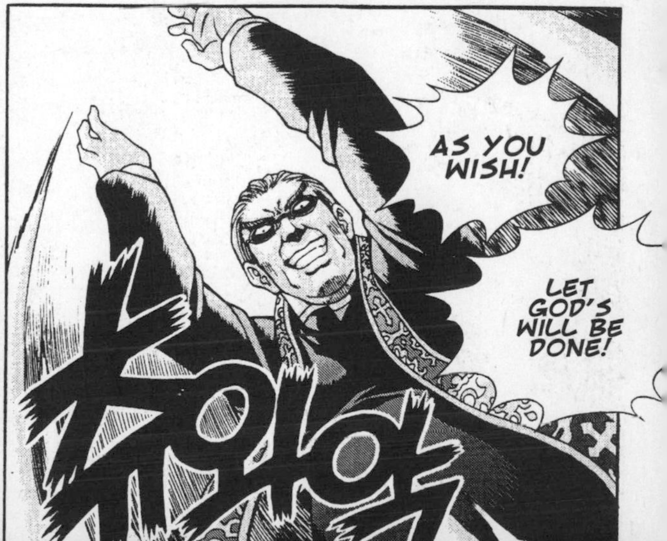
AS YOU WISH!
LET GOD'S WILL BE DONE!

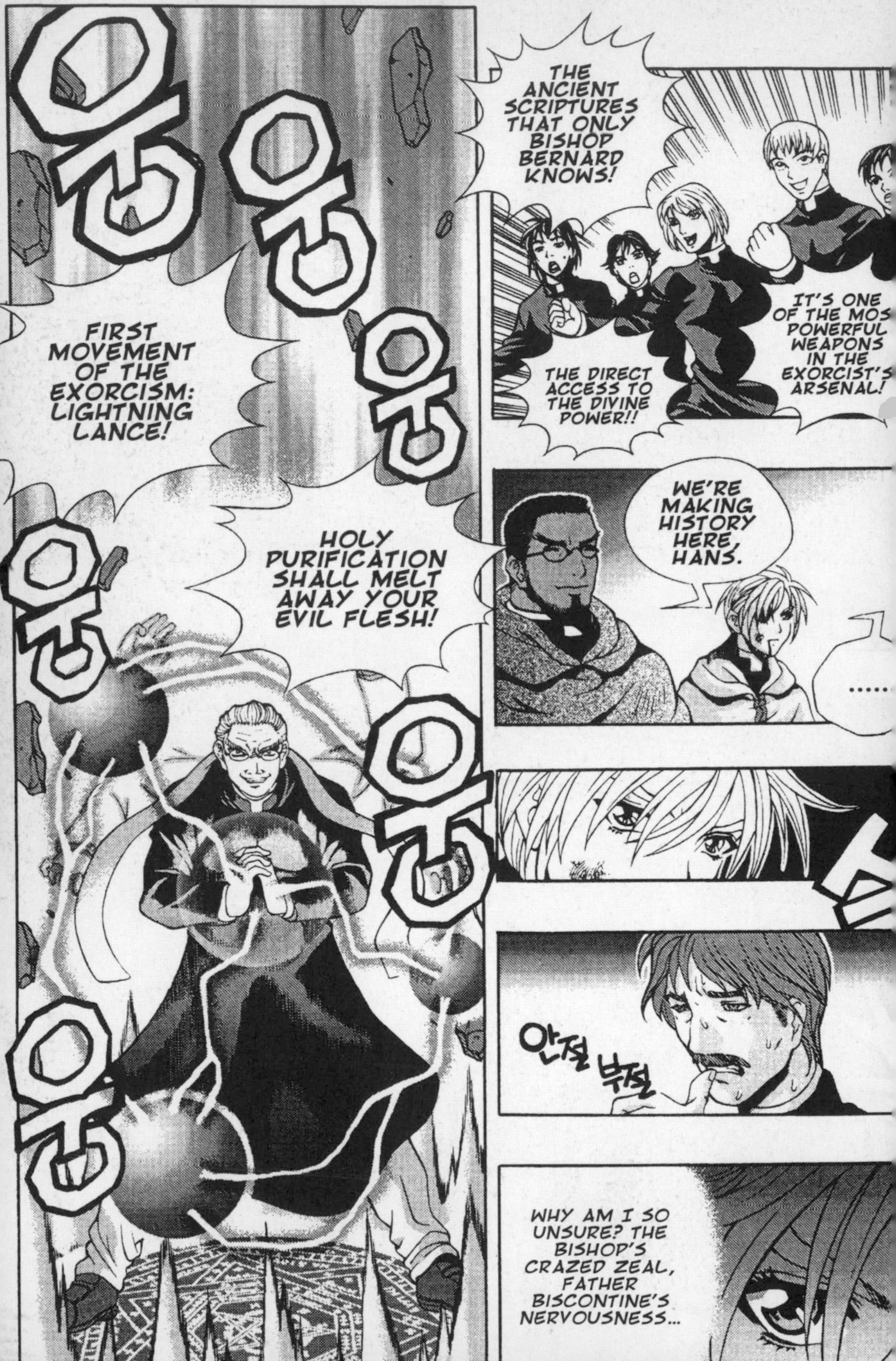
FIRST MOVEMENT OF THE EXORCISM: LIGHTNING LANCE!
HOLY PURIFICATION SHALL MELT AWAY YOUR EVIL FLESH!
THE ANCIENT SCRIPTURES THAT ONLY BISHOP BERNARD KNOWS!
THE DIRECT ACCESS TO THE DIVINE POWER!!
IT'S ONE OF THE MOS POWERFUL WEAPONS IN THE EXORCIST'S ARSENAL!
WE'RE MAKING HISTORY HERE, HANS.
......
안절 부절
WHY AM I SO UNSURE? THE BISHOP'S CRAZED ZEAL, FATHER BISCONTINE'S NERVOUSNESS...

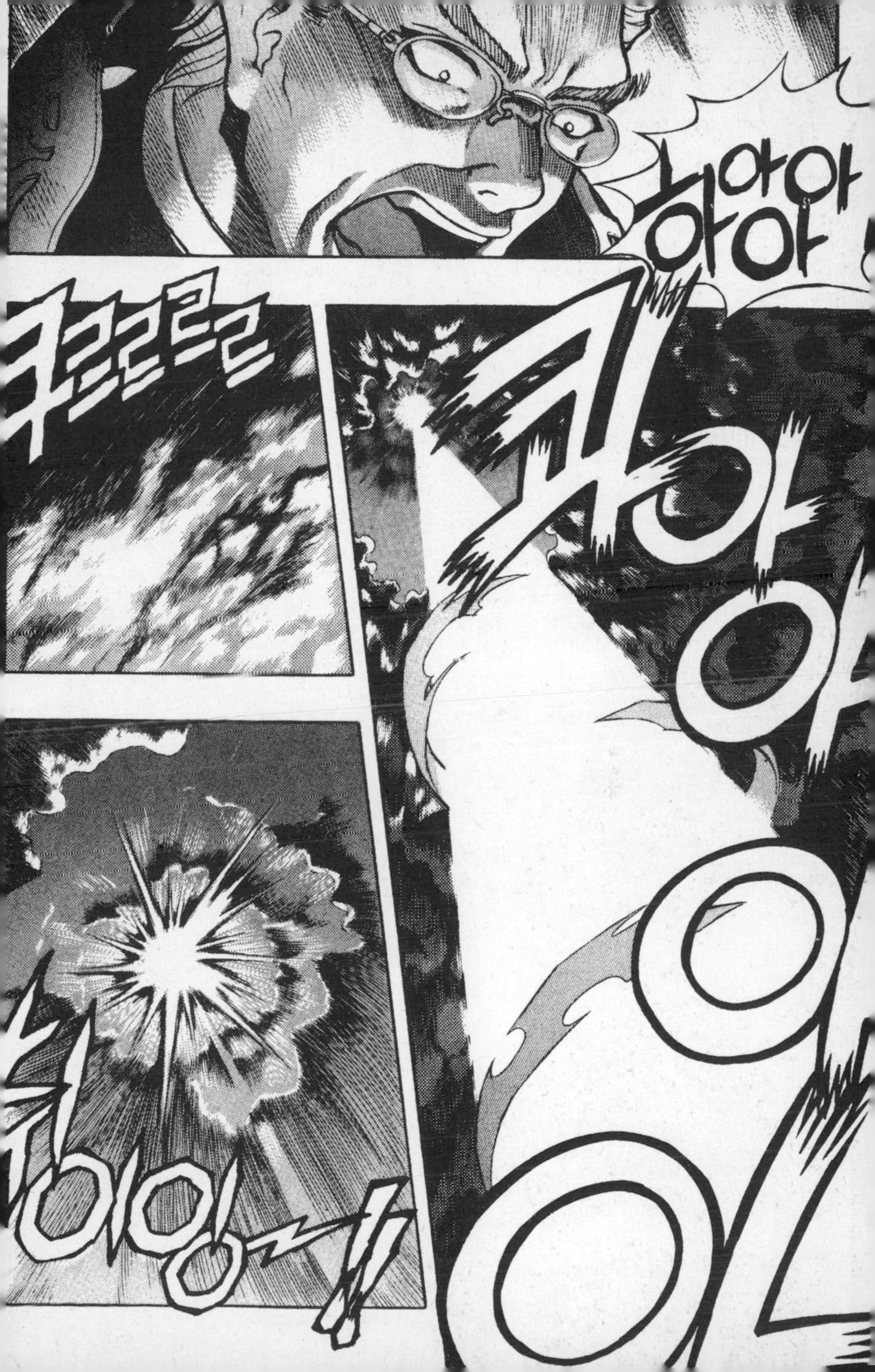

느아아
아아아!
카아아아
쿠르르르르
아아아앙─!

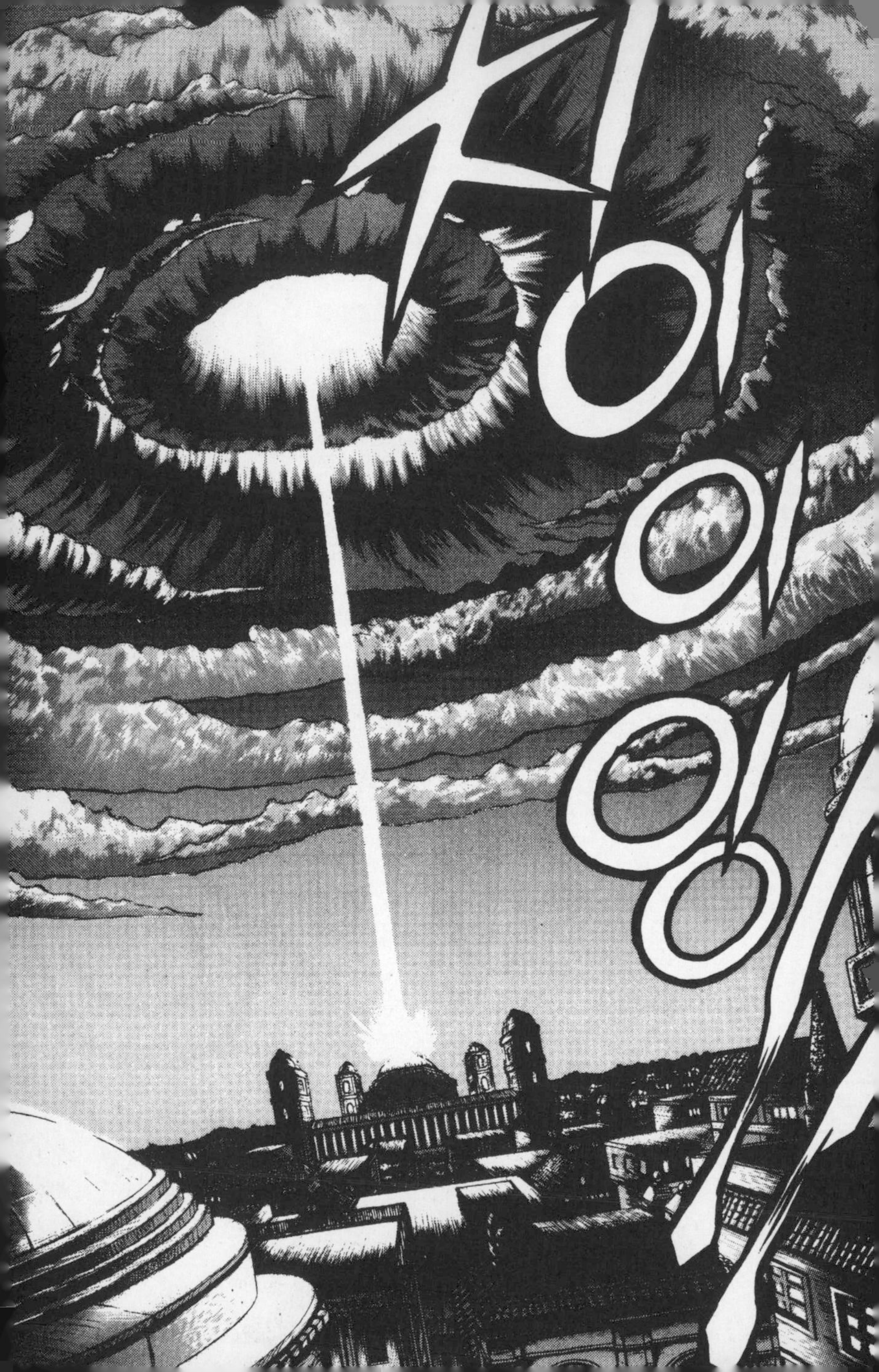

치이이이이

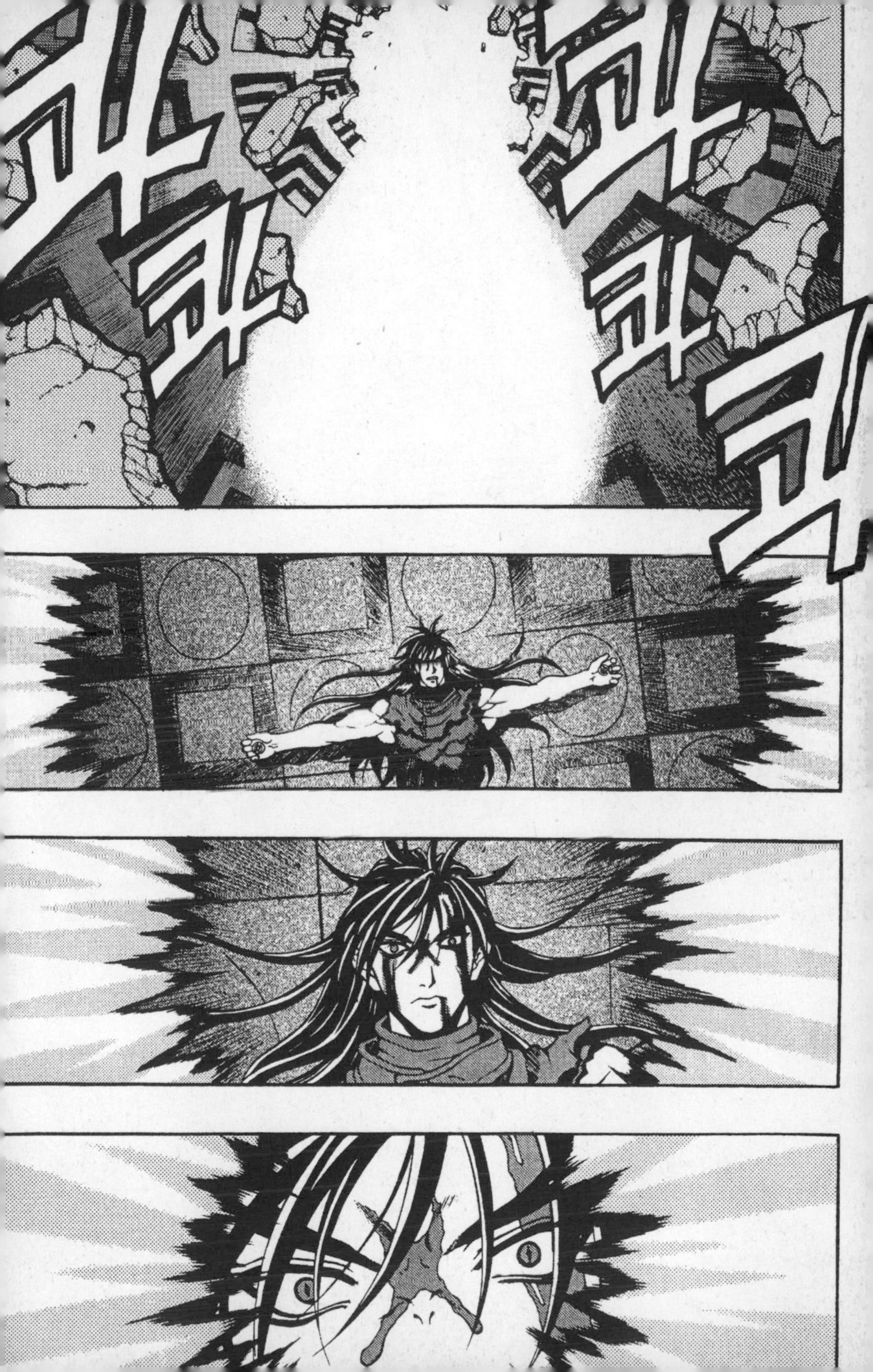
콰콰콰
콰콰

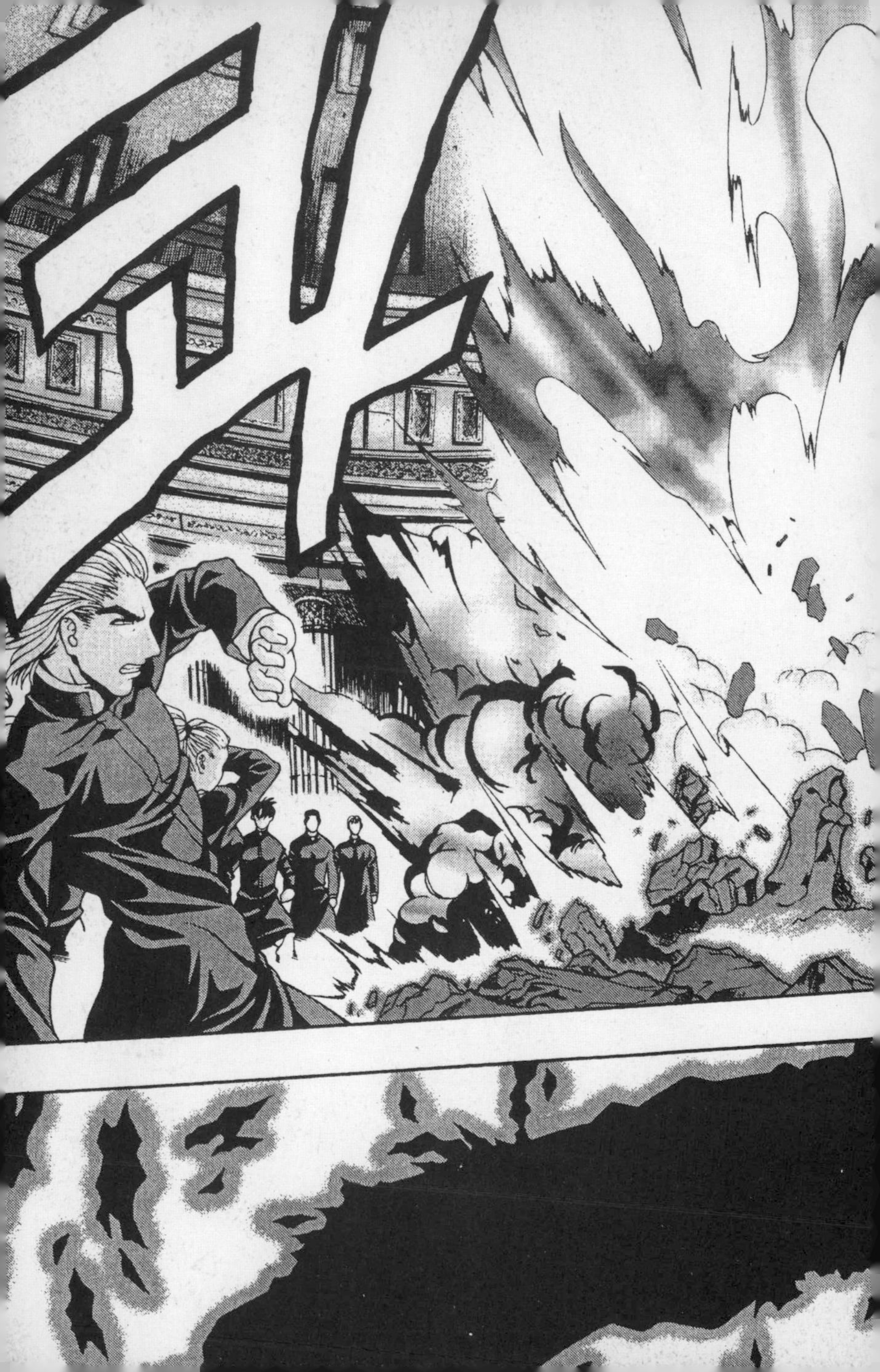

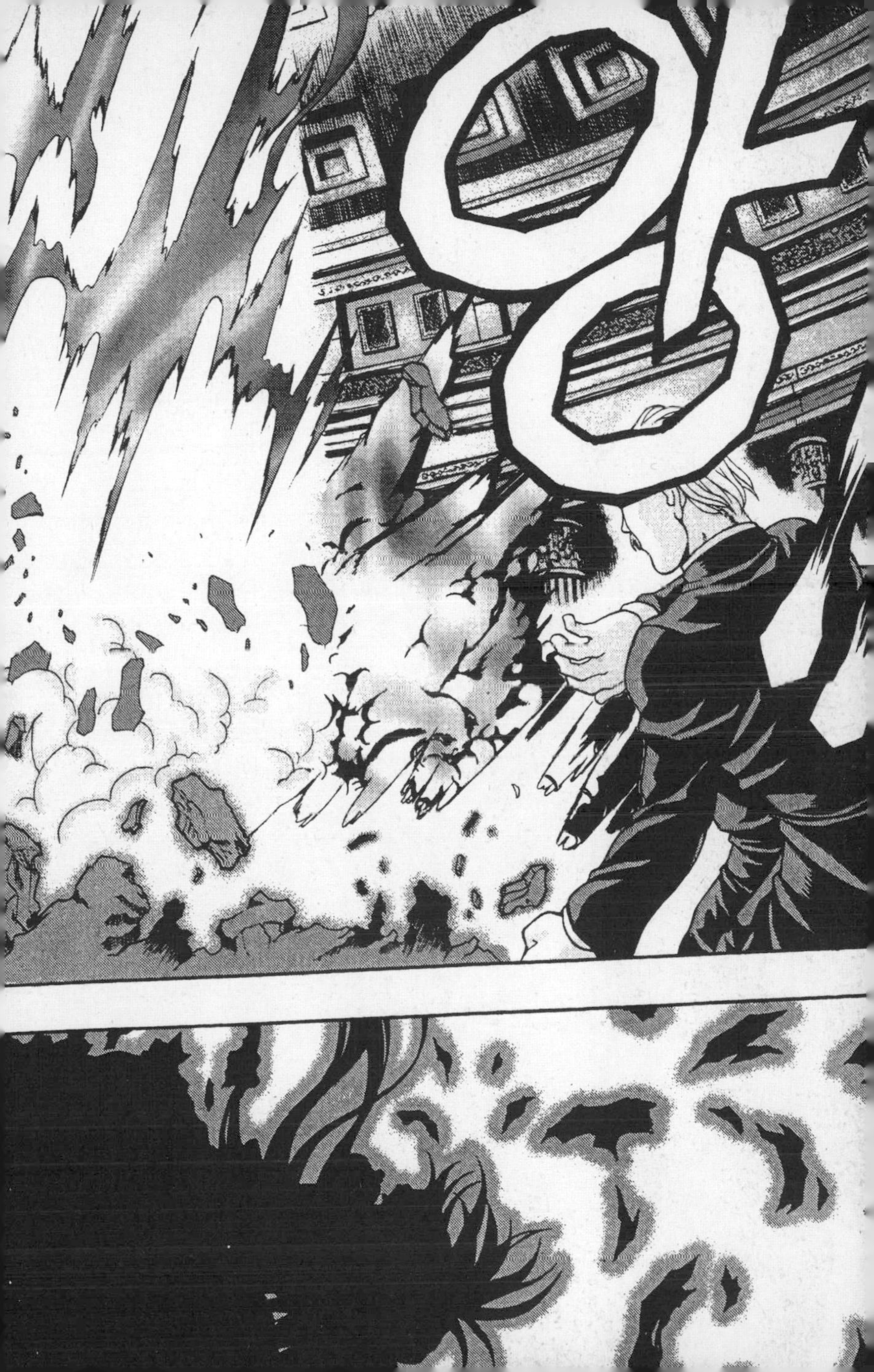

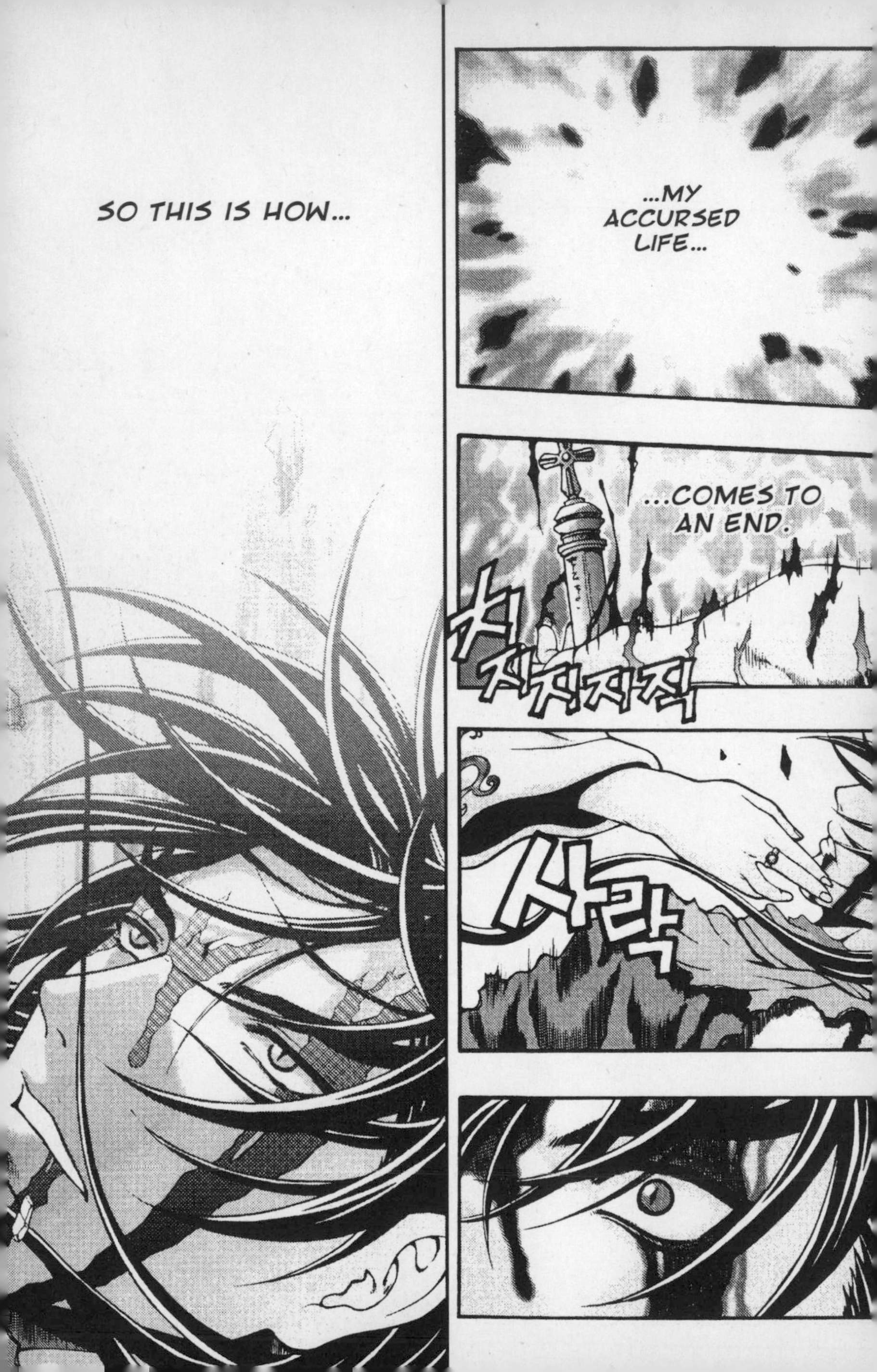
SO THIS IS HOW...
...MY ACCURSED LIFE...
...COMES TO AN END.
치지지지직
사락

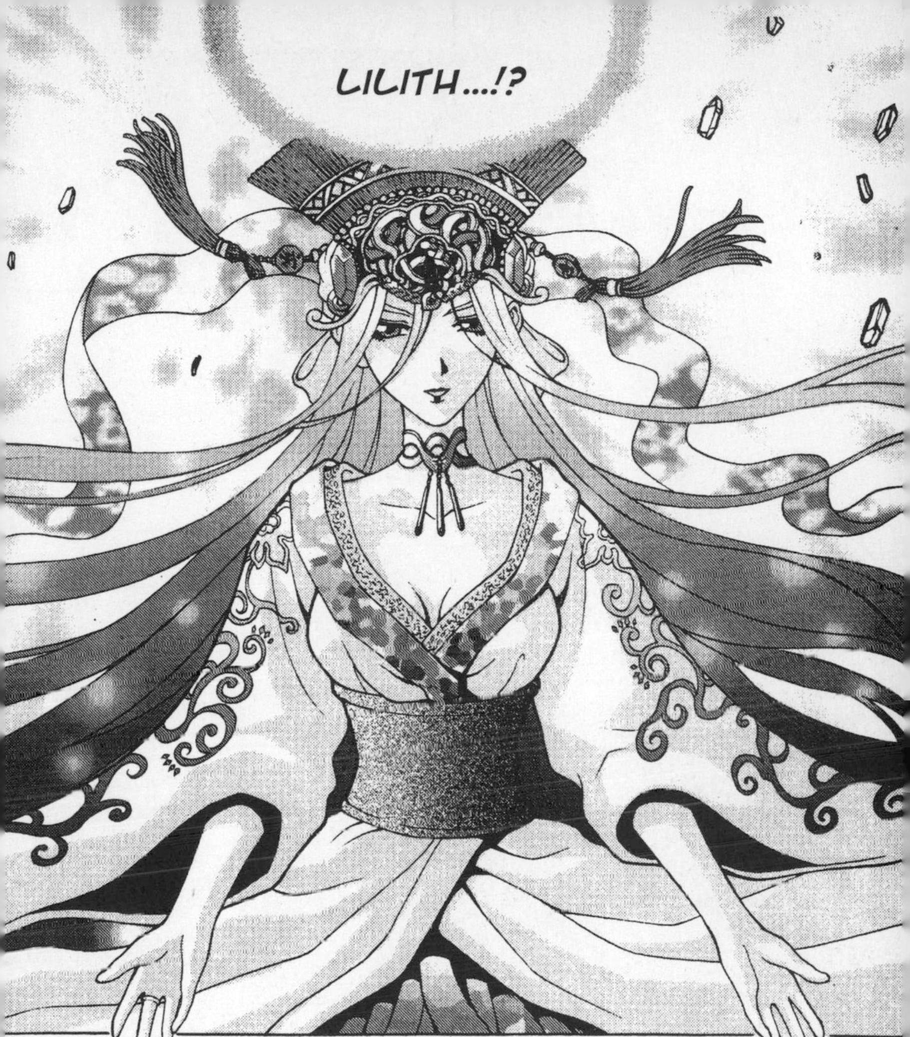
LILITH...!?
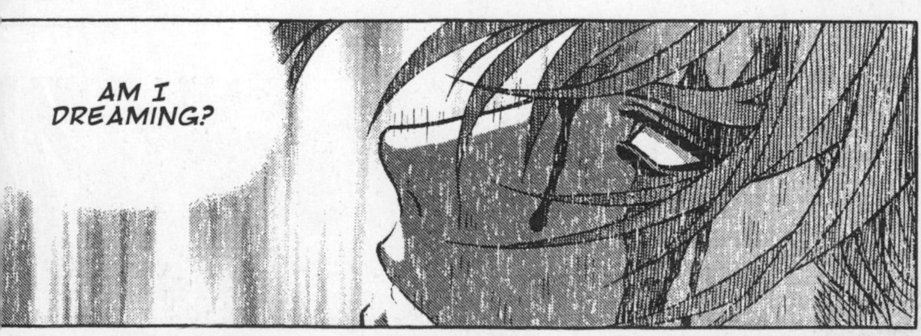
AM I DREAMING?

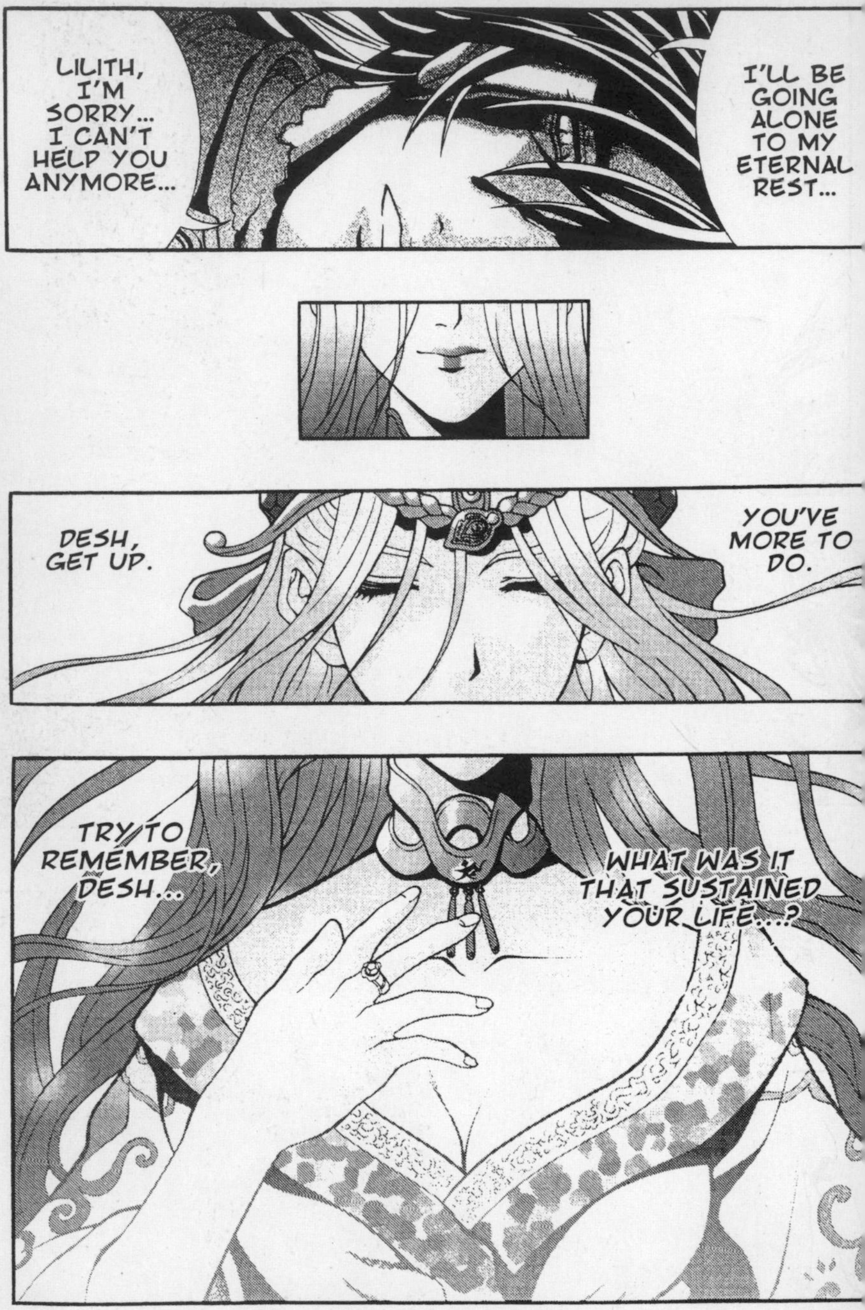
I'LL BE GOING ALONE TO MY ETERNAL REST...
LILITH, I'M SORRY... I CAN'T HELP YOU ANYMORE...
YOU'VE MORE TO DO.
DESH, GET UP.
WHAT WAS IT THAT SUSTAINED YOUR LIFE...?
TRY TO REMEMBER, DESH...

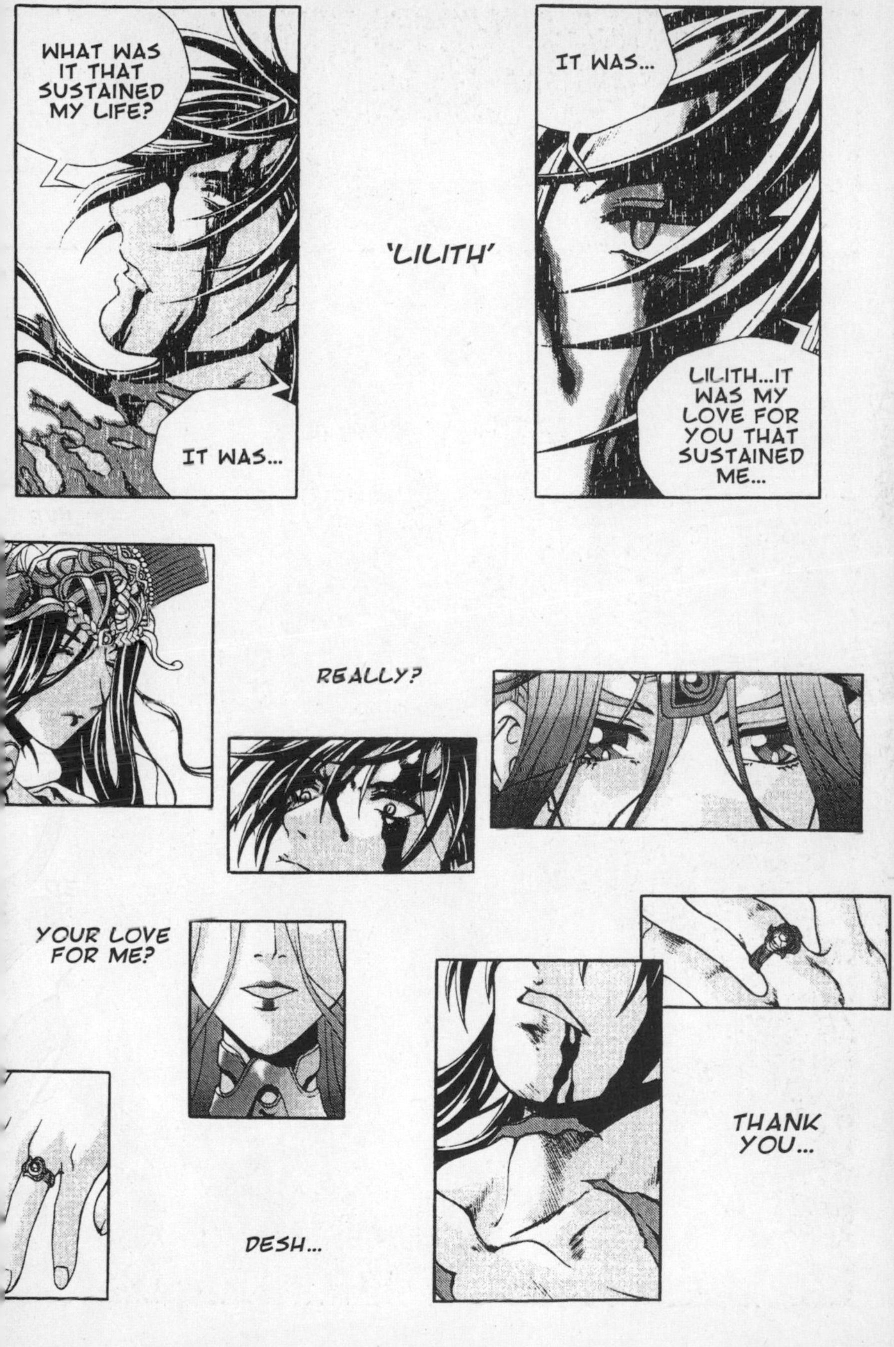
WHAT WAS IT THAT SUSTAINED MY LIFE?
IT WAS...
IT WAS...
LILITH...IT WAS MY LOVE FOR YOU THAT SUSTAINED ME...
'LILITH'
REALLY?
YOUR LOVE FOR ME?
DESH...
THANK YOU...

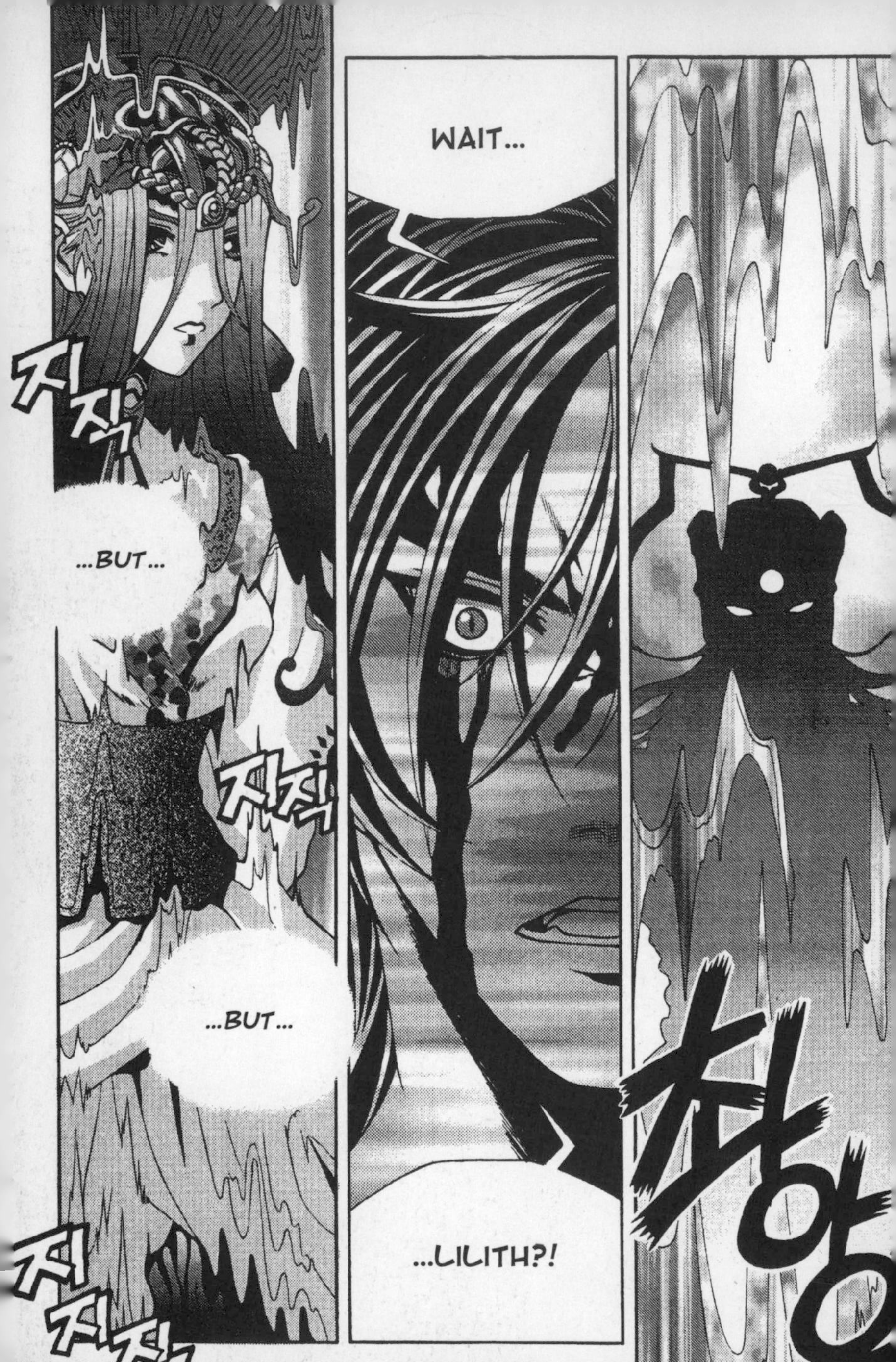
WAIT...
...LILITH?!
...BUT...
...BUT...

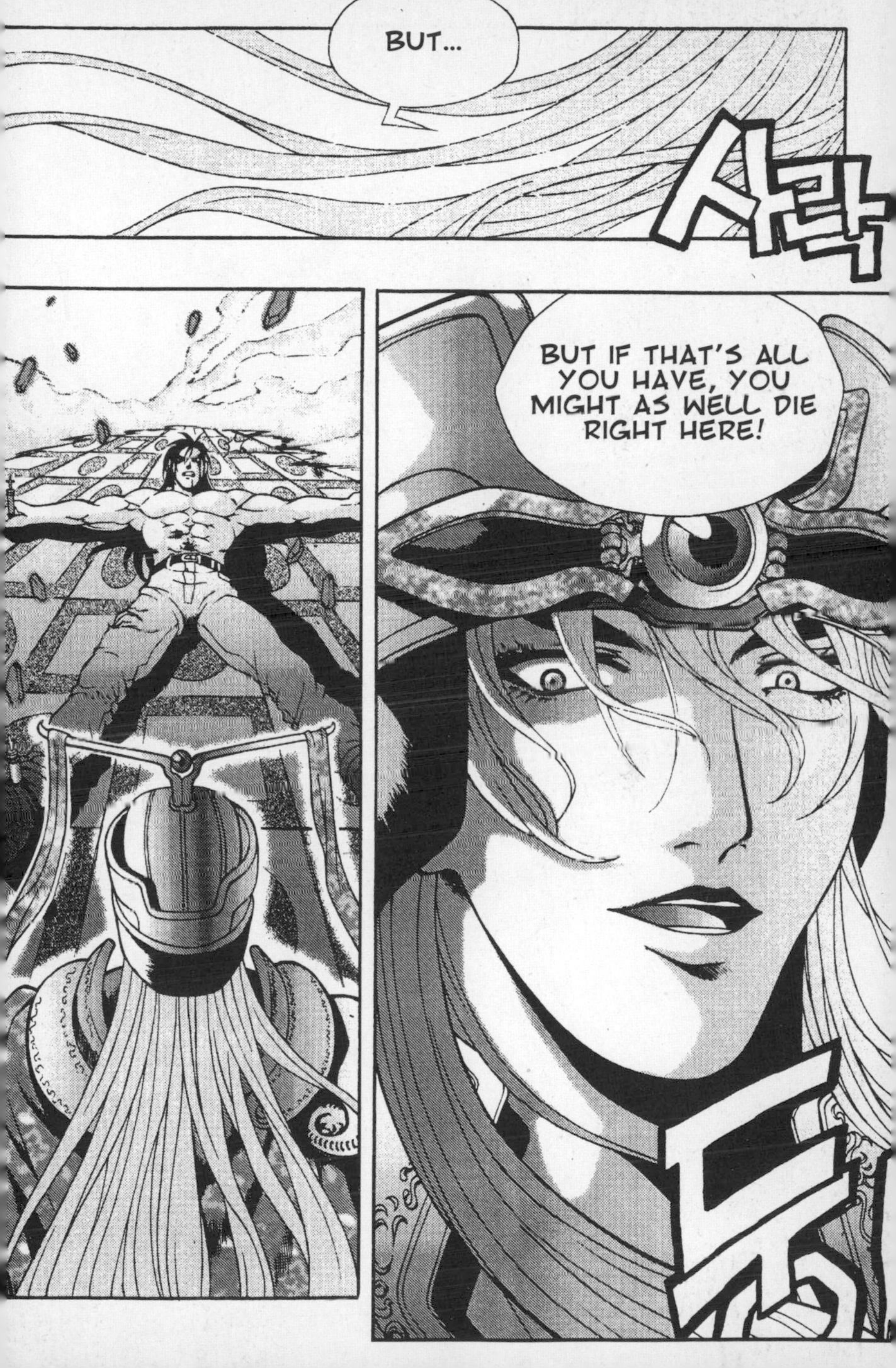
BUT...
BUT IF THAT'S ALL YOU HAVE, YOU MIGHT AS WELL DIE RIGHT HERE!

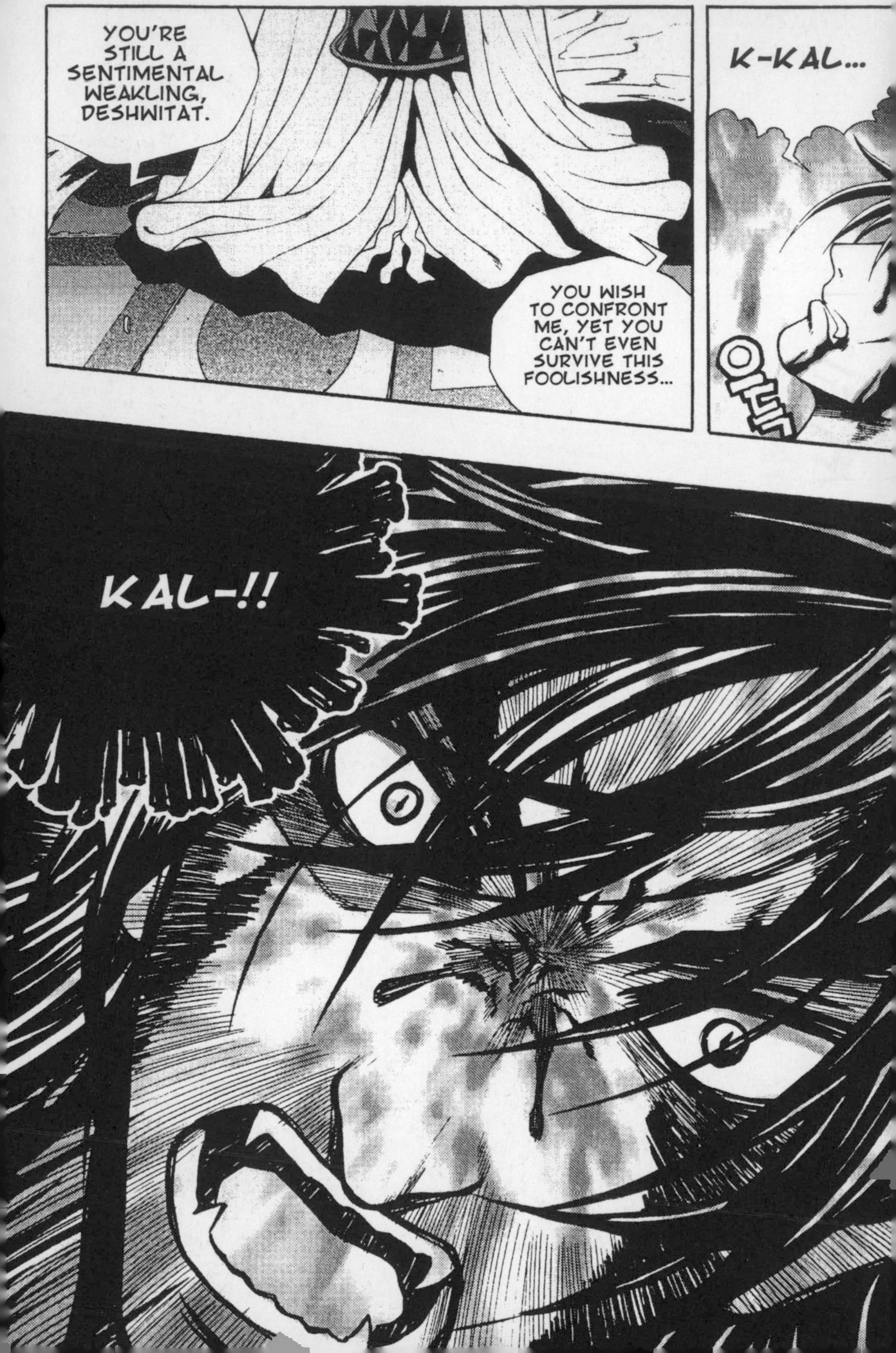
K-KAL...
YOU'RE STILL A SENTIMENTAL WEAKLING, DESHWITAT.
YOU WISH TO CONFRONT ME, YET YOU CAN'T EVEN SURVIVE THIS FOOLISHNESS...
KAL-!!

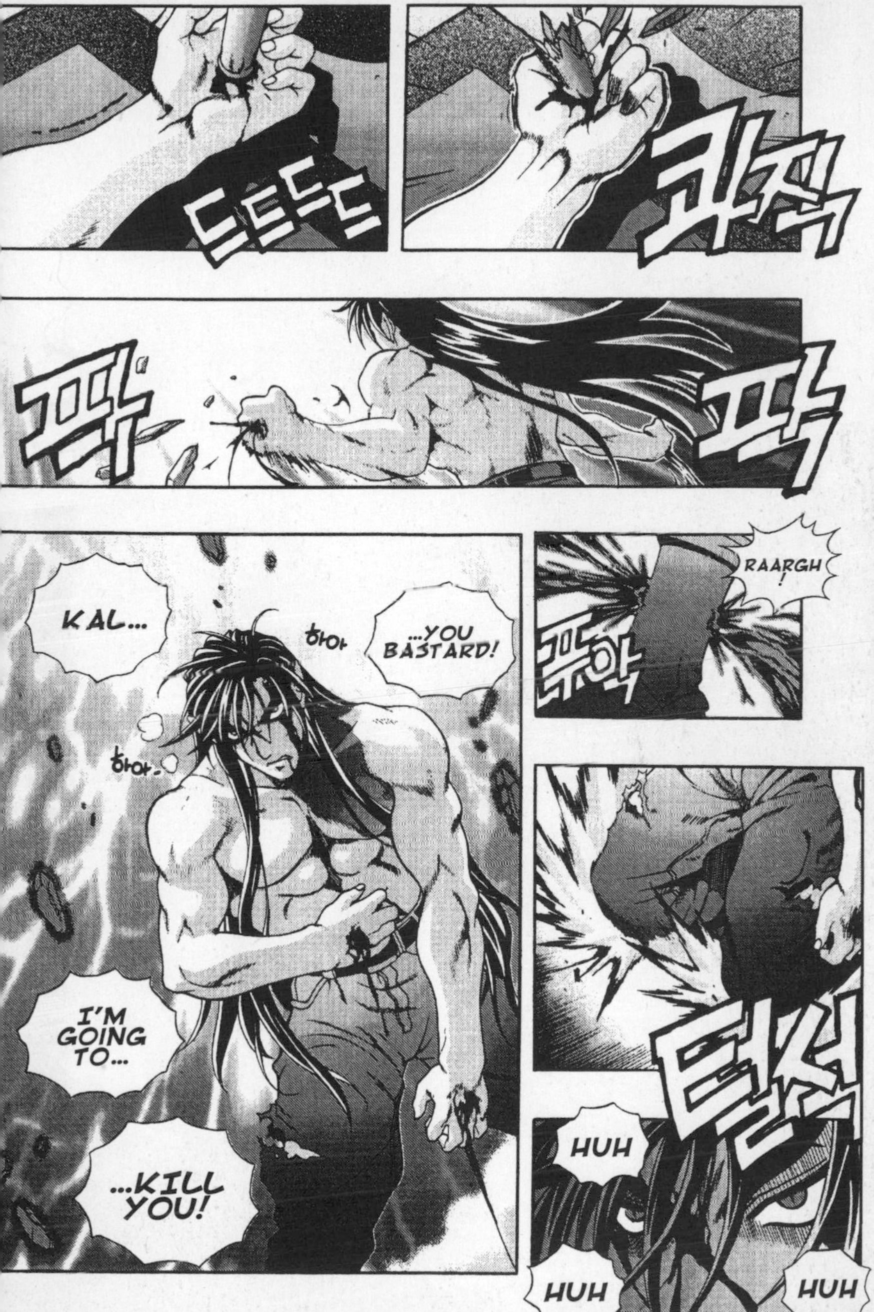
KAL...
하아
...YOU BASTARD!
하아
I'M GOING TO...
...KILL YOU!
RAARGH!
HUH
HUH
HUH

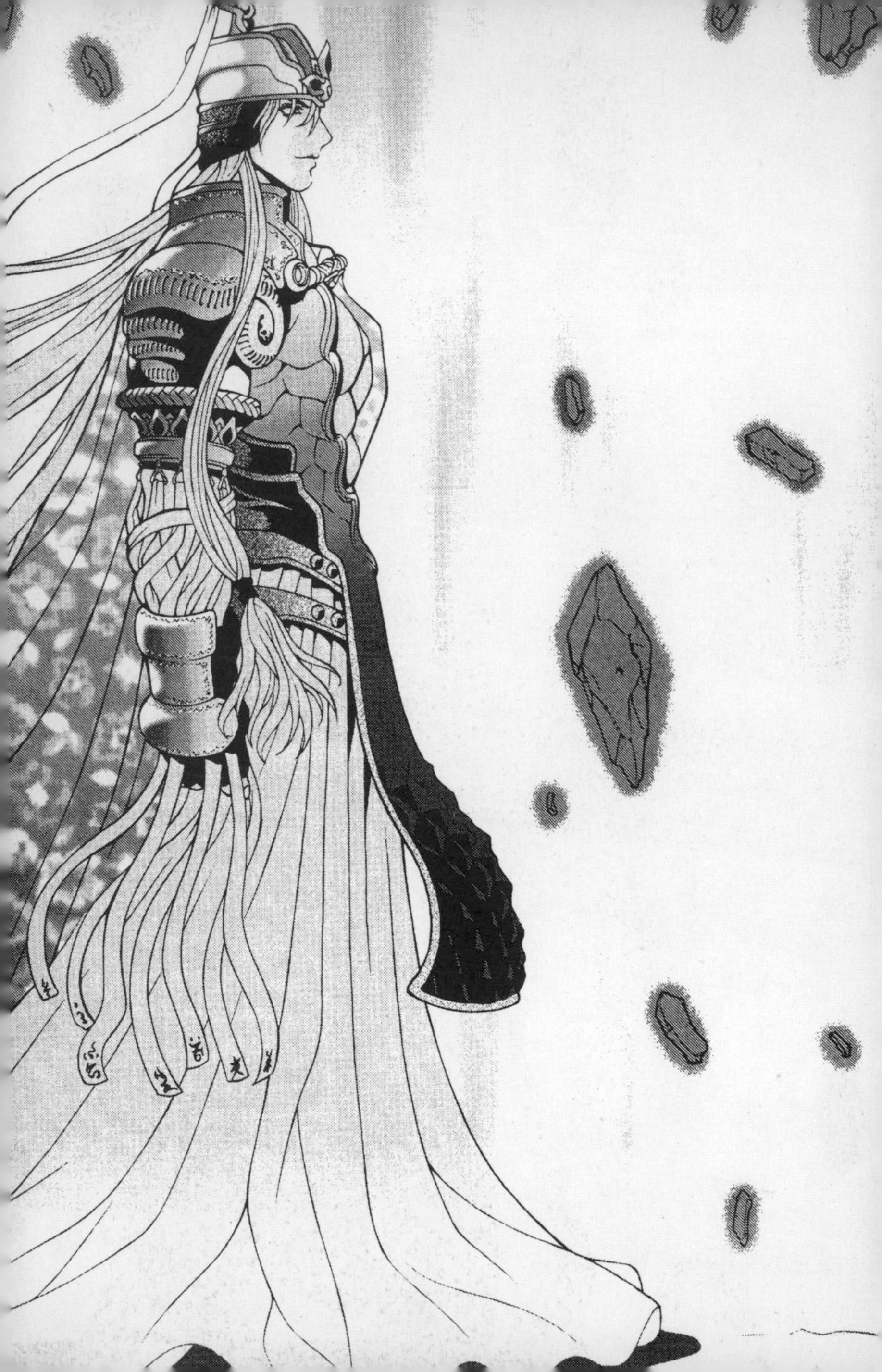

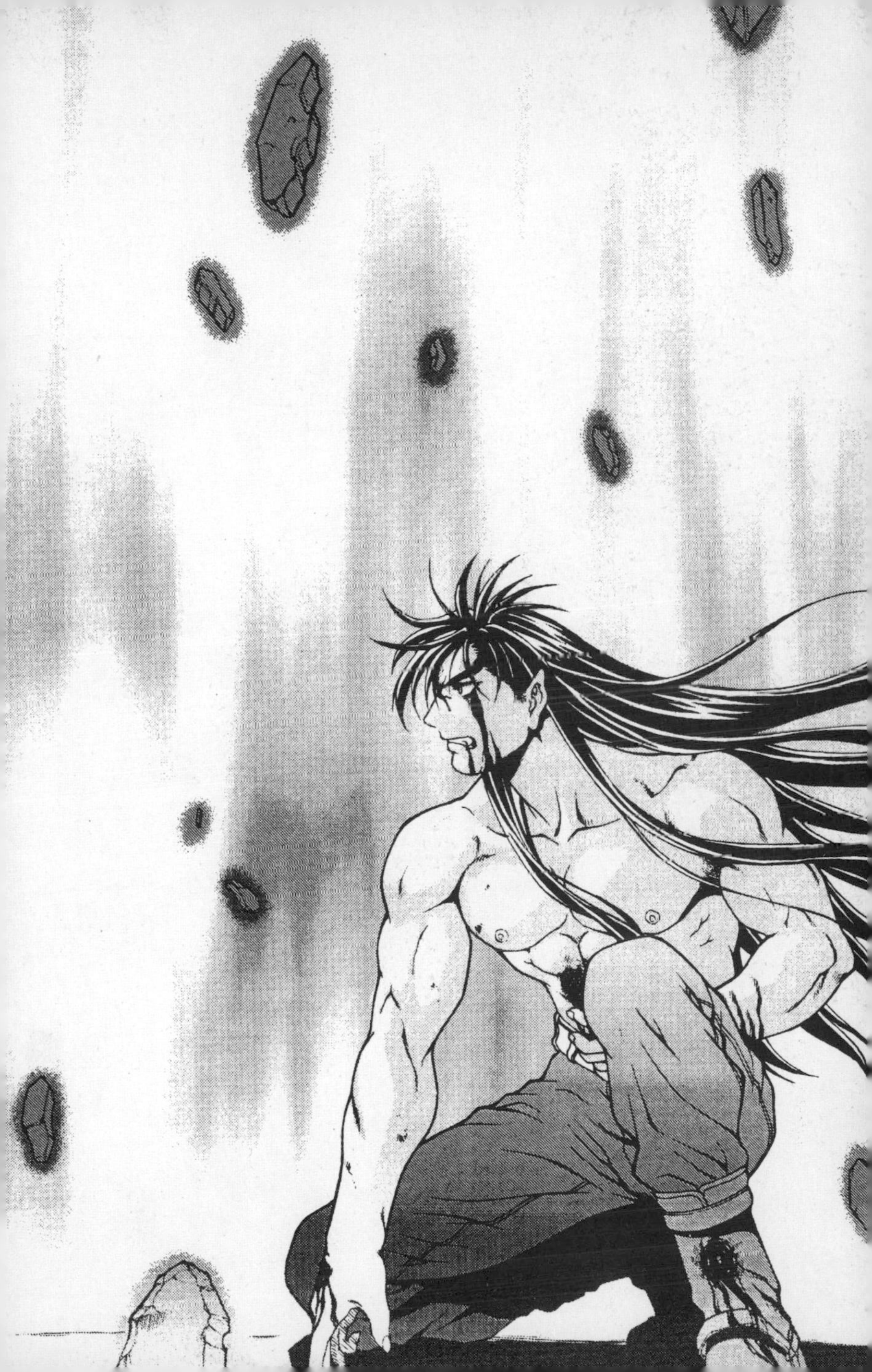

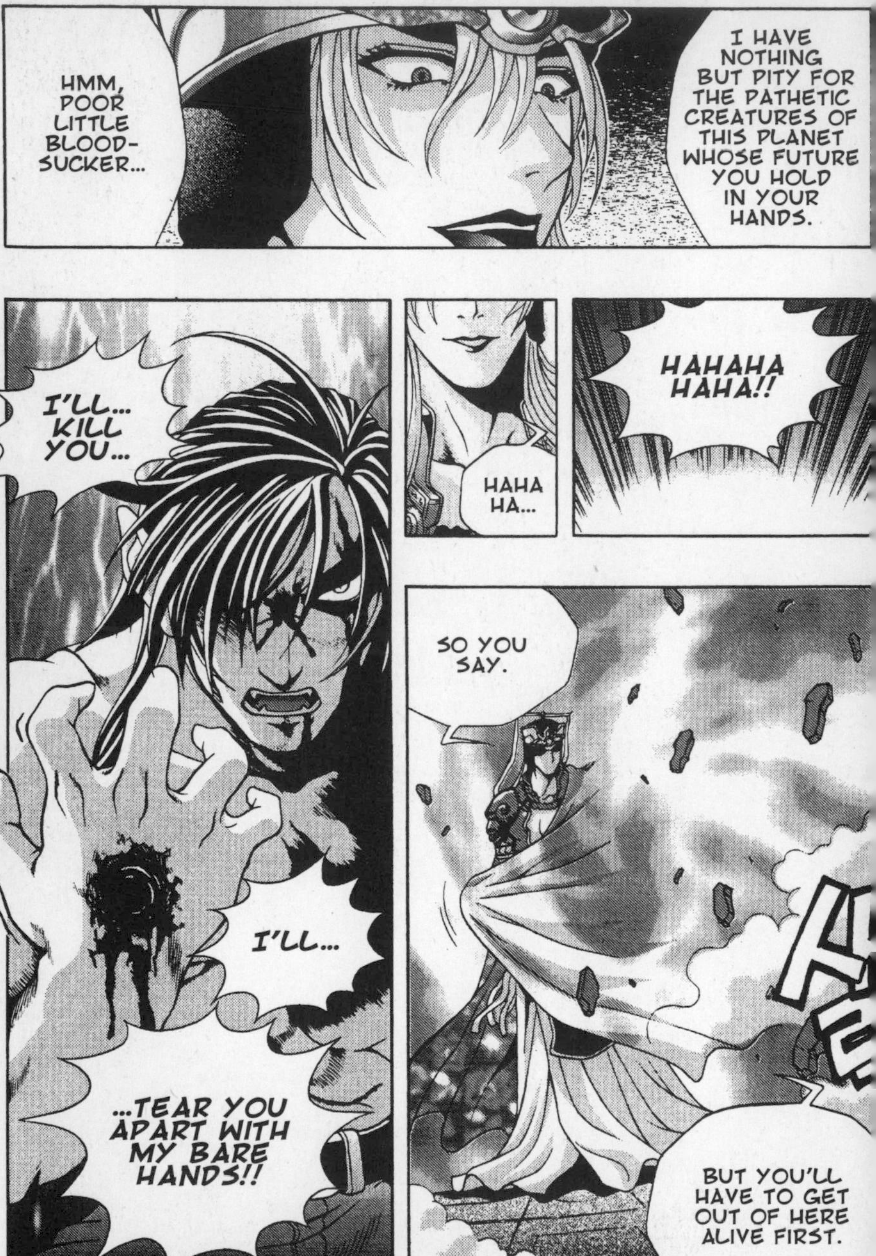
HMM, POOR LITTLE BLOOD-SUCKER...
I HAVE NOTHING BUT PITY FOR THE PATHETIC CREATURES OF THIS PLANET WHOSE FUTURE YOU HOLD IN YOUR HANDS.
I'LL... KILL YOU...
I'LL...
...TEAR YOU APART WITH MY BARE HANDS!!
HAHA HA...
HAHAHA HAHA!!
SO YOU SAY.
BUT YOU'LL HAVE TO GET OUT OF HERE ALIVE FIRST.

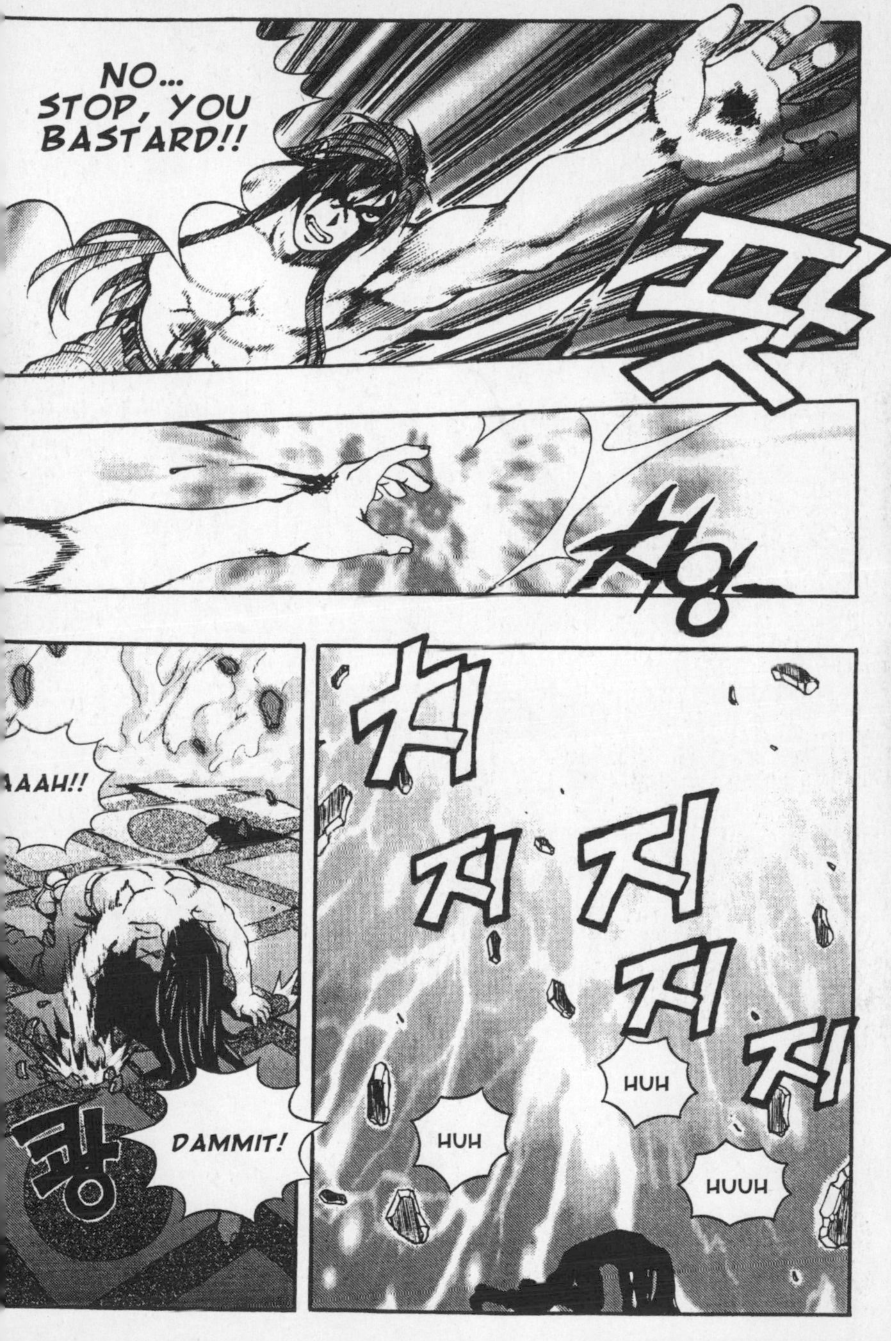
NO... STOP, YOU BASTARD!!
AAAH!!
DAMMIT!
HUH
HUH
HUUH

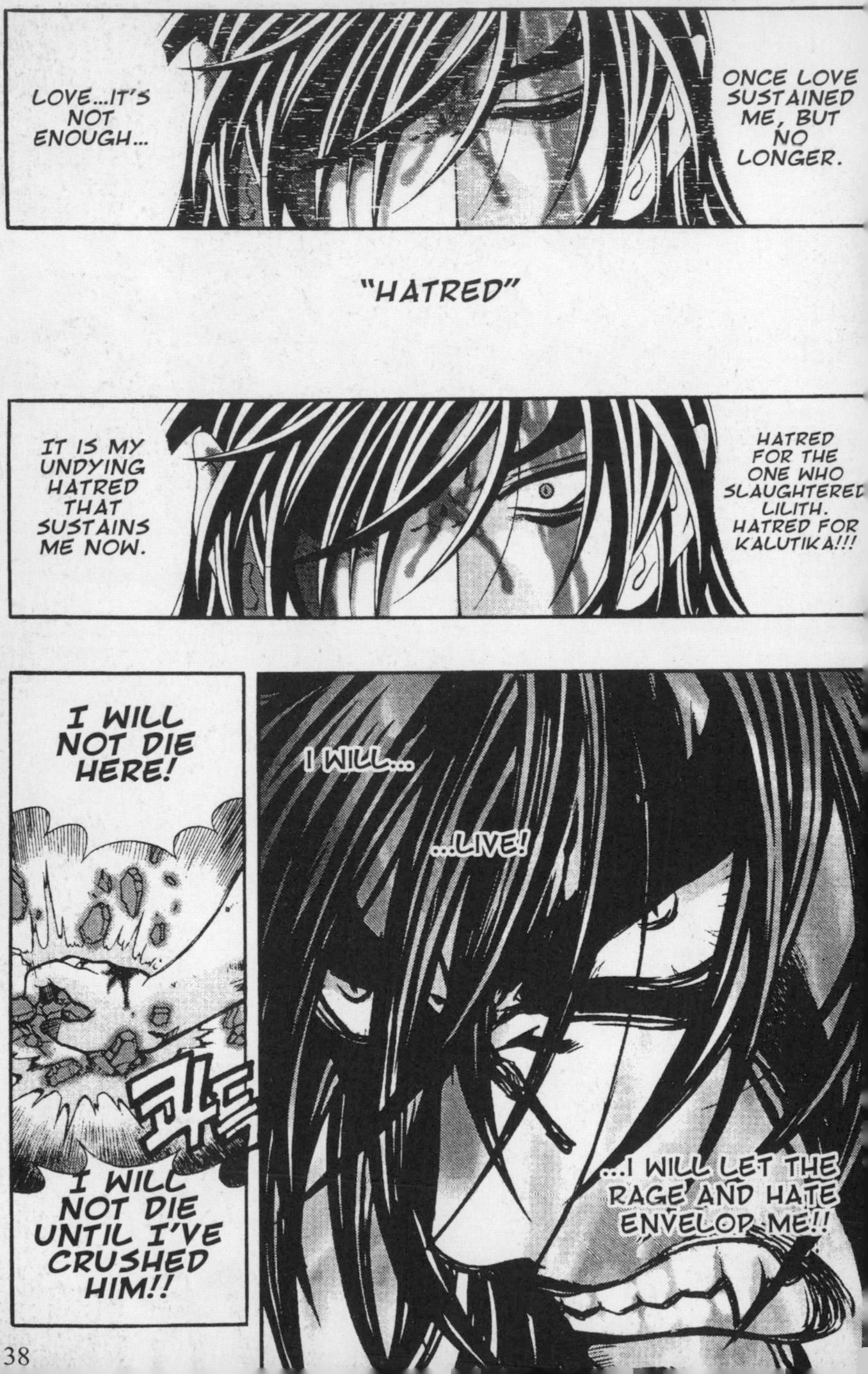
LOVE...IT'S NOT ENOUGH...
ONCE LOVE SUSTAINED ME, BUT NO LONGER.
"HATRED"
IT IS MY UNDYING HATRED THAT SUSTAINS ME NOW.
HATRED FOR THE ONE WHO SLAUGHTERED LILITH. HATRED FOR KALUTIKA!!!
I WILL NOT DIE HERE!
I WILL NOT DIE UNTIL I'VE CRUSHED HIM!!
I WILL...
...LIVE!
...I WILL LET THE RAGE AND HATE ENVELOP ME!!

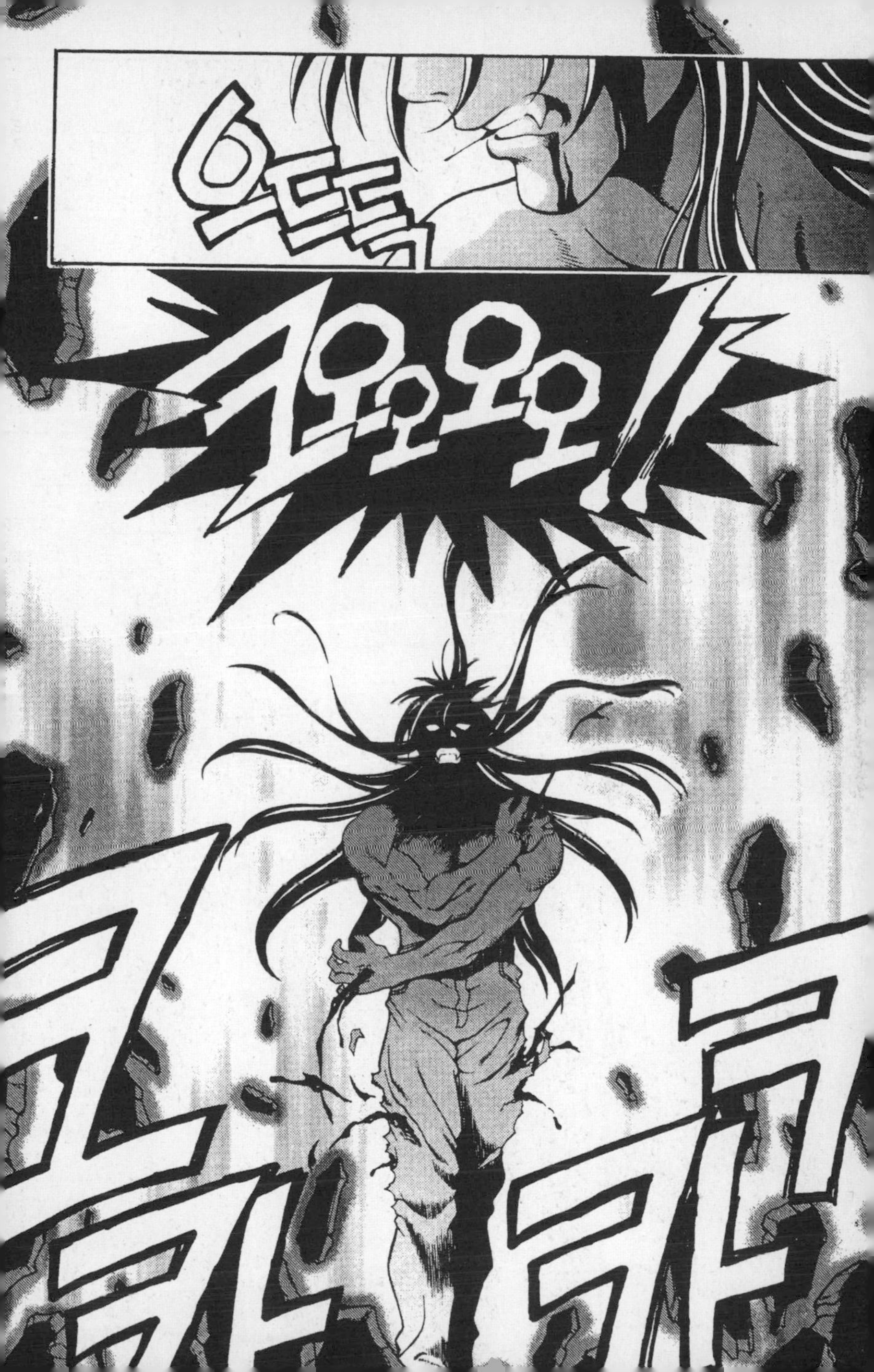
으드득
우우우우!!

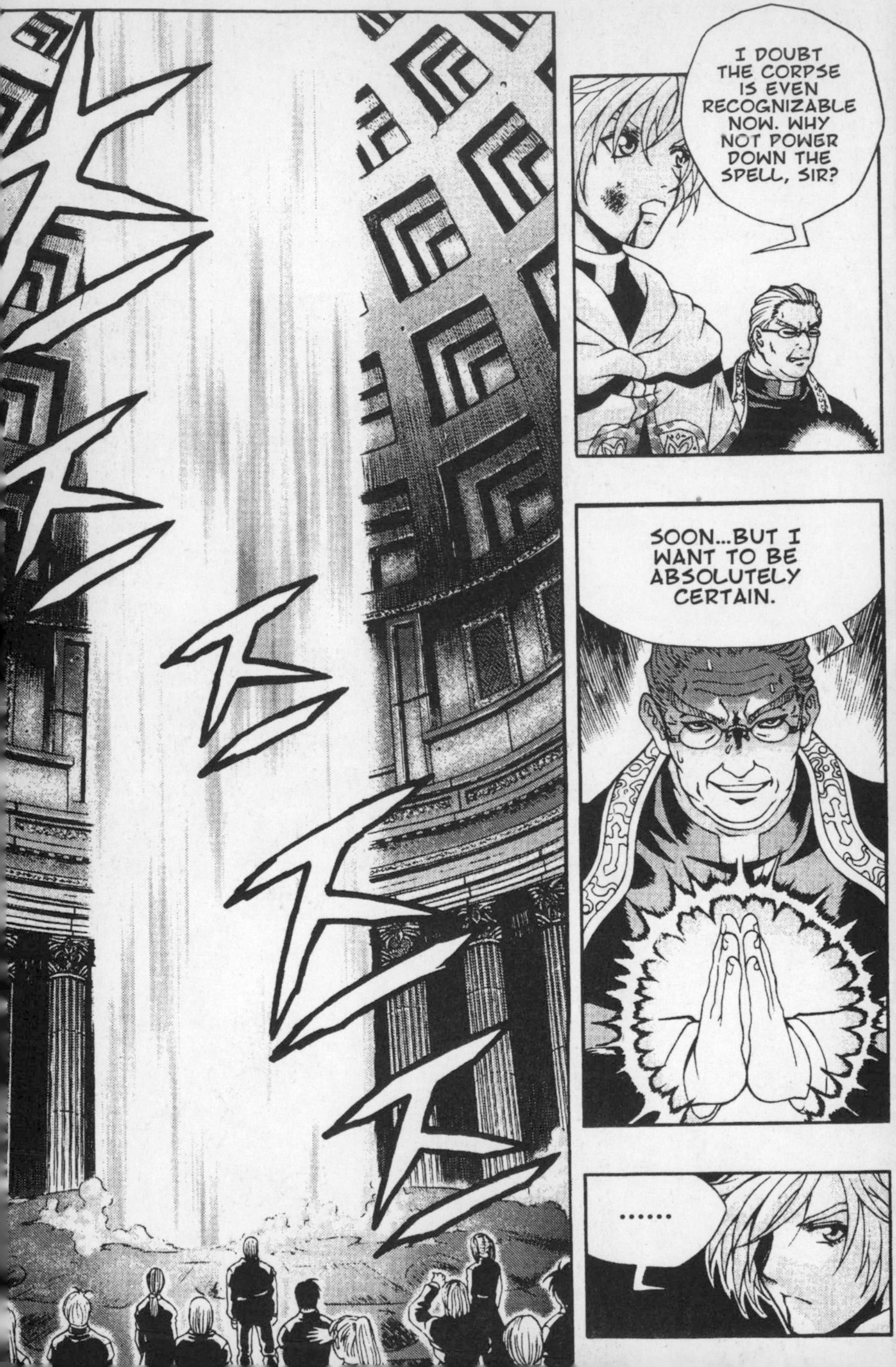
I DOUBT THE CORPSE IS EVEN RECOGNIZABLE NOW. WHY NOT POWER DOWN THE SPELL, SIR?
SOON...BUT I WANT TO BE ABSOLUTELY CERTAIN.
......

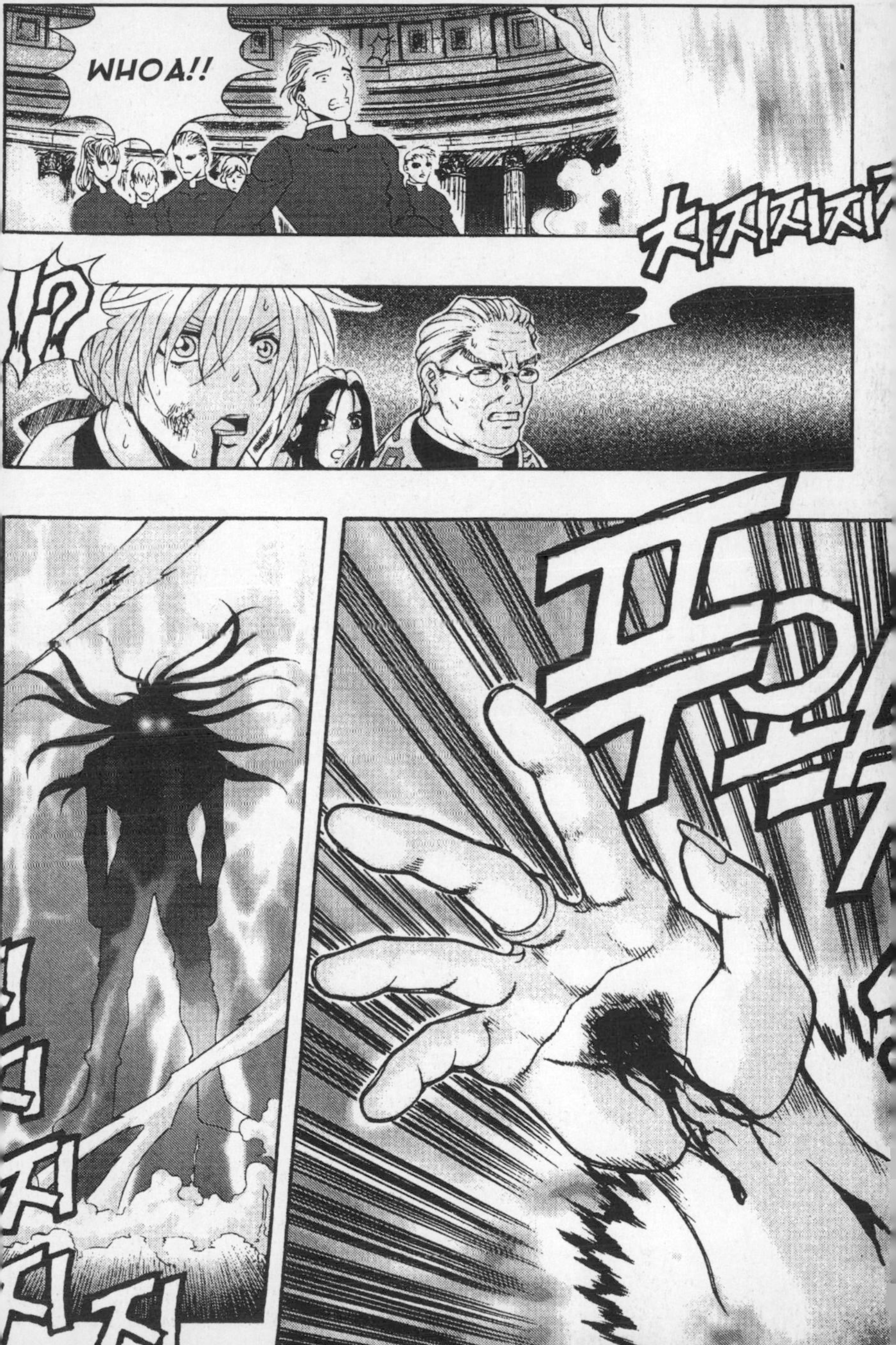
WHOA!!
!?

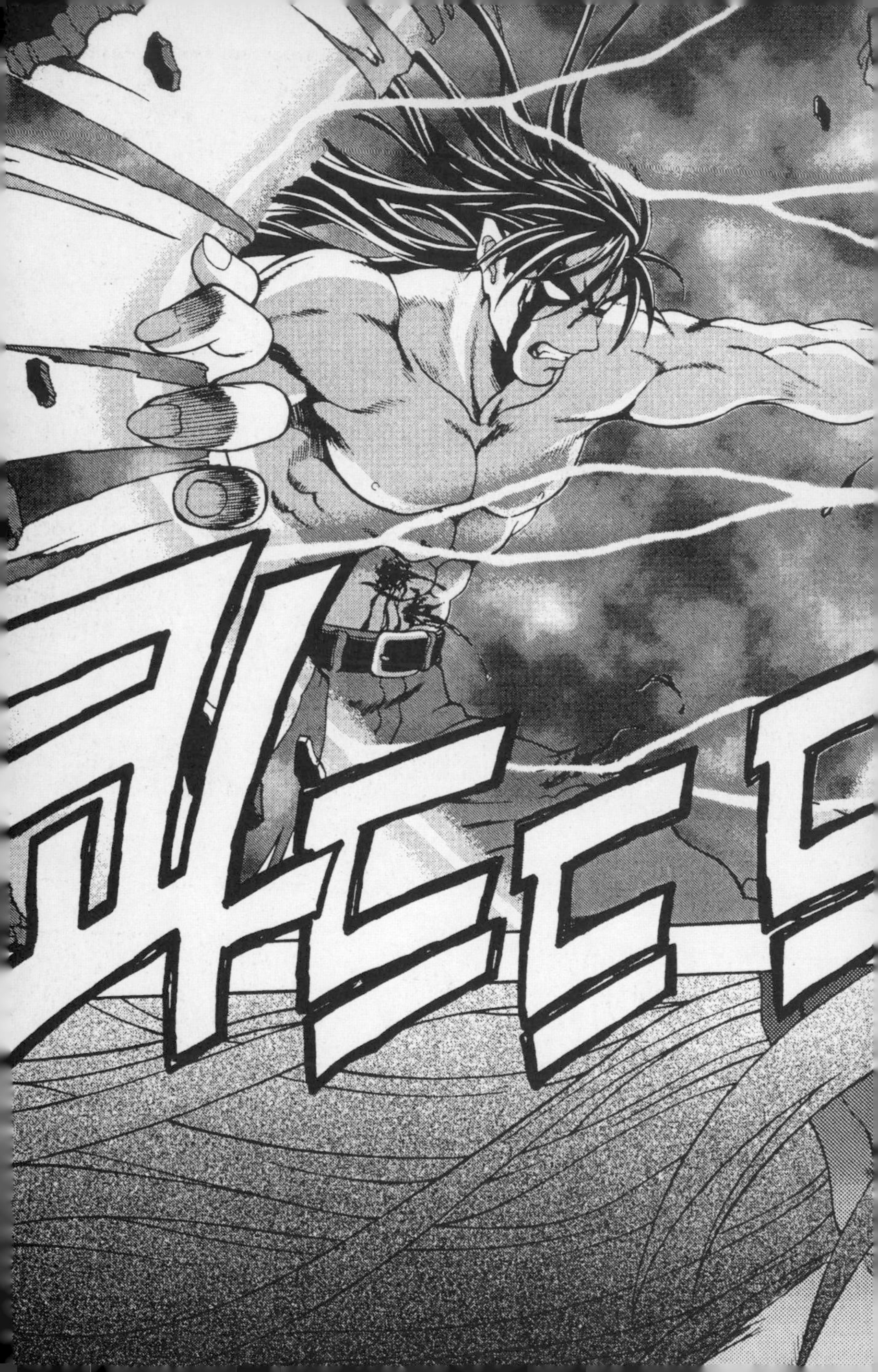

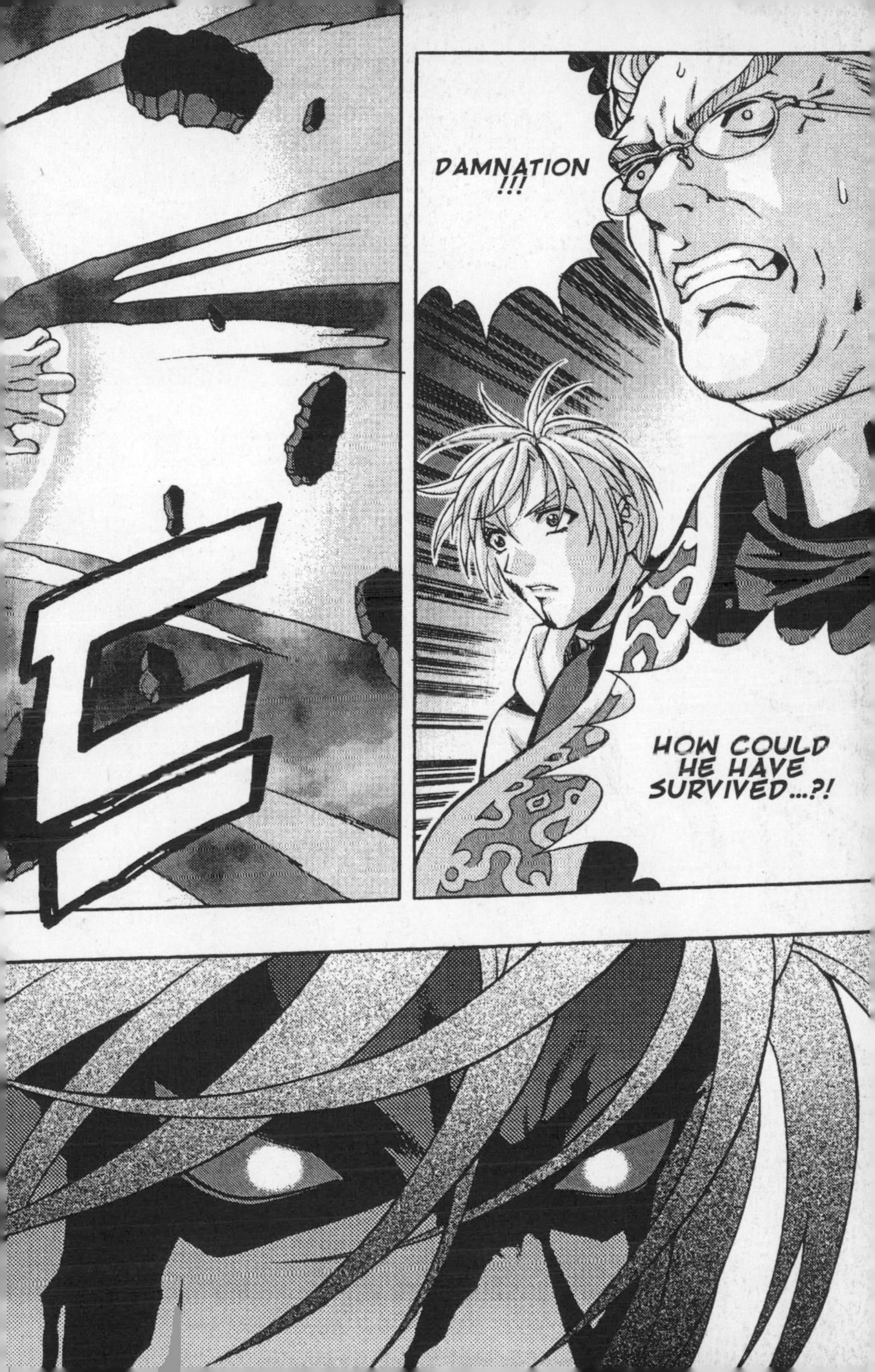
DAMNATION !!!
HOW COULD HE HAVE SURVIVED...?!

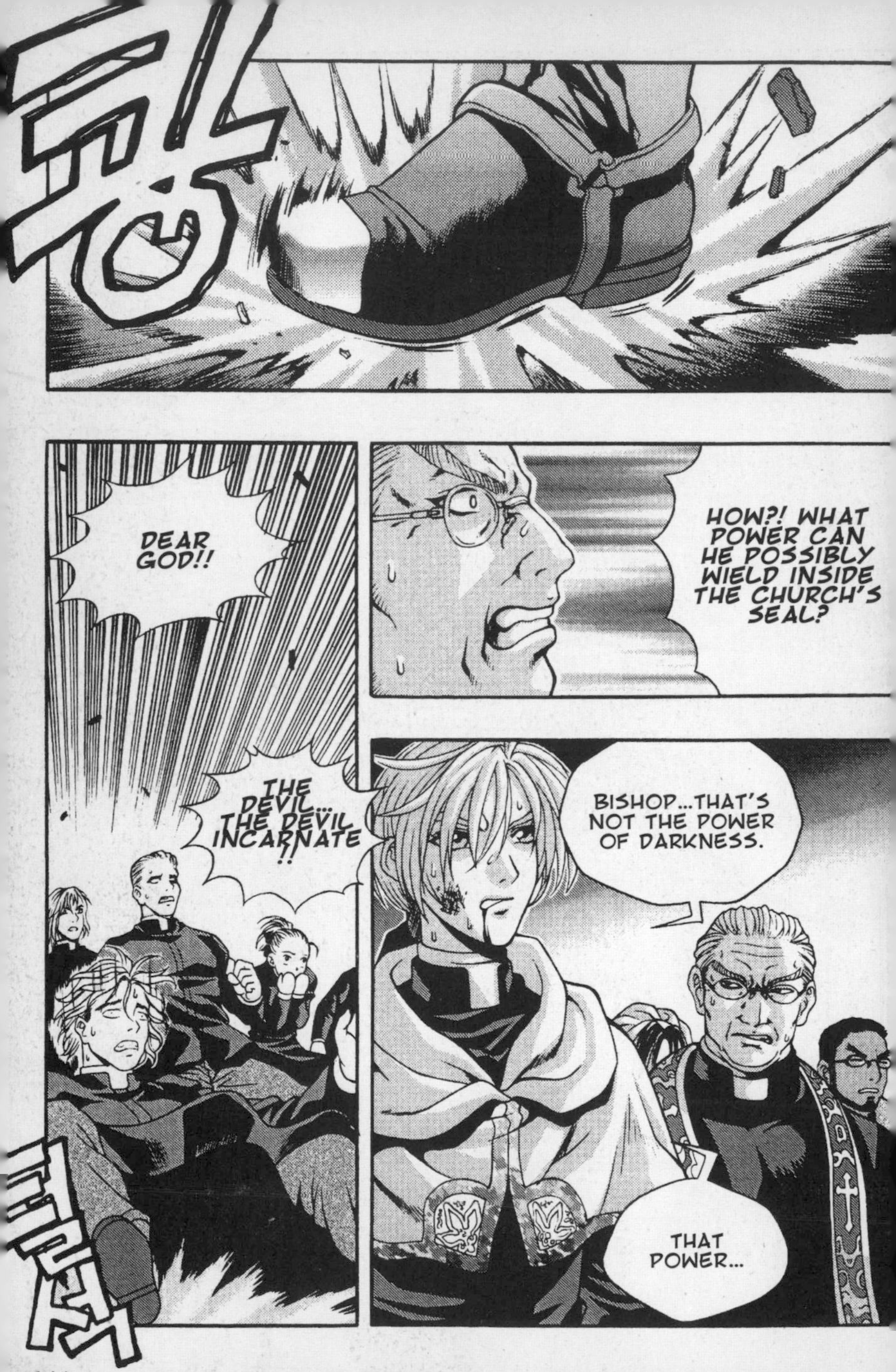
HOW?! WHAT POWER CAN HE POSSIBLY WIELD INSIDE THE CHURCH'S SEAL?
DEAR GOD!!
THE DEVIL... THE DEVIL INCARNATE !!
BISHOP...THAT'S NOT THE POWER OF DARKNESS.
THAT POWER...

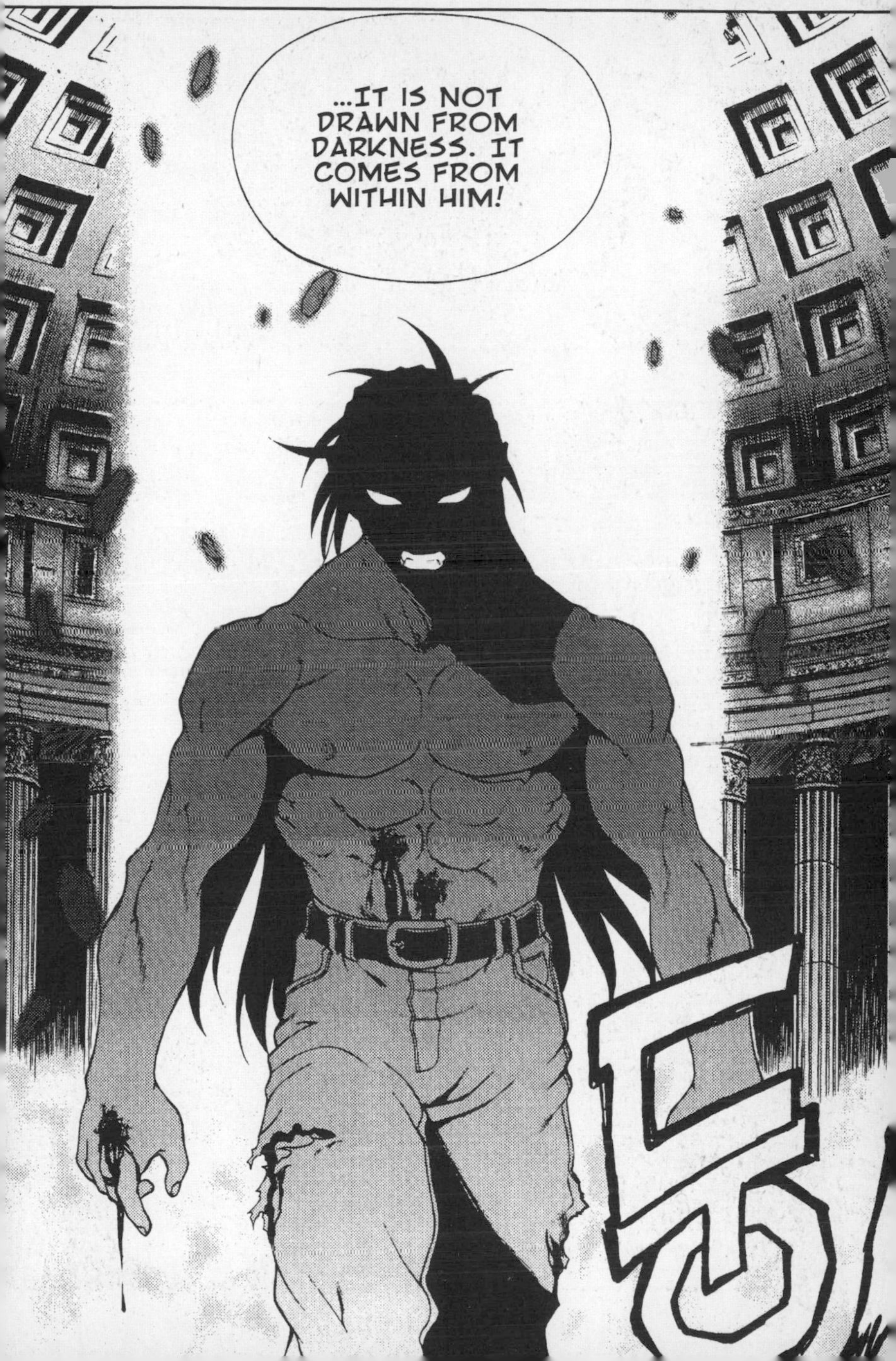
...IT IS NOT DRAWN FROM DARKNESS. IT COMES FROM WITHIN HIM!

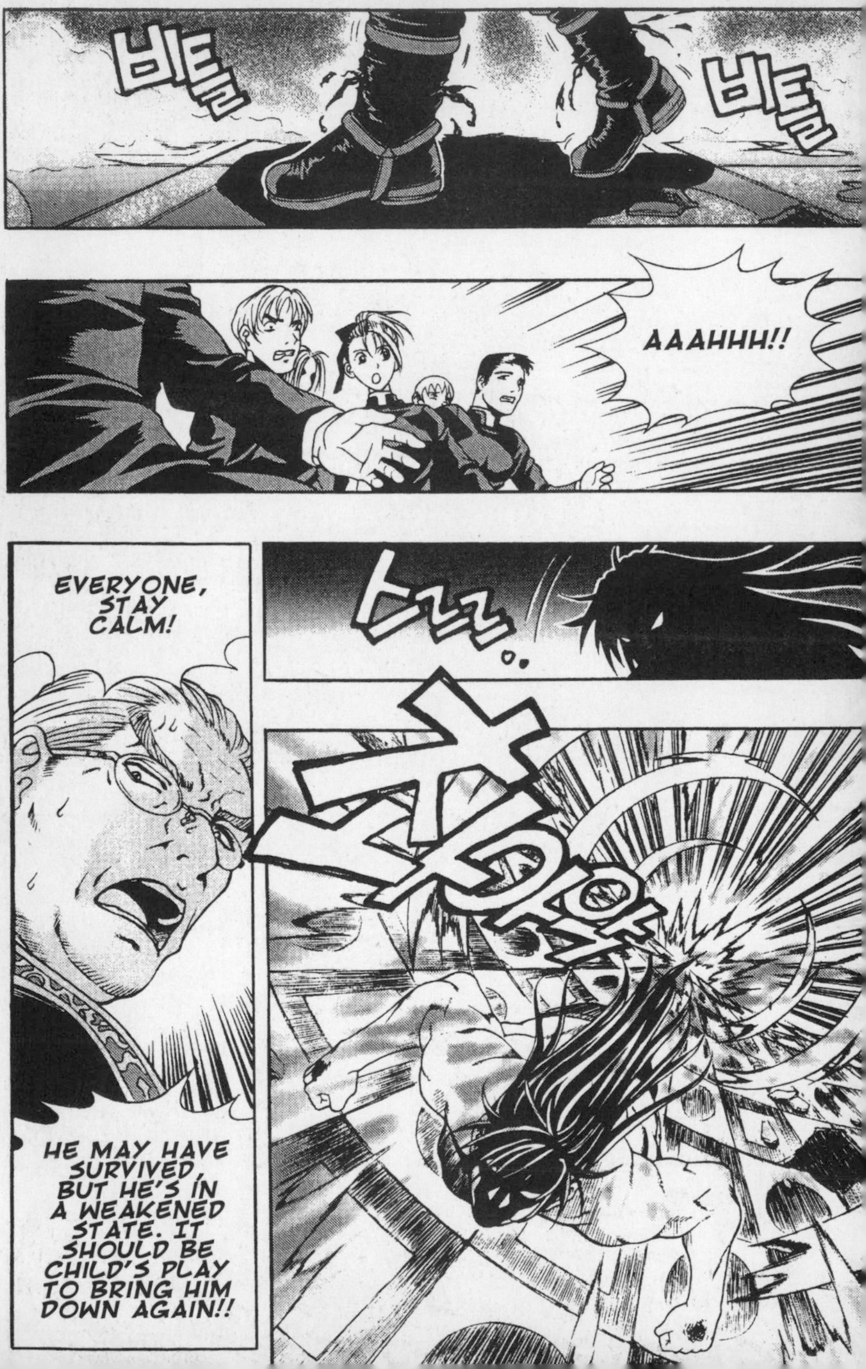
비틀
비틀
AAAHHH!!
EVERYONE, STAY CALM!
HE MAY HAVE SURVIVED, BUT HE'S IN A WEAKENED STATE. IT SHOULD BE CHILD'S PLAY TO BRING HIM DOWN AGAIN!!

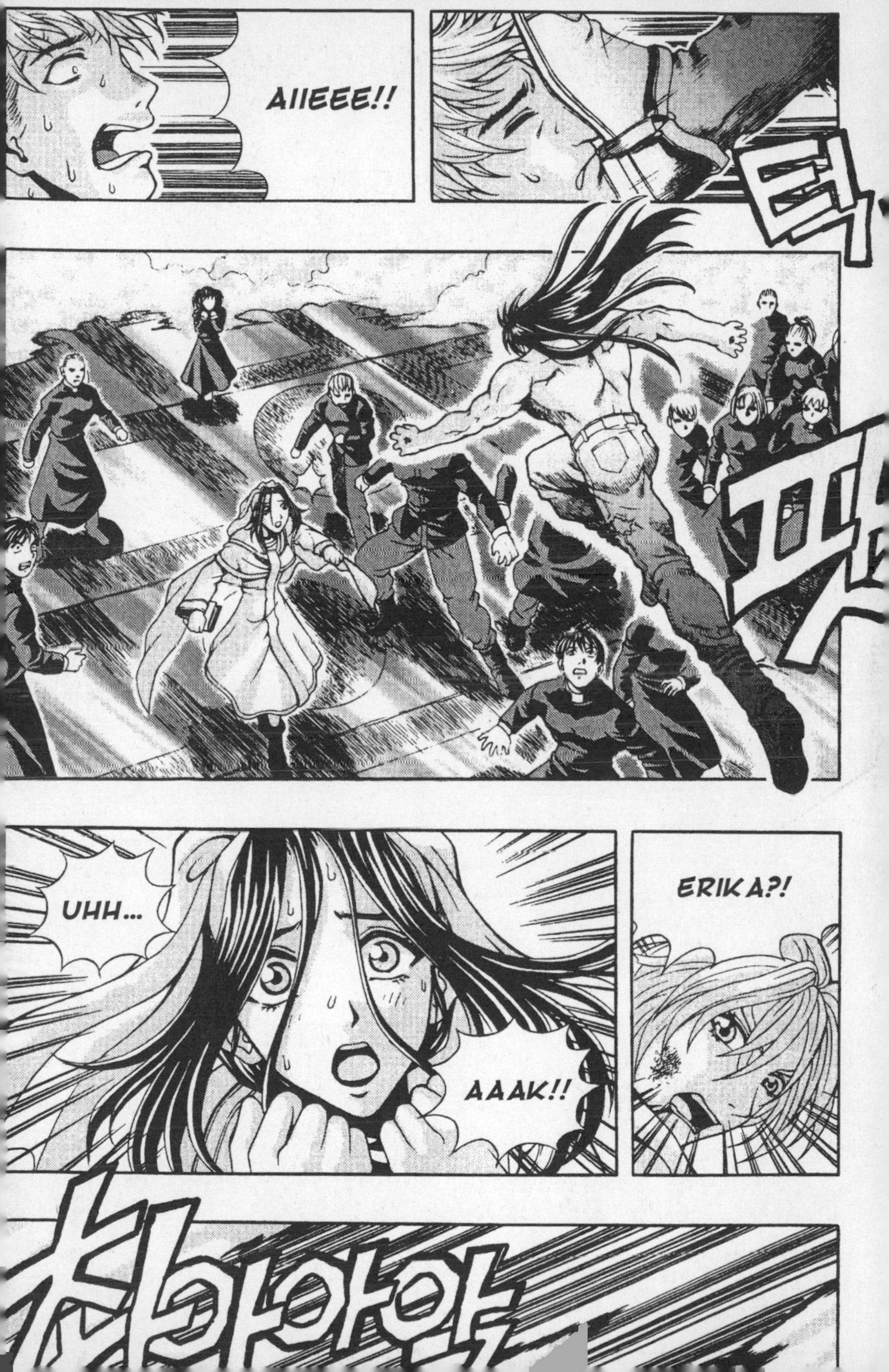
AIIEEE!!
UHH...
AAAK!!
ERIKA?!

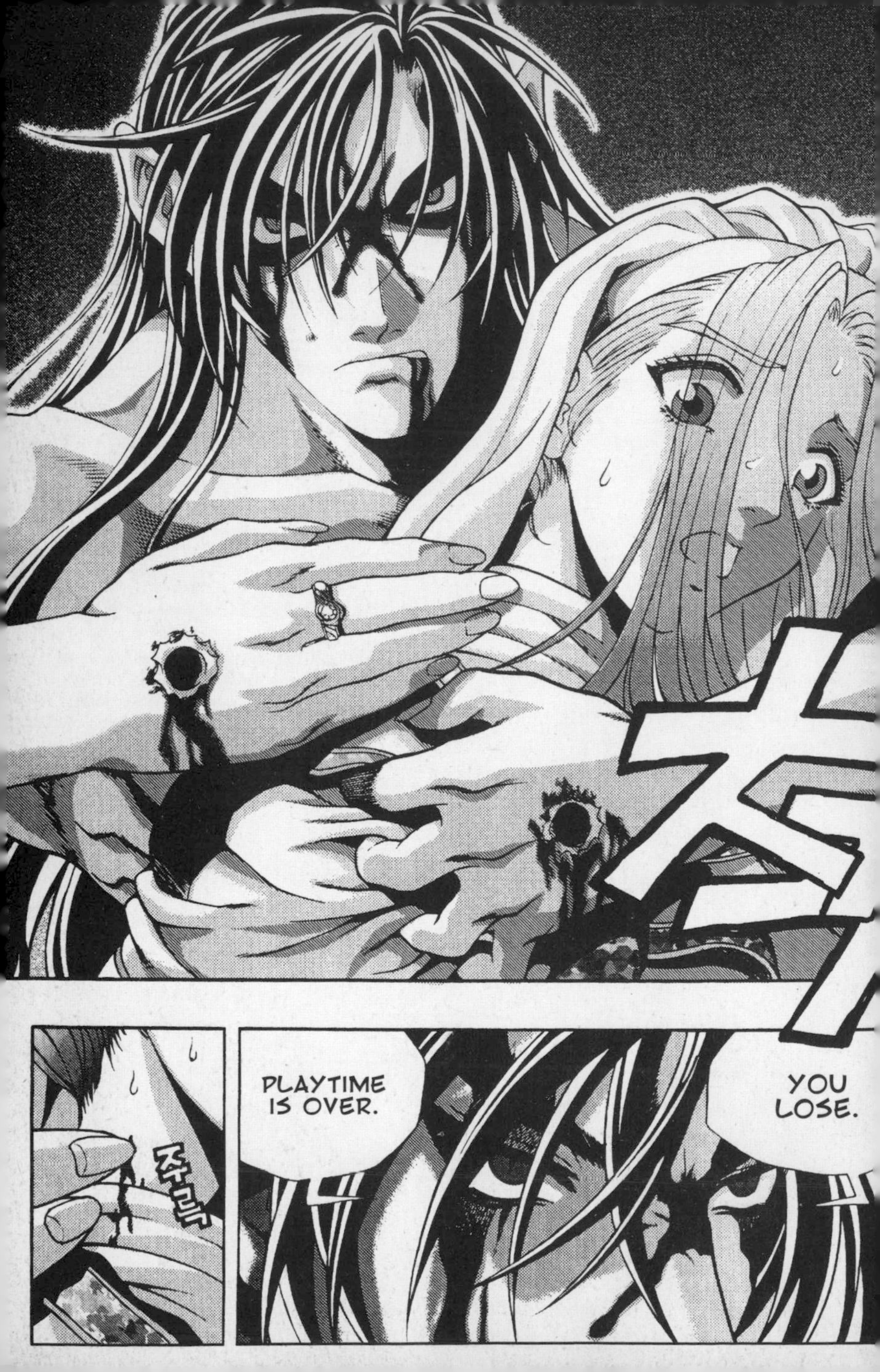
YOU LOSE.
PLAYTIME IS OVER.

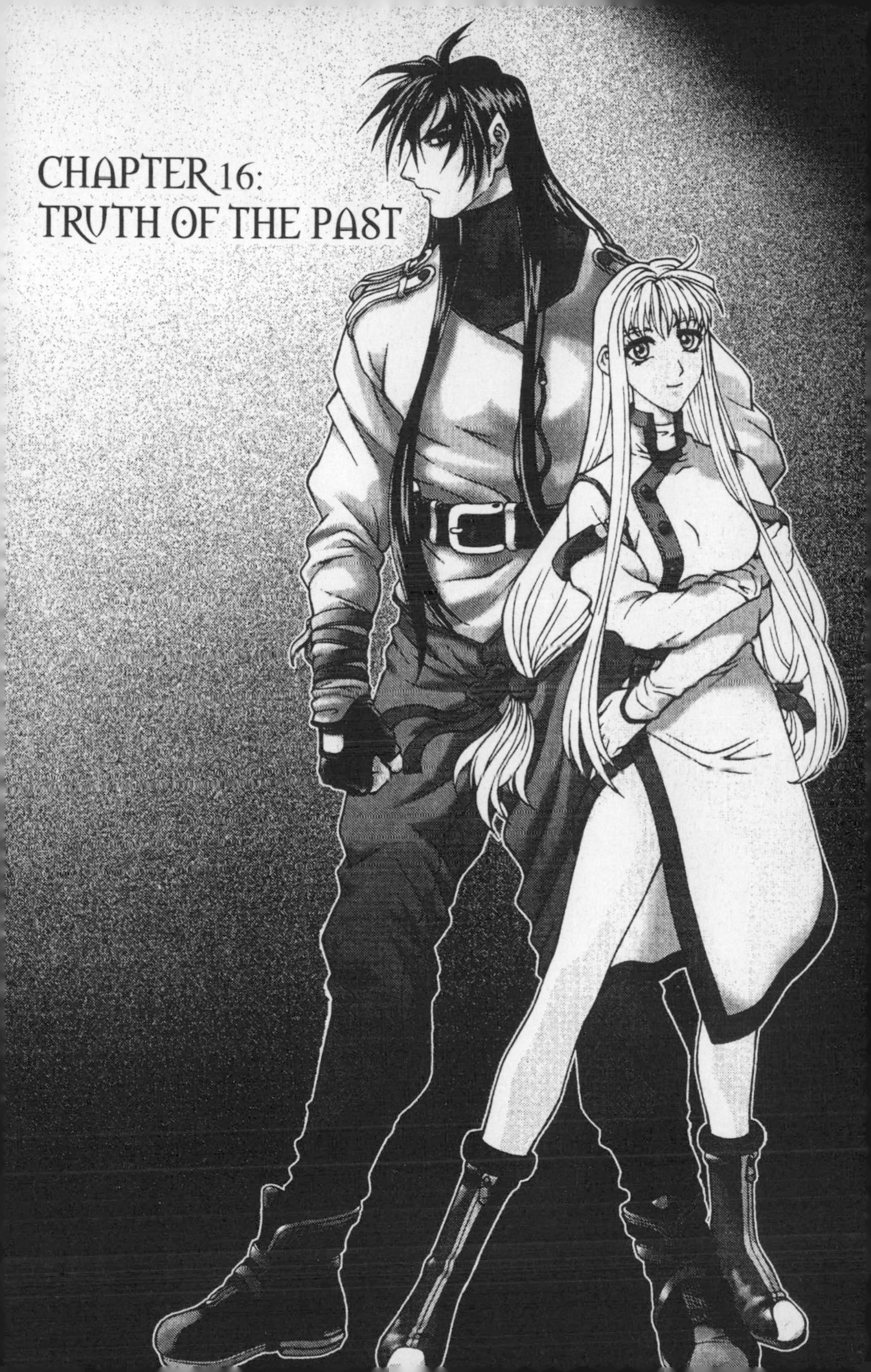
CHAPTER 16:
TRUTH OF THE PAST

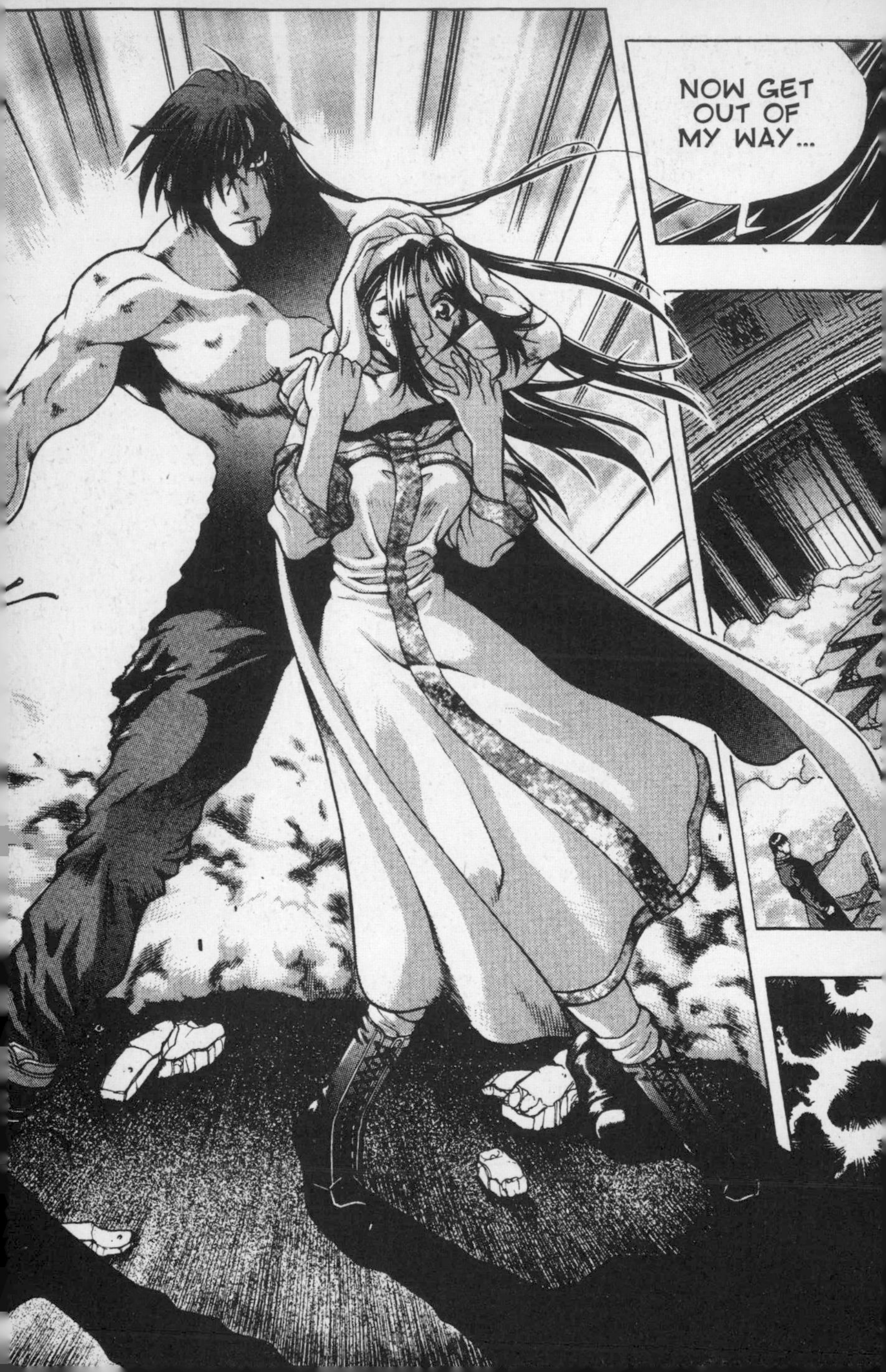
NOW GET OUT OF MY WAY...

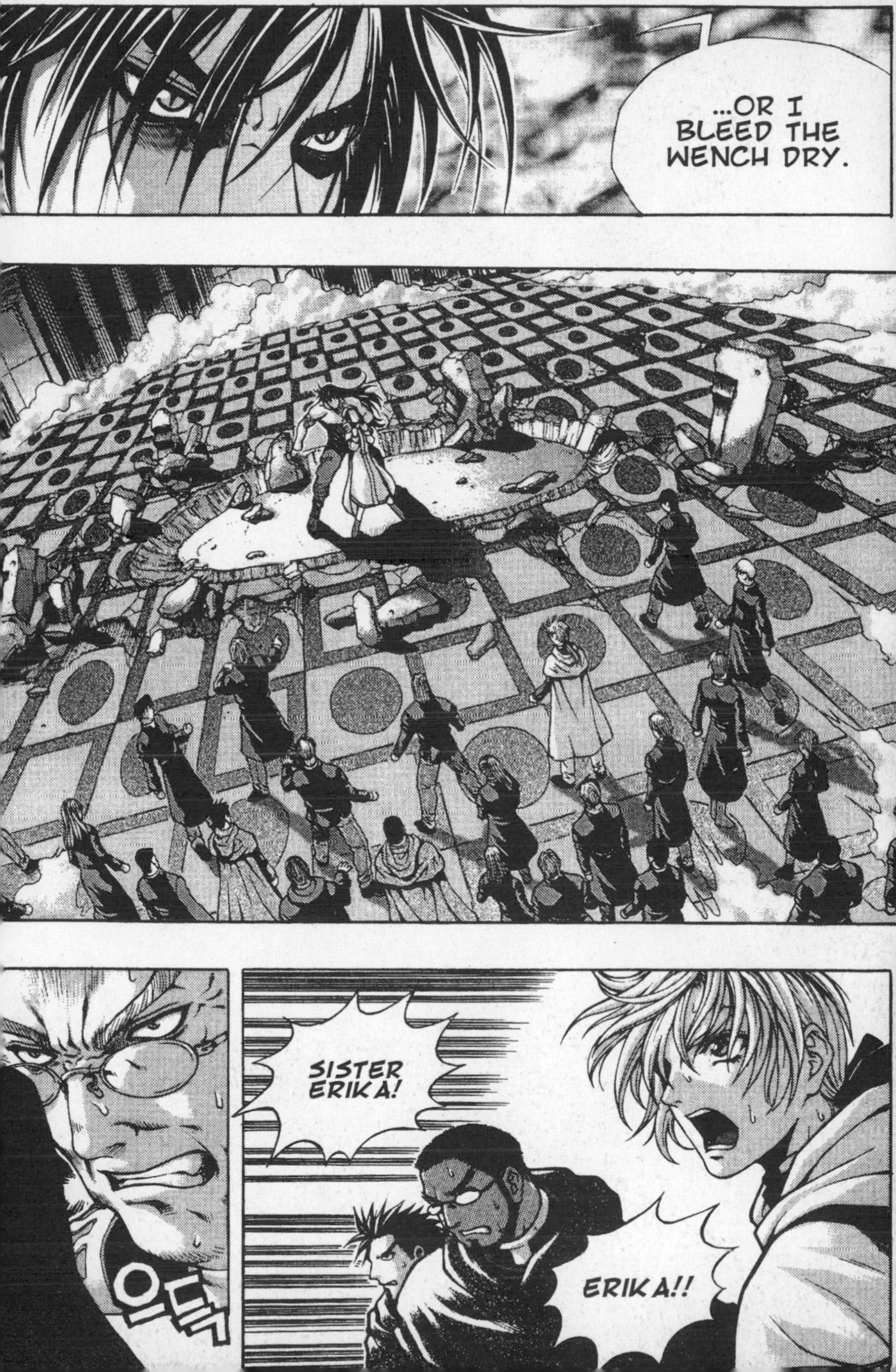
...OR I BLEED THE WENCH DRY.
SISTER ERIKA!
ERIKA!!

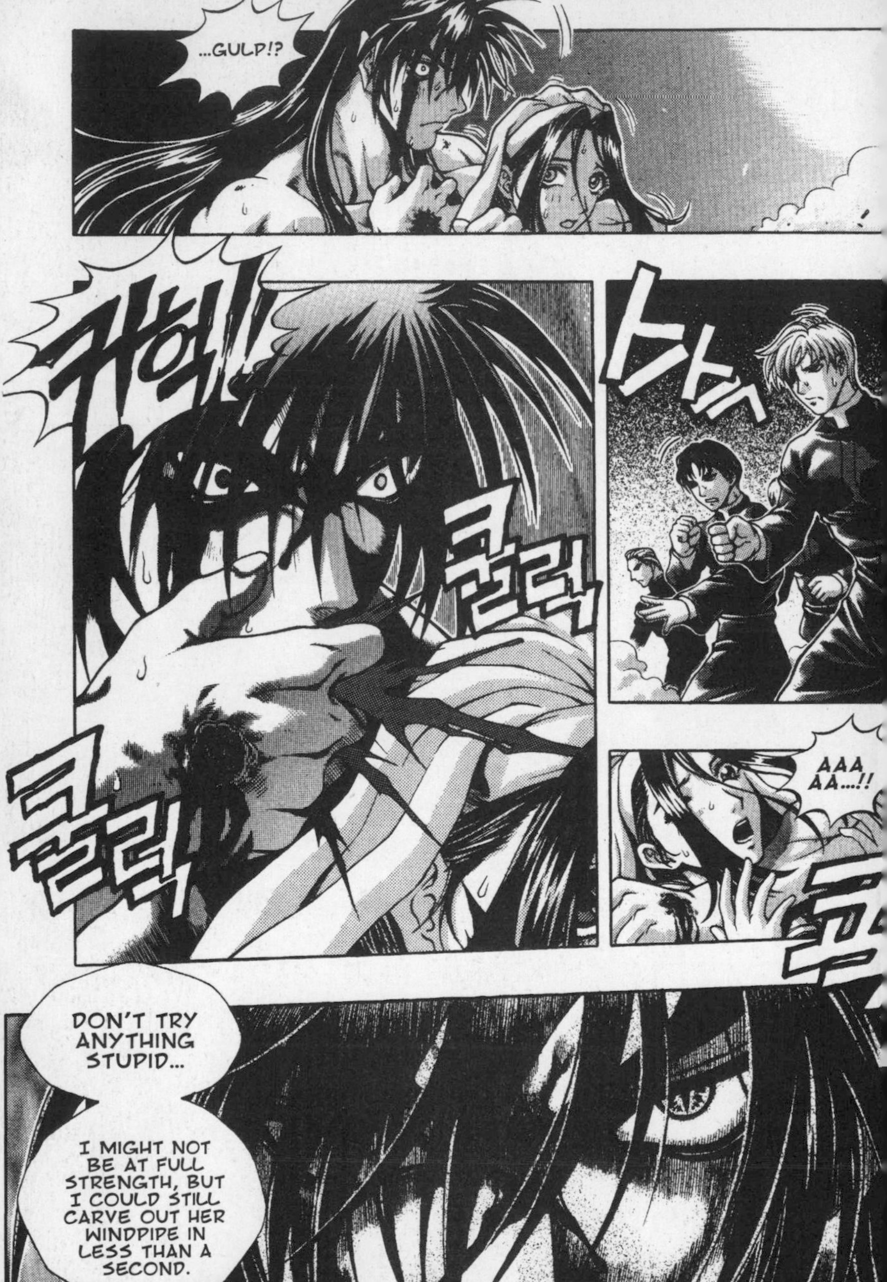
...GULP!?
AAA AA...!!
DON'T TRY ANYTHING STUPID...
I MIGHT NOT BE AT FULL STRENGTH, BUT I COULD STILL CARVE OUT HER WINDPIPE IN LESS THAN A SECOND.

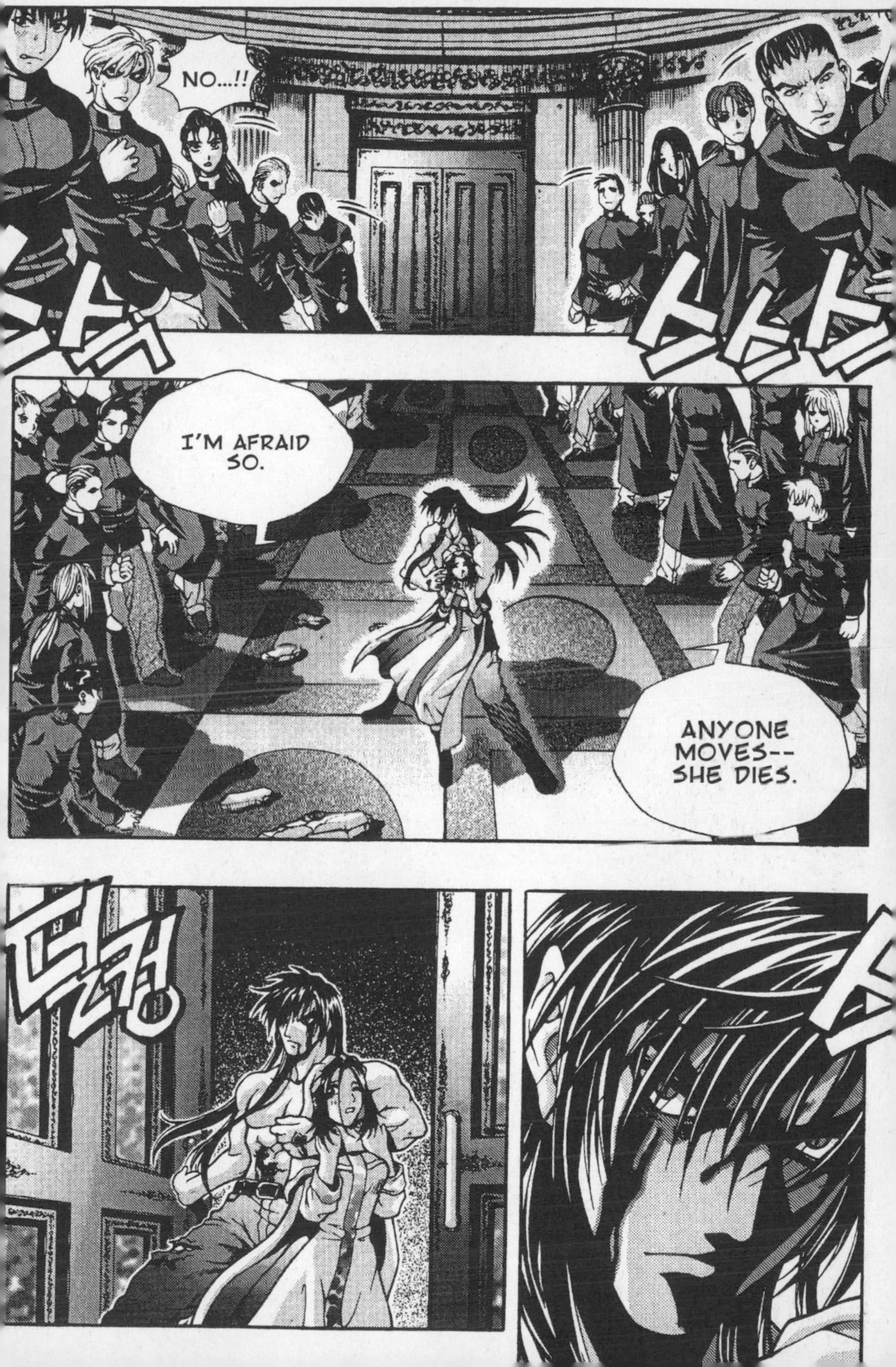
NO...!!
I'M AFRAID SO.
ANYONE MOVES-- SHE DIES.

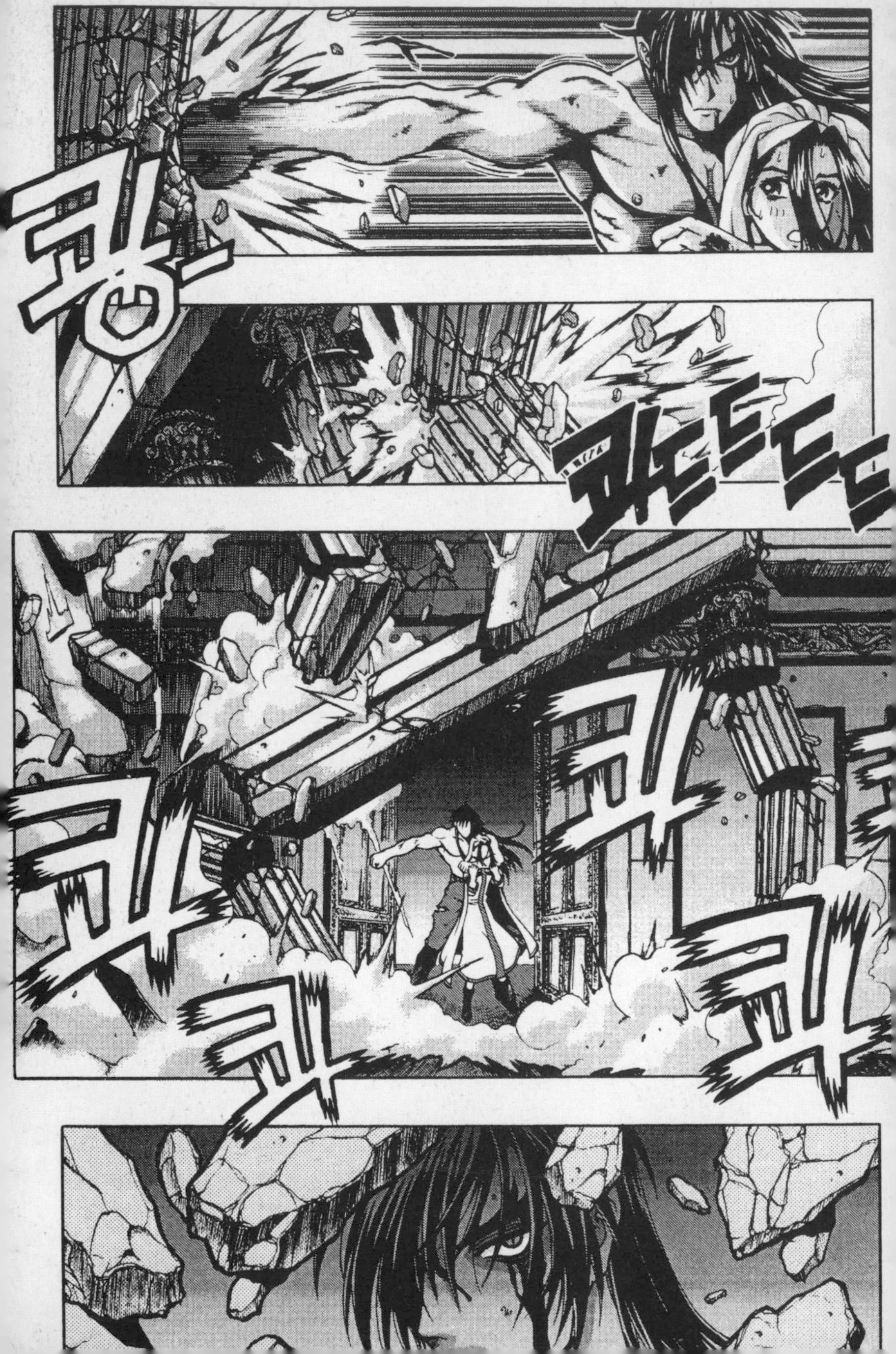
쾅
파드드드
콰
콰
콰
콰
콰

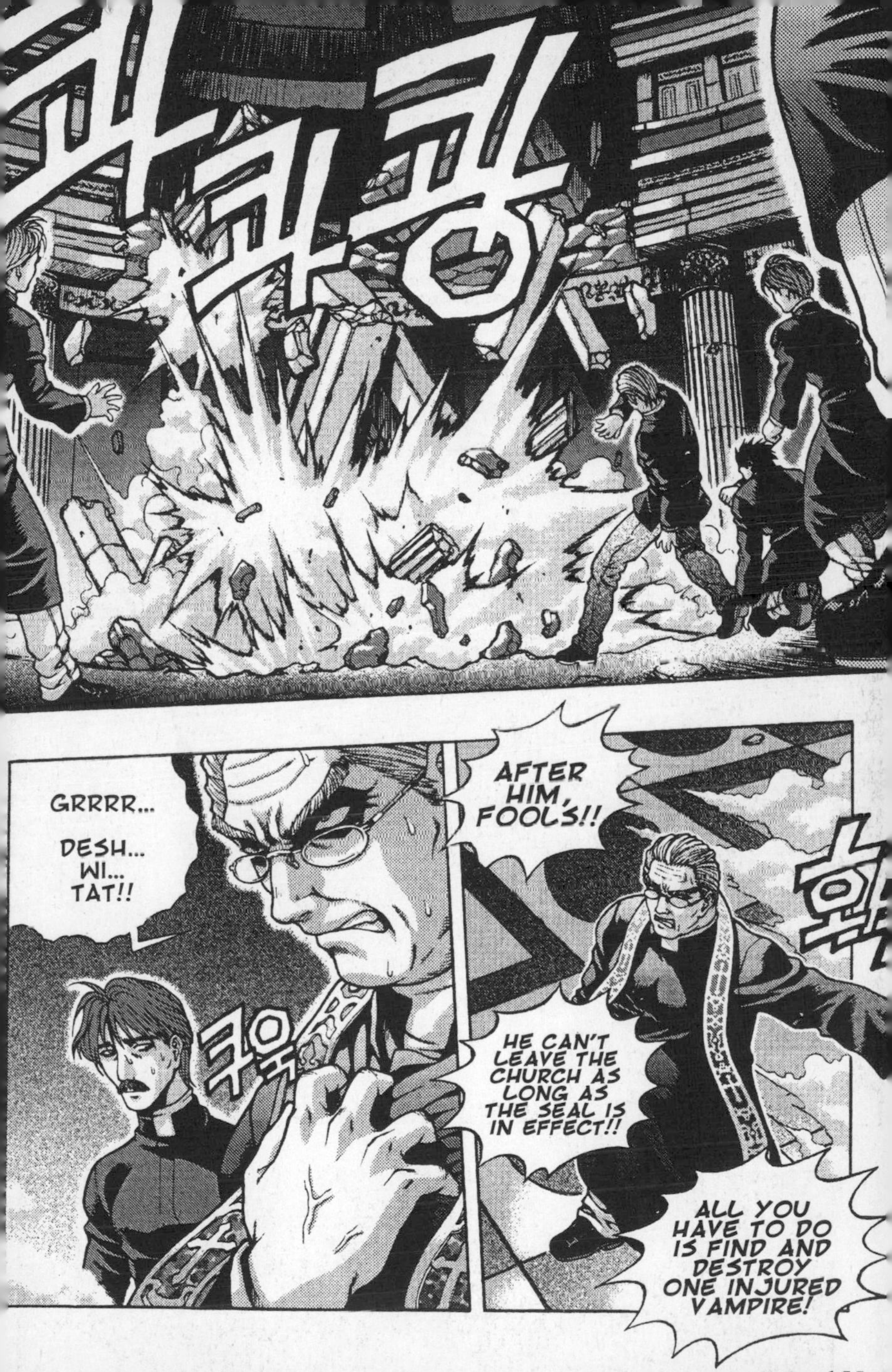
GRRRR...
DESH... WI... TAT!!
AFTER HIM, FOOLS!!
HE CAN'T LEAVE THE CHURCH AS LONG AS THE SEAL IS IN EFFECT!!
ALL YOU HAVE TO DO IS FIND AND DESTROY ONE INJURED VAMPIRE!

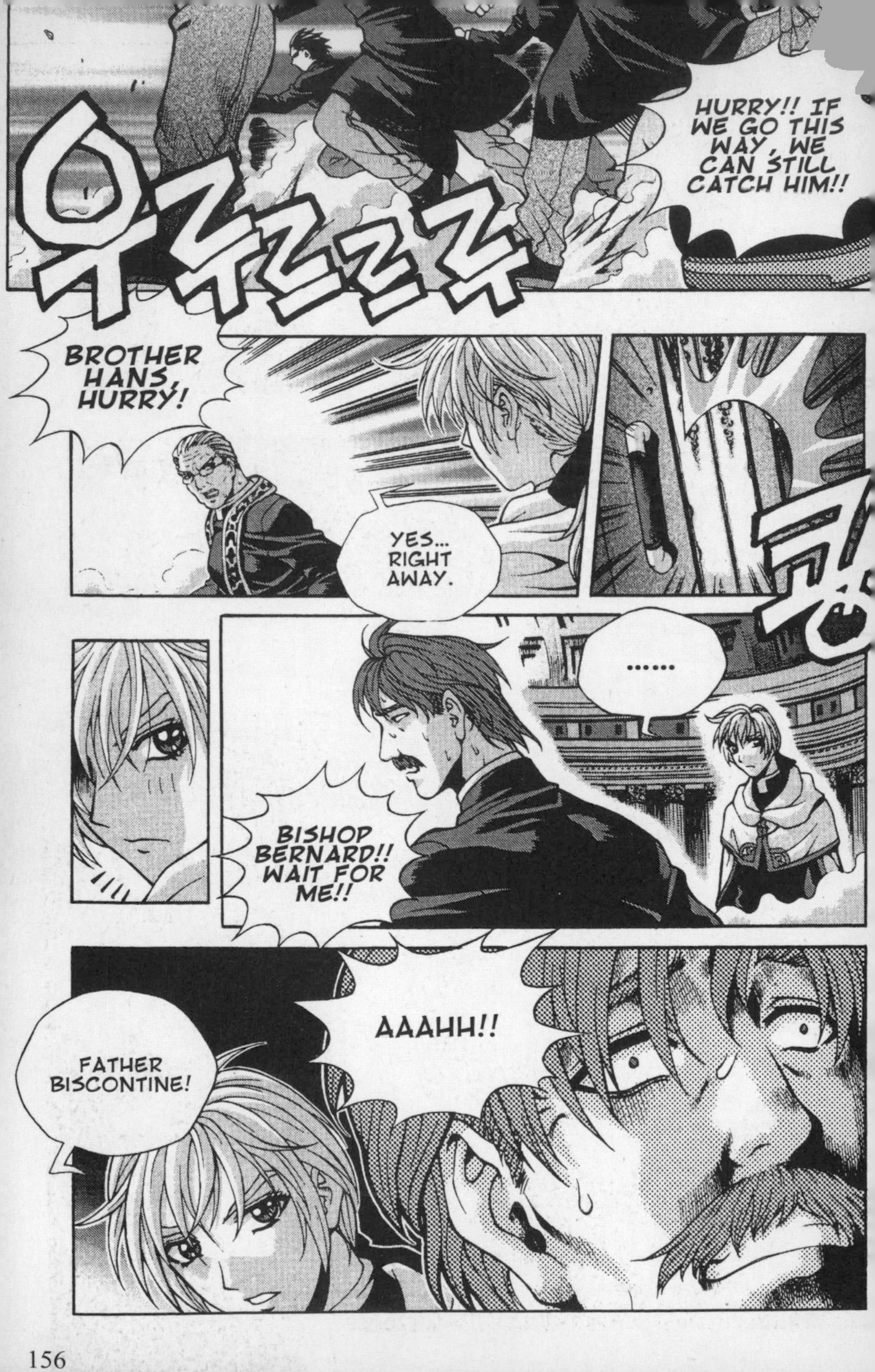
HURRY!! IF WE GO THIS WAY, WE CAN STILL CATCH HIM!!
BROTHER HANS, HURRY!
YES... RIGHT AWAY.
......
BISHOP BERNARD!! WAIT FOR ME!!
AAAHH!!
FATHER BISCONTINE!

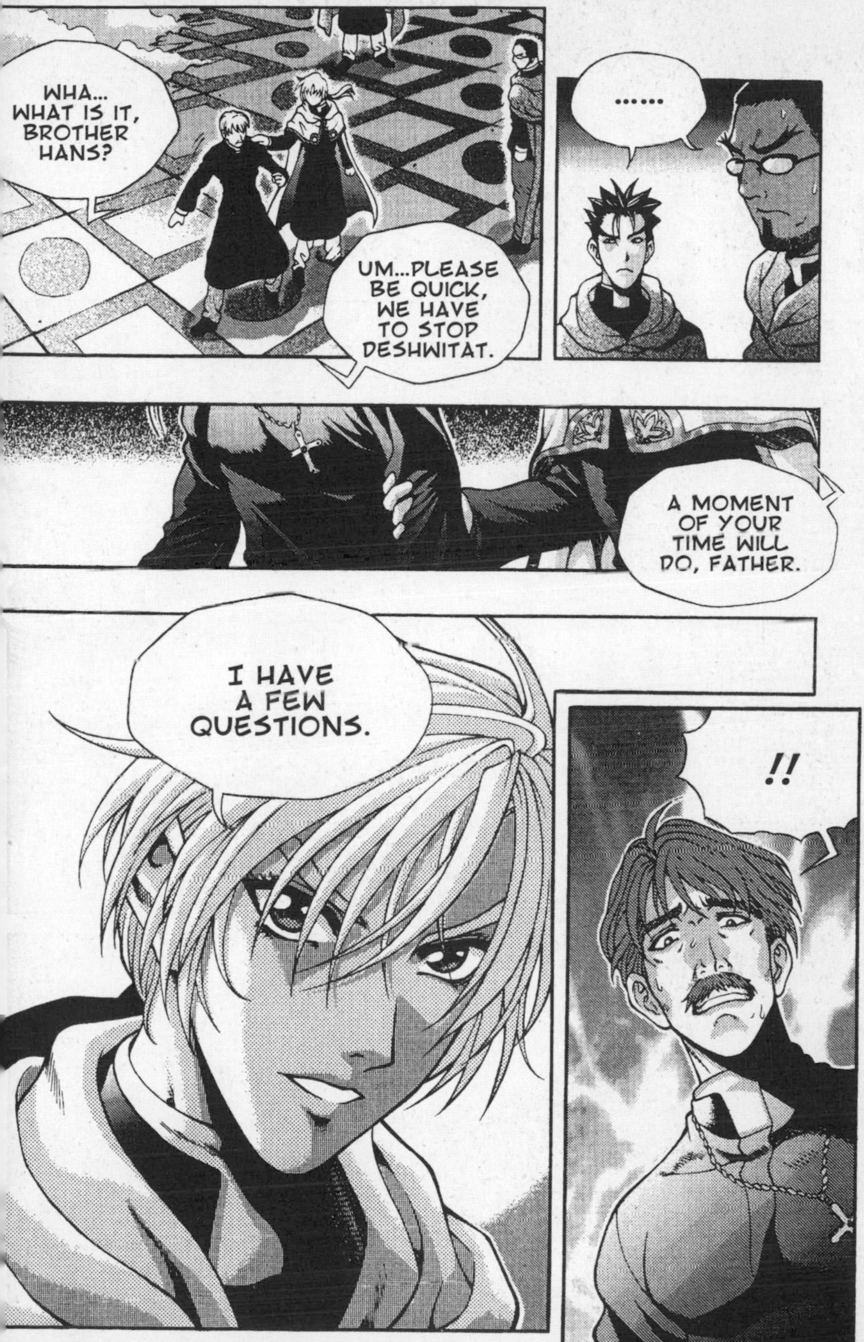
......
WHA... WHAT IS IT, BROTHER HANS?
UM...PLEASE BE QUICK, WE HAVE TO STOP DESHWITAT.
A MOMENT OF YOUR TIME WILL DO, FATHER.
I HAVE A FEW QUESTIONS.
!!

...WEIRD... THERE'S NO ONE HERE.

ALL I SEE IS A HANDFUL OF BLACK ROBES...

...I'M SO SORRY. I DIDN'T HAVE A CHANCE TO CONCENTRATE ON DESHWITAT'S ENERGY DURING THE CONFUSION OF THE BATTLE...

AND YOU, BERYUN?

I CAN'T SAY FOR SURE, BUT I DID JUST FEEL A SHIFT IN THE DARK POWERS.

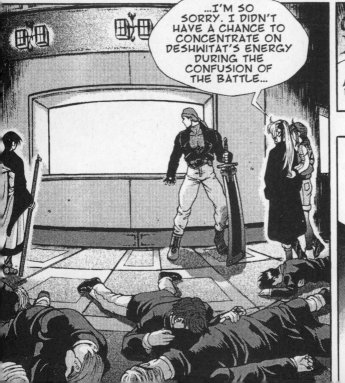

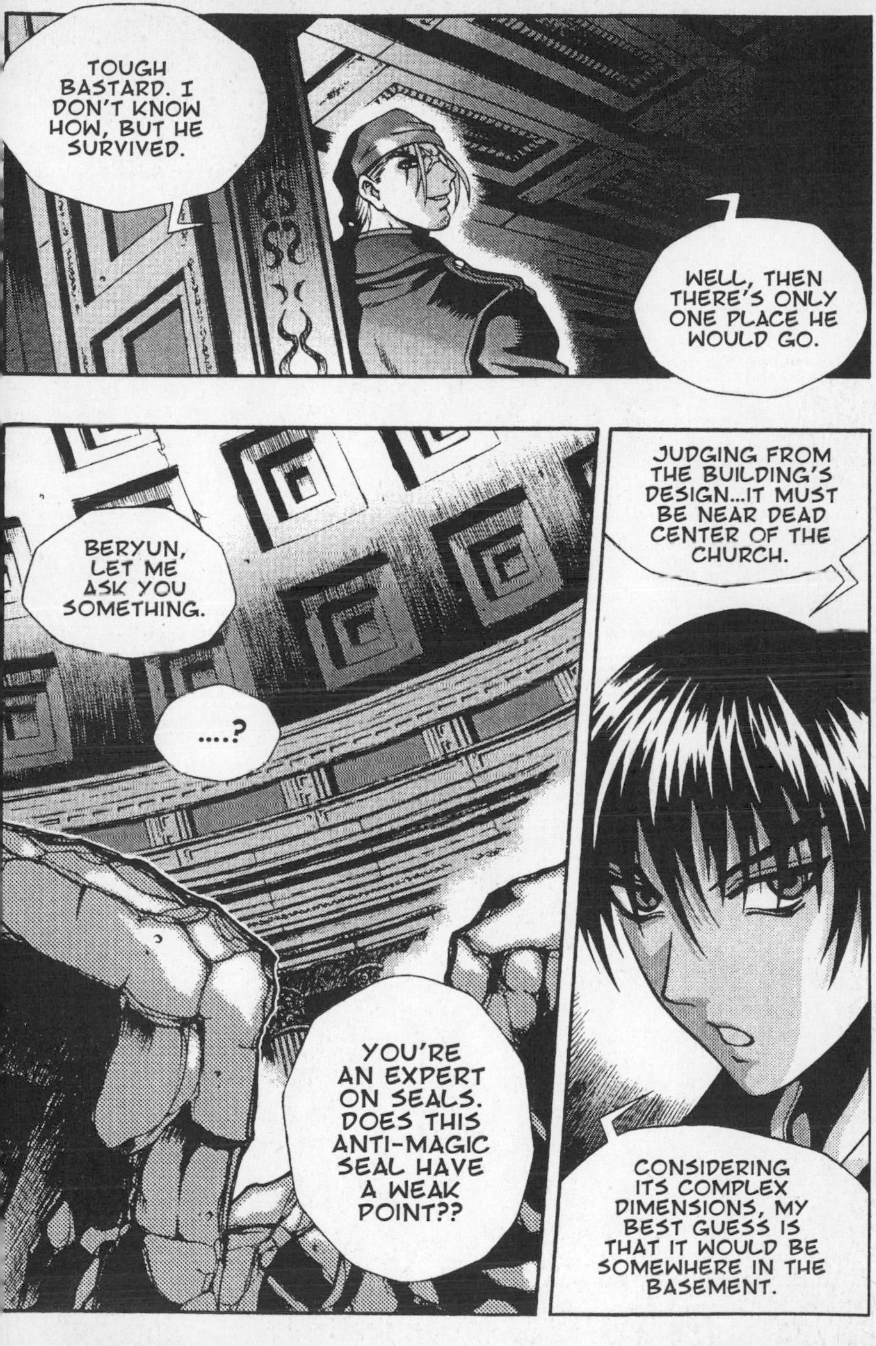
TOUGH BASTARD. I DON'T KNOW HOW, BUT HE SURVIVED.
WELL, THEN THERE'S ONLY ONE PLACE HE WOULD GO.
BERYUN, LET ME ASK YOU SOMETHING.
....?
YOU'RE AN EXPERT ON SEALS. DOES THIS ANTI-MAGIC SEAL HAVE A WEAK POINT??
JUDGING FROM THE BUILDING'S DESIGN...IT MUST BE NEAR DEAD CENTER OF THE CHURCH.
CONSIDERING ITS COMPLEX DIMENSIONS, MY BEST GUESS IS THAT IT WOULD BE SOMEWHERE IN THE BASEMENT.

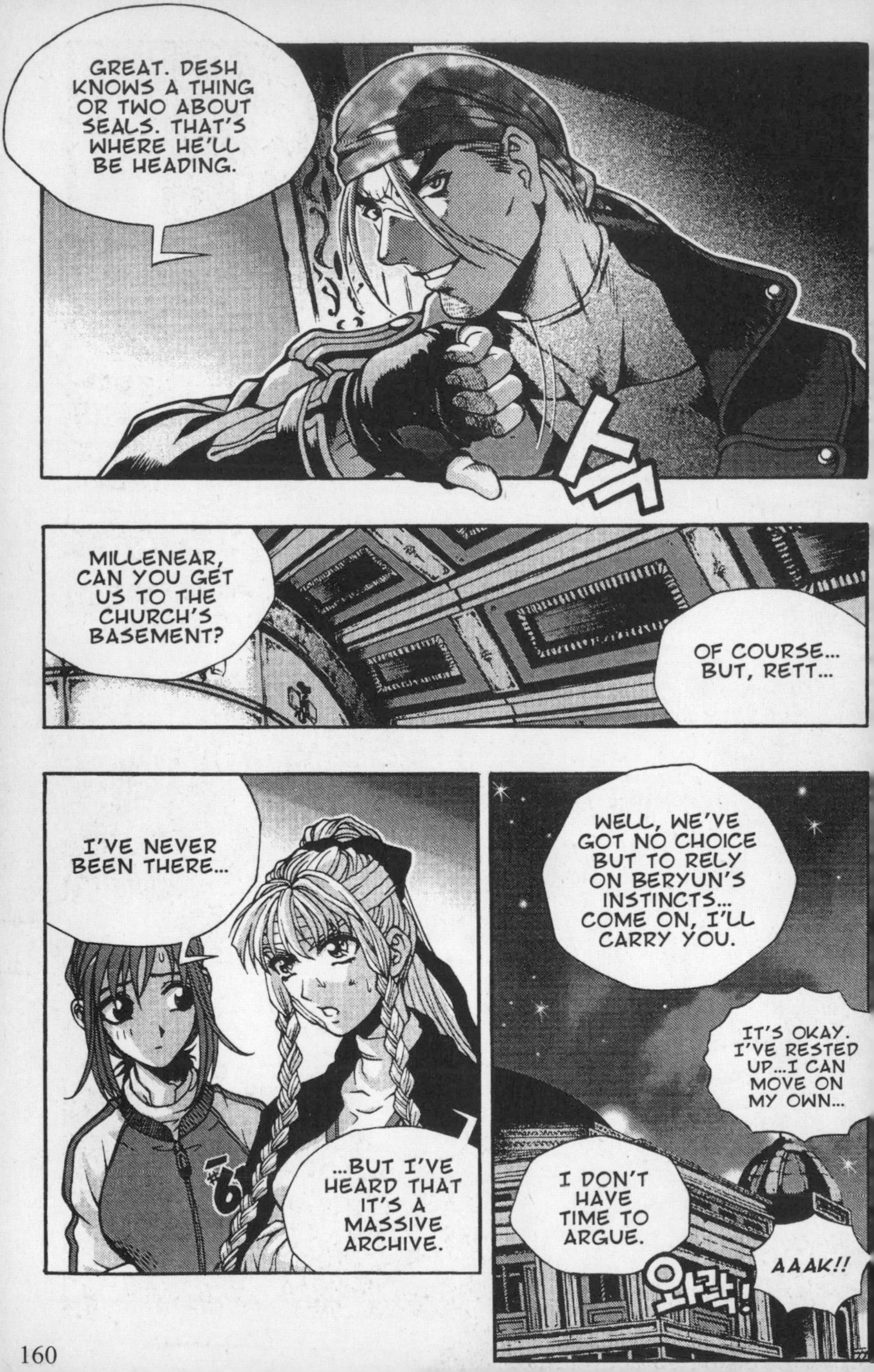
GREAT. DESH KNOWS A THING OR TWO ABOUT SEALS. THAT'S WHERE HE'LL BE HEADING.
MILLENEAR, CAN YOU GET US TO THE CHURCH'S BASEMENT?
OF COURSE... BUT, RETT...
I'VE NEVER BEEN THERE...
...BUT I'VE HEARD THAT IT'S A MASSIVE ARCHIVE.
WELL, WE'VE GOT NO CHOICE BUT TO RELY ON BERYUN'S INSTINCTS... COME ON, I'LL CARRY YOU.
IT'S OKAY. I'VE RESTED UP...I CAN MOVE ON MY OWN...
I DON'T HAVE TIME TO ARGUE.
와락!
AAAK!!

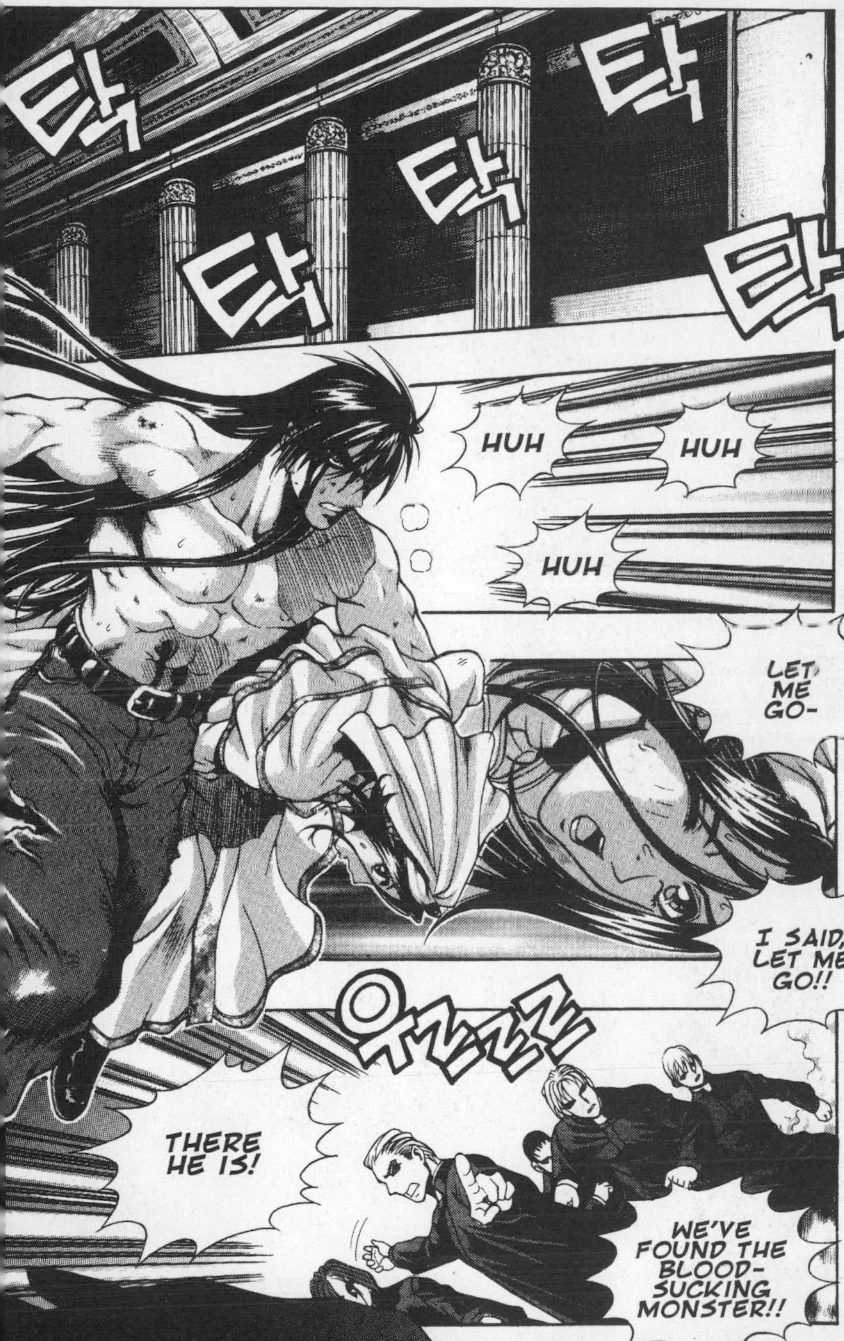
탁
탁
탁
탁
탁
HUH
HUH
HUH
LET ME GO-
I SAID, LET ME GO!!
THERE HE IS!
WE'VE FOUND THE BLOOD-SUCKING MONSTER!!

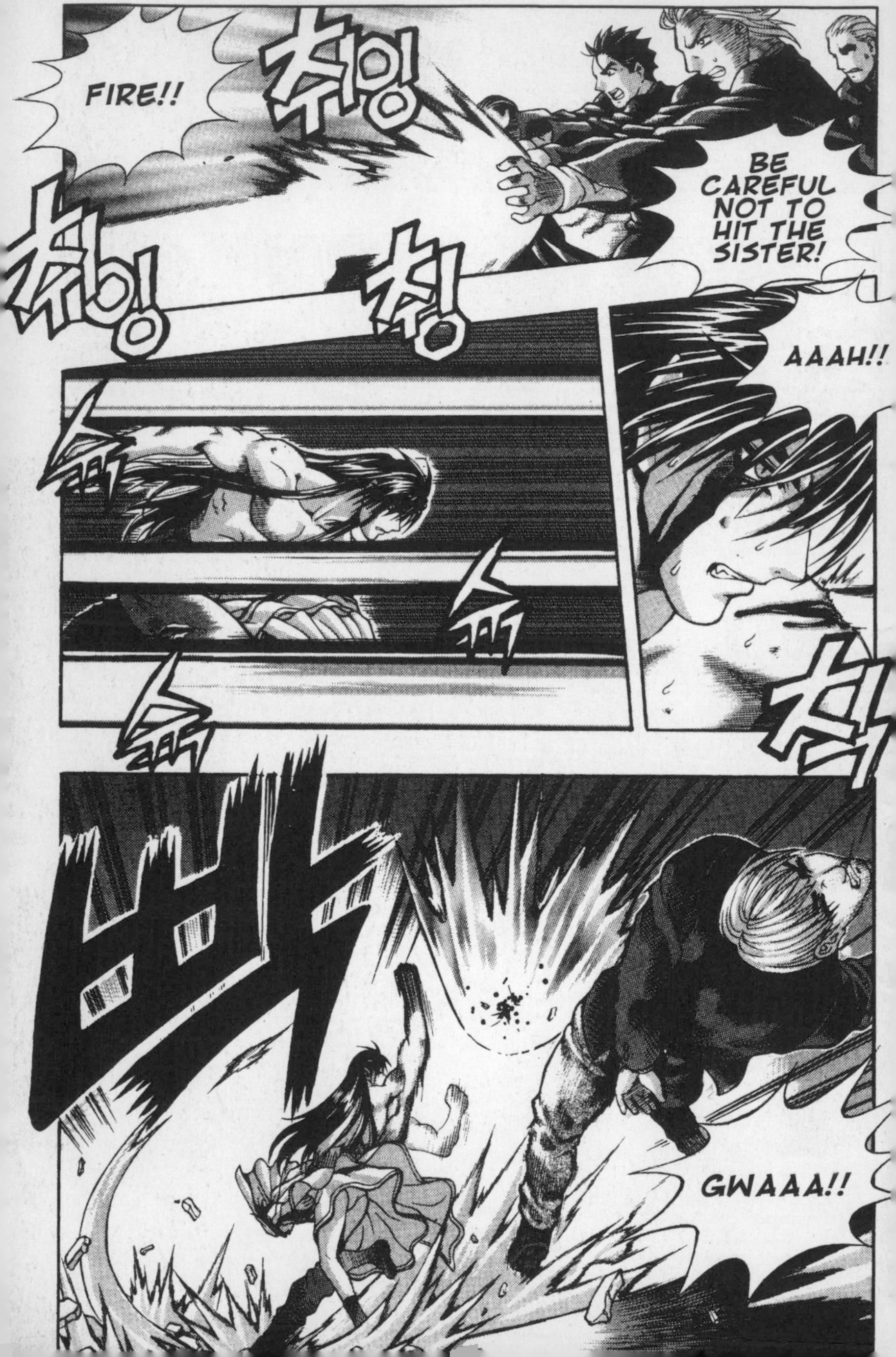
BE CAREFUL NOT TO HIT THE SISTER!
FIRE!!
AAAH!!
GWAAA!!

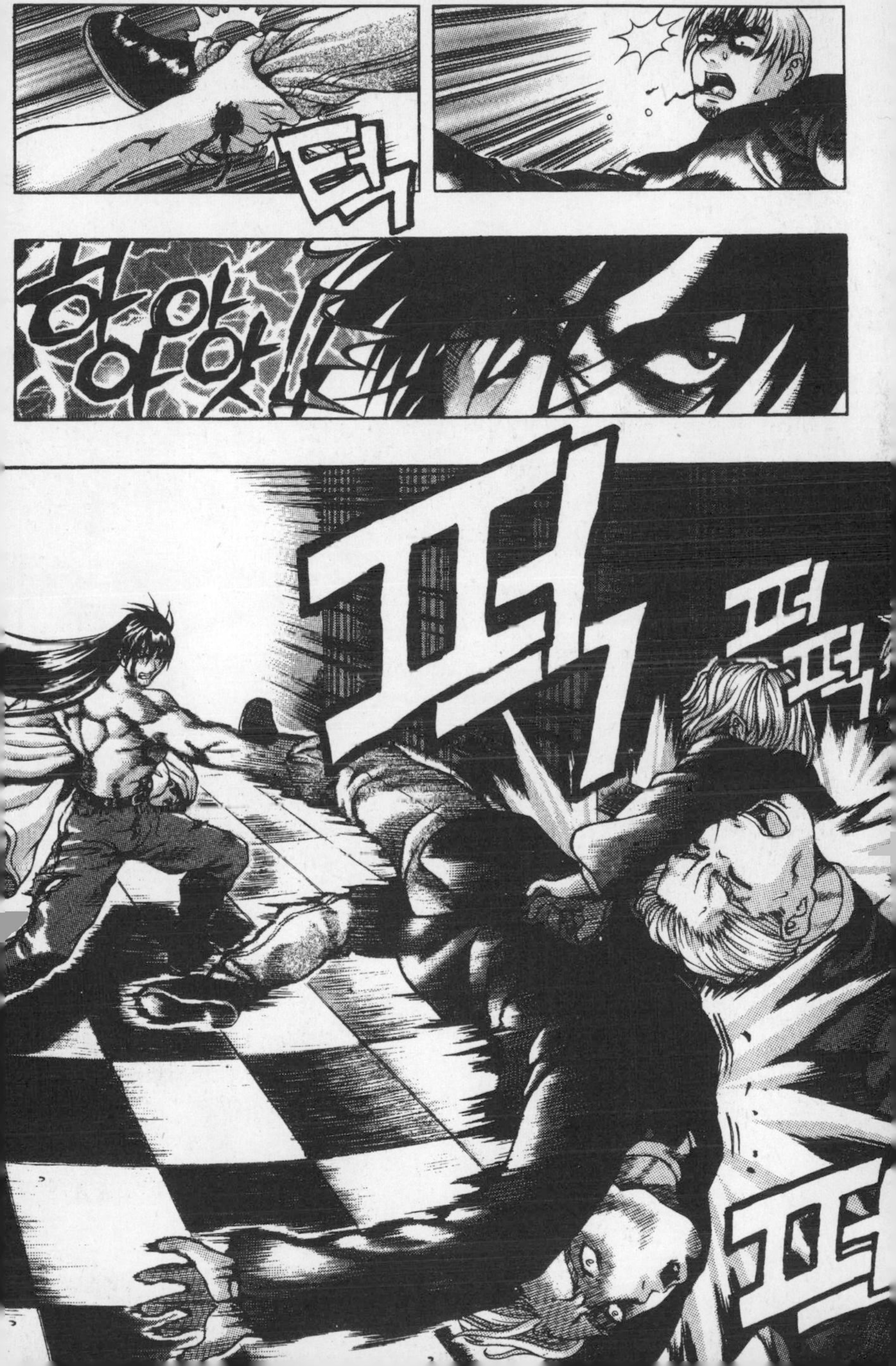
턱
하아아앗!!
퍽
퍼퍽!
퍼

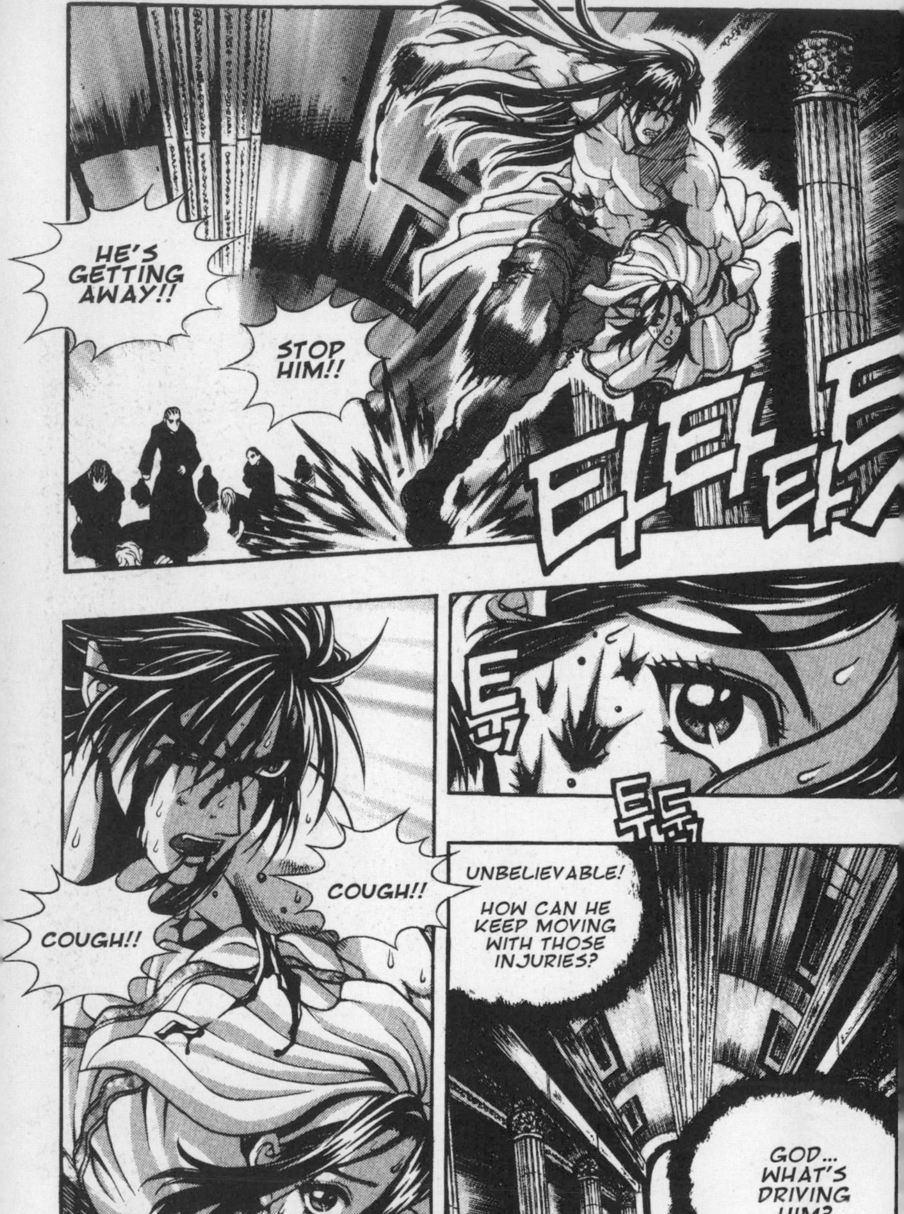
HE'S GETTING AWAY!!
STOP HIM!!
UNBELIEVABLE!
HOW CAN HE KEEP MOVING WITH THOSE INJURIES?
GOD... WHAT'S DRIVING HIM?
COUGH!!
COUGH!!

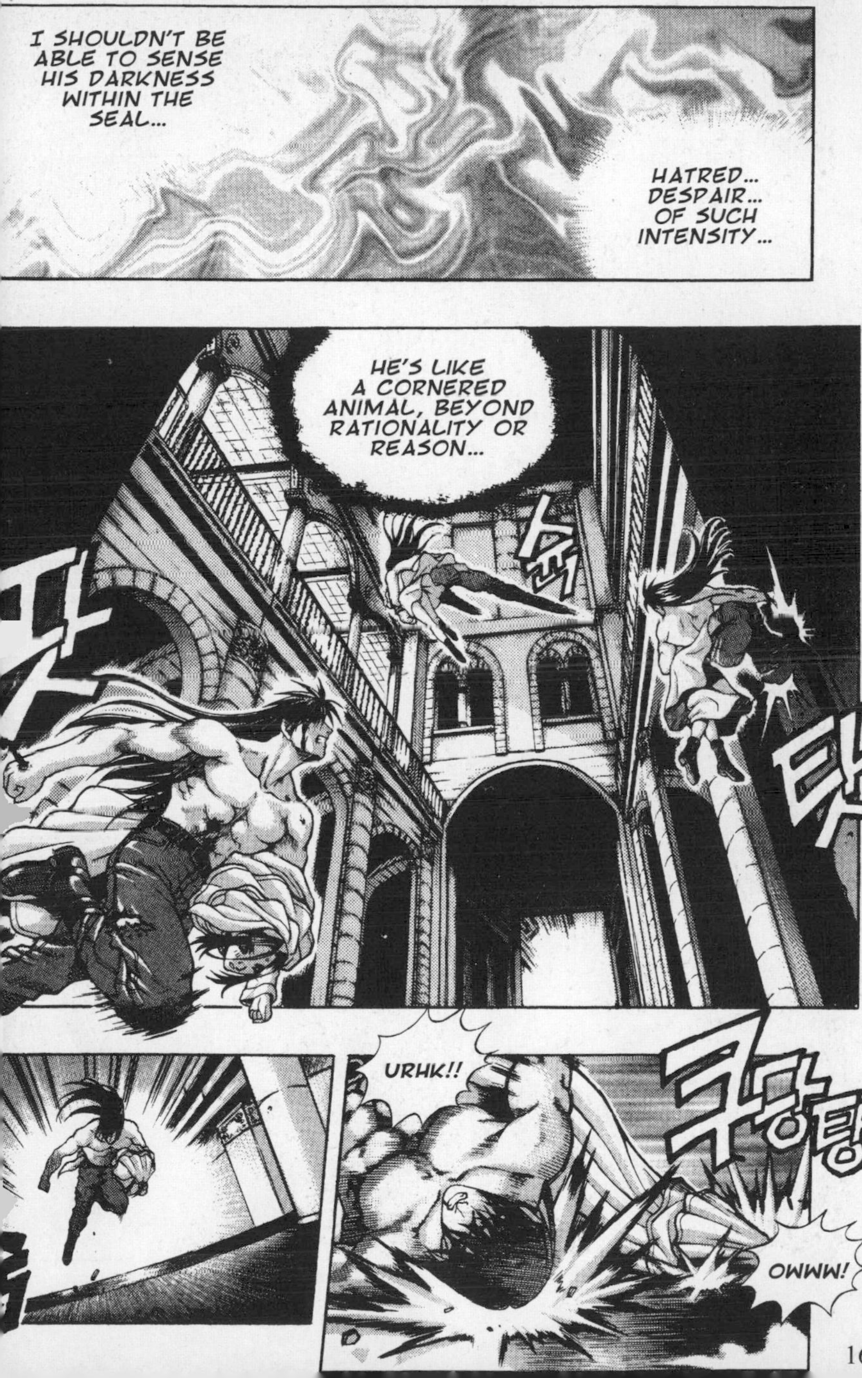
I SHOULDN'T BE ABLE TO SENSE HIS DARKNESS WITHIN THE SEAL...
HATRED... DESPAIR... OF SUCH INTENSITY...
HE'S LIKE A CORNERED ANIMAL, BEYOND RATIONALITY OR REASON...
탁
URHK!!
쿠당탕
OWWW!

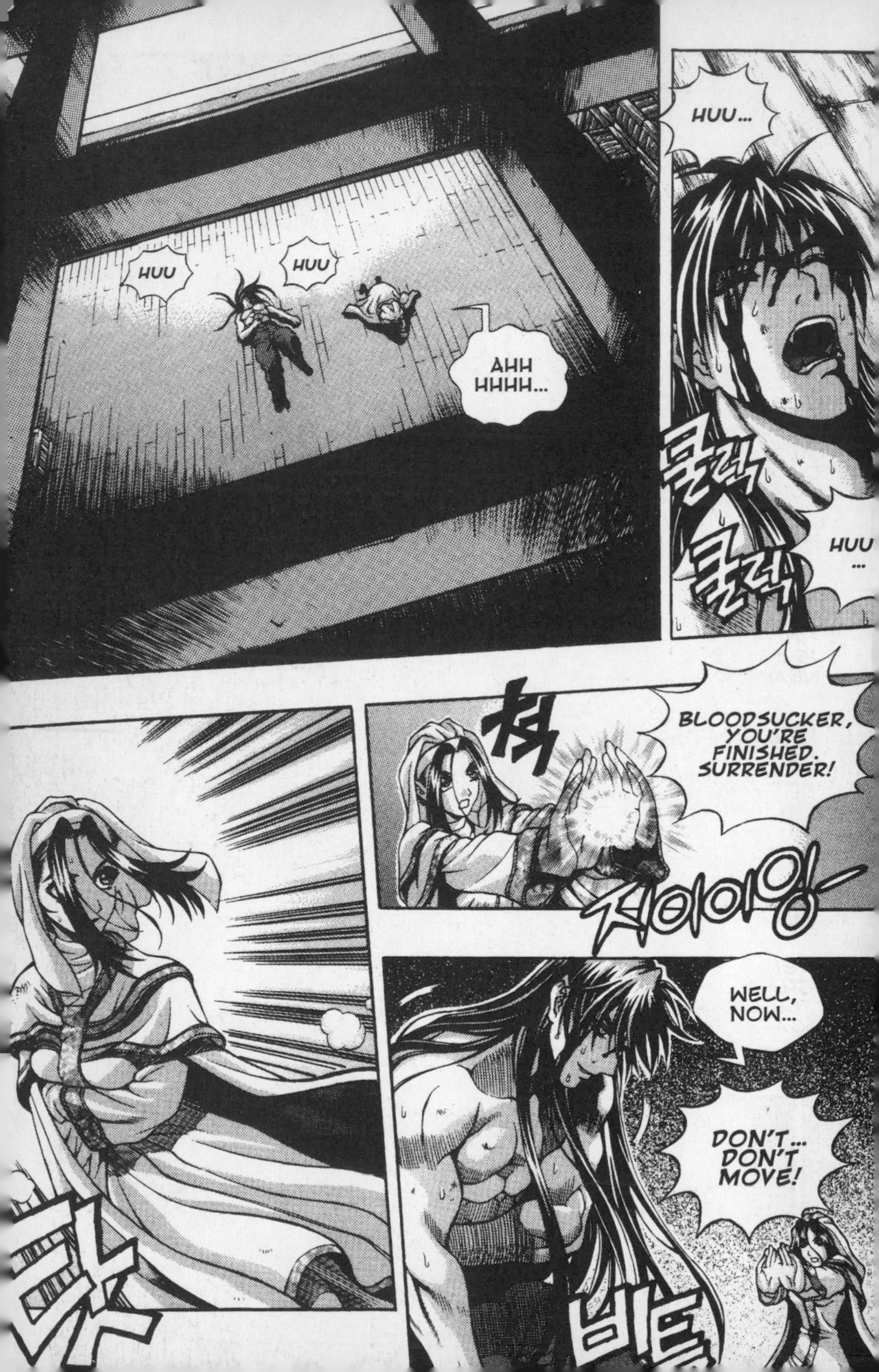
HUU
HUU
AHH HHHH...
HUU...
HUU ...
BLOODSUCKER, YOU'RE FINISHED. SURRENDER!
WELL, NOW...
DON'T... DON'T MOVE!

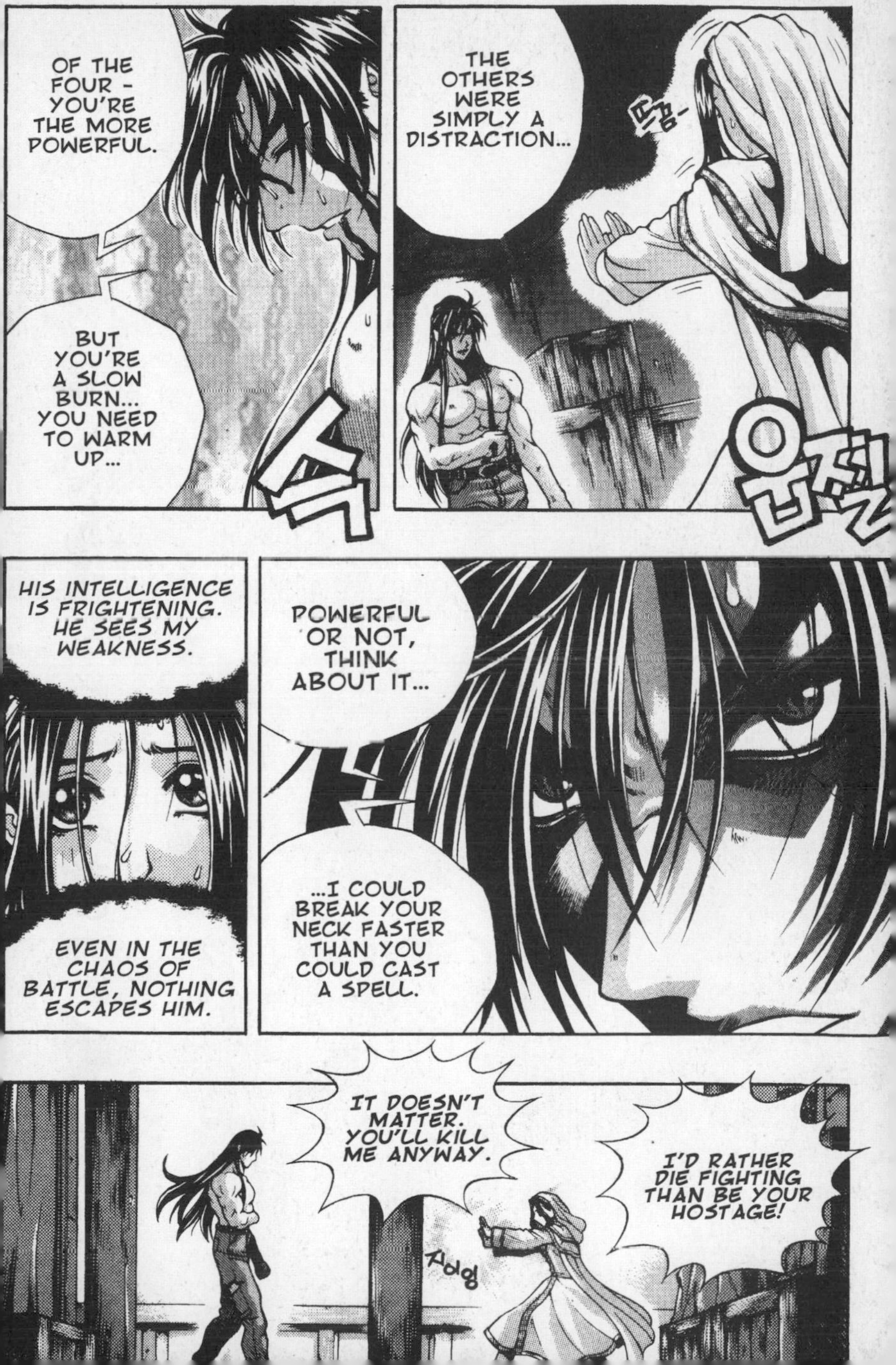
OF THE FOUR - YOU'RE THE MORE POWERFUL.
BUT YOU'RE A SLOW BURN... YOU NEED TO WARM UP...
THE OTHERS WERE SIMPLY A DISTRACTION...
HIS INTELLIGENCE IS FRIGHTENING. HE SEES MY WEAKNESS.
EVEN IN THE CHAOS OF BATTLE, NOTHING ESCAPES HIM.
POWERFUL OR NOT, THINK ABOUT IT...
...I COULD BREAK YOUR NECK FASTER THAN YOU COULD CAST A SPELL.
IT DOESN'T MATTER. YOU'LL KILL ME ANYWAY.
I'D RATHER DIE FIGHTING THAN BE YOUR HOSTAGE!

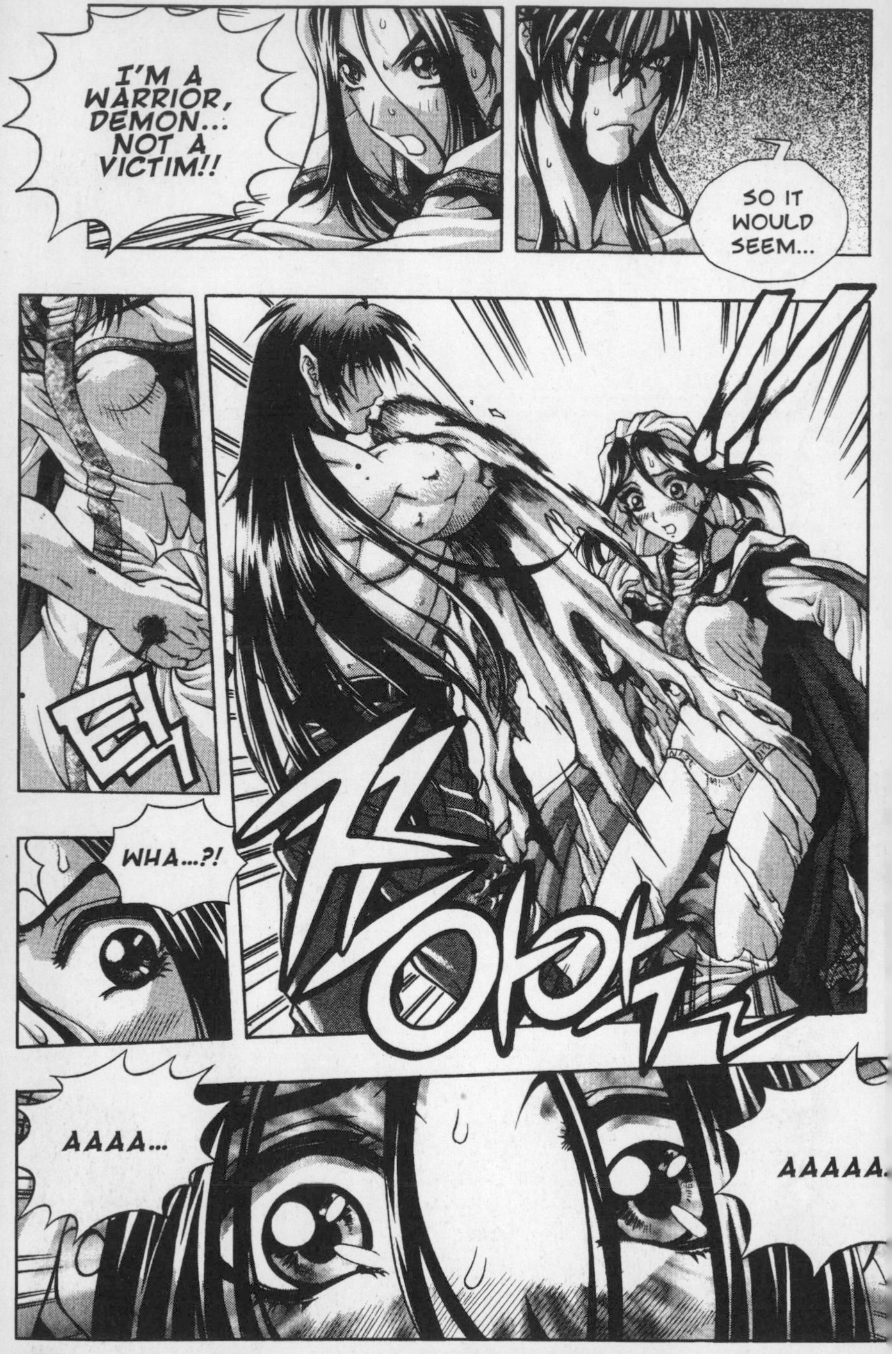
I'M A WARRIOR, DEMON... NOT A VICTIM!!
SO IT WOULD SEEM...
WHA...?!
AAAA...
AAAAA.

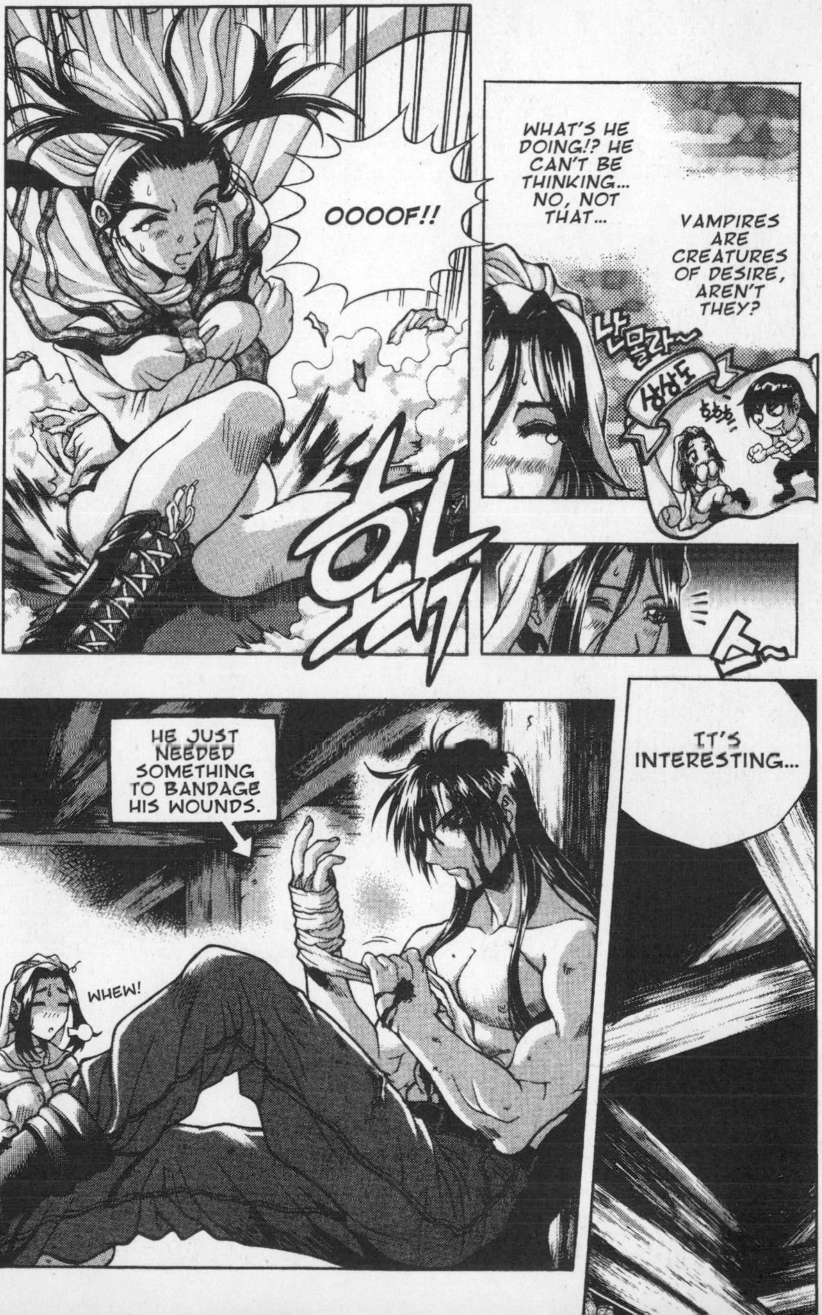
OOOOF!!
WHAT'S HE DOING!? HE CAN'T BE THINKING... NO, NOT THAT...
VAMPIRES ARE CREATURES OF DESIRE, AREN'T THEY?
난몰라~
상상도
HE JUST NEEDED SOMETHING TO BANDAGE HIS WOUNDS.
WHEW!
IT'S INTERESTING...

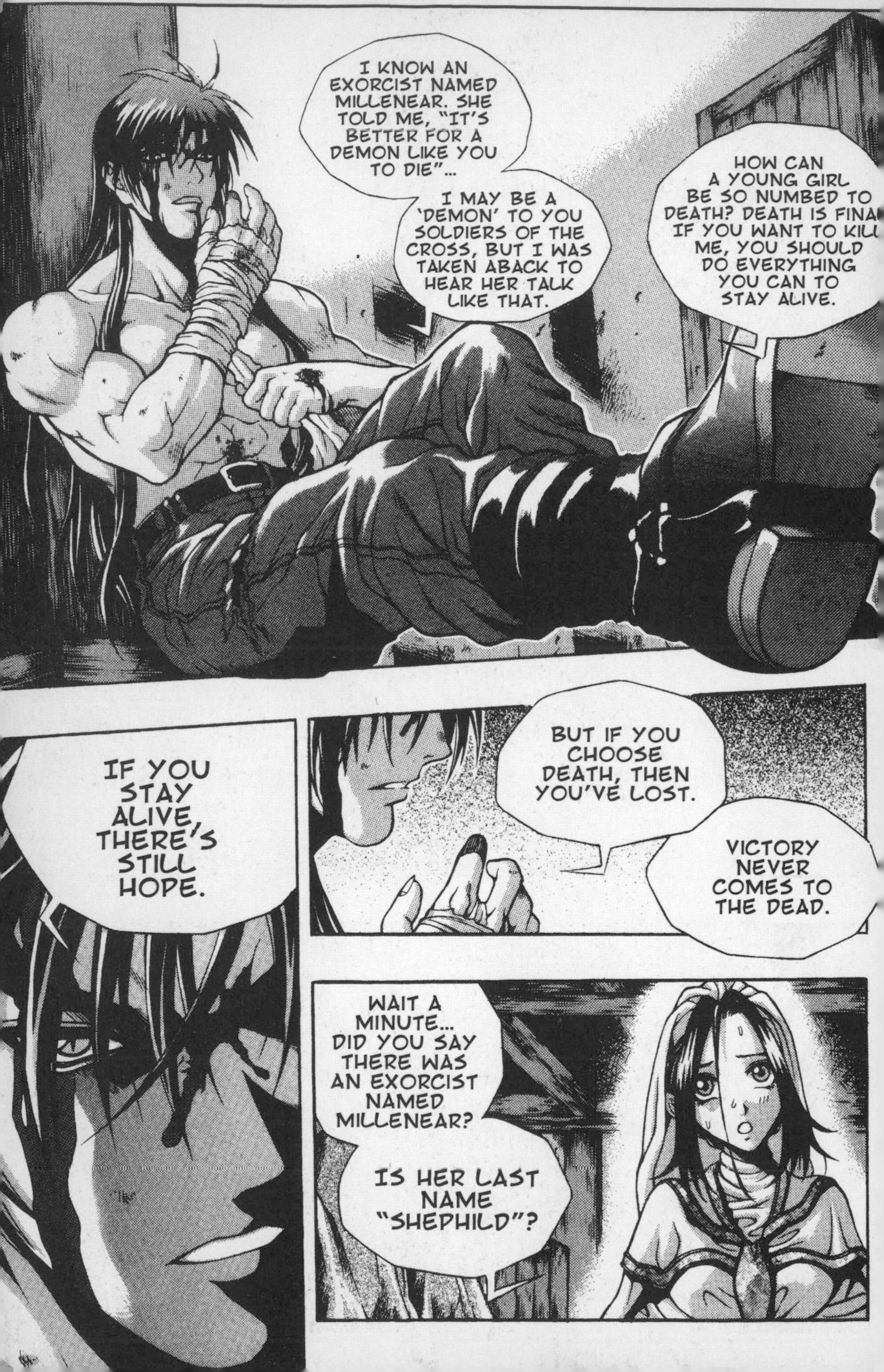
I KNOW AN EXORCIST NAMED MILLENEAR. SHE TOLD ME, "IT'S BETTER FOR A DEMON LIKE YOU TO DIE"...
I MAY BE A 'DEMON' TO YOU SOLDIERS OF THE CROSS, BUT I WAS TAKEN ABACK TO HEAR HER TALK LIKE THAT.
HOW CAN A YOUNG GIRL BE SO NUMBED TO DEATH? DEATH IS FINA IF YOU WANT TO KILL ME, YOU SHOULD DO EVERYTHING YOU CAN TO STAY ALIVE.
IF YOU STAY ALIVE, THERE'S STILL HOPE.
BUT IF YOU CHOOSE DEATH, THEN YOU'VE LOST.
VICTORY NEVER COMES TO THE DEAD.
WAIT A MINUTE... DID YOU SAY THERE WAS AN EXORCIST NAMED MILLENEAR?
IS HER LAST NAME "SHEPHILD"?

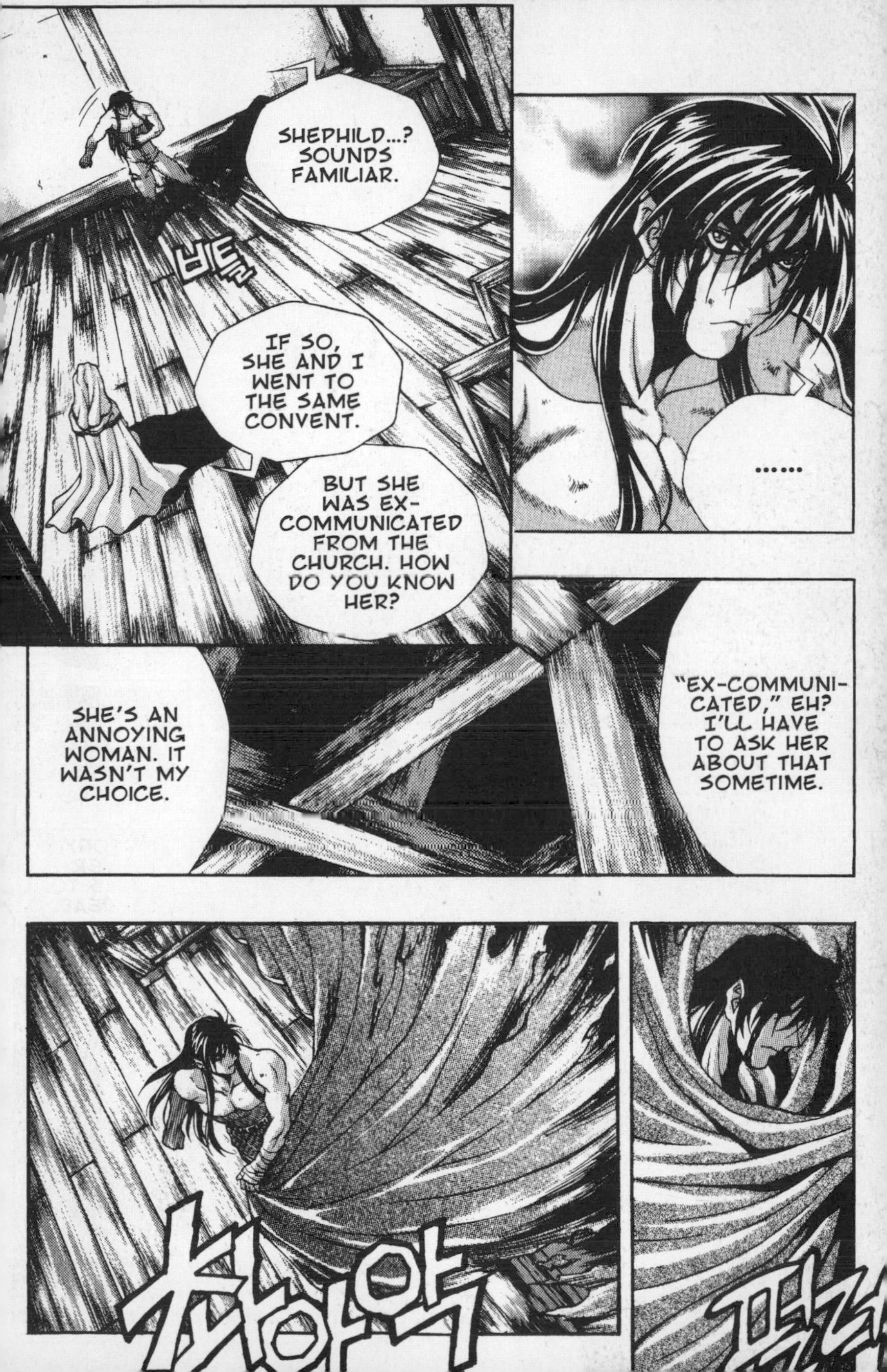
SHEPHILD...? SOUNDS FAMILIAR.
IF SO, SHE AND I WENT TO THE SAME CONVENT.
BUT SHE WAS EX-COMMUNICATED FROM THE CHURCH. HOW DO YOU KNOW HER?
......
SHE'S AN ANNOYING WOMAN. IT WASN'T MY CHOICE.
"EX-COMMUNICATED," EH? I'LL HAVE TO ASK HER ABOUT THAT SOMETIME.

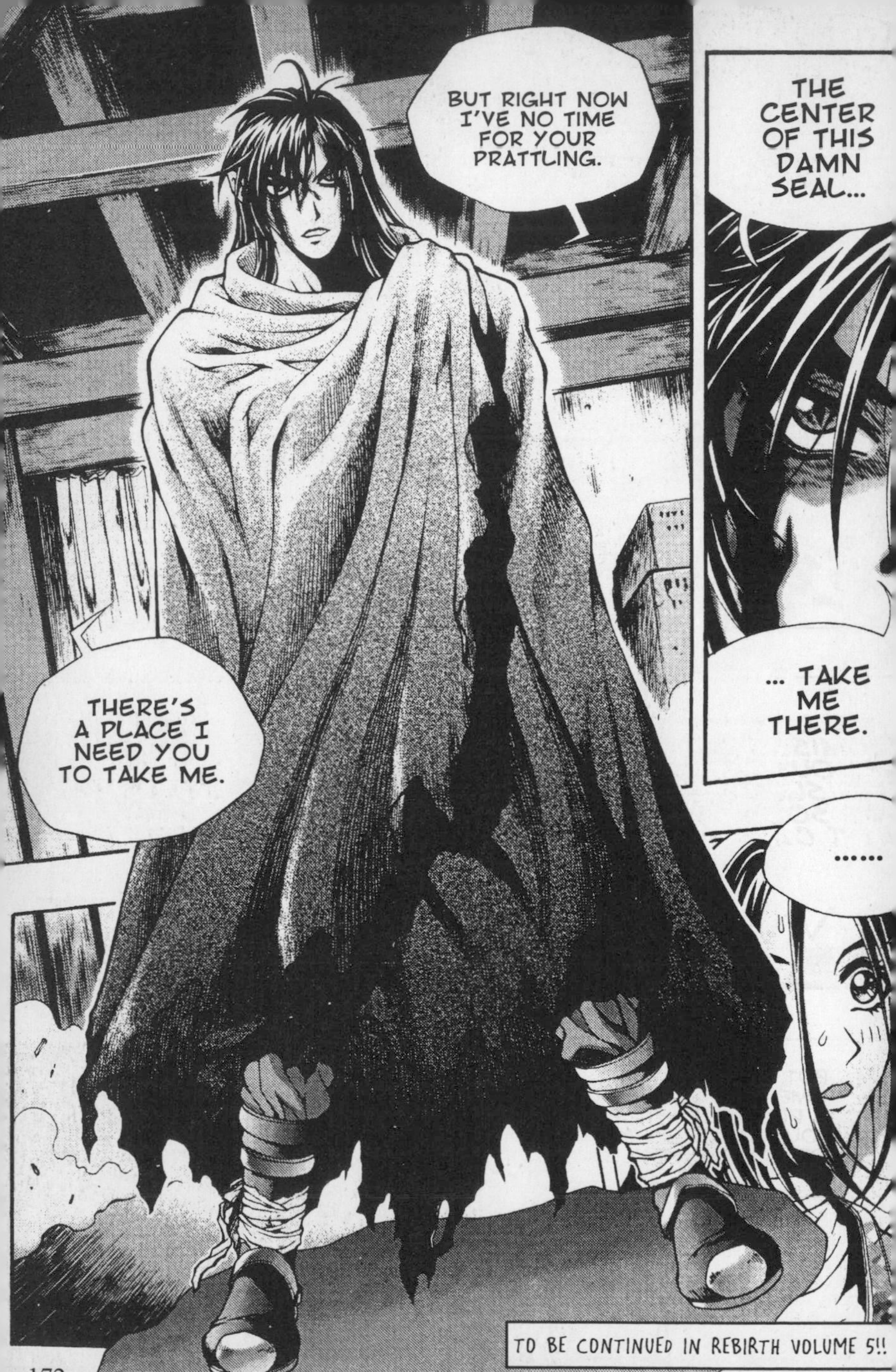
BUT RIGHT NOW I'VE NO TIME FOR YOUR PRATTLING.
THERE'S A PLACE I NEED YOU TO TAKE ME.
THE CENTER OF THIS DAMN SEAL...
... TAKE ME THERE.
......
TO BE CONTINUED IN REBIRTH VOLUME 5!!

마감특집인터뷰 ★

POST-DEADLINE INTERVIEW THE WRITER'S SITUATION

HELLO. MY NAME IS KANGWOO LEE, THE AUTHOR OF REBIRTH.

I APOLOGIZE FOR THE LESS THAN PERFECT QUALITY OF THE COMIC BOOK RECENTLY.

WOO.

TO TELL YOU THE TRUTH, I'VE BEEN IN A SEVERE SLUMP.

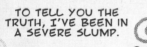

THE REASON, YOU ASK? WELL, DO SLUMPS REALLY COME WITH A REASON? AND WHAT'S WORSE, MY DEADLINES HAVE BEEN COMING.

KANGWOO, WHAT ARE YOU TRYING TO DO IN THIS CHAPTER?

DUNNO—!

MR. LEE, THE DEADLINE FOR THIS ISSUE WILL BE TWO DAYS EARLY.

GOOD GOD!

WELL, I PROMISE TO GET OUT OF THIS SLUMP AS SOON AS I CAN...

...AND SHOW YOU REBIRTH AS IT SHOULD BE!!

BUT CAN I REALLY COME THROUGH WITH THE PROMISE? I THANK YOU, THE READERS, FOR YOUR PATIENCE.

CHAN-HO PARK ALSO SEEMS TO BE IN A SLUMP...HOW DEPRESSING...

GOING, GOING, AND GONE! THE 20TH HOMERUN GIVEN UP BY CHAN-HO PARK THIS SEASON!!

HIS ERA HAS SOARED UP TO 6.19!

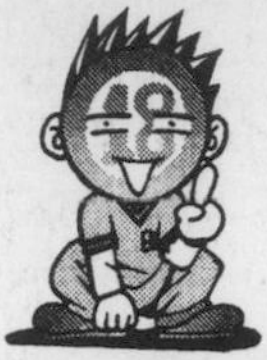

STAFF

INTRODUCING THE STAFF OF REBIRTH

(I'D JUST LIKE TO MENTION THAT THIS IS ME...) MY SELF-PORTRAIT.

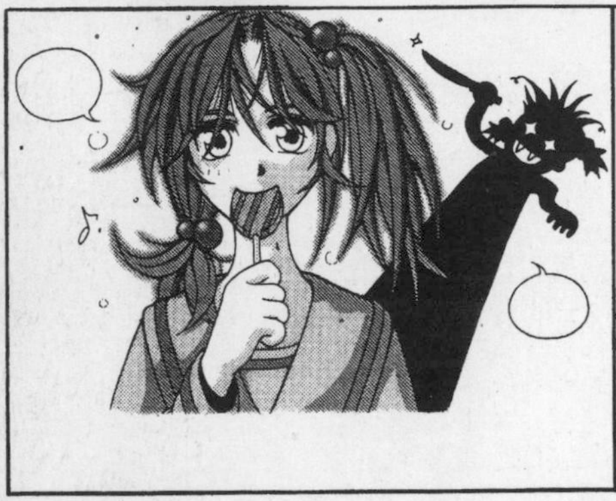

Minoru

I'M ALWAYS HAVING FUN WHEN I SHOULD BE WORKING. WHAT DO I DO FOR FUN? WHY DON'T YOU VISIT MY SITE AND SEE?

HTTP://WWW.HITEL.NET/ MINORU

THE ONLY FEMALE MEMBER OF THE STUDIO, MINORU IS ACTUALLY MY WIFE. SHE'S IN CHARGE OF SCANNING AND TONING.

석뽕이

*FLOWERS CANNOT BE USED AS PART OF THE BACKGROUND!

WHAT DO I WANT TO SAY? WELL, IF I HAVE TO SAY SOMETHING...

WHY IS THIS BACKGROUND SO BUSY?

SUKPPONG IS IN CHARGE OF BACKGROUND WORK. HIS DRAWBACK IS HIS LACK OF SPEED. AND, HIS GREASY LOOKS...

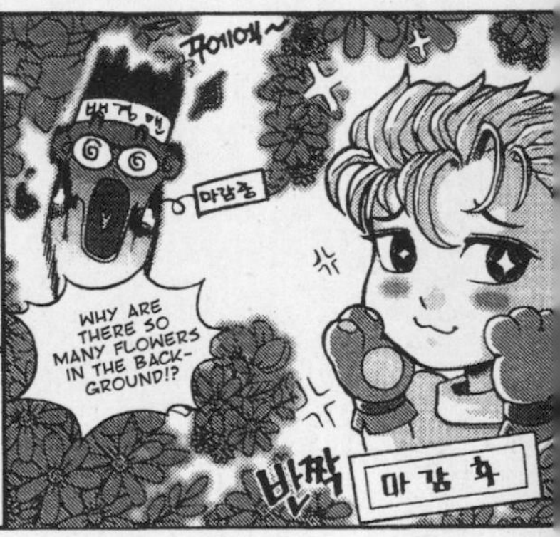
마감중
WHY ARE THERE SO MANY FLOWERS IN THE BACK-GROUND!?
반짝
마감 후

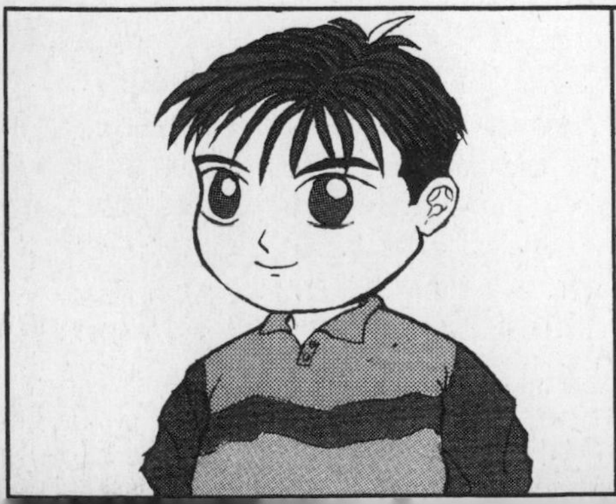

물봉이

HI. I'M A NEW INTERN (IT'S BEEN A MONTH NOW). PLEASE CONTINUE TO LOVE AND SUPPORT REBIRTH!

MULBONG IS THE NEWEST MEMBER OF OUR FAMILY. HE'S BUSY PRACTICING DRAFTING.

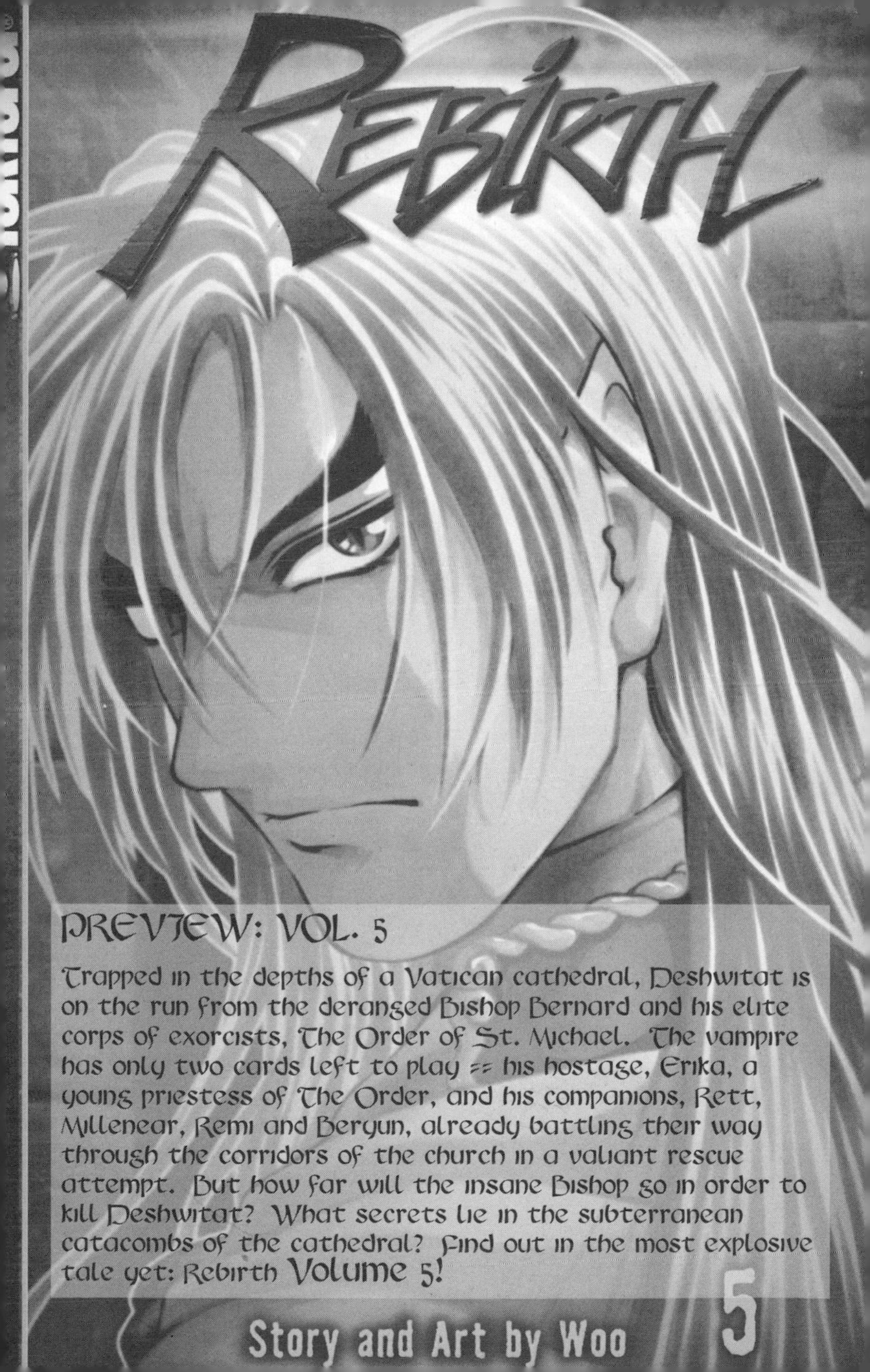
REBIRTH
5
Story and Art by Woo

PREVIEW: VOL. 5

Trapped in the depths of a Vatican cathedral, Deshwitat is on the run from the deranged Bishop Bernard and his elite corps of exorcists, The Order of St. Michael. The vampire has only two cards left to play -- his hostage, Erika, a young priestess of The Order, and his companions, Rett, Millenear, Remi and Beryun, already battling their way through the corridors of the church in a valiant rescue attempt. But how far will the insane Bishop go in order to kill Deshwitat? What secrets lie in the subterranean catacombs of the cathedral? Find out in the most explosive tale yet: Rebirth Volume 5!

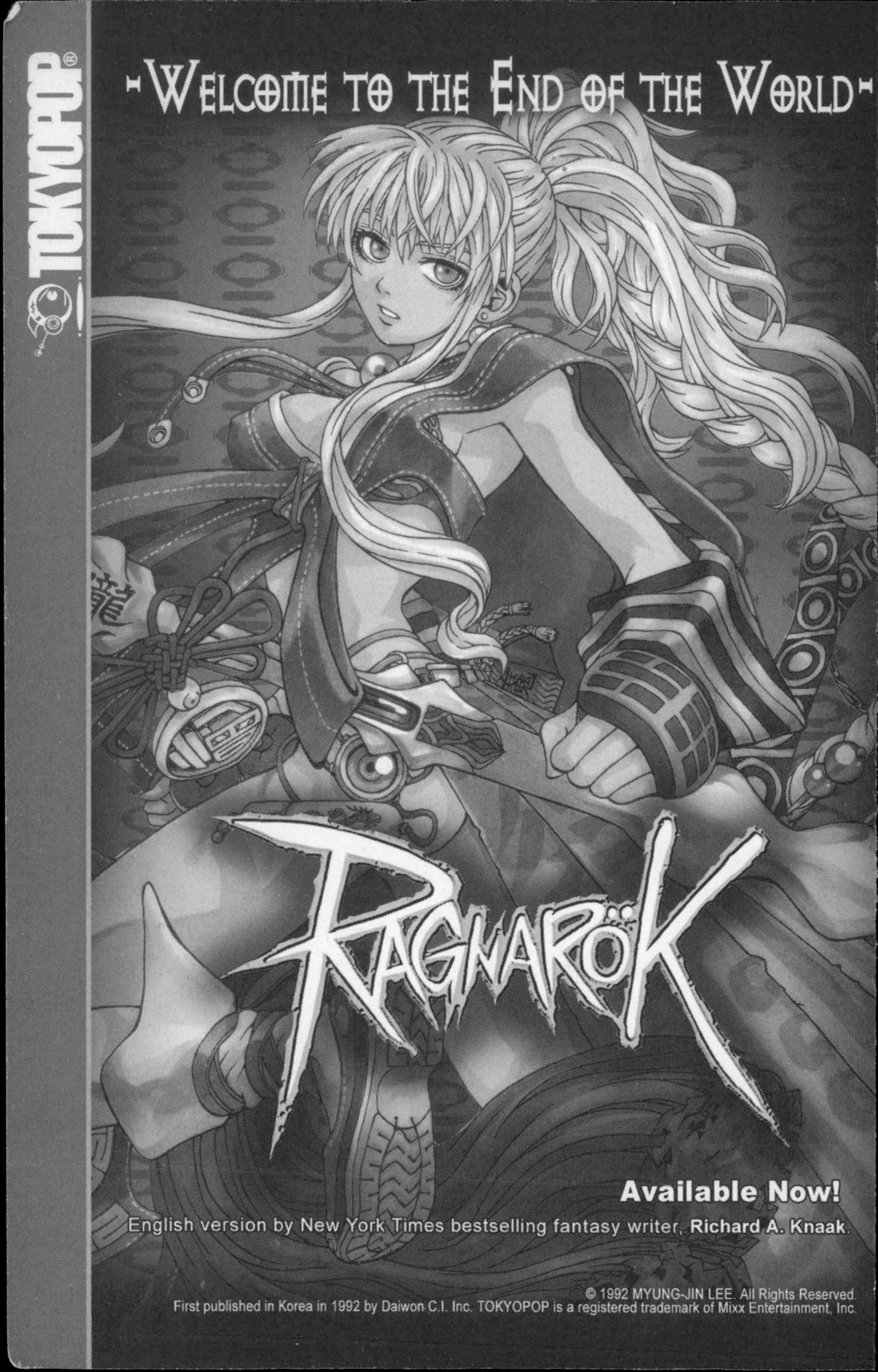
TOKYOPOP
-Welcome to the End of the World-
Ragnarök
Available Now!
English version by New York Times bestselling fantasy writer, Richard A. Knaak.
© 1992 MYUNG-JIN LEE. All Rights Reserved.
First published in Korea in 1992 by Daiwon C.I. Inc. TOKYOPOP is a registered trademark of Mixx Entertainment, Inc.

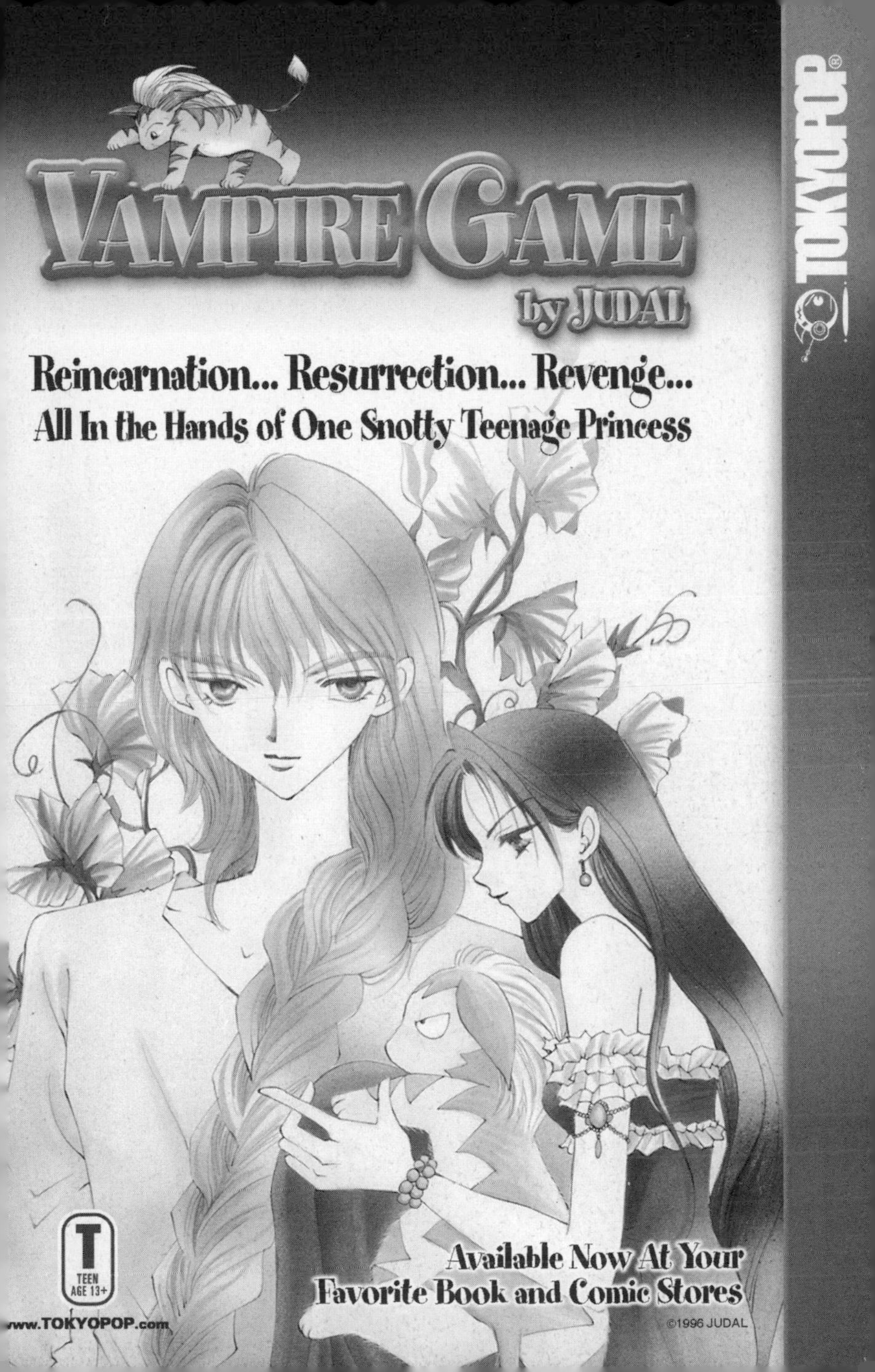
TOKYOPOP
VAMPIRE GAME
by JUDAL
Reincarnation... Resurrection... Revenge...
All In the Hands of One Snotty Teenage Princess
T
TEEN
AGE 13+
Available Now At Your
Favorite Book and Comic Stores
www.TOKYOPOP.com
©1996 JUDAL

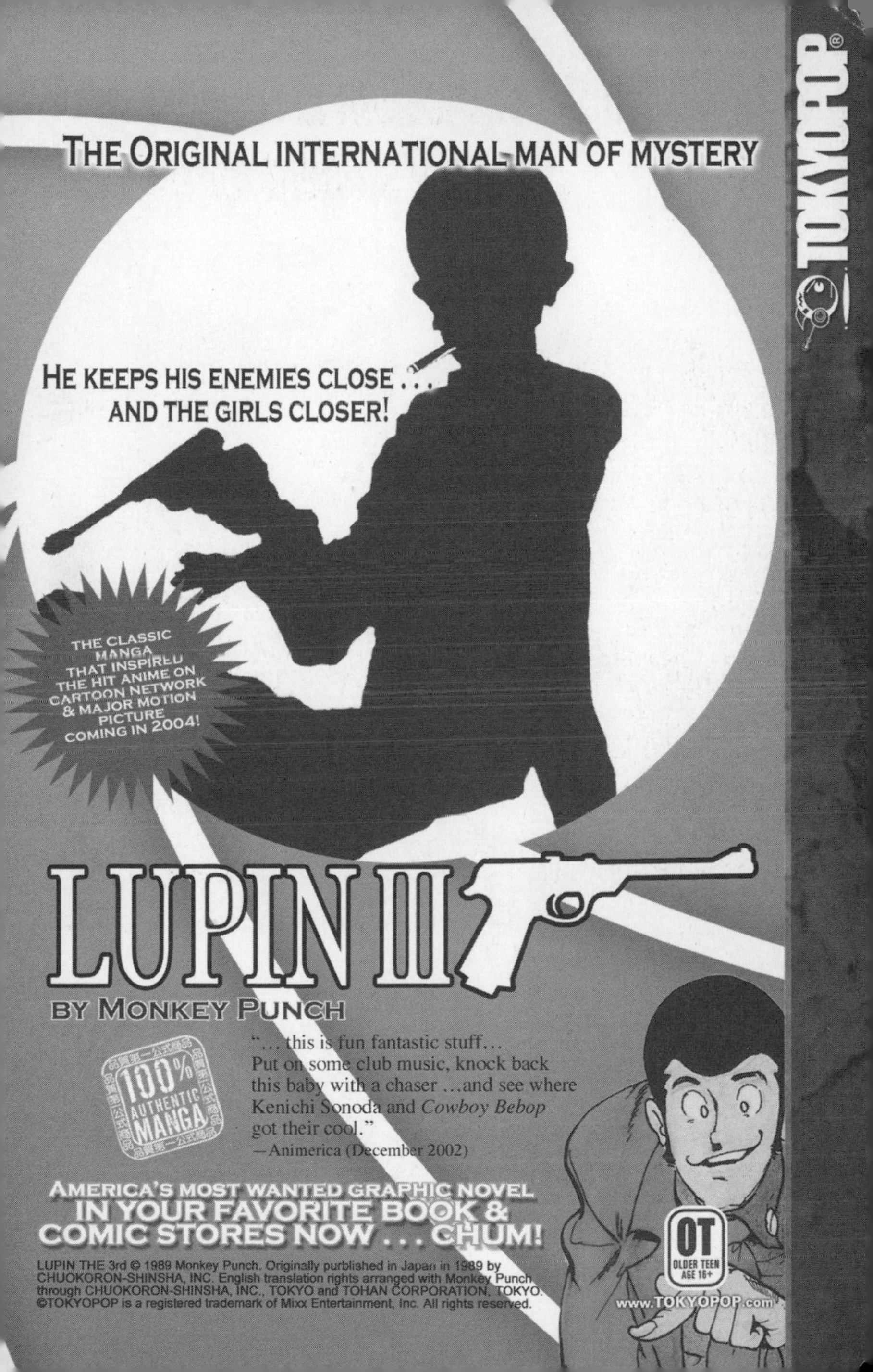
TOKYOPOP®
THE ORIGINAL INTERNATIONAL MAN OF MYSTERY
HE KEEPS HIS ENEMIES CLOSE . . .
. . . AND THE GIRLS CLOSER!
THE CLASSIC MANGA THAT INSPIRED THE HIT ANIME ON CARTOON NETWORK & MAJOR MOTION PICTURE COMING IN 2004!
LUPIN III
BY MONKEY PUNCH
100% AUTHENTIC MANGA
"... this is fun fantastic stuff... Put on some club music, knock back this baby with a chaser ...and see where Kenichi Sonoda and *Cowboy Bebop* got their cool."
—Animerica (December 2002)
AMERICA'S MOST WANTED GRAPHIC NOVEL
IN YOUR FAVORITE BOOK & COMIC STORES NOW . . . CHUM!
OT OLDER TEEN AGE 16+
LUPIN THE 3rd © 1989 Monkey Punch. Originally purblished in Japan in 1989 by CHUOKORON-SHINSHA, INC. English translation rights arranged with Monkey Punch through CHUOKORON-SHINSHA, INC., TOKYO and TOHAN CORPORATION, TOKYO. ©TOKYOPOP is a registered trademark of Mixx Entertainment, Inc. All rights reserved.
www.TOKYOPOP.com

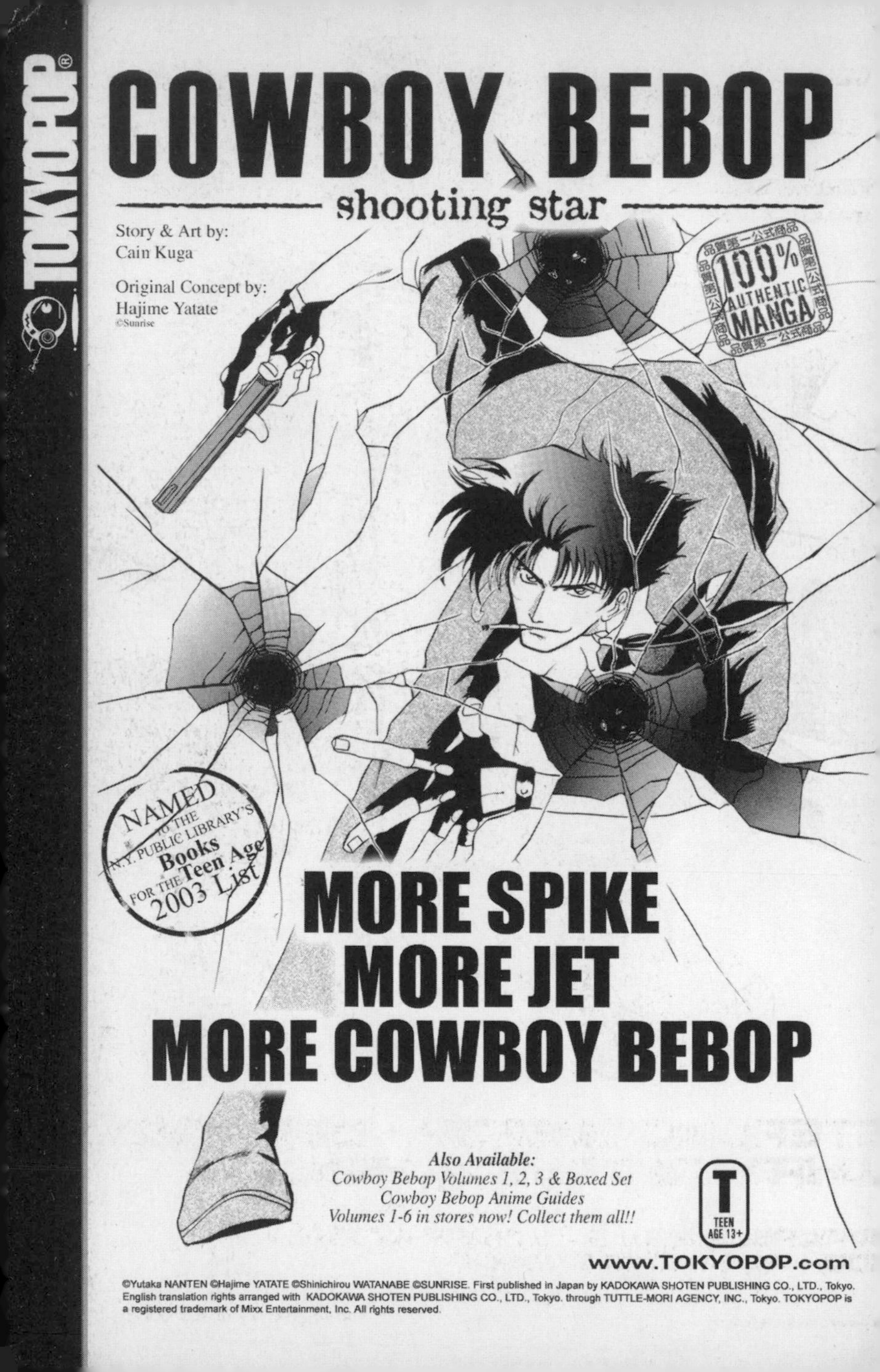
TOKYOPOP®
COWBOY BEBOP
shooting star
Story & Art by:
Cain Kuga
Original Concept by:
Hajime Yatate
©Sunrise
100% AUTHENTIC MANGA
NAMED TO THE N.Y. PUBLIC LIBRARY'S Books FOR THE Teen Age 2003 List
MORE SPIKE
MORE JET
MORE COWBOY BEBOP
Also Available:
Cowboy Bebop Volumes 1, 2, 3 & Boxed Set
Cowboy Bebop Anime Guides
Volumes 1-6 in stores now! Collect them all!!
T TEEN AGE 13+
www.TOKYOPOP.com
©Yutaka NANTEN ©Hajime YATATE ©Shinichirou WATANABE ©SUNRISE. First published in Japan by KADOKAWA SHOTEN PUBLISHING CO., LTD., Tokyo. English translation rights arranged with KADOKAWA SHOTEN PUBLISHING CO., LTD., Tokyo. through TUTTLE-MORI AGENCY, INC., Tokyo. TOKYOPOP is a registered trademark of Mixx Entertainment, Inc. All rights reserved.